SONG OF THE SAMURAI

C. A. PARKER

RUNNING
Wild
PRESS

To my late wife, Jeannine, and our wonderful children, Julia and Joshua: for all their patience in listening to years of shakuhachi practice and their enthusiasm and encouragement as I birthed this story.

I write in my notebook with the intention of stimulating good conversation, hoping that it will also be of use to some fellow traveler. —Basho (1644-1694)

TABLE OF CONTENTS

AWAITING CHERRY BLOSSOMS

ACKNOWLEDGMENTS

While most novels have a single author, they are never the product of one person. In writing this novel, I am profoundly grateful to many, many people who have supported and cheered me on. There is no way to adequately express my thanks.

In many ways this novel is the product of many years of *shakuhachi* practice under extraordinary teachers: Alcvin Ryuzen Ramos, James Nyoraku Schlefer, Yodo Kurahachi II, and, finally, the late Ronnie Nyogetsu Reishin Seldin, my first teacher and first guide to Japan. I also owe a profound debt of gratitude to Mitsugi Saotome, *Aikido* Shihan, and all the amazing teachers and students of the Aikido Shobukan Dojo in Washington, DC. They have taught me the meaning of *budo*.

This book could also not have come into being without the aid of four amazing early readers and friends. Christopher Yohmei Blasdel, Sensei (*shakuhachi* master and ethnomusicologist), Prof. Miyuki Yoshikami (koto master and specialist in the Japanese Performing Arts), Dr. Laura Lauth (poet and creative writing instructor), and John Taylor, IV (attorney and *Aikido* instructor). Each of them provided me with incredibly valuable feedback on the historical and musical content, as well as the technical crafting, of the story. Any mistakes are my own and these readers are the reason there are not far more.

One lesson from writing my first novel is that the actual writing is only the first (and, in many ways, easiest) stage of the journey. My deep thanks go to my literary agent Natalie Kimber of The Rights Factory for guiding me through this labyrinth and helping me craft a better text; and to Lisa Kastner, Founder and Executive Editor of Running Wild Press for taking a risk on a first-time author and shepherding this work to publication.

Lastly, my precious family has made all this work possible. In addition to plowing through this text multiple times and giving me invaluable advice, my late wife Jeannine supported our family financially all during the writing process, and gifted me with the space to create this story. It brightened her last days to know that the book would be published. Our wondrous children, Julia and Joshua, have been my primary cheering section throughout the journey.

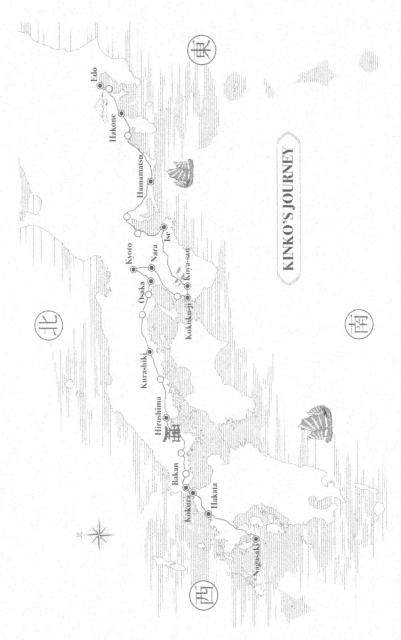

A map of Kurosawa's journey from Nagasaki to Edo

LAND OF FIRE AND WATER

PROLOGUE

JAPAN, 1745.

Only the steady beat of the horse's hooves broke the silent, pre-dawn darkness. The messenger had been riding swiftly for hours, with an intensity that carried him successfully through several official post-stations, despite his forged travel documents. The dead, joyless heat of summer made even his light armor stifling. Setting many hours earlier, the moon had abandoned the otherwise black and hollow night.

As he approached the Okayama station, he could see the sleepy guards rise to bar his way. Throwing his leg over the saddle with well-practiced ease, he slid off the horse even before it came to a halt. He tossed the reins to one of the guards, shouting—to no one in particular—"Quick, I need a fresh horse for the next stage. On the shogun's business!" This far west of Kyoto, the guards were used to a slower pace and were easily cowed.

The sentries looked at each other in some confusion, as a groom emerged to claim the tired horse and take it to the stables, whence—the messenger hoped—he would return with a fresh mount. Deliberately, and with an air of great importance, the messenger drew out his travel papers, saying, "Who is in charge here? I need food and water and must be on my way at once."

One of the guards took his travel documents, while the messenger endeavored to look imperious and put-upon. As the soldier unfolded the papers, an officer—wearing his armored cuirass and gauntlets, but no helmet—emerged from the wooden barrack inside the gate and walked with a studied indifference towards the commotion. Wordlessly, he held out his hand as the guard passed him the messenger's documents.

"I bear an important notice to the Shogun and require the utmost haste," the messenger insisted. The officer did not appear to find this compelling. He slowly unfolded the papers and examined them meticulously.

"The seal appears authentic, but this is not the accustomed signature from Kokura castle," he said, looking suspiciously over the paper at its bearer. "I need to check this with my superior."

"I am very short on time," the messenger repeated. "The usual officer was unavailable when the papers were drawn up, and his assistant signed them. Everything is clearly in order. Let me be on my way, or you will bear the consequences."

"I will also bear the consequences if I let someone pass through my post-station without proper papers," the officer replied. "Please follow me." He turned to walk back towards the building from which he had emerged.

"There is no time for this," the messenger persisted, stamping his foot as he raised his voice. The officer slowly turned and looked meaningfully at the two guards, who retreated a step from the messenger, leveling their spears.

Across the road, the messenger saw the groom emerge from

the stable with a fresh horse. On an impulse, he ran towards it, grabbing the reins from the startled stable hand.

"Stop him!" bellowed the officer as the two guards rushed forward. The messenger threw his leg over the horse and wheeled it around to his right, away from the guards. As the first guard grabbed hold of the horse's harness, the messenger drew his *katana* and slashed at the soldier, who dropped the harness and backed away, pointing his spear at the horse. The second guard lunged with his spear, while the horse reared, and the messenger slid off its back, managing to land on his feet before the horse fell.

He turned and fled between the stable and the adjacent building, hoping to escape in the darkness. Slivers of light shone through the slats of the ill-made barn; the air was heavy with the scent of wet hay and horse dung. On the far side of the building, he could see the ground slope sharply downwards towards a stream. If he could find a place to hide for a few hours, it would not be too difficult to steal a horse and continue his journey.

But the officer had already sped past his subordinates and lunged at the messenger with his *katana*, who parried the thrust on his left while stepping to the right and swinging his *katana* overhead to strike at the officer. At the apex of his stroke, however, a spear point tore through the exposed skin under his arm, twirling him around and throwing him off balance.

Before he could recover, the second guard's spear caught him in the side, under his chest armor. The spear point punctured his abdomen, and he fell, dropping his sword. Immediately, he felt the point of the officer's *katana* at his throat. It was over; his mission had failed. Raising his face, he locked eyes with his captor. Seeing the look of triumph and wishing to avoid the dishonor of capture, he thrust his head forward, impaling himself on the extended sword point. Everything went black.

The officer stood watching the dead man's blood pool on the dark ground. He wiped his sword carefully and re-sheathed it. Leaning over, he searched the dead man for any papers he might be carrying. Lifting a bundle wrapped in waxed rice paper, he sliced open the seal and read the first page. He then quickly refolded it, turned to the wondering guard, and said,

"Prepare a messenger for Edo."

THE KOMUSŌ

The deep magenta rays of the rising sun broke over the walls of Kuzaki Temple, reflecting off the tip of a raised *katana*, as it cut down through the still, morning air. Over and over, the sword rose and fell in a gentle rhythm, accompanied by the faintest hiss. Even this early hour heralded the oppressive humidity that would settle on Nagasaki as the day progressed. The heavy spring rains had long since come and gone, leaving the land trapped in the enervating heat of mid-summer.

The man wielding this particular *katana* was of moderate height, whose thin build belied surprising strength. His face was open and engaging, not exactly handsome but pleasing, and more youthful than his 35 years merited. The primary sign of his age was a receding hairline, about which he was more sensitive than he thought appropriate for a Zen priest. Fortunately, he wore the shaved hairstyle typical of most samurai, hiding his approaching baldness. He also benefitted—when he traveled outside the temple—by wearing a large, woven basket that covered his head.

This basket, called a *tengai*, was the sign of his Zen monastic order: the Fuke. The members of the Fuke-*shu* were known as *komusō* or "monks of nothingness," and they wore the basket as a sign of their humility and renunciation of the world. In the front of the basket, a more open weave allowed the monks to see out—if somewhat imperfectly—while not being seen. This alleviated the embarrassment that was a natural component of begging for alms—particularly among the proud samurai.

Just now, as Kinko Kurosawa[1] practiced his *suburi*—its gentle rhythm always calmed his troubled spirit—the rest of the temple residents were still asleep, awaiting the early bell that would wake them for their first session of meditation. In most Rinzai Temples, the monks would have been up for at least an hour by now, and probably beginning their first round of work. But, while Fuke temples technically fell under the umbrella of Rinzai Buddhism, their daily *zazen* meditation sessions were shorter, and the work requirements less demanding.

However, the Fuke had added one spiritual discipline to that of their Rinzai brethren: the practice of playing a flute called the *shakuhachi*, the hallmark of their order. This discipline was not simply musical; it was understood primarily as a meditative practice called *sui-zen*—"blowing meditation." From the first time he held the instrument—a nearly two-foot-long, heavy, end-blown piece of bamboo—Kurosawa fell in love with the *shakuhachi* and the music of the *komusō*. The music's long, melancholy phrasing and plaintive sound touched a place deep within him and resonated with the movement of his spirit.

Hard work supplemented his unusual talent, resulting in Kurosawa's speedy rise through the ranks of the temple's monks. Five years earlier, at the age of thirty, he became the senior musical instructor of the temple and the youngest priest on the abbot's council. This was an unheard-of honor for one so young and caused no small amount of grumbling among the older temple residents. Knowing himself to be talented and engaging, Kurosawa would have been dismayed at the resentment his swift rise provoked. In his more grandiloquent moments, he even imagined being elected abbot himself.... someday.

His coveted position, and—he feared—its imminent loss, had impelled Kurosawa to rise early that morning, take his *katana*, and go out in the predawn darkness of the temple garden to practice his *suburi*. All night, he had thrashed on his futon, unable to force his manic mind into stillness. Finally, he surrendered, arose, and gave himself up to the physical rigor of practicing a thousand sword strokes, clearing his mind and exhausting his body.

He knew better; he expected better from himself.

She had first visited the temple on a cool, autumn morning nearly two years earlier, with red and golden leaves chasing each other playfully across the central courtyard. Her family— her fleshy, arrogant husband, and her flower-like daughter— arrived to make a contribution to the temple in thanksgiving for a safe and successful family journey. At twenty-eight, she was no longer a child, but the glow of youth still clung to her skin, as if loath to relinquish a much-treasured favorite.

Although appropriately lowered, her sharp, intelligent eyes unobtrusively scanned the temple grounds, absorbing every detail. Observing Kinko leading the monks in their afternoon *shakuhachi* practice outdoors, those perceptive eyes gave him a rapid—and, he fancied, approving—appraisal. Likewise, watching her cross the temple yard caused him to lose his place in the music he was teaching, and—flustered—forced him to start from the beginning.

Within the week, she was back with only her daughter, ostensibly bringing flowers to decorate the *butsuden,* the main temple sanctuary. The morning was cold, with winter's first incursion on autumn's gentle beauty. His breath clouded as he exited the priests' dorm and recognized the woman and her daughter in the main courtyard as they looked around.

"Can I help you find anything, little sisters?" he asked companionably, as he approached them.

"I am looking for the abbot's office," she responded, as her face brightened with recognition.

"Let me walk you over," he volunteered. "My name is Kinko Kurosawa."

"And I am Matsu Ekken." She bowed. "Was that your beautiful playing I heard last week?"

"Group *shakuhachi* lessons are rarely beautiful," he laughed. "But, yes, that was me teaching."

"Well, I thought it very beautiful. It's quite a difficult instrument to play, is it not?"

"Oh, like anything else, it's just a matter of practice," he said, blushing slightly. Bowing as he left them at the temple's administrative building, he said, "I will look forward to seeing you again."

She smiled back, looking directly into his eyes.

The family visits to the temple—always now without the husband—became quite regular. The reasons for the trips varied from week to week, but gradually—and to Kinko's unacknowledged delight—Matsu's interest became more and more apparent. She always found some pretext to run across his path; and he found himself watching for her, fabricating excuses to engage her. Their talks became longer and longer, strolling in the temple garden, while her daughter played with a ball beneath the umbrella of manicured Cyprus trees.

Her family, he learned over time, were minor samurai from

the Hizen Prefecture around Nagasaki, vassals of the Nabeshima family who had ruled the prefecture since the Tokugawa became shoguns a century and a half earlier. Her husband's family had its roots in Kurosawa's home province of Kuroda on the northern end of Kyushu island and claimed a near relation to the famous scholar Kaibara Ekken.

One morning, as early spring took an undeniable hold, they strolled among the carefully sculpted plants as Matsu's daughter chased an errant butterfly.

"How I envy your life here, Kurosawa-*san*! The freedom to practice your art, to meditate, to teach."

"What would you do if you could choose, Ekken-*san*?"

"Oh, I would paint!" There was no hesitation, with an unmistakable finality at the end of the sentence. As an afterthought, she added, "My parents obtained lessons for me with the famous Shiseki Sō when he visited Nagasaki from Edo several years ago. The experience was world-shaking. The powerful way that he drew trees—it was like a sword-master doing calligraphy: dynamic and flawlessly precise. I asked my parents to let me return to Edo to study with him. It was all I wanted in life."

"And what did they say?" he ventured. She was silent for a moment, and he thought he could see her eyes well with tears, although not one fell.

"They stopped my lessons immediately," she spat out, as if expelling venom. "Painting professionally is for the lower classes—the artisans," she warbled, mimicking her mother's patrician voice. "Not at all suitable for a samurai daughter, who was to enhance her family's reputation through a good marriage and raise obedient children." Now the tears flowed down her cheeks. He reached out to comfort her, but caught himself before he crossed that invisible—yet obvious—line.

He learned of her marriage, which she found disappointing, though at least stable and safe. Arrogant, self-important, and unintelligent, Genzo Ekken was at least not a violent man, as were many samurai husbands; he was merely uninterested in his wife beyond her ability to bear a son and heir. As was typical of samurai of his station, he continued to carry on casually with several lovers that Matsu knew about. But it seemed to her that Genzo's primary emotional attachment was with a male lover, one of his samurai retainers.

In turn, Kurosawa shared his own story with her. He grew up in the region of Kuroda, on the northern tip of Kyushu island, the second son of a mid-ranking samurai retainer of Kuroda's local lord. Twenty years earlier, his father—knowing it was unlikely his lord could find enough work for a second son—sent Kinko south to the Fuke temple in Nagasaki, where his cousin had lived for a few years. This relocation was not entirely unwelcome to Kinko, since his persistently-disappointed father was difficult to live with, and his silent and submissive mother, little support. It was also a relief to leave his domineering older brother, although he missed his delicate, loving younger sister. And the move had ultimately proved a great blessing, since it led to Kurosawa discovering his talent for music and his great love of the *shakuhachi*.

The temple now felt more like home than his family household ever did. Kinko described life in the temple to Matsu, recounting the latest installments of the temple politics—always with an amused detachment. And he played his *shakuhachi* for her; which she seemed to love as much as he did. While he was aware of their mutual attraction, for a surprising length of time, he persuaded himself that their relationship was within the allotted bounds. He was, after all, merely a confidant, a spiritual advisor. He paid little attention to his own long-ignored needs for physical and emotional intimacy, as well as the gently budding joy that welled up like a spring cherry blossom every time he saw her.

One perfect afternoon in late spring, they were in the temple garden talking while Matsu played catch with her daughter. Caught up in her excitement, the little girl threw the ball so wildly that it missed her mother and landed on the far side of Kinko, who picked it up. Kinko admired the small *tamari* ball, woven together from scraps of silk and linen, noting its clever patterns of color and texture, before handing it to Matsu. Passing it to her, her open hand gently brushed along his, and Kinko felt a spark of energy run through his arm. Mores around touching a person of the opposite sex were quite strict, and drawing his hand back quickly, he saw the same shock in her eyes that he knew was in his own. Then his heart started again, and he saw a shy smile form on her lips.

Over the following weeks, there were several other times when one of the two "accidentally" touched the other, always out of view of any other people. Then one afternoon, as he played his *shakuhachi* in the garden for her, she teasingly took the flute from his hands, saying, "Teach me to play!" Placing the mouth of the flute—still warm from his lips—against her own, she tried to blow, eliciting no sound from the stubborn bamboo. She blew for several moments before abandoning the attempt. Placing the *shakuhachi*—now moist from her breath— against his lips, she said, "Show me."

As time passed, the touching became more regular, more needed, more insistent. They began to meet outside of the temple, "inadvertently" running into one another in town and then joining for tea or a meal. Matsu arranged one of these meals in a quiet tea house, far from the busy city center. The food was good and their conversation animated and far-ranging; but when they finished the meal, Matsu became quiet. Avoiding his gaze, she looked through the open window, as though engaged in some internal debate. Finally, she rose and, without speaking a word, took his hand and led him from the table, up a narrow set of stairs to a room on the second floor. Soft afternoon light filtered through the rice paper window panes, and the delicate scent of honeysuckle floated from the lit incense in the corner. A futon was laid out on the worn tatami mat.

Both still silent—fearful of the words that lay unspoken between them: the betrayal and risk of crossing this line—she undid the *obi* that bound his robes and carefully folded it, putting it aside. Pushing back the black robes over his shoulders, she followed them down as they fell off his back, kissing his chest lower and lower. Leading him to the futon, she undid her own *obi* and let her robe fall to the floor. She possessed a grown woman's body, but it showed little of the trauma of giving birth. Nipples with dark areola summited her small breasts; her hips were narrow.

The sounds of street traffic seeped through the rice paper windows, as from a world left far away. Although not Kinko's first sexual encounter, it felt as new and fresh as the flowers blossoming outside. There was no shyness or awkwardness in their coming together. It was as natural as two streams joining to become a river. She enjoyed him; she enjoyed being with him; she enjoyed loving him and being loved by him.

Lying on the futon, Matsu's naked body curled up next to his, with his arm around her shoulders, he felt as though he had never known such completeness. Gazing up at the ceiling, he watched the dust motes float gently in and out of the stripes of sunlight, dancing with the rising incense. He noted every detail of the room, wanting to lock it into his memory like a treasure he could take out and ponder when no one else was near.

Months passed, and their clandestine meetings continued. One afternoon, they had scheduled a rendezvous in a small marketplace on the other side of the city from the temple. While it was unusual for the temple's senior instructor to assign himself a time in the city to beg for alms, it was not unheard of, and ironically enhanced Kinko's reputation for humble piety. He found that he missed these forays into the city to play and enjoyed the thriving life around him. Settling himself on a well-trafficked corner on the edge of the market, he put the flute to his lips and launched into a popular folk tune—the best way to attract a paying crowd.

His fingers danced over the holes of the *shakuhachi* as he scanned the spectators for his paramour. The crowd was receptive and enthusiastic—this not being one of the usual spots frequented by the *komusō*. Soon he spied Matsu in the crowd, hanging back, near the edge, and lost his focus on the music, fumbling the end of the piece. Quickly he collected alms in his begging bowl and hurried to join her as she wandered away through the narrow, overhung alleys between the stalls of merchants. Catching up to her, he said, "I'm a little embarrassed at bungling the ending of the music just now."

She turned, observing him curiously for a moment before a broad smile spread across her face.

"*Anata,*" she whispered affectionately, "to me your music is always perfect."

The murmured words lay glowing in his ear, as the moisture of her breath dampened his cheek. His breath caught in his throat. A ray of sunlight seemed to break free of the clouds, as those simple words revealed a world of grace and freedom. Throughout his whole life, he had projected an image that—while not a lie—failed to convey who he really was: an image, built on his gifts as a musician, that tolerated no display of weaknesses or uncertainty. It was the image of a consummate priest and teacher, rising quickly and successfully through the ranks of the temple hierarchy, destined for positions of power and prestige.

Matsu already knew the worst about him and loved him anyway. And that love gave him permission to share all of who he was—the insecurities, the pettiness, the vanity, the ambition. She knew him thoroughly, loved him thoroughly; and in that knowledge and love was a freedom unknown before. He could shed the pretenses built up over years and reveal himself as he was. He looked at her with wonder and hastened them on to their rendezvous.

Months lengthened into a second year, with their love and connection deepening. Her visits to the temple fell into a regular weekly schedule. His visits into the city became part of his weekly pattern as well. Each day, he hoarded up his memories to share with her at their next meeting. Birds sang louder, and the colors were more vibrant on those days. He craved their stolen moments with the intensity of needing food at the end of a fast.

In his lucid moments—and there were many—he knew that there was no possible satisfactory ending to this affair. Countless times, he told himself that it must end. He told Matsu that it had to end. They agreed to never see each other. They agreed to run away together. They stopped. They clung. They wept. They fought. They loved. Their dance spun faster and faster, like water circling a drain.

Even in a city as large and bustling as Nagasaki, it was impossible that their ongoing rendezvous could avoid notice indefinitely. She was a prominent noblewoman; he was a *komusō* priest. They each knew too many people; they knew too many people in common. What madness kept them locked in such a mutually destructive embrace for so long? The sword stroke had to fall, eventually.

It had fallen the previous day and felt like a hundred years ago to Kurosawa as he cut the early morning air with his *katana*. As he had entered the temple precincts, one of his favorite pupils approached him—a young man with a solid musical ear and an appreciation of melodic nuance.

"*Shishō*," he ventured. "I thought you should know...."

"Yes?" Kinko responded. His heart began to hammer in such a way that the young monk must have heard it.

"Well..." the words dragged from his lips. "Several younger monks were buying soy sauce and miso in the market today, and the miso maker was teasing them about the local gossip about you and Genzo Ekken's wife. I know that you would never disgrace our temple in such a way, but thought you should know about the talk..."

"Thank you for your concern," Kinko laughed—perhaps too loudly? "These gossip mills are always speculating on one thing or another."

Walking away, he almost stumbled. His mind, frozen in dread, could hardly process what he heard. There were no smells, no sounds; the world went grey. His breath was trapped in his chest. They had been seen, they were being discussed. His life was over.

THE SUMMONS

F inishing his *suburi* cuts, Kurosawa hastened to the *onsen* —the bathhouse—a small wooden building toward the rear of the temple complex, used both for Buddhist purification rituals and ordinary bathing. Kinko grabbed a bucket, filled it at an outside well, and returned to the front room of the bathhouse, where he sat on a low bench and washed. When clean, he moved to the inner room containing the baths.

Originating from nearby hot springs, the water was scalding, and Kurosawa wrinkled his nose at the heavy sulphuric odor. Nonetheless, he soaked in the searing waters which relieved his sore muscles and tired body. He toweled off as the heavy, lotus-shaped bronze bell called the community to morning *zazen*, its reverberations suspended in the heavy morning air.

Tying his robes, he hurried across the courtyard to fall in line with the blurry-eyed monks stumbling to the *butsuden*, the main building of the temple complex, housing the large statue of the Buddha atop its altar. As Kurosawa approached the ancient structure, his breath slowed and took on a deeper rhythm. Silently, the community gathered. At the far end of the meditation room, the *jūshoku* took their place; these were the full priests and permanent temple residents. The *jūshoku* oversaw all the work of the community and cared for its spiritual needs. Most—like Kurosawa—had lived at the temple for many years. Next to them, on the cushions closer to the door, sat the much larger group of *kyogai*: the lay monks, whose residency at the temple was more temporary.

All the temple residents were—by imperial decree—of samurai status; and the *kyogai* generally planned on returning to a more typical samurai lifestyle in the service of some local lord. Many had wives and families to whom they would return after leaving the temple, and the norms for their behavior were fairly relaxed. By contrast, the *jūshoku* had committed themselves to a permanent religious vocation. For them, the monastic code was much more rigorous, and celibacy was extolled, if not always expected.

After meditation and breakfast, many of the monks donned their *komusō* attire with head baskets and headed out into Nagasaki to play their *shakuhachi* as they begged for alms, the temple's primary source of income. As a senior priest, Kinko normally spent this period of the day teaching *shakuhachi* lessons to individual monks. As a mendicant order, Fuke monks traveled from temple to temple across the countryside, and over time Kurosawa realized that his reputation as a player and teacher had spread quite widely. In fact, *komusō* made journeys to Kuzaki-*ji* specifically to learn from him. This elevated him in the eyes of the abbot, whose own power and prestige grew along with the reputation of his modest temple.

By afternoon, his teaching responsibilities completed, Kurosawa joined the other monks in the large courtyard in front of the great temple bell for *bujutsu* practice. Since most of the temple community would eventually return to secular life,

and because swordsmanship and military readiness character-
ized the samurai spirit, it was important for them to maintain
their martial skills. While Kurosawa had no ambitions to return
to the secular life of a warrior, he enjoyed the rigor of martial
practice and engaged in training most days.

A sweltering afternoon, the humidity made the air so thick
that Kinko felt as though he were swimming. Sweat flowed off
his forehead, and his wet garments clung to his body. While
they practiced, the moment came he had been dreading:
Hirata, the abbot's personal secretary, entered the training yard
and motioned for Kinko to join him. Kinko bowed to his practice partner and walked over to join the secretary.

"The Abbot would like to meet with you immediately
following the evening meal, Kurosawa."

"Of course," replied Kurosawa, trying hard to appear
unconcerned. "Is there anything that the abbot would like me
to prepare for the meeting?"

"No," Hirata answered, brusquely. "Please be prompt."

The arrival of evening did nothing to relieve the stultifying heat
of the day. Kinko dragged his feet over the tortured earth on his
way to the abbot's quarters. No bird's song broke the silence.
He was not sure what to expect when he arrived. In general,
the rules pertaining to sex were fairly forgiving. The great
fifteenth-century Zen monk Ikkyu even argued that sex was a
religious act. But sexual activity among the *jūshoku* priests was
expected to be occasional and discrete. Kurosawa was also
aware that his recklessness had political ramifications that
could be more problematic.

The abbot's quarters adjoined the larger building in which
the *jūshoku* priests lived together, though grander and with a
private entrance. In addition to a bedroom, the residence

included a large anti-room in which the abbot held smaller, private meetings—meetings like tonight's. Sliding back the lattice door, Kinko dropped to the ground in a deep bow, his nose almost touching the tatami flooring. The tatami was as immaculate as the abbot's conscience. Raising his head, Kurosawa's glance took in the abbot, seated on a raised platform, and flanked by his two closest advisors: Hirata, his personal secretary, and Iwakura, the priest charged with the administration and operations of the temple.

The abbot was a tall, balding man with a weak chin and protuberant eyes. His face was generally grim and dour, on which a smile usually seemed forced. At this moment, with his lips pressed together tightly, there was a warning fire in his eyes. His bearing and expression were both formal and severe. He motioned Kinko to come forward, which the latter did, keeping his eyes lowered. Without any preliminaries, the abbot began:

"We have heard some disturbing rumors about you and the wife of a certain samurai from the town. I am used to rumors about priests; it is part of the standard fodder of temple life. But these rumors come from enough sources that—combined with my own observations—I take them with deadly seriousness.

"I am not going to ask you the obvious question, for two reasons: I do not wish to put you in a position in which you might be tempted to lie; and I sometimes find it helpful to not 'know' a thing, so that I also do not have to tell a lie. Do you understand me?"

Kinko nodded.

"That being said, is there anything that you wish to tell me? Any word of explanation or extenuation?"

Kurosawa thought carefully and shook his head.

"I have frequent occasion to overlook indiscretions among our brothers here in the temple and do not take notice of periodic visits to the city's pleasure quarter and such. The lady in question, however, was both born into—and has married into—families of quality; families upon whose generosity this temple depends. Your indiscretion in this matter, therefore, not only reflects upon you, but places this temple's wellbeing at risk. Am I making myself clear?" the abbot asked, his voice rising.

Again, Kinko nodded.

"My anger and disappointment, brother Kurosawa, are such that I would like simply to expel you from our community. However, such an action would be perceived as an announcement of your guilt, and would further compromise the honor of this temple, and embarrass the noble families to whom I have referred.

"So, I am grateful that another solution has arisen quite independently: the head abbot of Ichigetsu Temple in Edo is seeking a *shakuhachi* teacher for his monks. He has heard of you from some of our traveling brethren and written to inquire whether I might send you to him. Because of the prominence of Ichigetsu-*ji*, his status is superior to mine, and I might have needed to submit to his request in any case. But this does provide me with a convenient way of ridding myself of you without causing any unwanted speculation.

"Let me be clear about several elements of this decision: you are hereby stripped of your status as a priest. You no longer hold the rank of *jūshoku* and leave this temple as a common *kyogai* monk, a status that your *komusō* identification papers will make plain. I will also write back to the abbot of Ichigetsu-*ji*, indicating that your departure was not entirely unwelcome on my part; I will let him imply from that what he will.

"Given your status and role here at Kuzaki-*ji*, I am giving you three days to conclude your teaching assignments and other responsibilities. I will expect a recommendation on a new senior instructor, and I expect that you will not leave the grounds of the temple before your departure. You are dismissed."

Without a word spoken, Kinko backed out of the abbot's room and turned down the hall to the front door. He was grateful that the falling darkness hid his face, so that his fellow residents could not see the tears streaming down his cheeks. Seeking to avoid the other monks, he made his way to the temple garden, losing himself among the darkening trees. Finally, he sat down on the perfectly manicured moss with his back against a broad cedar and sobbed. His body shook with the violence of his weeping until it abated through sheer exhaustion.

He expected a reprimand from the abbot, even a punishment. He anticipated a demotion; even a long assignment somewhere, getting him conveniently away from Nagasaki. He had not expected to be stripped of his priestly status and the permanent loss of his temple home. He never envisioned exile, the loss of everything he had built, everything that he was.

Deep in his being, Kinko loved Kuzaki-*ji*: the gracefully weathered eaves of the *butsuden*, the incense-soaked walls of the meditation hall. He loved the garden in spring; he loved the quirky assemblage of priests who guided the community. He grew up here; it was his home.

It had been his home. Now, in three days, he would never see it again. The teachers he learned from, the friends that he laughed with at dinner, they would all be part of his past, never known again. He could hardly comprehend the enormity of the abbot's punishment. He sat silently now with his back to the tree until all life in the temple slipped into the arms of sleep. Then he slowly picked himself up and stumbled back to his darkened room.

. . .

The following morning, Kinko could not bear to join any of the activities of the temple and asked one of his fellow teachers to take charge of the *shakuhachi* instruction for the day. Feeling lost and immobilized, he finally decided to visit his old teacher and mentor, Ikkei, who had been the temple's senior instructor when Kurosawa had arrived twenty years prior.

Kinko remembered his first meeting with Ikkei as though it were yesterday. He was seventeen and had been at the temple for several months. Up until that point, he had only participated in group *shakuhachi* lessons with the junior instructors. As he was leaving the lesson one day, the teacher said, "Chief instructor Ikkei would like you to join him for a lesson tomorrow morning after breakfast." The invitation pleased and flattered him, but left him ignorant of what to expect.

Arriving at the administrative building the next morning, he was directed to a small room towards the rear and followed the sound of flute music. Sliding open the *shoji* door, he saw an old priest with long, white hair and a wispy beard kneeling on the tatami mat with his eyes closed, resting his *shakuhachi* on his lap. Opposite him sat a young monk, playing with great intensity. At the opening of the door, both men turned. The older man nodded to Kurosawa, inviting him to sit and listen to the lesson. He motioned for the younger monk to continue, interrupting him periodically to correct some phrase or adjust the pitch of a note with the raising or lowering of the head.

After they finished the piece, the two men bowed to each other, and Kinko took his place before the old monk. "My name is Ikkei," his teacher began, "and I have heard that you are making unusually fast progress on our instrument." Kinko bowed, saying nothing.

"As you know by now, we call our music '*honkyoku*' or 'original music.' There are many of these pieces; no one knows how many. Most Fuke temples have a specific piece, sometimes two, that is their signature composition. But I like to start teaching the three oldest pieces, which virtually every temple also plays. These three are centuries old and date back to the beginnings of our order. They are *Kyorei* (Hollow Bell), *Kokû* (Empty Sky), and *Mukaiji* (Flute on a Misty Sea). Let us play *Kokû* together to begin; it is the easiest of the three."

Kinko had practiced *Kokû* before in group lessons. But when Ikkei placed the flute to his lips and played, the music was unlike anything Kinko had heard before. Whole worlds opened before his eyes, transporting him to another place and time. Or perhaps, out of time altogether, into a realm of perfect contemplation and peace.

Ikkei was a wonderful teacher, who combined superlative musicianship with a deep appreciation for the spiritual dimensions of the music. Over the subsequent years, he nurtured both of these in Kinko; although the former came more easily to the young monk than the latter. When Ikkei retired from his teaching position, he recommended to the abbot that Kurosawa fill the role. He still lived in the temple, though hampered by his old age, and Kurosawa now saw him infrequently.

As the old monk approached his eightieth year, he spent much of his time playing the *shakuhachi* in his room, or sitting alone in the *butsuden* meditating before the statue of the Buddha. He was still a talented player, but his lung capacity diminished over the years, leaving him unable to play the long complicated musical passages in a single breath, as he used to do. Kurosawa found Ikkei in his room, kneeling on the tatami, with his long *shakuhachi* resting idle in his hands.

"Shishō?" Kinko murmured as he slid back the *shoji* door.

"Ah, Kurosawa, I was hoping we would have a chance to see each other."

"The truth is, *Shishō*, have a matter of deep shame to share with you. I'm afraid that I..."

Ikkei cut him off with a wave of his hand.

"I am sorry too, for your predicament, my dear friend."

It did not surprise Kurosawa that Ikkei already knew of his banishment. The abbot would have immediately informed the rest of the council, and one of them would have informed Ikkei of the fall of his protégé.

Continuing, Ikkei said, "You have invested much of your life in this place, and you will leave it diminished without your brightness." He stopped as if to take pleasure from the reluctant breeze that wandered through the open window. Kinko also waited in silence. After so many years of friendship and mentoring, few words needed to pass between them. Finally, Ikkei continued:

"You are going to the most prestigious Fuke temple in Japan. Ichigetsu-ji is a magnificent place and magnificently aware of its preeminence. Yet it is not preeminent for any historical or spiritual reason, but by virtue of its proximity to the shogun. Do not confuse its political importance with spiritual substance." He took a deep breath, letting his words hang in the air.

"I hope I do not offend you by saying that you place too much significance on status. The trappings of power and rank draw you as a moth to a flame; so in many ways, Ichigetsu-ji will arouse your worst inclinations. You are a brilliant musician, and that brilliance will bring you to the attention of those in authority. But that is not always a good thing for your own spiritual growth." As the old man spoke, a lark began singing in the garden beyond.

"Your musicianship is technically exceptional, but it does not yet reflect your depth of soul. You are a dear friend, Kinko"—this was the first time his teacher had used his given name— "and a wonderful man. But that is not because of what is here..." Ikkei tapped the side of Kinko's head, "...nor because of what is here," Ikkei set his fingers on Kinko's lips. "You are wonderful because of what is *here*," said Ikkei, placing his hand on Kurosawa's heart.

And then, the old man took Kinko's face in his hands with surprising strength and looked into his eyes with a fiery intensity. "Claim that greatness of heart. Allow it to shape your music, then you will be on the path to Buddha-nature. You have it within you to be a source of enlightenment to the world."

Kinko did not know what to say. This was not the parting that he expected from his beloved teacher. What had he been looking for? Comfort? Sympathy? Understanding? He didn't know. But it was not this. This felt like a slap, a slap on a face already raw and exposed. He bit back tears, forcing a response out:

"*Shishō*, I am grateful for your wisdom, as I am grateful for your teaching over the years. You gave me the great gift of music, and I will try to use it worthily." With that, he bowed his head and backed out of the room.

AN EVENING IN NAGASAKI

The next three days were a blur to Kurosawa, passing with little sleep and less food. He spent his final afternoon bidding farewell to the rest of his friends and colleagues and was emotionally exhausted by evening. But one matter remained unresolved. The abbot had ordered him not to leave the temple; and he was certain that the political factors shaping the abbot's decision to banish him would likewise keep Matsu cloistered in her estate on the south side of the city.

Even though the country was largely peaceful, high-ranking samurai estates were still built to withstand an armed assault, so there was no way to gain access to the Ekken estate, even were there some plausible excuse. He was not sure how he could communicate with her, but he also knew that he could not simply disappear. Violent images filled his fevered brain, involving striding up to the estate and banging a heavily gloved fist on the high, broad, heavy wooden doors. In the fantasy, it was (of course) Genzo who opened the gate and rushed at him with his *katana* held high, while Kurosawa easily cut him down.

His fantasy required Genzo to initiate the attack, so that Kurosawa could enjoy the emotional luxury of a satisfying kill, without the moral awkwardness of being responsible for the death of the man whom he wronged in the first place.

On a practical level, Kurosawa was certain of his actual ability to kill Genzo. After one hundred and fifty years of largely peaceful Tokugawa rule, many upper-class samurai had transitioned from being warriors to serving as functionaries of the government. Genzo was one of these, and although he carried the two swords as a sign of his samurai status, he had not practiced with them since childhood. In fact, he saw his portliness as an expression of his wealth, the one-character trait that he loved to flaunt.

Although Kinko was deeply in love with Matsu, he harbored few illusions that they could ever have a life together. Matsu's highest priority was her beloved daughter, and she would do nothing to endanger the future of her child. Additionally, Matsu was from a prominent family whose members could never simply disappear in a nation as tightly controlled and monitored as Tokugawa Japan. And being part of that family— Kurosawa acknowledged—meant that Matsu would never want for food or clothing or a home. Kurosawa also knew that even if he flouted the authority of the abbot and fled the Fuke order, his only significant skill was useless outside its system of temples; the law permitted only *komusō* to play the *shakuhachi*.

Sitting in his darkening, half-packed room, with few options before him, Kinko took out a piece of heavily textured rice paper, his writing brush, and his ink-stone. Wetting the stone with the brush, he sat thinking for a few minutes, and with his steadiest hand, he wrote,

Laden clouds gather,
Heart heavy as summer air,

29

Tears like silent rain.

He wanted to say so much more: to unburden his over-flowing heart, to share his futile hopes, to mourn their shattered dreams, to apologize for the abuse that she was no doubt suffering. But the haiku would have to do. To say anything else would be to risk more pain for her; even her life. Besides, lovers traditionally communicated through the weighted words of poetry.

With little thought, he grabbed a *haori* jacket, straw hat, and his two swords, and cautiously left his room. The monks at this time would be settling in for evening meditation. Sneaking out the back door of the priest's quarters, he crept behind the surrounding buildings towards the back gate of the temple complex. The night was still heavy with humidity, and the leaves hung limply on the garden trees. A single nightingale sang.

Arriving at the gate, he stepped under the dark branches of a tree, threw the *haori* over his kimono top, tied his hair in a traditional samurai top-knot, and capped it with his straw hat. With the two swords thrust into his *obi*, he would easily pass for a shabby *rōnin*. He glanced around, and seeing no one, silently opened the gate, jamming a couple of leaves into the latch to keep it from locking behind him. As he stepped into the street, Kinko closed the gate carefully, relieved to hear no sound of the falling latch. Walking rapidly, he struck out in the opposite direction of the main temple gate.

Nagasaki, in the year 1745, was among the most vibrant and diverse cities in Japan. Its unique level of multiculturalism resulted from the city's role as the only port open to non-Japanese shipping. Over a century earlier, to stabilize Japan and isolate the country from its neighbors, the Tokugawa shogunate forbade contact with foreigners. But since some trade was essential, the *bakufu* in Edo designated Nagasaki as the primary port where foreign ships could land.

This gave the city a distinctly international flavor. Nagasaki was home to a dynamic Chinese community, responsible for building several of the city's largest Buddhist temples. A small, permanent Korean presence dominated one of the city's thriving commercial neighborhoods. Although shogunate had long ago expelled the Spanish and Portuguese from the city, the Dutch emerged as the trading intermediaries between Japan and Europe. Dutch merchants were confined to a small, artificially built island in Nagasaki harbor called Dejima, but one could occasionally see them clunking around the city in their large, heavy boots, swathed in stifling, smelly, woolen clothing.

Given the mercantile nature of the city, Nagasaki's activity extended late into the evening. So after leaving the darkened side streets near the temple, Kinko was soon lost amidst loud and thronging crowds—some finishing up the day's trading, and others preparing for the night's revelries (and some, both). Dressed as he was, and keeping his head bowed, Kurosawa blended easily into the mass of people.

Once away from the temple, he made his way towards the harbor on the southwest side of the city to a small kimono maker's shop. It was a shop that Matsu frequented and that he visited with her several times. Though merchants were the lowest social rank in Japan, Matsu always treated the widowed proprietress, Sagara, with great respect. In doing so, she had won the dress-maker's deep affection. A woman of significant life experience, Sagara seemed to intuit the nature of their relationship and gave Kurosawa a kindly, indulgent smile when she saw him in the past.

Kurosawa worried the shop would close before he arrived. With great relief, he turned the corner off the main thoroughfare into a small side street and saw the white rice paper lantern still lit and a soft, yellow glow flowing out of the little shop. After scanning up and down the quiet street, he slipped under the *noren* curtain and looked around. At this hour, there were no more customers. Young women apprentices folded up the bolts of silk, cotton, and linen cloth printed in patterns of flowers and birds. Not seeing Sagara in the front room of the shop, Kinko approached one of the young women.

"Is your mistress here this evening?"

The young woman bowed and scurried to the back room. A moment later, Sagara walked through the fabric-covered doorway. She looked at Kinko with abstracted eyes for a moment and then gave a start of recognition. Kinko nodded her over to an empty corner of the shop, and before she spoke, he took the haiku out from his kimono and handed it to her. He had fastened it with an unmarked wax seal.

"If you please, honorable mistress, there is a certain noblewoman of our mutual acquaintance who at times graces your shop." Sagara nodded her head in acknowledgment.

"When you see her next, could you please give her this message from an unworthy admirer?"

Sagara bowed low, accepting the rice paper letter. As Kinko handed it to her, she took his hand in both of hers, and delicately touched it to her forehead. As she turned from him with the letter, Kinko saw a single teardrop laying on the back of his hand. She vanished into the rear of the shop, and Kurosawa wandered back out into the night.

Having accomplished his mission, Kinko walked from the quiet side street towards the busier thoroughfare. Emerging into a bustling crowd, he realized how much he would miss this city in which he had spent his whole adulthood. While recently he spent more of his time teaching in the temple, in his early years he had spent a great deal of time out in the city playing his *shakuhachi* and collecting alms.

Impulsively, rather than returning to the temple lest someone notice his absence, Kurosawa found himself following his feet further south and west towards his old haunts around the harbor. In the back of his mind, besides the risk of violating the abbot's command, he also knew that there was a small chance of encountering some Ekken family retainer. To his surprise, he realized that one of the reasons he brought both swords was that a brawl would not be unwelcome. Shaking his head, he smiled at his callowness.

Even as these thoughts ran through his head, he heard his name called in the crowd, and his hand fell to the hilt of his *katana*. As he turned, instead of the feared and sought-for conflict, he saw his friend Okamoto San'emon working his way through the crowded street, his face alight with the genuineness of his smile.

San'emon was short and stocky, with a head of close-cut, bristly grey hair. Though he was around sixty, he radiated a captivating vigor. He made a modest living doing calligraphy for illiterate sailors and peasants, helping them with everything from correspondence home, to lists of merchandise, to love letters. Kurosawa had met him many years ago while playing for alms on a nearby street corner, close to San'emon's calligraphy shop.

On that long-ago day, the older man had dropped some coins in Kinko's begging bowl and stood for a long time listening to him play. When Kurosawa finished, San'emon invited him to a nearby tea shop. The two felt an immediate connection and fell into a surprisingly weighty conversation about Buddhist doctrine.

These conversations became a regular—if sporadic—part of Kurosawa's life. He was frequently surprised by the depth of

San'emon's knowledge, and after a year or so, San'emon finally confided the reason: he was secretly an active lay leader of the clandestine Roman Catholic community in Nagasaki.

Jesuits from Portugal first began missionary work in Japan in 1549. The faith had spread quickly, particularly on the island of Kyushu, and Nagasaki was the heart of a vibrant Japanese Christianity. However in 1637, the daimyo on Kyushu—many of whom were Christian—rebelled against the shogun. 125,000 troops descended on the small island to crush the rebellion, executing nearly 40,000 rebels. Expelling all the remaining Portuguese, the Shogunate forbade any expression of Christianity. After this suppression, Nagasaki became the center of Japan's *kakure kirishitans,* "hidden Christians."

Kinko deeply appreciated the trust that San'emon showed him by sharing this dangerous secret. It conversely gave him the freedom to share candidly with the older man in a way he was unable to do within his own religious community. This was particularly true as Kurosawa's career lifted him higher within the temple hierarchy, and he felt a greater need to conform to the theological orthodoxy of Rinzai Buddhism.

In San'emon's presence, Kinko could cast off the shackles of his position and ambition, and freely explore ideas and beliefs. The similarities between his Rinzai Buddhism and San'emon's Christianity intrigued him; such as how Buddhism rested on the three jewels of *Buddha, dharma,* and *sangha,* while Christianity rested on the triune authority of Jesus, scripture, and church.

He loved that the Christian mystics who San'emon revered practiced Christian prayer in a way that paralleled his own Buddhist meditative practice. And the first time he walked into the older man's calligraphy shop after San'emon's confession of faith, Kinko laughed out loud upon realizing that the statue in the corner of the shop—that he always took to be the goddess Kannon—was actually the Virgin Mary with a Japanese face.

And so, on this night, with hardly a word spoken, San'emon guided Kinko to a nearby sake shop. They took a table by the side wall, next to a window that opened onto the street, giving them a quiet space from which they could observe both the street and anyone entering the shop. This was a usual precaution for San'emon, and tonight it suited Kurosawa as well. They settled into the shadows and ordered two bottles of sake—cold, on this hot summer night.

"You are unusually attired, my friend," began San'emon, settling himself in for a long conversation. Kurosawa started to respond with a clever quip, but decided instead to share the whole sordid story. He spoke of his banishment and the road ahead of him to Edo.

Sake bottles were emptied and replaced. San'emon listened intently and without interruption. When Kinko finished, both men sat and drank for a while in silence. The grey-haired head nodded, and the older man said, "So this is our last meal together. I am grateful that you are spending your final night in Nagasaki with me." He waved the waitress over and ordered some miso soup, rice, and some pork *gyoza*. Kurosawa raised his eyebrows. Because there were so many foreigners in Nagasaki, it was one of the few places in Japan where pork was plentiful. But Buddhist priests lived on a vegetarian diet, which San'emon knew only too well.

"You are no longer a priest," he declared, somewhat louder than was strictly necessary. "You should get used to eating like a regular person." Kurosawa nodded in acquiescence. San'emon continued, "In our conversations in the past, you have occasionally mocked me for Christianity's obsessiveness about sexual morality." He paused, meaningfully. "You weren't wrong to mock me, but it feels to me as though our Japanese approach to sexuality may be—occasionally—somewhat too casual."

Lifting his sake cup to his lips, Kinko nodded smiling. San'emon laughed. "I'm not trying to take advantage of your misfortune to make a philosophical point," he added. "It's what struck me at the moment."

Kinko smiled in recognition. "You should absolutely take philosophical advantage of my misfortune. This is how philosophy works itself out."

San'emon chuckled again. "Yes, I suppose it is. Nonetheless, I am sorry for your loss," the older man added more somberly. "And I will miss our time together. You are one of the few people with whom I can be myself."

"You have given me that same gift," returned Kinko.

San'emon paused, and then added, "If I were going to see you again, I would just sit and commiserate with you tonight, and then offer you my thoughts when your pain was less raw." Kinko waited. The customers of the sake shop had thinned out during their dinner, and the few remaining patrons had settled in for a night's heavy drinking. The waitress blew out several lamps, causing the dark wood of the room to fade to black.

"But since I don't have that luxury, I'd like to offer you some thoughts before we part. First, as one of my favorite thinkers said—a German priest named Meister Eckhart— 'A human being has so many skins inside, covering the depths of the heart. We know so many things, but we don't know ourselves! Why, thirty or forty skins or hides, as thick and hard as an ox's or bear's, cover the soul. Go into your own ground and learn to know yourself there.'"

"We are all so complex," San'emon continued, "we cannot ever know even ourselves, much less another. Spend this hard time burrowing beneath all those 'skins' and seek to understand yourself better. It is a lifelong project, and the only worthwhile one." He paused again, closing his eyes and resting his grey head against the wall behind him.

"Eckhart also said, 'Truly, it is in darkness that one finds the light, so when we are in sorrow, then this light is nearest of all to us.' I know it does not feel like it amid your current darkness, but the light is there, as near as breath. Seek it out with all your heart."

The two sat for a while longer, sipping sake, in a companionable silence, each with his own thoughts. Finally, Kinko moved to get up.

"Thank you for this time, San'emon; I will miss our talks," he said with a bow, and then added in a whisper, "and may your Jesus bless you richly."

San'emon bowed and returned, "And may your Buddha bring you enlightenment."

The two men left the shop—a slight wobble in their steps— bowed to each other in the street, and took their separate paths into the darkness. The temple's rear gate remained unlatched, and sneaking in the priests' quarters, Kinko collapsed into a pleasant stupor on his futon.

Kinko awoke the next morning to a slate-grey sky and the steady drumming of rain on the roof; a drumming that felt as though it came from inside his head after the previous night's drinking. He wandered out on the porch to see a downpour churning the courtyard into a lake of mud, though it failed to wash away the oppressive heat of the nascent day. A jay, nestled in the branches of a nearby spruce tree, cried out harshly, mirroring Kurosawa's frustration and discouragement.

Turning back to his room, Kurosawa gathered together the last of his belongings for the trip. There was not much: a spare set of undergarments, a couple of pairs of straw sandals, a straw raincoat, a small wallet of paper handkerchiefs, a set of chopsticks and bowls, a rolled straw sleeping mat, and a wide segment of corked bamboo in which to store water. He wrapped his teaching *shakuhachi* in a length of cotton cloth and placed all his belongings in an oilcloth pack with straps to wear on his back.

He dressed in his black monk's robe, stuck his two swords in his *obi*, and slung the pack over his shoulder, grabbing his *tengai*—the straw-basket headdress that he would wear on the road. This *tengai*, the black robe, and the *shakuhachi* were known as the "three implements" of the *komusō*: the outward signs that distinguished their order. While, as a samurai, Kurosawa could carry the two swords as a sign of his rank, most *komusō* carried no sword, or only the short *wakizashi* sword, wishing to project a less martial appearance on their mendicant wanderings. However, because he did not know what else to do with his *katana*, and since he was in an angry frame of mind, he took both.

Waiting until the community was at breakfast, he threw the straw raincoat over his robes, walked out into the unremitting shower, and trudged through the muddy yard towards the tall *mon* gate that marked the entrance to the temple complex. Traditionally, *mon* gates—flanked by the two massive statues of protective deities—marked the boundary between sacred and profane spaces, setting the temple apart from the world. This morning, that transition—leaving the sacred to enter the profane—was a profoundly weighty one.

Wiping the water from his eyes, he saw two priests under the eaves of the closest building to the gate. Approaching close enough to recognize them, neither man's presence surprised him. The first was the abbot's secretary, Hirata. A tall, imposing monk, his grave demeanor and general reserve bestowed on him a reputation for spiritual depth. Over the years, Kurosawa had come to realize that his taciturnity was a mask for a thorough-going vacuousness and that Hirata's only deep thoughts were about how to best pander to the abbot.

"Thank you for taking the time to see me off," Kurosawa offered, with an ironic edge to his voice. Hirata ignored the edge and reached inside his sleeve to retrieve several objects, which he offered to Kurosawa. The Fuke referred to them as the "three seals." The *honsoku* was a small booklet that contained a summary of Fuke principles and history. That history came from an older, longer text called the *Kyotaku Denki*, describing the origins of the Fuke order and the rules that governed its members.

The second of the "seals" was the *kaiin*, a document that identified the holder as a member of the Fuke order. Kurosawa noted with bitterness that this *kaiin* identified him as a simple "*kyugai*" lay monk. It did not surprise him that the abbot would follow through on his threat, but seeing it in print nonetheless struck him like a blow.

The third and last "seal" was perhaps the most valuable. The *tsūin* was a travel permit allowing the *komusō* the right to travel freely and without hindrance, a freedom unparalleled in Japanese society. The Tokugawa *bakufu* maintained control over the sprawling nation of islands by carefully monitoring travel. All towns of any significance, and every major road, had inspection stations to check travelers' credentials. However, a *komusō* monk could travel anywhere, and no local official could question why. The travel permit also exempted a monk from paying tolls on the road or ferry fees when crossing rivers.

"We assume that you will meet your needs as our order always has: by begging alms," Hirata intoned.

"I am grateful for your thoughtfulness," Kinko replied. "Please share my thanks with the abbot. And with a simple bow, the two parted. Kinko then turned to his friend and mentor, Ikkei.

"*Shishō*, it was very kind of you to bid me farewell this morning," Kinko said with sincerity. "But you should not have come out in this rain." Ikkei shook his head and waved off the concern, smiling.

"I think that I would have been here regardless, but in truth, I was not happy with how we last parted. Please forgive an old man's propensity to preach." He bowed.

"I am grateful for any wisdom that you have to offer, *Shishō*," Kinko responded. "Even when I may not want to hear it," he added with a smile. Ikkei laughed.

"Then let me risk one more small suggestion for your time on the road." Kurosawa waited. "The legendary founder of our sect was the Chinese monk Fuke—or Pu'hua—who lived nearly a thousand years ago. Out of great love for the common people, he always spent time with peasants and farmers, even at the risk of offending the wealthy patrons who could have provided for his temple. Likewise, our Rinzai forebear Ikkyu spent years as a vagabond among commoners and mocked the senior students in his temple for seeking to sell Zen enlightenment to those with money.

"As you travel, you will receive invitations to stay in wealthy households and comfortable temples. Make sure that you follow in the example of these wise monks and seek out the wisdom of those with little. Accept their humble hospitality and open your mind and heart." Ikkei stopped, and let his words hang in the heavy air.

Finally, he continued, "And I have one last gift for you." From his belt, he pulled a long, heavy *shakuhachi*. "This is a true *komusō* instrument," he said. "It has a deep rich tone and a surprising weight. I made it many years ago when I was traveling."

Kinko had heard Ikkei playing this favorite *shakuhachi* many times over the years and always loved the resonance and gravity of its sound. "Thank you, *Shishō*; I will treasure this gift forever." Reflecting on both the advice and the gift made Kinko uncomfortable carrying his swords. On an impulse, he said, "If I could ask one small additional favor..."—and taking his long *katana* and short *wakizashi* out of his belt, he offered them to the older man— "I would be grateful if you could find a home for these swords. I do not think I will need them on my travels."

Smiling, Ikkei took the swords with a bow. Kinko slipped the long flute into their place in his belt; then, bowing deeply, he whispered, "Thank you, master." And turning from his teacher for the last time, he placed the *tengai* basket on his head and strode off down the quaggy road to the north.

Ikkei stood for some time until he lost sight of Kinko amid the rain and the flood of early morning workers preparing for a new day. "Goodbye, my dear son," he whispered. "May the Buddha smile on you all your days." And wiping away the tear-mixed rain, he turned and passed back through the tall *mon* gate.

CALLING BAMBOO

L ike his mentor, tears ran down Kinko's face as he trudged through the muddy streets, although unseen under his *tengai* basket. Traveling north from the temple, he planned to join the main Nagasaki Kaido as it exited the city. This road—the island's largest—began in the city's harbor, where goods unloaded from ships traveled to Kokura City on the northern tip of Kyushu Island, and thence to Japan's main island of Honshu. It would, therefore, carry Kinko both past his family's home and onward to the ferry that would take him on the next stage of his journey.

Not having breakfasted, he stopped at a food cart which was setting up for the day's business and purchased a rice ball filled with pickled vegetables. He ate as he walked, while the deepening mud slowed his pace and soured his mood. Even at this early hour, carts and people transporting goods crowded the city. Most of the two-story wooden buildings along the street incorporated living quarters on the top floor, with shop space on the ground floor. As Kurosawa walked, he watched storekeepers sweep dirt from their shops and hang out signs advertising their wares.

Even at a slow pace, it did not take Kinko long to reach the Nagasaki Kaido, which was far wider and better maintained than the city streets. As he neared the edge of the city, he came to the first government post station and checkpoint, Yagami-*shuku*. These stations occurred every few miles along all the country's major roads, which allowed for regular horse changes for the shogun's messengers and served as security checkpoints to monitor travelers.

Early after taking power, the *bakufu* government had instituted a policy requiring the country's powerful *daimyo*—who governed the provinces throughout the nation—to establish a permanent residence in Edo where they would spend one year of every two. Their families, however, needed to stay in Edo continually, effectively acting as hostages against any potential rebellion. Checkpoints along all the major roads enforced this system—called *sankin kotai*—by carefully monitoring all travelers. However, given the heavy traffic of the morning and the foul weather, when the guards saw Kurosawa in his traditional *komusō* dress, they waved him through without even asking to see his travel permit.

As Kurosawa passed through the gate, he turned for one last look at his home of nearly twenty years, and taking a deep breath, said a mental farewell. The hard-packed road was firmer than the streets of Nagasaki, although the mud was still slippery and made for difficult traveling. Kurosawa let his thoughts wander as he walked past the maturing rice paddies and outlying farms around the city.

Komusō did not carry umbrellas, as virtually everyone else. Their *tengai* was supposedly enough head cover, and the lack of an umbrella was a sign of their indifference to physical comfort. In reality, the open weave of the basket provided little protection from the rain. And at the moment, Kinko did not feel indifferent to comfort at all. Drenched by the downpour and sweating from the humidity, he was thoroughly dissatisfied with life.

Thickets of maple, acer, and hemlock trees lined the flat road. Raindrops glistened from the needles of the hemlocks like countless jewels. The traffic thinned farther from the city, but the steady rain continued to impede his progress. Although playing the flute while walking was a part of the *komusō* tradition, Kurosawa could not bear to pull his *shakuhachi* out and play. Midday passed without the prospect of food, so he focused on moving one foot in front of the other.

It was mid-afternoon by the time he reached the next post station, at a little crossroads village called Eisho. Kurosawa hoped to reach the large town of Omura that day on the north coast of the bay, but the road led through a steep pass that would prove difficult in the rain.

Uncertain how to proceed, Kurosawa found a spot under the eaves of a building near the checkpoint. Pulling Ikkei's *shakuhachi* from his belt, he began to play. It took Kinko a few minutes to get the feel of his new instrument, but he quickly fell in love with its deep resonant first octave, which performed with great clarity and power. The upper octave was solid and strong without being shrill.

After warming up the bamboo, he played a piece of local *min'yo* folk music, a tune everyone from the area would know. Even in the rain, people soon gathered to listen. He could see people keeping time with their feet and smiling. When a sufficient crowd gathered, he began to play *Kokû*, one of the old traditional Zen pieces. The mood of the crown immediately became more somber, recognizing the religious nature of the music.

Most of the people listened quietly, but as he finished, several members of the crowd began to wander off. Before he lost his audience (and the prospect of some food), Kurosawa started another folk tune. With a crowd already gathered, people started to clap in time, and several joined in singing the familiar words. As the crowd warmed up, Kinko continued with another tune called "wet clothes," a song that was popular in the pleasure quarters. A bawdy tune, several of the men in the crowd loudly sang along.

As soon as this song was over, without even setting down his *shakuhachi*, Kinko grabbed his begging bowl and handed it to the closest person. While they passed the bowl, he played *Hifumi Hachigaeshi*— "Returning the Bowl"—the traditional Fuke piece to express gratitude for alms collected. To Kinko's delight, the bowl came back with two rice balls and a number of copper coins; more than enough for his immediate needs.

Locating the village bathhouse, he gave a few coins to the attendant who ushered him inside to a room dominated by a deep wooden tub of hot water. A young girl brought in a bucket of cold water and a bag of rice bran for washing. Alone, Kinko stripped off his soaked garments and washed, shivering—even in the heat—at the splash of the cold bucket. Then he gingerly climbed into the hot tub and sank down, letting the tension drain from his limbs.

When the attendant knocked on the door to tell him his time was up, Kurosawa was nearly asleep. He dressed hurriedly in his spare set of undergarments and with great reluctance, pulled on his soaked outer clothes. The bathhouse owner directed him down the street to a small inn, where Kurosawa rented an upstairs room for the night. In the trough of water in the back, Kurosawa washed his soaked undergarments and returned to his room to lay out his wet clothes to dry. He then settled himself into a half lotus on the tatami floor and meditated, watching his breath and centering his fractured spirit. At first, thoughts of Matsu clamored for his attention. What must she be doing? Was she being punished? Was she even aware that he was gone yet? Gradually, as he focused on his breath, the tension in his body ebbed, and he released the worry and frustration he had carried all day.

As the late afternoon ripened into evening, the rain slackened. Kinko descended to the main room, bringing his new *shakuhachi* with him. He seated himself at a low, rough, wooden table near an open window and held the instrument in both hands to carefully inspect it. It was a dark, mottled segment of madake bamboo, a little over two feet long—about three inches longer than the standard instrument. The bell of the flute was large and heavy, cut from the root ball of the bamboo plant. The tale, as Kurosawa remembered it, was that a bandit from the Osaka area who loved the *shakuhachi* first cut the instrument from the root end so that the heavy root bulb could double as a club.

The *shakuhachi* had gone through many incarnations since arriving in Japan a thousand years earlier. When the Fuke sect adopted the instrument in the previous century, they regularized it, so that monastic communities could play together. Now, the standard size of the instrument was about the length of a man's arm, one shaku (roughly a foot) and eight sun (roughly eight inches). Oddly, this is how the flute got its name: from its measurement *i-shaku-hachi-sun*. The teaching *shakuhachi* that Kurosawa carried in his pack was this exact size, allowing him to play in tune with any of his students. Since many monks made their own instruments, however, they often crafted longer flutes with a lower tone for the slow, meditative Zen music. Ikkei's flute was one of these.

Kurosawa waved over the young woman cleaning tables,

probably the owner's daughter, and asked for supper. Within a few minutes, smiling coyly, she returned with a small tray of miso soup, steamed daikon radish and cabbage, and a large bowl of rice. Lastly, she set down a pot of green tea. Kurosawa asked for a bottle of sake as well and launched into his meal. Not yet ready for company, as other patrons gathered for dinner, Kurosawa retreated to his room, where he sat in a formal *seiza* position and played. The rain had lightened to a drizzle by the time Kurosawa unrolled his mat and drifted off to sleep.

The next morning arose with the air thick and heavy, though at least the rain had ended. Kurosawa—still on the temple schedule—woke up early and took advantage of the silent inn to meditate before leaving. He gave most of what he collected the previous day to the innkeeper.

"Thank you for the lovely concert last night, your reverence," said the old man, nearly bent at the waist. Confused, Kinko hesitated for a moment before realizing that probably everyone heard him play the previous night through the thin walls of the inn.

Kurosawa bowed. "I hope that I did not disturb your guests," he said.

"Not at all," the innkeeper insisted. "It was very beautiful and made our humble inn into sacred space." Kurosawa bowed again, slung his pack on his shoulders, and set off down the road at a brisk pace.

Leaving the village of Eisho, the road bent steeply uphill to the Suzutza Pass. Though the walking was easier than the previous day, the road was still wet and slippery. Over the next few hours, the maple and hemlock trees gave way to ancient cedars and pines, towering over the road like pillars in a temple. The forest pressed close on either side of the road, and when Kinko stopped for a breath, all he could hear was the ominous dripping of water from trees draped in grey.

Cresting the mountain pass, the air became cooler as he descended on the north side of the bay. The road ran close to the escarpment, and from time to time, the trees opened, granting a view of the water below. Scattered about the bay, small fishing boats plied their trade, while the cries of eager gulls struck his ears. He could smell a hint of salt in the wind. As the road flattened out, small farms appeared, covered by the square rice patties that fed the country. Far ahead, off to his right, he could see Mt. Tara raise its noble head, still wreathed in clouds.

Foot traffic increased as Kurosawa reached the town of Omura. He paused there to collect alms near the harbor before he pushed on to Matsubara-shuku in the north, home to a vibrant community of blacksmiths.

The next few days were much the same: long hot walks, interspersed with begging for alms when he happened upon a village. Twice listeners offered the mendicant monk a place to spend the night. One night, a farmer, with nothing to offer for the begging bowl—his rice was not yet ready for harvest— offered the *komusō* his barn to sleep in. On another occasion, a weaver opened his home, allowing Kinko to spread his mat in the family's main room, next to the fire.

In both instances, Kinko remembered Ikkei's final advice and engaged the families with a variety of questions about their lives. Their simple but deeply held faith impressed him, as well as their gratitude for the prosperity and security provided by the rule of the shogun. They were thankful for the political stability that allowed them to grow and harvest crops year after year. They valued the ability to travel the roads in relative safety.

This revelation surprised Kinko because in his samurai world, the heaviness of the shogun's hand engendered significant discontent. Samurai chafed at their taxes and lack of freedom. Nagasaki still bore the physical scars of the previous century's ruthlessly crushed rebellion. Everyone understood that only the unvarnished fear of the power of Edo kept local lords at peace. Even the Fuke, with their close ties to the *bakufu*, resented how the government intruded into religious life.

For peasants and farmers, however, the shogun provided a stability unknown in previous generations. Most remembered the family stories from before the Tokugawa shogunate, when feuding between rival *daimyo* ravaged the land, and roving troops of bandits and soldiers stole what they wanted. The life of a farmer was always hard and precarious, but under the shogunate, it was far more predictable and prosperous.

Kinko continued to play his *shakuhachi* as he traveled. He found that his shorter teaching instrument was easier to play while walking, since its smaller bore required less breath. He had not met any other *komusō* yet on his journey; and so, was surprised one muggy afternoon to hear—off through the woods to his right—the distant music of another flute.

At first, it sounded like the player was deep in the forest. Kurosawa then met another road converging with the Nagasaki Kaido from the East and realized that the player approached from that road. He stopped and waited, listening to the haunting melody as it wafted down the empty woodland corridor.

Eventually, as he rounded a bend, the player appeared. A *komusō* of slight build, but unusual height, he looked like a slender stalk atop which a flower was about to bloom. When he saw Kurosawa, the stranger immediately halted his music and began a new piece. This was a traditional piece called *Yobitake-uketake* played when two wandering *komusō* met. It was call and response music in which one player performed the first set of phrases, and the second *komusō* responded with the next. Then the two would play the third section together.

This piece, "Calling bamboo, receiving bamboo," was a way of honoring the occasion of two monks meeting, but served two additional practical functions. The first was to reveal which temple each *komusō* was from, since every temple possessed its own variant on the piece. The second, and more important function, was to distinguish real *komusō* from counterfeit *komusō*.

In the previous century, when the shogunate had granted the Fuke sect the special permission to travel the country freely, there was a price: the *bakufu* would periodically make use of traveling *komusō* to deliver secret messages, and occasionally to spy. While the Fuke resented this imposition, they also recognized that it was the cost for their freedom to travel without hindrance.

However, sometimes the *bakufu* sent out their own spies masquerading as itinerant *komusō* monks, which greatly affronted the Fuke. Given the inherent difficulty of playing the instrument, *Yobitake-uketake* evolved as a code for weeding out these spies. When two *komusō* met, one played the first section —*yobitake*—and the other needed to respond with *uketake*. If the first monk played *yobitake* three times without receiving a response, he could assume that he had encountered a spy, and was obligated to punish him. Depending on the mood of the monk, that punishment occasionally meant death to the imposter.

On this occasion, Kinko immediately recognized the *yobitake* as coming from Rinseiken Temple, a Fuke temple almost due east from where he was now. Kurosawa raised his *shakuhachi* to his lips and played the *uketake* response, and then the two played the final phrases in unison.

There being no one else around, Kurosawa lifted the *tengai* basket and gave his fellow traveler a smile and a bow. His comrade, likewise, took off his basket, and returned the bow. Bright, active eyes shone beneath thin brows, above a mouth that seemed used to smiling.

"Greetings, brother," he called. "May the Buddha smile on you."

"It is a joy to encounter another of our fellowship," Kurosawa responded with unaffected pleasure. "You are traveling from Rinseiken Temple?"

"Yes, on my way to Hakata city—to Itchōken Temple."

"Then we travel together," Kurosawa responded cheerfully.

"I am Yoshin Shizu, and my family is from Kumamoto, vassals of the Hosokawa clan."

"My name is Kinko Kurosawa from Kuzaki Temple, although my family is from the north near Hakata and are vassals of the Kuroda clan."

On hearing Kurosawa's name, Shizu raised his eyebrows in recognition. "Are you the head instructor at Kuzaki-*ji*?" he asked.

"I was," Kinko quickly answered. And then, he deflected any further questions by adding, "I am on my way to teach in Edo at Ichigetsu-*ji*."

"Ah," Shizu responded, bowing, "a great honor."

"Come," suggested Kurosawa, "let us travel together."

Over the next days, the two *komusō* found themselves of similar temperament and quickly became friends. Like Kurosawa, Shizu was also the younger son of a low-level samurai whose father placed him in a Fuke temple, although a much larger one than Kurosawa's. Shizu was also ranked as a *jūshoku*, a full temple priest, and assumed that Kurosawa was the same. Kurosawa did not correct him, for fear of having to share his embarrassing story—their friendship being too new, and his emotions too raw.

One day, soon after they began traveling together, Kinko asked, "What was that beautiful piece I heard you playing the day we met?"

"*Chikugo Sashi*," Shizu responded. "It is the signature piece of our temple and a prayer to the bodhisattva Kannon to have mercy on this suffering world."

"Will you teach it to me?"

"I can try."

Over the next days, while they walked the Nagasaki Kaido, phrase by phrase, Shizu taught Kurosawa Rinseiken-*ji*'s sacred song. In addition to being an extraordinarily gifted player, Kinko possessed a remarkable memory and mastered the new music at a speed that elicited the surprised admiration of his companion.

"There are so many temples across our land," Kinko wondered aloud, "I wonder how many different pieces of *honkyoku* music there are?"

"As many as there are temples, I suspect," said Shizu.

"A life would be well-spent trying to hear them all," Kurosawa mused.

"Indeed it would," his companion agreed.

The season continued hot, the air heavy with late summer humidity. While the traveling was more pleasant with a companion, their alms collecting suffered. Shizu was a good player, and whenever the two passed through a village in which to beg, they inevitably collected a respectable crowd. But while their listeners enjoyed having two musicians, they were not inclined to contribute twice as much as they might have to a single player.

One night, as evening fell and the warmth of the day abated, the road broke out of the forest into an open field. Off to their left, the dying sun stained the high clouds with a deep orange glow. The two monks stopped for a moment to take in the glory of the dusk. Then Shizu shielded his eyes and pointed ahead and off to the left where they could just make out the roof of a small shrine under the eaves of the wood before them.

"That might be a place to stay for the night," he suggested, and the two men picked up their pace, arriving before dark. Walking under the red *torii* gate, they saw an older man, bent with age, sweeping the steps of the main shrine. The building only consisted of a small room with a serene Buddha sitting on the altar, before which sat some simple food offerings left by local peasants. Small *sessha* shrines dedicated to local *kami* and ancestors littered the surrounding grounds.

"Excuse me, *Obo-san*," Kurosawa said to the old monk. "We two unworthy travelers hoped to spend the night under the eaves of your honorable shrine." The old man jumped in surprise at the sound of Kurosawa's voice and, turning, bowed to his two visitors.

"Ah, worthy *komusō*, it would be a great honor to have you stay in our humble shrine. Please let me show you around the precincts." Kurosawa thought to himself that "precincts" seemed a somewhat exalted term for the paltry yard that surrounded them. Nonetheless, he listened attentively to the monk as he conducted the two *komusō* around the grounds proudly pointing out the small shrines to the *kami* worshipped in the nearby village, and the deceased members of local families venerated as bodhisattvas.

Eventually, the older man stopped and escorted the travelers back to the porch of the shrine. "You should be comfortable rolling out your sleeping mats here, brethren. Give me an hour, and I would be honored to return home to my wife and then bring you a little dinner." Both men demurred—but not too strenuously—and the old monk persuaded them to accept his hospitality.

Kurosawa and Shizu sat on the shrine porch and played for the hour as Kinko sought to perfect *Chikugo Sashi*. In what seemed a very short time, the old monk returned with a simple dinner and a bamboo flask of sake. The three men ate together companionably for some time while the older monk chatted about the goings-on in the local community. He had inherited his role as caretaker of the shrine from his father and was sad that he had no son on whom to pass the office.

Kurosawa asked him, "Do you consider yourself primarily a Buddhist monk or a Shinto priest?"

The older man looked at him blankly. "I'm not sure what you mean," he finally said.

"Well," said Kurosawa cautiously, "do you understand your primary role to be that of a Buddhist monk, observing and teaching Buddhist *dharma*, or primarily that of a Shinto priest officiating at those religious rituals?"

The old man thought for a while. "I'm not sure how those are different. I share the Buddha's words, and I preside over coming-of-age ceremonies and weddings. It is all one."

Kurosawa pushed a little harder. "For example, what do you teach people about the *kami*? Are they beings who—like us—are trapped in the cycle of *samsāra*? Or are they people who have achieved buddha-hood? Or are they the spirits of the Buddhas?"

The older man's face bore a look of troubled consternation. "I'm not sure that I've taught any of those things," he finally admitted—to Kurosawa's smug satisfaction. "Nor, honestly, am I sure that I've reflected much on them myself." He fell quiet.

After an awkward silence, Shizu began to talked about his own family, and the conversation fell into comfortable channels again. As the night deepened, the old man picked himself up and prepared to return to his home.

"Thank you both for your company," he said shyly. "And for your beautiful playing. You have hallowed this sacred space." His two guests rose and bowed to their host.

"We are grateful for your generous hospitality," Shizu said. "Please accept these few coins as our unworthy donation to your shrine and pass on our gratitude to your wife for this wonderful meal and for allowing you to spend the evening with us. Your company has been a gift to us." The men all bowed to each other, and the older man walked down a path into the darkness.

After their host had passed out of sight, Shizu chuckled softly and said, "You have high theological expectations for a local shrine priest, Kurosawa."

Kurosawa reddened. "Do I?" he said somewhat defensively. "Is it wrong to hope that religious leaders be able to articulate their own beliefs? This odd patchwork of doctrines is sloppy thinking. For instance, it bothers me to see this yard full of people's ancestors portrayed as bodhisattvas, when they were likely no nearer to enlightenment than we are."

To Kurosawa's consternation, Shizu burst out laughing. "Kurosawa, I make no pretense of being the theologian that you are, but I wonder if it is a terrible thing for a family to believe its ancestors were bodhisattvas? Couldn't that give a person the sense that enlightenment was possible for them too and maybe cause them to seek it a little harder? Might that make the world a little more beautiful and hopeful?"

Kinko thought for a few moments before shrugging his shoulders and acknowledging, "Perhaps I can get a little intellectually arrogant."

"Now what would the Buddha have to say about that?" Shizu needled.

"Perhaps something about the wisdom of humility," replied Kinko, with some embarrassment. "Or about gentleness towards all sentient beings. Or probably just, 'Shut up and sit,'" he finally acknowledged. And that is what they did.

That night, Kinko lay on the shrine's porch which faced the grounds, his back to his friend, when he felt Shizu's hand placed gently on his hip. Sexual relationships between monks were quite common—even encouraged in some temples, particularly between younger initiates and more experienced residents—and Kinko recognized this as an overture. Not wanting to offend his new friend, but also with images of Matsu still fresh in his mind, Kinko patted his hand affectionately and pulled his cloak more closely over his shoulder. After a moment, Shizu took the hint and rolled over on his other side.

Neither mentioned the events of the night the next morning. They made good progress over the next few days and continued to benefit from local shrines at which to spend the night. No peasants were willing to take in and feed two wandering monks, so there were also nights that they found themselves forced to spread their tatami sleeping mats on the forest floor and sleep under the hazy stars.

After traveling for some days together, and as their trust deepened, Kinko asked, "What is it that takes you away from your temple?" Shizu's face clouded, and he paused for such a long time that Kinko wondered whether he heard the question.

Finally, Shizu responded, "Well, it's a delicate task, which I am not supposed to discuss; but I can't see why you shouldn't know: some of the local lords in Kumamoto have heard rumors of a plot against the *bakufu*. Two weeks ago, several came together to hold a conference at Rinseiken-*ji*. There was a great deal of apprehension and disquiet about the question. My abbot dispatched me to see if the abbot at Itchōken has any information that would be helpful to us."

Kinko absorbed this news in taut silence. Uprisings against the *bakufu* were more frequent in the years immediately after the battle of Sekigahara established the Tokugawa as shogun, but there had been none for quite some time. It was true that Kyushu—because it was a separate island with a long and rich history—enjoyed a strong independent spirit. But the regional *daimyos* were so closely monitored and restricted that any sort of uprising seemed like a futile, far-fetched idea.

Eventually, Kurosawa replied, "I have heard no such whisperings in Nagasaki. But Itchōken-*ji* is a more prominent temple and undoubtedly monitors the politics of the island more closely." Shizu nodded, and the two walked together in silence for some time. Shizu finally continued, "It hardly seems possible that any *daimyo* would consider such treason, given the power of the shogun."

"True. South in Nagasaki, people still visit the charred remains of Hara Castle, burned to the ground by the shogun's troops a hundred years ago. The shogun never allowed anyone to build on that spot again. I assume, because he wanted it to remain as a monument to the *bakufu*'s invincibility."

Shizu nodded again, and added, "I know from listening to my father, that the *daimyo* bitterly resent having to support a second set of estates in Edo. And having to leave their families there as ransom. But they also seem to jockey with each other for proximity to the shogun. They simultaneously take umbrage at being kept away from their own lands and seek to be close to the power of Edo. When I think about it too hard, it makes me grateful to be a priest."

Kurosawa winced slightly at Shizu's mention of "priest,"

but agreed that it was a gift to avoid worrying about politics. He knew that abbots, particularly abbots of Fuke temples, could easily get drawn into these power struggles; but since his dreams of professional advancement had been stripped from him—at least for the moment—he could still enjoy the blessings of obscurity.

HOMECOMING

The next days brought a comfortable rhythm of walking, begging, and sleeping—or at least as comfortable as the ebbing summer's sultry heat would allow. With packs on their backs and *tengai* baskets covering their heads, the two *komusō* sweltered under their robes throughout most days. To make matters worse, out in the rural areas, bathhouses or *onsen* hot springs were less frequent, leaving Kurosawa uncomfortably aware of his growing odor.

As the days wore on and they drew nearer to their destination, the villages became larger and more numerous. Many were large enough that the two *komusō* could split up and beg for alms in different neighborhoods, allowing them to collect a little more money before meeting at an inn for the night, or on the far side of the village to continue their journey. And some had bath houses.

As they entered the Kuroda domain—the province of which Hakata was the capital—Kinko began to experience a feeling he gradually recognized as anxiety. Puzzled by it initially, he realized the anxiety was about seeing his father.

Kurosawa senior was an exacting man, with a strong sense of duty, and a defensiveness of his family's honor that stood in inverse proportion to the family's status in the social hierarchy.

Samurai, by definition, were at the top of the social ladder, as defined by decree of the shogun. Below them, in social rank, were farmers; below farmers were artisans; and below artisans —and at the bottom of the social structure—were merchants; a position that reflected the samurai distaste for anything having to do with money. Marriage was limited to those in a person's social rank, although in practice, that was rarely enforced.

Within the broad class of samurai, however, existed many gradations in rank. The shogun, of course, was at the top of this hierarchy. While there had been shoguns in Japan for a thousand years, for the last century and a half, the title belonged to the Tokugawa family, who had effectively supplanted the Emperor as the rulers of Japan. The current shogun, Ieashige Tokugawa, came to power earlier that year, although it was largely understood that his "retired" father Yoshimune continued to make the decisions. The extended Tokugawa family joined the shogun resting at the top of the samurai social pyramid.

Below them were the great *daimyo* families, who ruled the disparate regions of Japan on behalf of the shogun. Many of these families received their positions because they supported Ieyasu Tokugawa at the Battle of Sekigahara in 1600. On that historic day, he defeated Hideyoshi Toyotomi and consolidated control over all of Japan. All of these *daimyo* were supported by networks of minor lords bound to them by proximity or family history. A host of samurai retainers, in turn, supported each of these minor lords.

Kurosawa's father—Korenobu Kurosawa—was near the bottom of this complex network of relationships; so that while he was of the samurai class, his financial circumstances were more difficult than many of his farmer and merchant neighbors. His outrage at this perceived injustice resulted in a great sensitivity regarding his family's honor.

Korenobu was in the employ of Lord Kagae Akisada, one of the minor lords who supported the Kuroda *daimyo* family. One hundred and fifty years earlier, Nagamasa Kuroda had the foresight to support Ieyasu Tokugawa at Sekigahara, and the province of Chikuzen was his reward. While the territory was still occasionally referred to by this older name, it was generally called by the family name Kuroda. Nagamasa built his great fortress of Fukuoka Castle on the outskirts of the provincial capital of Hakata, high on a bluff overlooking Hakata Bay, a visual reminder to the city of his power.

In part, Kinko's tortured relationship with his father resulted from the normal temperamental differences between fathers and sons. But the elder Kurosawa also seemed perpetually frustrated with his younger son. Kinko was never sure why he was such a great disappointment to his father. Occasionally, the elder Kurosawa expressed his dissatisfaction with Kinko's inadequacies in fierce diatribes; but more often it was a subtle, insinuated, ongoing critique of his son's actions.

Kinko often remembered the day in his mid-teens when his father had returned home from a meeting with Lord Akisada, pensive and brooding. As usual, dinner that night was largely silent, until his father threw his chopsticks on the table and spat out, "I met with our Lord this afternoon, and he has no positions available to support you, Kinko." A subtle smile played on the lips of Kinko's older brother, who would inherit their father's position in the Lord's household. His mother's head bowed lower, as though suffering an unexpected blow.

"What will I do, father?"

"I am sending you to the Fuke temple in Nagasaki, where cousin Tanjuro resided for a few years. You can continue your *budo* studies there until we can find a lord whose service you can enter." Kinko recognized his father's embarrassment and disappointment, but it still felt like anger—anger directed at him. When his father finally sent Kinko far south to Kuzaki-*ji*, the younger Kurosawa knew that the temple's great distance would be a relief for both of them.

All these thoughts flooded Kurosawa's consciousness as his feet bore him closer and closer to his family's home on the southern edge of Hakata city. And while Kurosawa planned to stay there, he knew that he must first report to the abbot of Itchōken Temple in Hakata proper. Itchōken-*ji* was the largest and most prestigious Fuke temple on the island of Kyushu, and its abbot would be indignant if Kurosawa did not report to him immediately upon his arrival. Kurosawa did not need more difficulty with the Fuke hierarchy at this point. And so, as Kurosawa and Shizu passed by the road leading to his father's home, Kurosawa did not even mention the fact to his new friend.

The two drew near to Hakata city in the early afternoon of a late summer's day, and their pace slowed in anticipation of this final stage of their journey.

"I have enjoyed our travel together, Kurosawa," Shizu offered. "You are an easy companion, and I have learned much from your playing." He paused for a few moments. "You have been quieter and more reflective the past few days," he noted hesitantly. "Are you feeling unwell?"

Kinko began to brush the question aside, but then thought the better of it.

"Truthfully, Shizu, returning to my home has me conflicted. I look forward to seeing my sweet mother and younger sister, but my father will be more difficult."

"Will he not be proud of your promotion to Edo?" Shizu asked. Kinko laughed.

"I do not remember him being proud of anything I ever did," he admitted. "I'm sure that he will relish the enhanced status of the position, but I doubt that he will let me know."

Shizu laughed this time. "Ah, the eternal struggle between fathers and sons," he said, nodding. "I hope it goes well for you."

They soon crossed the post-station checkpoint on the southern edge of the city, making their way towards the city center. Built in the middle of the provincial capital, Itchōken was a huge complex. Kuzaki Temple in Nagasaki often felt like a large community to Kinko, but Itchōken-ji could have contained several Kuzaki Temples within its walls. The gate-keeper offered them a bow as they approached, but did not pay them much attention, being too used to the multitude of *komusō* who made their way to the temple.

When Kurosawa and Shizu asked where they might find the abbot, the monk raised his eyebrows in surprise and pointed towards a building in the middle of the temple complex. As soon as they entered the temple precincts, Kurosawa let a wave of familiarity wash over him. He could hear a group of monks playing a lovely, but unfamiliar *shakuhachi* piece in a building off to his right. It seemed like a brighter, more vigorous piece than was usual for *honkyoku* music.

As they approached the main temple hall—the *butsuden* —they noticed off to its right a large building bustling with activity, with all the appearances of an administrative center. They walked up the smoothly worn cedar steps, and deposited their sandals with the others, hoping they could distinguish theirs when they left the building.

Entering into a large room, falling dark in the late afternoon shadow, they saw an attendant kneeling to the left of the door. Both bowed to him, Kurosawa speaking first.

"Two humble travelers from Rinseiken-*ji* and Kuzaki-*ji* beg the favor of an audience with the abbot to convey greetings from our abbots."

This was the standard formula for requesting a little of a busy abbot's time. Generally, wandering monks would not trouble the abbot of such a large and prestigious temple for an individual meeting; one of his assistants would simply find accommodation for them. But with monks of Kurosawa and Shizu's rank, it would be a grave affront to fail to extend formal greetings upon arrival.

The attendant bowed and withdrew up the stairs behind him. A few minutes later, he returned and beckoned for Kurosawa and Shizu to follow him. He led them up the stairs and ushered them into a large audience room, where the abbot sat with several of the temple officials. He did not glance up as the two monks entered. Kneeling, they bowed their heads to the tatami floor of the room, awaiting his acknowledgement.

The abbot was a tall, thin man, whose large, bulbous head seemed to balance precariously on his fragile neck. After a short time, the abbot raised his eyes to his two visitors and beckoned them forward. As they knelt before him, pressing their foreheads again to the tatami, he wordlessly opened his hand to them.

Both men offered the abbot their *komusō* identification papers, which would tell the abbot their temples of origin and status. On reviewing Shizu's papers, the abbot nodded gravely, adding, "Your errand is known to us. We will summon you later this evening for conversation." Shizu bowed and edged backward. The abbot opened Kurosawa's identification papers and raised his eyebrows at noting Kurosawa's status as a simple lay monk. Kinko flushed with embarrassment. If Shizu noticed any of this, he was delicate enough to show no indication.

"It is an honor to have you here, brother Kurosawa," the abbot said. "What brings you to our unworthy temple?"

Bowing, Kurosawa responded, "Your humble servant is on a journey to Edo, at the invitation of the abbot of Ichigetsu Temple, to instruct the monks there in *shakuhachi*."

The abbot frowned. Given Kurosawa's obvious demotion, he knew that there was more to this story. There was also a long-standing rivalry between Itchōken-*ji* and Ichigetsu-*ji*, each coming from different lines of the Fuke sect, so that Kurosawa was in the awkward position of leaving Kyushu for a rival temple. Curious about both of these unusual circumstances, the abbot paused for some time reflecting, but refrained from voicing any of his questions in this public venue.

"Perhaps you will honor us with your playing this evening, Kurosawa," the abbot said. "You are both welcome here. The gatekeeper will direct you to our guest quarters."

"Your unworthy servant will be honored to play this evening, Lord Abbot," Kurosawa replied. "Thank you for your hospitality." The two guests bowed again to the tatami and backed out of the room.

Their guest quarters, reserved for traveling *jūshoku* priests, were clean and comfortable. Regular lay monks slept in a separate, more crowded building. Kurosawa was grateful for the abbot's generosity in assigning him this lodging, despite his diminished status. The two men deposited their traveling belongings and headed to the bathhouse to clean off the dust of the journey.

Relaxed and settled, they then made their way to the refectory for dinner, followed by evening meditation in the *zendo*. After the *zazen* session, one of the abbot's assistants—an awkward young man with an acne-covered face—led Kurosawa to the elevated platform where the abbot and governing council sat. Inviting Kurosawa to kneel, the abbott's assistant said as he turned to the assembled congregation, "Itchōken-*ji* is pleased to receive the esteemed teacher of Kuzaki-*ji* in our humble temple. He will honor us with his playing tonight."

A low murmur rippled across the room, as Kinko got up and walked forward. He sat in *seiza* on the platform at the front of the *zendo* and raised Ikkei's long *shakuhachi* to his lips. He began by playing a long, slow, low-octave *tsu* note, introducing the oldest of the three classic *honkyoku* pieces: *Kyorei*, or "Empty Bell." *Kyorei* harkened back to the founding myth of the Fuke sect. According to the stories, the Chinese monk Fuke would ring a bell to awaken enlightenment in his followers. The music of *Kyorei* sought to imitate the ringing of that bell. A deceptively simple piece played entirely in the lower octave, Kinko always felt that it captured the great tension of *zazen*: being at peace and yet fully awake and present. In the presence of the monks of Itchōken-*ji*, it would also invoke the bond that all the Fuke shared.

He could see the monks before him settle back into a meditative frame, as they closed their eyes, enjoying the familiar piece. After finishing, he kept both hands on the instrument, slowly drew his upper hand along the *shakuhachi* to his mouth, ceremoniously withdrew the flute from his lips, held it horizontally, and bowed over it. This was the traditional way to close a *honkyoku* piece. The *zendo* was as silent as the night.

He paused for a moment; and, glancing over at the abbot, saw him nod his oddly shaped head slightly. Taking that as an invitation to keep playing, he raised his *shakuhachi* again and played *Chikugo Sashi*, as a way of honoring his friend Shizu. Out of the corner of his eye, he could see Shizu smile, his head towering over his neighbors. After this piece was over, Kurosawa again glanced at the abbot, whose eyes remained closed and his head motionless, which Kinko understood as a dismissal. Bowing deeply to the gathering, he returned to his seat.

After the monks dispersed for the evening, Shizu followed the abbot and three of his inner circle back over to the abbot's quarters in the administrative building. As he watched his friend retreat, Kurosawa felt a gentle touch on his elbow. Turning, he saw a priest of about his own age and height with a prominent nose below a high forehead.

"Good evening, *Shishō*," the stranger began. "I am Hitoshi Taizen, the chief instructor here at Itchōken-*ji*. It was wonderful to hear you play this evening. I hoped that you might be willing to meet with a few of my senior students during your stay here."

Kurosawa bowed "It would be my honor, Taizen. Could I ask a small favor in return?"

Taizen waited.

"When I entered the temple this evening, I heard a group of monks playing a piece that was new to me." Kurosawa stopped and tried to hum what he remembered of the tune. Taizen's face lit up.

"*Kumoi Jishi*," he exclaimed. "It is a piece arranged by one of the earliest teachers here at Itchōken, named Iccho Yoshida. They say that the playful melody came to him while watching a group of clouds that looked like Chinese lions. Our monks often play it in the late afternoon, since it seems a bit too light-hearted for Zen practice. I would be honored to teach it to you."

The two made arrangements for Kurosawa to teach the following morning and to meet Taizen for a lesson in the afternoon. They bowed and parted for the night. Aware that teachers were often guarded with each other, Kurosawa appreciated Taizen's openness, which also provided a reason for Kurasawa to extend his time in the temple before returning to his home.

It was quite late by the time Shizu returned to their shared room. Kurosawa was almost asleep on his futon. Shizu quietly slid back the door and prepared for bed in the dark.

"How was your conversation with the abbot?" Kinko asked his companion. Shizu continued disrobing in silence. After several moments, he replied.

"The abbot has also heard several rumors of an insurrection plot. They appear focused here in Hakata, but he has no information on who or how high their rank might be. There is some indication it could even involve people in the house of the *daimyo* himself. The Kurodas have been allies of the Tokugawa since the beginning, but they have always been independent. No alliance lasts forever."

Shizu lay down on his futon, remaining thoughtfully quiet. "Another Kyushu rebellion would be disastrous for the island," he finally said. And then, as an afterthought, "Please, Kurosawa, keep this information to yourself. I am not to speak of this to anyone but my abbot."

"Of course, Shizu. It remains with me." And with that each man rolled over, pretending to sleep.

The following days passed pleasantly. Kurosawa enjoyed teaching again, and several of Taizen's students were strong musicians. He also relished learning *Kumoi Jishi* from Taizen, who was a very solid, if unimaginative player. Additionally, Taizen taught him one of the more traditional Zen pieces from Itchōken called *Banshiki*: a quiet, mournful piece intended to help deceased souls transition from this life to the next. He also learned the basic notes for two more pieces that were new to him: *Sashi* and *Azuma no Kyoku*.

Kurosawa possessed a remarkable memory for music. Over the years of learning from Ikkei, he easily memorized the musical repertoire of Kuzaki-*ji*. Given how thoroughly he knew those pieces, it was simple to add Shizu's piece from Rinseiken-*ji* to his memory. But with several new pieces—all acquired in such a short period—Kurosawa realized that he would need some written aid. So, he began jotting down his own rough notation of the music on a piece of rice paper. The notation would be meaningless to anyone else reading it, but it was enough to jog Kurosawa's memory.

Kinko enjoyed the beauty of the temple and the process of falling back into the daily monastic rhythm. The quotidian rituals of temple life felt safe and familiar. As traumatic as was his departure from Nagasaki, he found comfort in knowing that ultimately, he would be returning to some form of temple life. He felt an urgency to settle into the stable patterns that had nurtured him for so long.

Itchōken Temple possessed a long, rich monastic history, tracing its roots to the revered temple of Myoan-*ji* in Kyoto. Ichigetsu-*ji* and Reihō-*ji* were the two large temples in Edo which dominated the political life of the *komusō*, drawing their power from their proximity to the shogun. Myoan-*ji*—an older temple—was reputedly established by the Japanese founder of the Fuke sect, the Zen master Kichiku, in the 13th century. Its venerable history gave it a justifiable claim to be the spiritual center of the Fuke sect.

In the early seventeenth century, a priest named Ichio had traveled from Myoan-*ji* to Hakata—even then the most prominent city on the island of Kyushu—and established Itchōken Temple. Itchōken-*ji*, therefore, traced its lineage back to Japan's oldest Fuke temple and took great pride in that ancient association. While Kurosawa's journey would lead him to the political center of the Fuke, the monks at Itchōken were as smugly superior about their spiritual heritage as all those who find themselves excluded from political power.

Shizu spent many nights in conversation with the abbot, collecting what information the latter possessed about the political unrest in Hakata. One evening, a week after their arrival, Shizu returned to their room and said, "It is time for me to return to Rinseiken-*ji*, my friend; tomorrow will be my last day here."

"I have little to keep me here, either," Kinko responded. "Let's take our leave from the abbot tomorrow, and I will join you as far as my father's house."

The next morning, the two monks visited the administrative building one last time and asked leave from the abbot to continue on their journeys. The abbot bid them farewell and thanked them for their service. He then asked Kurosawa, "I assume that on your way to Edo, you will travel through Kyoto. Could I ask you to take some correspondence from me to the abbot at Myoan-*ji*?"

"Of course," Kurosawa replied. "It would be my honor."

"I will send the packet to you within the hour," the abbot said, bowing. Both travelers touched their foreheads to the tatami and left the abbot's presence.

True to his word, about an hour later, as the friends packed their belongings, an assistant came from the abbot with a small bundle of written material. Kurosawa tucked it safely away on the inside of his pack, protected from the rain and dust of the journey. Then, as unobtrusively as they had arrived, the two monks left through the *mon* gate and set off back towards the southern checkpoint of the city.

The day was bright and less hot in these waning days of summer. The two friends did not talk much, each lost in his own thoughts. A few miles outside of Hakata, they came upon the side road that led to Kinko's home.

"Well, my friend," Shizu began, "it seems our journey

together has come to an end. I will miss your companionship and your music."

"I will miss you as well," Kinko returned. "You have made this stage of my journey a joy. May Buddha smile on all your endeavors."

"And may Buddha cause the rains to fall upon you lightly," Shizu responded. The two men bowed deeply and turned down their separate roads.

Kurosawa walked on for some time. He let the ripening rice patties hold his attention, and avoided the anxiety rising in his breast. It was hard knowing that his father would assume that he had somehow failed in his work in Nagasaki (and harder still knowing that he would be correct). Still, he hoped to cast his journey to Edo as a reward for his musical skill with the promise of social advancement. Even so, his pace slackened the closer he came to home.

The Kurosawa home was one of several low-ranking samurai houses on the large estate of Lord Kagae Akisada. At the center of the Akisada estate was a large and graceful manor house, in which the Lord's extended family lived. Lord Akisada's parents were dead, but his in-laws lived in the manor house, along with his wife, and their four children, who were roughly Kinko's age and with whom he had grown up. Several of Lord Kagae's retainers, like Korenobu Kurosawa, lived within the walls of the estate, while others lived in the nearby village.

As Kinko drew near, he saw that the large double gates into the estate were open, guards stationed on either side of the heavy wooden doors. Having the gates open was usual, except in times of unrest. Approaching the gate, Kinko removed the *tengai* basket from his head. Mopping the sweat from his forehead, he bowed.

"I am Kinko Kurosawa, here to see my father Korenobu Kurosawa," he told the guards. The guards glanced at each other with what seemed to Kinko a look of understanding, and then one led him into the estate, accompanying him to his father's home. Their mutual glance caused Kinko some anxiety. He had not been home in several years and did not recognize either man. Certainly, he was not expected, was he?

As he climbed the steps to his home and took off his dusty sandals, Fusa Kurosawa met him at the door. An older, unmarried cousin of his father's who lived with the family to help raise their children, she had been a fixture during Kinko's youth and was like a second mother to him.

"Niban!" she exclaimed, throwing her arms around him, just as when he was a child, though now she barely reached his chin. As the second of Korenobu's sons, everyone called Kinko "Niban" throughout his growing up. "It is so good to see your beautiful smile!" Fusa's smile would—sadly—never be called beautiful, being somewhat gap-toothed, and residing under an oversized nose. And yet, a luminosity radiated from her soul, untroubled by anything but love.

"Dearest, Fusa," he replied, holding her tightly, "it is good to see your face as well. How are you and the family?"

There was the slightest of pauses before Fusa exclaimed, "Everyone is well." So slight was the pause that almost anyone would have missed it. Kinko did not, but decided to bide his time and wait for an opportunity to have a more frank conversation.

"Is my mother here?" Kinko asked.

"Yes, she's in the back, working in the garden," Fusa replied. "Set your things down. I'll have Tome bring you some tea while I get her."

Fusa shuffled out of the room, leaving Kinko to take in the changes to the home of his youth. All the furniture was in the same place, but it all looked older and more worn—not shabby, exactly, but well past its prime. The tatami mats needed replacing, and the calligraphy on the wall looked faded and dingy.

Shortly, the family maid, Tome, arrived bearing a small pot of green tea on a tray with two cups. She bowed, setting the tray down next to Kinko and poured a cup.

"It's nice to see you, Tome," Kinko said. "I hope your family is well." Appropriately silent until now, Kinko's acknowledgement allowed Tome to respond.

"Everyone is very well, young master. It is nice to see you, too." She stayed tidying the room while Kinko sipped his tea.

Moments later, his mother bustled in, cleaning her dirt-stained hands on a rag. She had always been a diminutive woman; today, she appeared much frailer than Kinko remembered, as though his father's belligerence was taking its toll. Despite her fragile demeanor, however, her face lit up on seeing her younger son. Holding open her arms, she cried, "Niban!" and Kinko enfolded her gently in his arms. Neither said anything, but took comfort in the other's presence and touch. When they separated, she held him at arm's length, looking him up and down.

"You look healthy, Niban," she finally said. "It is good to have you home." She sat down and joined her son in a cup of tea. "Have you been to Itchōken-*ji* already?" she inquired. Her lack of surprise at seeing him contributed to Kinko's rising apprehension, but they chatted normally about the happenings on the Akisada estate.

Eventually, his mother turned to the maid. "Tome," she said, "please take my son's pack to his old room." Then turning back to Kinko, she said, "Why not take a bath and get cleaned up. We can catch up more over dinner."

There was a surreal quality to the conversation: on the one hand, almost pointedly normal; on the other, not a single question about what brought him home. Kinko followed Tome to his old room, which was being used for storage in his absence, and made his way to the bathhouse.

When Kinko arrived at the dining room that evening, his father was already seated at the low table drinking resolutely from a bottle of sake. In the doorway, Kinko paused and bowed.

"It is a joy to be back home, honorable Father," he said. His father did not raise his eyes, but continued drinking.

"I would have hoped that it might be under better circumstances," Korenobu finally responded. Kinko's heart sunk. So even here, they knew of his disgrace. He sighed and knelt on the pillow at the table.

"My coming was not a surprise to you?" he began.

His father raised an eyebrow. "Of course not. For good or ill —with spies everywhere—there are few surprises in Tokugawa Japan. I suspect that I heard of your disgrace at the same time that you did. If you're going to be led around by your cock, couldn't you have found a more discrete way of doing it? Nagasaki has a decent pleasure quarter, if memory serves me. How is it possible to have screwed up being a simple monk?"

Even if Kinko had an appropriate response, the arrival of Kinko's mother and Tome laying out their dinner cut the conversation short. Dinner was a simple, but comfortable affair, including miso soup with tofu, dried daikon strips, marinated clams, pickled plums, and a large bowl of rice. When Korenobu showed no inclination to share his bottle of sake, Kinko motioned to Tome, who brought out another bottle that Kinko and his mother shared.

Growing up, there was never much free and open conversation at the Kurosawa dinner table. Tonight, the tense silence, broken by sporadic questions from Kinko or his mother, seemed normal. Finishing, Kinko's mother excused herself to help Tome clear the plates away, bringing out another bottle of sake that she positioned carefully between her husband and son. When the women were gone, Korenobu began where he had left off.

"Did you not even consider the difficult position that you put our family in through your irresponsibility?" he demanded.

"In all honesty, Father," Kinko replied, somewhat more combatively than he intended, "of my various worries, that particular one never occurred to me."

"Well, it should have," his father snapped. "The Ekken family have been significant vassals of Lord Kuroda for generations. Our own Lord Akisada is friends with Lord Ekken. Your indiscretion—even involving a distant branch of the Ekken family—makes my position with Lord Akisada very awkward. Not to mention the fact that there is some talk that the Ekken family has arranged for you to have an 'accident.'"

Kinko was tired, and tired of this conversation, and burst out, "If they feel their honor has been compromised, there are easy solutions to that: why not challenge me?"

"Fool!" his father fumed, "Because they don't have to. Your status is too low to merit a formal challenge, and they have the money to take care of it quietly. I don't know why the husband didn't challenge you in Nagasaki, but at this point, it's easier and quieter to have you disposed of on your journey."

Kinko desperately wanted to say, "Genzo Ekken didn't challenge me because I could kill him without a moment's thought." But he realized how petty and pathetic that sounded, so he kept his silence, his face flushed with rage.

"All of which means," his father continued, "that you should continue on your journey as quickly as possible. Every moment you are here brings risk to me of embarrassment with Lord Akisada, and risk to you of an untimely death. You should stay in the house tonight and be on your way in the morning."

Kinko said nothing. Waves of disappointment rolled over him. He had planned on spending some time enjoying his family home and resting before the next stage of his journey. But he acknowledged the prudence of his father's command, remembering the knowing expression on the faces of the guards at the gate. His father rose slowly and unsteadily from the table. "Your abbot gave you another chance, my son; try not to bungle it."

"Yes, Father," Kinko responded, bowing his head. His father exited the room, leaving Kinko hurt and distracted. His mother joined him a few moments later. She knelt next to him, put her thin arm around his shoulders, and laid her head gently against his.

"I'm sorry, my sweet Niban. Your father is a hard man, but he cares for you; and though he might not admit it, he worries about you. Can I get you some tea before you retire?"

"I don't need his concern," Kinko responded bitterly. "And I don't wish to retire. If I need to leave in the morning, I would like to at least see my sister." Tsuyu, the youngest Kurosawa child—now thirty-two—lived in the village with her husband, another low-ranking retainer of Lord Akisada.

"Oh, no," his mother gasped, covering her mouth. "Your father didn't want you to leave the house tonight. Perhaps I could send for Tsuyu and ask her to come to see you off tomorrow morning."

"I will not be a prisoner in my own house," Kinko shot back, his voice rising. "I am going to see my sister tonight." He arose, somewhat unsteadily, and left his mother kneeling by the table.

· · ·

Striding out into the evening's deepening shadows, Kinko walked to the gate and exited without giving the two guards even a glance. He turned left down the dirt road to the village. The cool air, beginning to hint at the autumn to come, helped him regain his equilibrium.

He soon recognized how rash it was to leave his father's house, particularly with nothing but his *shakuhachi* thrust into his obi—a precarious situation if he were to meet someone intending him harm. He immediately began to pay close attention to his surroundings. A gentle wind whispered through the darkening trees, and a hazy moon hung low in the azure sky. The cacophony of crickets seemed far louder than on a normal evening.

Happily, he met no one on the ten-minute walk into town. Less a village and more of a small hamlet, all the businesses were already closed for the night, leaving only the local tavern lit with a red lantern. Boisterous conversation spilled out into the deepening twilight. Two unkempt young men sat at a small table on the outside porch and suspiciously eyed Kurosawa as he walked by. Feeling their eyes still on him, at the next corner, he turned left down the street where his sister lived.

Pushing open the wobbly gate, Kurosawa walked up to his sister's house and knocked at the door. He heard muffled sounds within the house and waited for a long time before footsteps approached, and a young girl's face peeked up at him through the doorway.

Kurosawa bowed, and announced, "I am Kinko Kurosawa, and I am here to see my sister Tsuyu." The girl looked at him blankly for a moment before turning to run back into the house calling, "Mama, mama, it's for you." Within a few moments, a heavier tread approached the door and his sister's familiar face appeared.

She stared at him for a brief moment before she flung open

the door and threw her sinewy arms around her older brother. Like her mother, Tsuyu was of a slight build but unlike her mother, her lithe frame belied great strength and even greater force of will. Tsuyu was the one member of the family who never allowed her father to bully her, and would not cede an inch of ground in an argument. Korenobu made no secret of his delight when he was able to marry his challenging daughter off to another of Lord Akisada's minor retainers.

Tsuyu's husband was a stolid, steady man, with few aspirations above his current station, but a deep appreciation for his formidable wife. Their affection was palpable, and their life together was good.

Tsuyu ushered Kinko to the back of the house, where their rear porch overlooked a small but elegant garden. Like their mother, Tsuyu loved to have her hands covered in rich earth. She sat him at a low table and said, "Would you like some tea or sake?"

"Tea would probably be the wiser choice right now, dear sister," he responded. She smiled and disappeared back into the house. A few minutes later, she was back carrying a tray with a large teapot and followed by her husband and the daughter who had answered the door. The four of them chatted pleasantly for some time, and—at a signal from Tsuyu—her husband excused himself and his daughter to let the siblings talk more freely.

"So," Tsuyu commenced with a twinkle, "was she at least pretty?" Kinko could not keep from smiling. He always envied his sister's ability to cut to the core of any issue.

He rolled his eyes, admitting, "Yes, she was very pretty. But," he added quickly, "I did not fall in love because of her appearance." Now it was Tsuyu's opportunity to roll her eyes.

"You were really in love with her, then?" she asked, more sympathetically.

"Yes, I was. Am—I suppose. But it was all hopeless from the beginning, and I can't keep from kicking myself. For once, our father's fault-finding seems appropriate."

"That must sting," she laughed. Then, settling down again, she added, "I'm sorry. This must all be so painful and embarrassing." Falling quickly into the well-worn tracks of intimacy, the two siblings continued talking until the moon was well high. Tsuyu brought her brother up to date on the happenings around the estate and village. Kinko spoke of music, pulling out his *shakuhachi* and playing for a bit. Tsuyu closed her eyes and listened to him appreciatively. She was the one member of the family who always valued music and recognized her brother's gift.

"So, what now?" Tsuyu asked, the conversation winding towards a close.

"I don't know," Kinko admitted. "I guess I move on to the next chapter and try to rebuild the life I had planned. I keep trying to make our father proud."

"Well, perhaps you should keep your goals a little more realistic," Tsuyu laughed. "Maybe your answer should have less to do with rebuilding what you've lost, and more to do with exploring the new path that you've been set on." The two sat in silence for a while.

"I should get back home, so Mother can sleep," Kinko sighed, smiling.

"Yes," Tsuyu agreed. "Let me show you out the gate at the back of the garden."

Kinko looked at her in surprise. "Why would I go out the back?" he countered.

"Because, *genius*, my maid tells me that two seedy-looking goons have been hanging around the corner and keep watching our house."

Kinko reddened and shot back, "I'm perfectly capable of

dealing with a couple of local ruffians, if they are looking for me."

"I'm sure you are," soothed his sister. "But our mother has enough to worry about without you endangering yourself and risking more embarrassment to our father—who, I don't need to remind you, is easily embarrassed. Please humor me and go out the back gate, and sneak into the estate over the rear wall, as we did as children."

Though bristling at the indignity of the suggestion, Kinko conceded its wisdom. Embracing his sister, he slipped out the darkened back gate. Avoiding any prying eyes, he followed the back streets to the edge of the village, where he regained the main road. Pausing in the shadow of the last building, he carefully surveyed the placid street behind him. Seeing no movement, he slipped quietly onto the road and disappeared into the darkness of the forest.

He followed the main road to the estate, where he turned right off the road at the high enclosure wall and then walked along the open space on its outside. When they were young, the Kurosawa children had discovered a tree that was growing too close to the wall, with a branch that extended over it. They used it regularly for various games and indiscretions.

Kinko acknowledged his relief at seeing the tree untouched and managed to hoist his adult frame into its lower branches, climbing up to the overhanging limb. Once he shimmied over to the wall, it was a simple matter to swing down from the branch to the grounds of the estate. Undignified, perhaps; but unharmed as well.

PASSAGE TO HONSHU

The next morning dawned bright and clear, and somewhat less humid than the past weeks. Accustomed to early rising, Kinko was up before the household and spent some time in meditation. When he heard the rest of the house moving, he packed his things and joined his parents at the table for breakfast. Everyone ate in silence for some time until Kinko finally spoke.

"It has been good to see you both; thank you for your hospitality." He bowed.

"I would suggest," Korenobu offered, "that you take one of the side roads northwest to the Nagasaki Kaido. I have heard rumors that the Ekken family has hired some thugs to salve their wounded egos by giving you a good beating." Noting his son beginning to redden, he added, "I don't worry about your ability to handle yourself, it's just that there's no use causing a further ruckus about this matter. Better to let it fade away."

There was silence between them for a time. As Kinko's mother arose to clean away some dishes, Korenobu continued,

"Since you are on your way to Edo, could you do me the favor of carrying a letter to your uncle Kazunori, who works in the Edo household of Lord Kuroda."

"Well, as it happens," Kinko smiled, "since I am already acting as a postal carrier for the abbot of Itchoken-*ji*, it will not be an inconvenience to provide you with the same service." Korenobu reached inside the bellowed sleeve of his kimono and pulled out a sealed letter, handing it to his son.

As Kinko lifted his hand to take the letter, his father paused; and with an unexpected intensity, added, "This letter has no address, and I want you to make sure that you place it only in the hands of your uncle. Directly. No servants, no other family members. Only him."

This seemed an odd request to Kinko, but he nodded. "I understand, Father. I will make sure he gets it. Is there anything else I can do for you before I leave this morning?"

"No, thank you." And then, unexpectedly, Korenobu arose, embraced his son, and left the room. Kinko sat for a few moments finishing his tea and then collected his pack.

Little remained to do except to begin the last leg of his journey in Kyushu. He visited the kitchen to collect some food for the trip, and then walked slowly to the front of the house, absorbing all the familiar details and smells. He paused, closing his eyes, and took a long, deep breath. "Will I ever see these walls or these people again?" he wondered. A sadness settled on his heart that he could not quite pinpoint: an ending, a loss, a surrender...he wasn't sure.

As he expected, his mother awaited him at the front door of the house. Additionally, he discovered with surprise and pleasure that his sister was there. Both women held him long in their embraces without speaking. Finally, his mother let him go and reached to pick up something behind her. Turning back, she held out to him a solid oaken staff, the bottom shod in iron.

"I appreciate that you do not want a *katana* on your journey, but it would ease my mind if you would carry this with you," she said. "It will aid your steps and may ward off some dangers." Kinko smiled, nodded, and bowed. While he had always enjoyed sword practice, and while a *katana* was the soul of a samurai, he loved his training with the *jo* staff even more. Its greater length gave it some advantages over a sword; and as a Buddhist, it provided good protection without the lethality of the edged weapon.

"This is a beautiful gift, Mother," he said. "It will be a great comfort on the journey and a remembrance of home." He embraced her again, and she slipped a string of silver coins into his sleeve.

His sister then handed him a small package wrapped in rice paper. "Some *mochi*, for when your sweet tooth gets the better of you, big brother," she smiled. "I made them this morning, and they are best eaten fresh; so don't wait too long before you succumb." Then, leaning in closely, she whispered, "And watch out for pretty faces."

He smiled back at them both, slung his pack over his shoulders, and turned away to hide the tears forming in his eyes. He briskly walked to the gate, nodded to the guards, and turned west toward the Nagasaki Kaido. He waited until he was past the gate to put on his *tengai* head basket. He wanted the guards to have no doubt who it was that left, so they could report with certainty to Lord Akisada, or whomever else they might be spying for.

He kept a brisk pace for some time after leaving the estate, making as if to head directly west on the main thoroughfare. After about forty-five minutes, with no one in sight, he ducked off the road onto a small path leading to the north. While the woods were generally more dangerous, until he left the island of Kyushu, they were probably safer than the public roads. He did not know this path, but calculated that if he worked his way north and west, he would meet the Nagasaki Kaido. Ideally, he might even strike it north of Hakata, which would minimize any risk of running into Ekken family retainers.

The narrowness of the footpath made rapid progress difficult. Leafy trees pushed close on either side. Kinko was grateful for his mother's gift, which eased the walking. From time to time, he caught the sound of galloping hooves on the road to his south or off to the west and was glad for the anonymity of his route.

Kurosawa's path grew steep as he climbed. The last throws of a dying summer made for uncomfortably hot hiking. Except for a brief mid-day halt to eat a little of his food, Kurosawa progressed steadily all day. Although he crossed several trails leading west to the Nagasaki Kaido, he maintained his northward direction, trying to emerge on the far side of Hakata. He encountered no one on the small woodland path and felt his safety increase with each step.

Evening quickly fell in the dense wood, and rather than seek out shelter in some local peasant's hut, he rolled out his tatami sleeping mat in a small clearing off the path. On the warm summer night, and with several *onigiri* rice balls for dinner, there was no need for a fire. Amidst the darkening trees, before sleep overtook him, he pulled out Ikkei's long flute, and began playing *Kumoi Jishi*, in honor of his new friends at Itchōken-*ji* and to commit the tune to memory. Before long, full night embraced him and, rolling himself in his traveling cloak, he drifted off to sleep.

Kinko had barely closed his eyes when he heard the sound of footsteps following his path from the south. Instinctively, he pulled his pack around the tree that shielded him from the forest track. Sneaking a glance through the low undergrowth, he soon saw a rice paper lantern held aloft by a young, barrel-chested man, followed by a smaller man of indeterminate age. Both carried clubs with long knives slung at their waist. As they neared the place where Kurosawa left the path, the smaller man said, "We missed him; he wouldn't have come this far from the main road."

"Idiot," barked the larger man, "I'm sure I heard a flute playing. Keep your eyes open for any sign of a campfire."

"Have been," snapped his companion, "and ain't seen nor smelled a thing. This whole job is stupid. He's sure to show up on the main road. Let's call it a night."

"Fine," grunted the other. "At the next crossing, we'll head back and report." The two men continued their journey, and the lantern faded into the distance. Kurosawa, grateful to have forgone a fire, listened long after the two were out of sight. He slept fitfully for the rest of the night.

In the morning, Kurosawa rose early and followed the path of his two would-be assailants north. Upon reaching the first crossing, he turned back eastward, deeper into the forest. The path narrowed even further as he moved further away from the Nagasaki Kaido. Progress was slow enough that at the next opportunity, he turned north again. By mid-day, the trail began to descend, and the trees opened up. Passing over a small brook, Kinko was able to refill his bamboo water container. The air was motionless under the canopy of branches, with even the birds silent.

As the sun fell, the trail reached a ridge overlooking a valley to the north. Kinko looked down upon the countryside dotted with farms. Gazing off to his left, he could see no sign of Hakata. Assuming that he must be north of the city by now, he decided that it was finally safe to work his way west again. The footpath dropped steeply, and he saw occasional cottages amidst the trees, but he decided to spend another night in the woods rather than risk being seen.

The following morning, Kinko tied a scarf around his head to hide his samurai topknot and stuffed his robes in his pack, taking on the appearance of a common laborer. Soon he met a larger east-west road and turned left to make his way back to the Nagasaki Kaido. Before long, the woods opened up onto fields, and the path became a straight road raised above the surrounding rice patties. Farmers carted their produce to local villages, and day laborers became common. Kinko stopped one of these, "How far is it to Hakata?"

"If you travel quickly, you can be there by nightfall," the peasant answered. "You will need to continue west along this road about ten miles to the Nagasaki Kaido; then turn south on the Kaido for about four more miles to the city."

Kinko smiled, pleased to have come this far north and east of the main road. It was very likely that his detour would throw off any immediate pursuit. He set off at a brisk walk with the warm morning sun at his back.

After trudging through the forest on the narrow path for so long, walking on a straight, flat, open road was a welcome change. He made good progress and by early afternoon reached the Nagasaki Kaido, turning north towards the coast and passage to the island of Honshu. The traffic on the Kaido was notably heavier, but Kurosawa was not worried about recognition this far north of the city. Only on one occasion did he meet another *komusō* traveling south towards Hakata and playing his flute. As the monk approached, he slowed and seemed to take note of Kurosawa, though it was hard to tell with the *tengai* over his head. Kinko pretended to mop his face with a handkerchief until the other man passed by.

That night, he took the chance of staying at a roadside inn, where he quietly ordered dinner and promptly retired for the evening. The next morning was grey in anticipation of a cleansing rain. He was on the road early, dressed again in his robes and donning his *tengai* basket. He would need to make use of his monk's status if he was to pass through the two remaining checkpoints on the Kaido.

The day passed uneventfully, and he begged some alms at another tavern on the outskirts of Kokura, the castle town for the Ogasawara clan, the *daimyo* rulers for this part of Kyushu. A century earlier, Lord Tadezane Ogasawara had invited the famed swordsman Miyamoto Musashi here to duel with the lord's lance expert Takada Matabei. After defeating Matabei, Musashi settled briefly in Kokura, living in the castle.

Kokura was also the termination point of the Nagasaki Kaido, and the departure point—by ferry—for Honshu, the largest island of Japan. The city encircled a major port, with a crowded, bustling harbor. It was towards this harbor that Kinko made his way, hoping for greater anonymity in an area filled with strangers and travelers.

As the guards waved him through the last post station checkpoint on the Nagasaki Kaido, the slate sky that had been threatening rain all day finally opened up. It released a deluge that sent people scattering for shelter, and Kurosawa hurried to a nearby inn. A large wooden board hung in the inn's front, painted with a red caricature of a demon, under which was the name *Oninosumika*, the "Devil's Den."

Kurosawa smiled to himself, thinking that this would be an unlikely place for anyone seeking a Zen monk, and walked through the wet *noren* curtain into the crowded main room. It was a large space with a raised platform in the center, in the middle of which was a cooking fire. Many of the patrons sat cross-legged around low tables on the platform. Scattered straw covered the hard ground surrounding the platform to absorb the rainwater. This narrow space would ordinarily have been a walking area, but because of the crowd, the owner had wedged several small tables in to accommodate more guests. The noise was overwhelming, as Kurosawa squeezed into an empty seat at a small table, and ordered a bottle of sake from a young waiter.

When the young man returned with the bottle, Kurosawa asked him, "would it be possible to rent a room for the night?"

He laughed in response, "Not unless you were the shogun! But if you're willing to share, I'm sure we can add you to one of the common rooms."

Kurosawa smiled and nodded. "I am grateful." After ordering some dinner, Kurosawa made his way upstairs despite the early hour, and carved out some space for himself in the corner of the common sleeping room furthest from the door, and unrolled his sleeping mat.

It was not long before his fellow travelers filled the room, and Kinko was soon surrounded by the heavy breathing of sleeping men. Kurosawa was about to nod off himself when the last resident of the room arrived, apparently stumbling from too much sake. Still anxious from his journey, Kurosawa waited until the stranger settled down and had begun to snore before letting himself drift off into a restless sleep, with the rain drumming steadily on the roof.

The next morning dawned grey and wet. Both the rain and wind had picked up during the night. Kurosawa took his time packing his belongings and made his way downstairs for a tavern breakfast. Unusually busy, Kurosawa asked his waitress, an older woman, why so many travelers were still at the inn.

"The weather has the ferries locked in the harbor this morning, good Sir," she answered. "It's stranded all the travelers here until the storm breaks."

Kinko did not relish the idea of spending the day in a cramped tavern. Leaving his pack in the care of the inn-keeper, he threw his straw rain-coat over his robes, donned his *tengai* basket, and stuck Ikkei's flute in his obi, venturing out towards the harbor. As his hostess said, no ferries were leaving for Honshu that morning. Kurosawa gazed out over the open water. The wind whipped the strait into a frenzy of white caps that would have quickly swamped any of the low, flat-bottomed ferries.

Eager to continue on the next stage of his journey and frustrated at the delay and the miserable weather, Kinko turned back to the city and found a row of street shops with a straw overhang extending the length of the block. Positioning himself at the end of these eaves, just out of the flow of shoppers, he took out his flute and played.

He continued for the next several hours, while the subdued foot traffic of the rainy day passed him by. Usually, when *komusō* played, a crowd gathered, and a monk would play a few pieces, and then pass his bowl for offerings. In this weather, no one stopped, but passers-by tossed him coins, and one shop owner brought him out a bowl of rice around mid-day. It felt to Kurosawa more like private meditative practice than a performance.

Even so, by late afternoon, as Kurosawa walked back to the "Devil's Den," he had collected a fair amount of money. Leaving his raincoat, sandals, and *tengai* out on the porch, Kinko entered the large, full main room. The atmosphere was thick with tension. Waving over the young waiter from the previous night, he ordered tea and asked what was going on.

"Two of your roommates were arguing over a pair of missing sandals," the youth whispered. "We were afraid that they would become violent." A large group of travelers trapped together by rain was bound to result in some outbursts of frustration, Kurosawa thought. While his tea was prepared, he found the inn-keeper, reclaimed his pack, and exchanged Ikkei's long *shakuhachi* for his standard 1.8 teaching flute.

He sat down cross-legged on the raised platform and, warmed by the tea and the nearby hearth-fire, he began an old folk melody called *Mogamigawa Funa Uta*, the Mogami River Boat Song. By the time he played it through once, an older man, who looked like a traveling merchant, joined him, singing in a raspy baritone. As Kinko continued, several more voices joined in the second verse. By the time the third verse started, another traveler had produced a *shamisen*, playing with Kurosawa while the rest of the room clapped and sang along.

One song led into another, with other travelers jumping in to join with their own songs. After a few phrases, Kurosawa could generally pick up the right key and play along with the singing. The *shamisen* player was also good and could pluck along with the melody.

Soon, sake replaced tea, and the room was lively and boisterous with clapping and some dancing. The tension dissipated along with the rain outside. Finally, Kinko put down his *shakuhachi*, too much applause, and retired to a quiet corner of the room. Several of his fellow travelers came by to thank him, and one brought him a bottle of sake—not, Kurosawa noticed smiling, entirely full. After a while, the young waiter approached him bearing a large plate of food.

"My father thanks you for honoring us with your playing and would be grateful if you would accept this gift of dinner."

Kurosawa bowed and accepted the tray from him. "Please thank your father for his generosity and your gracious hospitality," he returned. Smiling, the youth backed away and returned to the kitchen. Kurosawa gratefully polished off his dinner and sat for the rest of the evening, enjoying the warm buzz of the room until taking himself to bed.

The morning dawned bright and new, as he knew it would. Kurosawa was up early, loaded his pack, paid his bill, and left before most of his fellow travelers were awake. He knew that the overflow of travelers would battle for seats on the ferries for much of the day, and he hated waiting.

There were enough early risers that he was still forced to contend with crowds at the ferry docks. His *komusō* status and the travel permit he carried exempted him from paying ferry fees. But with this crowd of paying patrons, the day would be long gone before a ferrymen would offer him a free spot. So, he pulled out a handful of copper coins and made his way onto one of the first transports across the Kanmon Straits. Kinko sat in the front of the low, wide boat, and watched the gulls dip over the white-tipped waves, still high from the night wind, but calming with the warmth of the rising sun.

As he looked over the rippling sea, his mind traveled back six hundred years, to the great Battle of Dan-no-Ura—fought just where the ferry crossed the straight. That battle had established the Genji clan as the first shoguns of Japan. He remembered the six-year-old emperor, Antoku, carried in the arms of his grandmother, as she leapt from the defeated Heike flagship to their death. So much violence; so much loss.

His mind ran to the poet Basho's lines: "The past remains hidden in clouds of memory. Still, it returns us to memories from a thousand years before. Such a moment is the reason for a pilgrimage: infirmities forgotten, the ancients remembered, joyous tears trembled in my eyes."

That was the word: pilgrimage. He was on a pilgrimage. Just naming it made the journey feel different somehow. A strong breeze tugged at his robes, as Kinko looked back on the island of Kyushu, where he had spent his whole life. People called it the "Land of Fire and Water": an island born of volcanos, and home to a fiery people. He watched the shoreline recede before his eyes; and he saw a lone leaf—blown from some anonymous tree on the shore—drift across the waves, landing next to the ferry, to take its own path to a new harbor. Autumn had arrived.

THE SUNNY SIDE OF THE MOUNTAINS

LIGHTS IN A GRAVEYARD

The port of Bakan was the first in a string of villages south of the castle town of Chofu, capital of the Nagato Province and home to the powerful Mori *daimyo* family. Climbing off of the boat, Kinko looked around, absorbing the bustle of travelers and merchants as they took their goods to and from Kyushu. On the edge of the harbor, facing the Kanmon Straits, lay a beautiful Shinto shrine, its large *torii* gate standing off the shallow waves of the beach. Wishing to give thanks for his safe crossing, Kinko elbowed his way towards the temple through the milling crowds.

The temple entrance was unusual: a bright red lacquered roof, which sat atop walls of rounded, whitewashed plaster. Passing through the gate, Kurosawa sought out the main sanctuary, where he placed several coins in the offering box accompanied by the customary bow. After reciting a prayer of thanksgiving, he wandered around the temple and enjoyed its fascinating architecture. Very different from shrines on Kyushu, these buildings were all white plaster, crossed with wooden beams of a vivid, almost garish, red.

He discovered that the shrine—*Akama jingū*—was dedicated to the child emperor Antoku, who had died at the Battle of Dan-no-Ura. The temple was originally built to appease the spirits of the dead Heike warriors who drowned in that disastrous military engagement just off these shores. As Kurosawa wandered the temple grounds, he spotted an odd statue of a *biwa* (a short-necked lute) player with no ears, sitting in a small *sessha* shrine. As he examined the unusual monument, a young priest approached him. "I see you are appreciating our statue of Hoichi the Earless. Do you know his story?"

"No, I'm new to Bakan—and Honshu, in fact."

"Well, it's an odd little story, as many ghost stories are; but it supposedly took place in this very temple." The young priest, enjoying a fresh audience for his narrative, sat down on the broad, grey stone step in front of the little shrine and settled in for his tale.

"As you know, long ago—in the year *Bunji* 1 (1185)—the Gempei War came to a dramatic end here in the straits of Kanmon, when the superior numbers of the Genji fleet overwhelmed the Heike navy. The Heike clan initially held the advantage that fateful day, until the faithless general Shigeyoshi Taguchi betrayed the Heike, attacking them from the rear. He had also informed the Genji forces on which ship the child Emperor Antoku sailed. The Genji were then able to focus their archery on that vessel.

"As the Heike watched the battle turn against them, many of the warriors—along with the young Emperor and his grandmother—leapt into the sea, rather than face the dishonor of capture. As a result, the angry ghosts of the Heike have long haunted these shores. Local legends claim that their wrathful spirits appear as lights called 'demon fires' on the shore and in the water. The shells of the crabs in this area are also said to look like human faces. And ghosts would sometimes try to drown unwary swimmers.

"To appease these spirits, the people of the village built this temple and its cemetery with seven large mounds raised in honor of the dead Heike warriors. Shinto priests conducted funeral services and built monuments in their honor. Although these efforts were largely successful in appeasing the spirits, to this day, lights still periodically appear in the graveyard.

"Well, many years after the temple's construction, the head priest invited a local *biwa* player named Hoichi to live here. The head priest extended the invitation both as an act of charity—because Hoichi was blind and homeless—but also because the priest loved *biwa* music, and Hoichi was an extraordinary performer.

Now it happened one night that the priest was away from the temple, and Hoichi was sitting on the porch of his living quarters playing his *biwa* in the darkness. He heard a heavy tread in the garden and stopped playing, waiting for his visitor to announce himself. A deep voice said, 'Hoichi, an important Lord is traveling through this province. Having heard of your musical skill, he desires a performance from you.'

"Hoichi picked up his instrument and followed the samurai, who led the blind musician on a long route. Although Hoichi knew the town of Bakan well, he soon lost track of where he was going. Finally, his guide arrived, ushering Hoichi into a large room full of people at a banquet. A sharp-voiced woman coordinating the dinner approached Hoichi.

"'Since we are here in Bakan, the Lord would like you to sing from *The Tale of the Heike*.'

"'I am happy to sing of that sad story,' Hoichi replied, 'but it is a long one. Is there a particular portion that the Lord would like to hear?'

"'The ballad of the Battle of Dan-no-Ura.'

"Hoichi then settled himself and began to perform the ballad of that disastrous battle. And as he sang, the people in the room wept at the beauty of his playing and the sadness of the story. He sang for hours, having to pause many times to wait for the sobbing to end. Finally, the woman who requested the music approached Hoichi again.

"'The Lord is grateful for your singing and invites you to perform again tomorrow night. Since he is traveling incognito in this part of the county, he also requests that you tell no one what you have been doing tonight.'

"Bowing before his host, Hoichi traveled back to his shrine escorted by his samurai guide, returning shortly before dawn. He slept much of the day and left again that night with his attendant. As on the first night, his singing and playing brought the assembled guests to tears; and again, the Lord invited him to return the following evening.

"By the next day, the head priest became suspicious, being unable to persuade Hoichi to divulge where he was spending his nights. So, he ordered two of his adepts to follow Hoichi and discover where he was going. That night, the two young men watched until the *biwa* player left. They did not see anyone with him, but were amazed at how sure-footed he traveled for a blind man. They followed him through the village streets until he made his way back to the cemetery at the rear of the shrine complex. There, he knelt before the seven mounds dedicated to the Heike warriors and began to play. The young men watched long in amazement, before returning to the head priest to report their discovery.

"The following morning, the head priest sat down with his friend and said, 'Brother Hoichi, you are in grievous danger. A wrathful spirit has deceived you into performing for the dead Emperor Antoku. Having obeyed the summons of the dead, you are now subject to their vengeance. But I can help you.

Strip naked and I will write the words of the Heart Sutra all over your body. When you hear the ghost come for you tonight, you must be absolutely quiet, and you will be invisible to him.'

"With that, the priest took some ink and copied the words of the holy sutra all over Hoichi's body. In his haste, however, he neglected to write them on the musician's ears. That night, when the ghostly samurai arrived, he called for Hoichi, and—receiving no answer—climbed up on the porch of the house. 'How odd,' Hoichi heard the samurai say to himself, 'I see the *biwa*, but not the player. All that remains of him are these two ears. I will take them back to the emperor to show him that the *biwa* player is no more.'

"And with that, the samurai grasped Hoichi's two ears, ripped them from his head, and strode off into the darkness. Despite the pain, Hoichi remained silent and still for the rest of the night. The priest arrived the next morning, mortified by the sight of his maimed and bleeding friend and at having caused the grievous injury through his oversight. He immediately brought a doctor, who treated Hoichi's wounds. Eventually, the *biwa* player recovered and became renowned throughout Honshu as the musician who could make the dead weep. He lived in honor here at the temple for the rest of his days."

With that, the young monk sat silent. Mirroring him, Kurosawa quietly sat, nodding at the poignancy of the tale. "What a wonderful story," he finally volunteered.

"Well, in truth," the young monk continued, "The cemetery continues to be an unsettling and perplexing place. I believe that the dead are not entirely at peace."

"I have just the solution for that," Kinko offered. "We have a piece of *komusō* music called *Banshiki Cho* that I learned recently in Hakata, played to help souls transition to their next life. Perhaps I could play it tonight in the cemetery to quiet some restless spirits."

The young monk's face lit up. "That would be marvelous. Perhaps you would do us the honor of joining in evening prayers and dining with our community tonight."

Kurosawa bowed. "Gladly."

Kinko spent the afternoon wandering around the port town and purchased some supplies for the next stage of his journey. The pufferfish of Bakan—its largest commercial seafood harvest —were considered a great delicacy throughout Japan. Called *fugu* when eaten raw in *narezushi*, it was extremely poisonous —even quite deadly—if not precisely prepared. Kurosawa had often desired to sample this delicacy and reasoned that it must be safer to try it in Bakan than anywhere else in Japan. So, he found a reputable-looking tavern to indulge his curiosity. The proprietress, a portly, middle-aged woman, was very proud of her *fugu* and served it with great fanfare.

Hovering near his table, to better assess his appreciation, she asked, "What is your destination, *Obo-san?*"

"I am going to Edo, by way of Kyoto."

"That's quite a journey," she returned. "If you don't mind some advice from a meddling old woman, I'd recommend you link up with some other travelers. The roads become less safe as you get north of Chofu. Distance undermines the authority of the shogun this far west." Kurosawa thanked her for the concern and excellent *fugu* and left the tavern, poorer than he had planned.

As evening fell, Kurosawa returned to the Akama Shrine, delighted to find his new friend waiting for him at the gate. Together they walked to the sanctuary and climbed the broad, dark wooden steps, joining a mix of monks and neighbors who were gathered for the evening prayer service. Since *Akama jingū* was a Shinto shrine, Kinko joined the people in their traditional prayers for the *kami* and the ancestors. It was a perfunctory service, attended by a handful of older women, for whom this was part of their daily ritual.

After the service, Kurosawa joined the other monks as they made their way to the temple's refectory. The meal was the standard fare of soup, rice, and fresh and pickled vegetables. The atmosphere of loud, raucous conversation, however, was dramatically different from his home temple. Rather than the muted conversations of a Zen refectory, this community understood their meal to be a social event. Most of the members were lay monks with families and lives outside the temple; only four monks were residents of the shrine.

All were full of questions about Kurosawa and his life at Kuzaki temple and of his journey. No Fuke temples were in this part of Honshu. In fact, no Fuke temples existed between Hakata and Kyoto at all. With very little knowledge of *komusō* practice, the conversation felt very free and un-fraught to their visitor.

When they heard that Kurosawa planned to spend the night in the cemetery playing his *shakuhachi* for the restless spirits, they were both delighted and impressed. All the men seemed to have stories of seeing ghostly lights there at one time or another or hearing voices in high storms. It was a little difficult for Kurosawa to tell how seriously they took these tales. It was clear, however, that they believed it would be a blessing to the fallen Heike warriors to receive assistance in moving on to their next incarnation.

Night had fallen by the time the meal ended. Kurosawa thanked the head priest, took Ikkei's long *shakuhachi,* and left the refectory. A warm, dense mist rolled in from the Kanmon Straits and enveloped the temple complex and cemetery. Glad that he had visited the site during daylight, Kurosawa crept along the flagstone path through the maze of raised monuments. It was far too dark and murky to read any of the inscriptions on the tall, thin tombstones. He could barely make out the small flower holders at the base of the markers—some of them filled by pious relations. Families had placed incense burners and the tall, narrow strips of wood—called *sotōba*—next to the central grave pillars to commemorate significant anniversaries.

He found his way to a long wall covered with small *jizo* statues, following it to the end. Seven tall earthen mounds which honored the fallen Heike warriors loomed large out of the surrounding darkness. Was it his imagination, or did the mist seem denser at these monuments, as if rising from the ground? Shivering, he wondered about the wisdom of this enterprise—the image of Hoichi the Earless rising unbidden to his memory.

Kneeling before the center mound, Kinko's knees became wet from the fog-soaked moss which covered the flagstone. He touched his head to the ground and sat for some time before the mound. Then, breathing deeply to calm his mind, he brought the *shakuhachi* to his lips. He blew the opening *tsu-re* notes of *Choshi*, a traditional piece used to warm up the instrument and check its tuning. In the thick fog, the leaden notes dropped like weights from the flute to the ground.

He then played *Banshiki*, a quiet, slow, melancholy tune structured like a mountain. Starting in the lower octave, the music gradually climbed into the upper octave before descending back to return to the lower octave. It finally ended in a gentle silence—a silence magnified by the eerie mist. Kurosawa played the piece twice more before stopping. His knees were sore from sitting *seiza* on the hard stone, so he moved across the path and sat cross-legged on the edge of the grave opposite the largest mound. He meditated for some time, staring at the mound with its forbidding air.

Then, off to his left, towards the sea, he saw a small dancing light on the edge of the cemetery. Intrigued, he picked up his flute, holding it more like a club, and ventured down the flagstone path. Although he moved quietly, he heard no sound from the direction of the light, and it seemed to recede before him, gliding out towards the water.

Following, Kinko stumbled on the low stone wall which enclosed the cemetery before he expected to, and stood there, watching several lights dance down the beach. Turning back towards the mounds, Kinko spotted another light in the fog. Large and bright, contrasting with the small dancing lights, this flame did not move. He returned up the path to his original spot and found a lit torch thrust deep in the ground before the central mound.

Kurosawa did not remember seeing an unlit torch in the ground before he arose, but given the darkness of the night, he might have missed it. Perhaps some young monks were playing a trick on their visitor. Or perhaps the grateful dead had accepted his offering. Whatever the source, Kurosawa was glad for the comfort of the light and settled himself again on the edge of the stone step facing the mound.

He began to play again, this time a variety of *honkyoku* pieces from his own temple and from his travels. He played for many hours and allowed the music to move him into a deeper state of reflection. As the night wore on, the mist lifted, and myriad stars shone forth. Eventually, the torch burned out, and the deep darkness enfolded him.

Kurosawa arose with the sun, having fallen asleep sitting, and found himself wet with dew. He stretched his sore body and made for the temple bathhouse, emerging clean and refreshed to take breakfast with the four resident monks. If any of the monks played games with the lights the previous night, they made no indication. Morning prayer followed breakfast, after which Kurosawa took his leave of the head priest.

"Thank you for your hospitality, *Gūji*," Kurosawa bowed. "You have a beautiful temple, and I pray the Buddha's blessings on you."

"It has been a joy having you here, Kurosawa, and I am grateful for your beautiful music, and your offering to the dead. Please travel safely on your journey. The road is easy through the local villages on the way to Chofu castle; beyond that, however, it becomes less secure. A traveling monk is hopefully safe, but please take care."

Kinko took his staff and swung his pack over his shoulders, setting off at a brisk pace through the harbor. The crowds were lighter this morning, and the sun was bright without being too hot. As soon as he was clear of the harbor, the crowds dissipated even more, and he walked comfortably through the village.

The harbor village of Bakan never really came to an end before it merged, almost seamlessly, into its neighbor to the north. One village turned into another as the road flowed into the castle town of Chofu to the north. Arriving by late afternoon, Kurosawa visited the famous Iminomiya Shrine, the oldest Shinto shrine in the province, renowned for its beauty.

A vast number of birds made their home there, and their raucous music filled the evening air. Outside the front gate of the shrine was a tall, thin stone pillar of roughly fifteen feet high with a stone cap on its top, which gave it a phallus-like appearance. Called the "demon stone," it kept unfriendly spirits at bay.

Kinko found accommodations towards the north side of the town—a large, respectable establishment called the "Castle Inn." Entering the main room, he found a crowd of merchants preparing for their trips along the San'yōdō, the long road that ran from Chofu to Kyoto over 300 miles to the east. Though the San'yōdō was a heavily traveled thoroughfare, it was not large enough to warrant the designation "*kaido.*" Its name meant "Road on the Sunny Side of the Mountains" since it ran on the south side of the range of mountains which bordered the sea.

Kinko found an empty table and motioned to the innkeeper to bring him a bottle of sake. He sat for some time and sipped his sake while he watched the whirl of life as it eddied and flowed around him. Picking up bits and pieces of the conversation from fellow travelers, Kinko distinguished two groups that were making arrangements to travel together to various cities along the San'yōdō.

He gave some thought to following the advice of the tavern proprietress and shrine priest to join one of these bands. But he preferred the freedom of traveling by himself, and dismissed being a target of bandits. Mendicant monks generally carried little money with them, and he hoped that any potential assailants would avoid the dreadful karma resulting from such an action—to the degree that bandits worried about karma.

SWORDS IN THE MOONLIGHT

The following morning dawned clear and bright, and Kurosawa got an early start, donning his *tengai* basket and setting off down the road. Many of the merchants and wagons milled about the front yard of the inn as they assembled for their journey. With a cool breeze flowing down from the mountains off to his left and a luminous, cloudless sky above, Kinko reflected that San'yōdō was aptly named and was grateful for an auspicious start.

While the San'yōdō was largely an east-west thoroughfare, just as the road left Chofu, it ran north. Kinko climbed sharply to a pass at the north end of the bay, where the road, the mountains, and the sea came together with a spectacular view which overlooked the water. The monk pushed back his basket, mopped his head, and breathed the deep, cool air. With a gentle slope downwards now, the walk was easy, and Kurosawa kept up a vigorous pace for the rest of the day, pausing only briefly to eat.

Wishing to conserve his meager resources, Kurosawa passed the night at a deserted shrine just off the road. The second day went much as the first, with the monk encountering little traffic. Around mid-day, he happened upon a crossroads where the San'yōdō intersected with a thoroughfare which led north through the mountains. On the far side of the pass, the road would meet another east-west highway called the San'in: "the shady side of the mountains." At this southern crossroads, a cluster of homes and businesses had grown up, and a lovely, well-located inn seemed to do a brisk business.

The inn yard was full of people, so Kurosawa found a spot in the front of the entrance porch and took out his *shakuhachi*. As he played, out of the corner of his eye, he noticed two men sitting on the porch of the inn watching him closely. With the basket over his head, Kinko could observe them without their knowing. Both were ill-shaven, with an unsavory look. They did not carry the dual swords of the samurai, but looked like *rōnin*, masterless samurai.

He watched as one of the men left to enter the inn, only to re-emerge shortly thereafter with a third man. This one was clearly a samurai, bearing both swords and wearing his hair in the traditional top-knot. He watched Kurosawa for a few moments, and then the two re-entered the inn.

Nervous and uncomfortable, Kurosawa brought his playing to a halt, taking up a hasty collection. Having lost his appetite and with no desire to meet the men in the inn, he quickly set off. Rather than continue east on the San'yōdō, however, he departed on the northern road—towards the mountains—in the hopes of confusing anyone who might follow.

Simultaneously berating himself for over-reacting and keeping an eye behind him, he walked for about half an hour. Taking off his *tengai* and abandoning the thoroughfare, he crossed a narrow pathway separating rice paddies towards a thin line of trees on his right.

As he suspected, the line of trees bordered another narrow

lane, which Kinko followed until reaching a small farm. An old, bent woman swept in front of the house.

"Excuse me, Mother, can you tell me how to get to the San'yōdō?"

It took her a moment to react, before she slowly looked up at Kinko and pointed down the road. "If you go about a mile, you'll reach another narrow lane going to your left. Take that and in about two miles, you'll reach a small crossroads. Go right, and shortly you'll meet the San'yōdō."

"Thank you, Mother," Kinko bowed. His brief detour may have been foolish and unnecessary, but it cost him little more than an hour and might have helped to avoid a conflict. Replacing the *tengai* on his head, he set off down the road. He reached the San'yōdō by mid-afternoon, and when he saw no one else on that particular stretch, continued his journey to the east. As a gentle evening arrived, he passed through a modest town, but decided against stopping at its inn. Instead, he bought several *onigiri* from a street vendor and continued on his way.

The evening ripened into a deep purple, and far ahead Kinko heard a brown-headed thrush off in the woods and wondered how well he could imitate its sound on his *shakuhachi*. The San'yōdō was still empty, and the monk began to laugh at his anxiety from that afternoon. He stowed his *tengai* in his pack so that he could see better in the waning light, while he ate one of his *onigiri* as he walked and softly hummed to himself.

It was nearly dark under the trees, and by this time, he had hoped to encounter a farmhouse or a small shrine where he could sleep. His path led him out of the wood into a bright, open field, illuminated by a nearly full moon high in a cloudless sky. He slowed. Something seemed out of place. Looking around, all seemed at rest; but his spirit was unsettled. He stopped; he breathed; he listened. All was quiet.

Too quiet. He heard no melodious thrush singing. Was it because he had left the shadow of the woods and was plainly visible? Perhaps. But a breath of anticipation hung in the night air.

All the while fearing that he was over-reacting again, Kinko abruptly turned to his right and walked back into the darkness of the forest's border. As soon as he had cleared the first line of trees, he stopped, slipped behind a large, low-hanging elm, and waited. There was no movement from the road ahead of him.

After several minutes, he quietly slid into a seated position and continued waiting. Zen Master Dōgen had taught monks to meditate with their eyes open, and while intended for monastics facing a blank wall, it was a technique well-suited to a moment such as this. Kinko sat, watched his breath, and stretched his awareness as far around him as possible.

Still, there was no movement, and still Kinko felt uneasy. "Well, if I need to sleep under this tree, at least it is a pleasant night for it," he said to himself. And he waited.

It was nearly an hour later, and Kinko had started to move from meditation to dozing, when out of the corner of his eye, he saw movement to his left. He dropped his hand out of its meditation position in his lap and found the thick oaken staff on his right side. Two dark figures had abandoned the forest shadows on the far side of the field and begun to move towards the point Kinko had entered the shelter of the woods.

They quietly moved to the place where he had forsaken the road and paused, looking around as if seeking a hidden path that he might have taken. Kinko saw them put their heads together, but could not make out any words. After consulting, they moved towards the spot where he had entered the wood.

Slowly—silently—Kinko raised himself from his seated

position and held his staff high on the right side of his body. He shifted further behind the tree as the two men approached. The first man walked past, casting about in the mottled moonlight for any sign of a path. Kinko let him go by.

As the second man passed the tree, Kinko moved forward and struck him hard from behind with his staff, knocking him to the ground with a groan. Raising his staff rapidly he made to strike at the man's companion, but the latter spun, swiftly drew his *katana,* and deflected the blow aimed at his head.

The speed and fluidity of the man's movement told the monk that he faced an experienced swordsman, so he paused before striking again. In the shadows of the trees, the two men stood motionless; the ends of the sword and staff nearly touched. Neither spoke, and neither moved; each watched for the slightest waver in his opponent's focus, leaving an opening for an attack. The only sound was the rustle of leaves on the forest floor as they shifted their stance.

After a moment, Kinko realized that he could not hesitate for too long. His opponent could afford to wait until the second man awoke from his stupor.

"Why were you waiting for me?" Kinko asked.

"Orders," the other answered.

"Orders from whom?"

The samurai smiled and assumed a *gedan kamae* (with his sword held in a low guard position), biding his time. He could wait.

With the advantage of the longer weapon, Kinko thrust a feint at his opponent's face. The latter jumped back out of range, snapped his blade against the heavy oaken staff, and then moved in for his sword thrust, as the monk had expected. Kinko stepped towards him and to the right, which allowed the momentum of his opponent's strike to push the staff over his left shoulder, and form a shield between the sword blade and

SONG OF THE SAMURAI

his body. The motion of his body and the staff drew the sword thrust past his body—gently, without effort—as he closed on his opponent.

Bringing the staff quickly around and over his head, Kinko struck down and hard. This time, the length and weight of the staff prevailed: even though the swordsman retreated while trying to parry the blow, the top of Kinko's staff still caught his head and knocked him off balance. He tried, vainly, to cut at Kurosawa, who easily deflected it, knocking the sword away.

"Now, who sent you?" Kurosawa demanded, overwrought by the fight and the adrenaline coursing through his body.

The samurai laid flat on his back with his arms spread wide and looked at him, silent and unsmiling. He could still wait.

Kurosawa could not and struck him smartly on the head—hard enough to render him unconscious, but not to kill him. Then, dropping to his knees, he searched the listless body until he found the man's travel documents, which he pocketed. He did likewise to the man's unconscious comrade, knowing that without these documents, they could not travel on major roads. Lastly, he took their swords and placed them against a large tree, then snapped them both with a kick of his leg. He flung the pieces deep into the woods.

Returning to the road, Kurosawa hurried eastward on the San'yōdō before either man could recover consciousness and follow. The moon was quite low and while he could easily make out the road, he could not see much to either side. Fortunately, the road at this point was level and straight, and Kinko kept up a good pace. He passed several farmhouses, but was far too anxious about being overtaken to stop so he decided instead to keep marching through the night and get a significant lead on his pursuers.

All the while he walked, he wondered how it was possible that the enmity of the Ekken clan could have followed him this

111

far from Hakata. Certainly, intricate networks of alliances existed between *daimyo* across Japan, but for the Ekkens to have requested such a favor from a *daimyo* on Honshu seemed surprising for an offense done to a minor member of the family in far-away Nagasaki. Could the samurai have been tracking him all the way from Hakata? None of it made any sense.

Wracking his brains, however, he could see no other explanation for the attack. Although wearing unmarked tunics, those samurai were obviously in the service of some lord and not random brigands' intent on robbery. Besides, the one acknowledged to Kurosawa that he was under orders. But orders from whom?

When the moon disappeared, Kurosawa's progress slowed; but he was confident that he was miles ahead of his assailants. Passing over a broad stream in the dark hours before dawn, he took out the plundered travel papers, tore them into small pieces, and dropped them into the swiftly moving water. While he was curious to examine them by daylight, he could not afford to be caught with stolen travel permits should he happen upon a checkpoint before daylight.

As it happened, it was well past dawn when he crossed the next checkpoint. His anxiety diminished: his pursuers—if they followed him at all—would not be able to get through the checkpoint without their papers, and would be detained for some time. Even so, he passed through the town and did not rest until he found an abandoned shrine in the mid-morning where he felt safe sleeping for a few hours.

He set off again in the mid-afternoon and traveled until he found a town large enough for him to go unnoticed. He chose the town's largest inn for the night. Entering the spacious main room, the usual assortment of travelers and merchants met

Kinko's eye. Kinko claimed a spot at a loud, busy table, filled with talkative merchants.

Ordering walnut dumplings and sake, he engaged a broad, burly man in conversation. As it happened, the man was a merchant from Hakata, transporting a shipment of *yukata* from his brother-in-law's sewing business on Kyushu to his cousin in Hiroshima. Kinko chatted casually about his own recent visit to Hakata, while he kept his connections vague. The man's name was Harushige Asano, a surname whose fame caused Kurosawa's eyebrows to raise, though he said nothing.

After the drama of the past two days, Kinko decided it was time for company, and Asano looked to be a good and stout traveling companion. "Asano," he ventured, "I am traveling to Kyoto, and wondered if I might join you on your journey tomorrow, since we share the same path for a period."

"I would enjoy the company," his new friend responded. "I am accompanied by several other merchants already, but it is always helpful to have another pair of hands on a trip like this." With those arrangements made, the two men bade each other good night and retired to their rooms.

RŌNIN

The following day dawned grey and cool; ideal traveling weather from Kinko's perspective, assuming the rain held off. He met his new companion in the inn's main room, eating and laughing with a rowdy group of merchants. The men on the trip had all been strangers two days before, but now treated one another as family, their conversation filled with mockery and good-natured jibes. They were a ragtag lot; some carried on businesses that were in their families for generations, others were simply in search of steady work.

After the last few stragglers arrived, the party gathered outside with their carts of goods. An ox pulled Harushige's cart, and Kurosawa gratefully accepted his offer of a seat beside him. After much adjusting and jockeying, the group started. Given the events of the past two days, Kinko decided to store his *tengai* basket in his pack to travel more anonymously. He wore his *kesa* robes, however, knowing that when they came to a check-point barrier, he would need to use his Fuke travel permit.

Harushige was an outgoing man, and the two fell into the

easy conversation of seasoned travelers. Kinko was surprised by how quickly the flask of sake emerged, but not so surprised that he declined to share in it. After riding together for a few hours, Kurosawa asked his question from the night before: "Are you connected to the famous Asano family whose vassals were the forty-seven *rōnin*?" Even though the actual events of the forty-seven *rōnin* had taken place only forty-five years earlier, the story had already acquired the status of national legend.

With a very thinly disguised satisfaction, Harushige acknowledged that he was from a distant branch of the same family. The famous Lord Naganori Asano had lived in the city of Ako, while the branch closer to Harushige governed Hiroshima. Several generations earlier, a younger son of the Hiroshima family gave up his samurai status to become a merchant, launching Harushige's family line. Nonetheless, Kinko's companions overheard the question and beseeched him to tell the story, although little urging was necessary. With practiced ease, Harushige launched into the well-worn tale.

On the death of his father, Lord Naganori Asano had traveled to Edo to take over his role as head of his family. He was young and a relative novice to the political corruption of the capital, unaware of the many pitfalls of navigating the complex court dynamics. So, when the shogun gave him an important assignment, Asano sought the assistance of the powerful Lord Yoshinaka Kira, a favorite of the shogun. Unfortunately, he unwittingly offended the Lord by not offering him a sufficient bribe for his help. Kira, therefore, publicly ridiculed Asano, who responded to the taunt by drawing his short sword and attacking Kira within the palace precincts. Although Kira provoked the attack and was only slightly wounded, the shogun condemned Asano to commit *seppuku* (ritual suicide) for the offense of drawing his sword within the royal house and assaulting the shogun's official.

Kira knew that Asano's retainers were likely to seek revenge, and took exhaustive steps to ensure his own protection. He kept his residence heavily fortified, while carefully monitoring the activities of Asano's samurai. After two years of dissembling their intent, forty-seven of Asano's former retainers (who were now *rōnin* by virtue of their Lord's death) attacked Kira's heavily guarded estate by night, cutting off his head and laying it at their Lord's grave.

Rather than dishonor the samurai with execution, the shogun allowed the *rōnin* to follow their Lord into death by committing *seppuku* with honor. It was a wild, romantic tale that Harushige told with gusto, and his companions reveled in hearing it again—imagining each unfamiliar detail to be the private legacy of Asano family tradition.

When Harushige finished, he sighed philosophically, and noted—to the surprise of his listeners: "I must admit that I have always found the story a little unsatisfying." And with their full attention, he continued, "So much death and sacrifice for a simple insult. I mean, I know that a samurai's honor is paramount, but—really—why not just wait to draw your sword until you get outside the shogun's house? Or challenge Kira to a duel of honor? It's a lack of self-control on the part of my distant relation. Still," he admitted, chuckling, "a good story."

His companions nodded sagely in agreement. The conversation turned naturally to the foibles of samurai and their destructive notions of honor. Several of these men were successful merchants, whose wealth gave them a sense of superiority to their poorer samurai neighbors. But they also knew that any sign of disrespect to those neighbors would likely result in their swift—and perfectly legal—death.

Kurosawa quietly listened and said nothing of his own family history, feeling a wave of defensiveness rise in his breast. He was aware of the toll that pride could take on a poor samurai family like his own. He had also certainly spent enough time criticizing his father's excessive vanity. But the fist of anger in his stomach betrayed his unwillingness to share his right to criticize with these merchants, who knew nothing of the values that bound the samurai as a class.

The rest of the day passed easily, and Kinko's anger faded away with the deepening sense of comradeship, facilitated by the free-flowing sake. Other than a brief stop to rest the animals and have a hurried mid-day meal, the caravan made consistent progress, stopping for the evening in a small town. Two of the group spent the night with local friends, while the rest found accommodation at the town's main inn. There, the men continued the day's conversation through dinner and far into the night.

Over the next several days, the temperature dropped, and the leaves began to turn color. Autumn had always been Kinko's favorite time of year, infusing him with a sense of quiet serenity, tinged with melancholy. It was the quintessential Buddhist season: a time to reflect on the inevitable transience of life and the indescribable beauty of the natural world.

On their fifth day together, as they crossed a barrier checkpoint, the cooling air brought with it a hard cold rain. It was late in the day, and the guards at the checkpoint—for no obvious reason—detained the travelers far longer than necessary. The company was tired, frustrated, and grumpy. Disinterested in traveling anymore that day, they took refuge in an unused guard shack at the barrier.

Little more than a roof with walls, their accommodations provided no comfort other than minimal shelter from the rain. They built a small fire in the cooking pit for warmth and shared their modest provisions.

The morning brought no relief from the rain, which settled into a steady rhythm and showed little interest in moving on. A few more travelers joined them throughout the day, making the guardhouse cramped and noisome. Too congested to play his *shakuhachi* or to meditate, Kinko found himself sitting dully with the others around the fire. He remembered some lines from the poet Basho in a similar situation:

> Eaten alive by
> Lice and fleas—now the horse
> Beside my pillow pees.

That night, a brisk wind whistled through the broad chinks in the ill-constructed shack, intensifying the cold. Like the rain, Kinko's companions seemed inclined to hunker down, their mood as foul as the weather.

By the third day, the rain eased enough that the residents of the tiny guardhouse broke free, and Kinko's company continued on their way. They traveled slowly on the muddy roads, and their dwindling food and sake made the companions laconic and surly. By late afternoon, the rain stopped, and they picked up their pace.

As they discussed their plans for the night, a group of horsemen came upon them from behind. Swords and topknots identified them as samurai, but their unkempt appearance and lack of clan crests confirmed them as masterless *rōnin*. Kinko's companions drew closer together, and Kinko himself dropped his head low.

The five *rōnin* passed the company, stopping in front of them while they assumed an air of indifference. "Greetings, travelers," their leader began. "Do you have any food to spare for some hungry samurai?" The tension between the two groups was palpable.

"Forgive us, masters," returned Harushige. "The rain has trapped us for three days, and we have not enough food remaining for our own meal." Two of the *rōnin* broke off from the group and guided their horses on either side of the company of merchants, prodding at their carts to see what the group might be carrying.

"Come now," the *rōnin* leader continued, as his face tightened. "You must have a few morsels you could share with a group of peacekeepers, maintaining the safety of these roads."

One of the merchants audibly snorted at this pretense, and instantly, the feigned smiles disappeared from the samurai's faces. They all dropped their hands to their swords. This was a dangerous moment for everyone. By law, a samurai—even a *rōnin*—possessed the legal right to strike down a commoner for disrespect. On the other hand, they were far from witnesses, and the group of sturdy merchants outnumbered the samurai, so attacking them would be a risky venture.

Before too many heartbeats passed, Harushige chuckled good-naturedly. "Come, noble samurai, in truth, this storm marooned us, and we have no food. But take this," he said, tossing the leader a string of coppers, "as a sign of our gratitude for your protection, and have a drink with your comrades at the next inn."

The *rōnin* leader—being in no mood for a fight—dropped his shoulders, shook his head, and laughed as well. "You are right, friend. This rain has worn all our nerves a little raw. We will be happy to drink to your good health." The *rōnin* gathered together and started to turn down the road when the leader's eye happened to fall upon Kurosawa.

"And who is this monk traveling with you?" he asked suspiciously.

"My idiot cousin," laughed Harushige. "I am conveying

him to a temple in Hiroshima, where we are having him cared for."

"Hmmm," the *rōnin* pondered. "One should be careful about traveling monks; they are often more than they appear."

"Perhaps so," acknowledged Harushige. "But I can vouch for this one, at least."

Nodding, the *rōnin* leader turned his horse, and the troop trotted off down the road.

As soon as the *rōnin* passed out of sight around the next bend, Kinko's companions let out an audible sigh. The rice merchant, who had feared for the fate of his stock, aggressively spat on the ground.

"Good-for-nothing thugs," he grumbled. The men all collected a few coppers for Harushige so that they would share his loss for the bribe.

"Your boldness amazed me," Kinko admitted to Harushige with admiration as he handed his friend some money. The others in the group murmured their assent.

His companion smiled. "*Rōnin* like that are little more than brigands. They have scant interest in asserting the privileges of their rank, and less in risking a brawl they aren't certain to win. Cowards are easily bluffed."

For the second time on this trip, Kurosawa found himself discomfited by this frank talk about people of his rank. Nonetheless, he was also dismayed by the craven bullying of the samurai. He knew it happened and knew that *komusō* monks were occasionally accused of the same thing. But from his sheltered view in the temple precincts, he did not have much occasion to see it. He was grateful for Harushige's cool head and leadership, as well as for his mother's gift of a stout staff.

"I'm not sure how much I like playing your 'idiot cousin,'" Kinko said to Harushige, smiling.

"Well, you certainly look the part," laughed his friend, slapping him on the shoulder. Then, more seriously, "One never knows who might be a spy, and it's generally best to avoid unnecessary questions."

The next several days were a slow and steady slog along muddy roads with modest traffic. The little company passed through several villages where they replenished their supplies. Most boasted inns and bathhouses where the troop could get clean and spend the night—albeit in shared rooms. Once they slept in the open on the ground under their carts. As they neared the castle town of Hiroshima, travelers on the road became more frequent and the journey felt safer. Their group began to break up into smaller bands, depending on how fast they traveled. By the time they arrived at Hiroshima, only Kinko, Harushige, and an itinerant carpenter remained.

The night before entering Hiroshima, the three stayed at a comfortable inn, doing a brisk business. Since leaving Chofu, Kurosawa had done very little playing or begging for alms. In part, it seemed too dangerous to draw attention to himself, but the logistics of playing and begging were also more complicated with a large group of fellow travelers.

Now, low on cash and feeling an almost physical need for the *shakuhachi*, Kurosawa settled himself outside the front of the inn to play, while his companions made arrangements for their lodgings. He played long enough to take a couple of collections, during which time, Harushige came out of the inn and sat down on the wooden plank steps. Plucking a long piece of grass and sticking it between his lips, he listened with his eyes closed. After Kurosawa finished, the two men entered the inn and took a table together.

"Let me buy your dinner tonight, my friend," said the

monk, pleased with his collection. "It is the least I can do for the comfort of your cart over the past days."

Harushige laughed. "Well, I will accept your offer with pleasure, though I'm not sure how comfortable the cart was. I'm fairly certain that you would have made faster progress walking."

"For a Zen monk, speed is rarely the goal," replied Kurosawa, laughing.

"That's an interesting point," responded his companion, becoming thoughtful. "My house in Hakata is not too far from Itchōken-*ji*, so I have heard *komusō* playing over the years. I am, of course, no musician—much less a monk—but as I listened to you play just now, I recognized some of the *honkyoku*, and it seemed that I have generally heard them played more slowly." And then, as though he could sense Kurosawa's rising defensiveness, he added, "Please, don't mistake me: I've never heard a sweeter or clearer tone in my life—I didn't even know that the instrument could sound that pure. It's just that the tempo seemed fast and some of the passages a little ornate."

Kurosawa was still orienting himself to this unexpected turn in the conversation. In all their time together, Harushige had never mentioned he was familiar with the Fuke sect or asked Kurosawa a single question about it. Nor did he indicate that he was well-versed in music. Perhaps reflecting the arrogance of his rank, the monk assumed the merchant's ignorance in both areas.

He raised his eyebrows in surprise and his lips tightened into a subtle frown. What could this uneducated shopkeeper— at the lowest end of the social hierarchy—understand about music or the life of a *komusō*? What gave him the audacity to criticize Kurosawa—widely acknowledged as one of the finest players in the Fuke community? Kurosawa, who even now was on his way to becoming an instructor at the most prestigious temple in the country? In the world?

And yet, at the same time, Kinko recognized the truth in his friend's observation. He had played the pieces a little faster than *komusō* generally performed them, perhaps with a little more ornamentation than strictly necessary. But why? And why was he now so defensive about it? After a long pause, he sighed.

"You are very perceptive, Asano. I'm not exactly sure why I chose to play like that. I think I assume the speed and ornamentation makes the music more interesting for those less familiar with the meditative impetus behind the music." Kurosawa punctuated this statement with a nod of his head.

"So, are you entertaining them, or teaching them?" Harushige asked. Again, Kurosawa felt ambushed by the question.

"Perhaps both," he responded tightly. And then—taking a deep breath—added, more reflectively, "I'm not sure that I always differentiate between those two."

Harushige sat thoughtfully. "Both may well be happening when you play, but they seem like different goals to me. Obviously, I could be wrong; you're the expert." And after a moment of silence, he added, "It's just that listening to you felt more like being at a performance than a religious service."

In his own mind, Kurosawa always played for a religious purpose, so his friend's words cut deeply. But they were clearly intended as honest reflections, and Kinko sat quietly and pondered them.

After a few moments of silence, Harushige, with no apparent sense of Kinko's internal conflict, changed subjects. "Kurosawa, you have a long trip ahead of you, going to Kyoto. If you have the time, please stay with my family for a little while in Hiroshima. We have plenty of room, and your presence would be a blessing."

Involuntarily, Kinko heard Ikkei's advice: "As you travel, you will no doubt have invitations to stay in wealthy households and comfortable temples. Make sure that you follow in the paths of these wise monks and seek out the wisdom of those with little. Accept their humble hospitality and open your mind and heart."

"I would be honored to accept your hospitality, Asano. Thank you so much for the offer."

"Excellent!" exclaimed his companion with gratifying enthusiasm. And with that, the two men retired to their room. Kinko sat for a long time in the dark, meditating and reflecting. There were times when his lack of self-awareness was unsettling.

DANCING BY LANTERN LIGHT

Kurosawa took an instant liking to Hiroshima—a thriving, energetic, and beautiful city. Harushige navigated his way, with years of familiarity, to his cousin's business in the heart of the commercial district. Like many merchants, the Asano clothing business occupied the ground floor of a three-story building, with the family living quarters on the two floors above.

The Asano family greeted Harushige's arrival with great festivity. He was clearly a favorite among his younger cousins, who called him "Uncle Haru" and immediately surrounded him with shrieks of delight. After passing out gifts to all the children, he joined his older cousins in unloading the cart of the bundles of *yukata*. The clothing was an astounding variety of colors and patterns: purple with silver dragonflies, pink with light blue peonies, green with golden dragons. Even Kinko, with little knowledge of such things, appreciated its high quality.

Kinko was immediately accepted into the family; if he was a friend of Uncle Haru, he was vouched for. The two men shared the guest room on the top floor, which was small, but adequate for two bedrolls. Still, it was not exactly what the monk imagined when Harushige had mentioned "plenty of room."

The Asano's were an extended family with several branches of cousins, all of whom lived and worked in the same neighborhood. The branch of the family that was hosting Kinko owned the *yukata* shop. Another branch owned a cloth dying business, and another ran a kimono shop that catered to a higher class of patrons. Because all the businesses were inter-related, members from all the branches pitched in to get any large job done quickly—such as unloading and storing a cart-load of *yukata* from Kyushu. Children from the different families all ran around together between the businesses and homes. Kinko was never entirely clear about which children belonged to which parents.

Harushige spent the rest of that first day helping his cousins with the business; Kinko pitched in where he could. Having spent most of his life amongst fellow samurai, Kuro-sawa realized how much of his class's disdain for merchants he carried. But the Asano family impressed him: their compelling work ethic, the pride they took in their products, and the satis-faction they derived from the service to their customers.

That evening, to welcome Uncle Haru back to Hiroshima, several of the family branches gathered for a large, raucous dinner. The food and sake were plentiful, and graciously shared. The table was the center of a prolonged flurry of activ-ity. As different dishes arrived and disappeared, children dashed around the room, and lines of conversation continually interrupted each other.

Given Kurosawa's smaller family and more taciturn upbringing, as well as his life in the temple, the chaos and cacophony caught him by surprise. But he was more bemused by how much he enjoyed it. He took great pleasure in watching the scampering children and could engage in a spirited conversation with his dinner table neighbors, or sit quietly, picking up bits and pieces of several competing conversations.

Just when the meal—and the evening—seemed to be winding down, several of the older male cousins suggested that they go to a nearby tavern. Harushige's enthusiasm for the idea carried Kinko along, and the smaller group was soon ensconced around another table in a bustling local sake house.

The conversation quickly turned to business and catching up on family stories. Kurosawa found himself talking to a younger cousin named Masahiko Asano, a member of the family branch that owned the cloth-dying business. All the young man could talk about was his upcoming marriage to a young woman from the neighborhood, whom he had loved since childhood. Kinko listened politely, charmed by his enthusiasm.

Some time after they arrived, across the broad room, a young woman pulled out a *shamisen* and began playing and singing. The tavern quieted as the patrons turned their attention to her. She was short, dressed in a simple grey kimono, and appeared to be approaching thirty. Not conventionally pretty, she possessed a lively and mobile face and drew her listeners in with her engaging presence.

Kinko listened, captivated by the music, until he felt his friend tug on his sleeve. "Kurosawa, you should pull out your *shakuhachi* and join her." Kinko demurred, but Harushige's cousins joined his prodding. Reluctantly, he pulled his flute from his sash and walked over to the *shamisen* player. He was not worried about his ability to play with her, but he was unsure of his reception. She played to earn a few coins and might not relish a partner who would want a share.

Sure enough, when the musician first saw him approach

and assumed that he was going to give her some money, she flashed him an appreciative smile. When she noticed him carrying an instrument, however, her look became withering. She was not employed by the tavern and could not deny him the chance to perform with her, but she was also unhappy about having to share any of her proceeds.

When her song came to an end, she quickly pocketed the donations already before her. Grudgingly, she slid over to provide Kurosawa some room on her bench. With barely a nod of acknowledgment, she launched into her next song. It was a familiar one to Kinko, and he quickly joined her. Their audience enjoyed the addition of the *shakuhachi* and clapped and called out requests as the two performed.

When the *shamisen* player realized that Kinko knew what he was doing and was not—at least—going to detract from her performance, she warmed up a little, turning to him slightly to engage him as a partner. The two played for some time, much to the delight of the tavern-goers, who expressed their pleasure with generosity.

Finally, the two musicians were ready for a break and bowed to the audience, who whooped and clapped. As the *shamisen* player began to divide up the coins in front of her, Kinko smiled and bowed, indicating that he did not expect to share in the takings. At that, her demeanor significantly thawed. "I thank you for your generosity, as well as for your fine artistry, good sir. Will you at least share a bottle of sake with me?"

"It would be my pleasure," Kinko responded.

The two sat down at a small table in the corner, and a waitress, without being signaled, brought over a bottle of sake and two cups. "You're quite good," she began.

"As are you."

"I wasn't sure what to expect when you approached."

"I know that you weren't looking for a partner; you were very gracious about letting me join you."

She laughed. "Gracious is not the word that comes to mind, but I appreciate your understanding. My name is Taka Kudo, by the way."

"And I am Kinko Kurosawa, from Nagasaki." Taka raised her eyebrows in surprise. "I'm here for a brief visit on my way to Kyoto and then to Edo."

"You have quite a journey ahead of you, then."

The two musicians chatted for some time about Hiroshima and music. Eventually, the woman paused, apparently reflecting for a moment.

"I don't know how long you are here in Hiroshima, but if you have the time, I play with a handful of musicians several evenings a week in the pleasure quarter just across the bay on Miyajima Island. It's a little inconvenient to get to, but the pay makes it well worth the trip. You should join us. I'll be leaving by ferry from the west side of the port late tomorrow afternoon." She paused, adding, "Oh... and don't dress like a monk."

Kurosawa pondered the offer throughout much of the next day, and finally only decided when Harushige expressed an interest in joining him on the excursion. Many years prior, near the beginning of the Tokugawa shogunate, to better control the illicit activity associated with prostitution in Edo, the shogun decreed that all prostitution must happen in a single area of the city—designated *yukaku*, the "pleasure quarter." The residents of Edo called their pleasure quarter the "*Yoshiwara*." This policy benefitted the *bakufu* in several ways: since all prostitutes needed a license, it was easier to monitor them in a single area. Additionally, since no one entering the pleasure quarter could carry weapons, government officials could easily contain any associated violence.

Yet the shogun never foresaw that this isolated island of pleasure would develop its own distinct culture, transforming the surrounding city. Its name, *ukiyo*—the floating world—alluded to the transitory nature of pleasure, and—more broadly—to the transitory nature of life. This insular realm developed its own music, painting, social norms, literature, and clothing styles. And—in a perverse twist of fate—those fashions became a driving force in fashionable Edo society. Artists imitated the paintings of the *ukiyo*; poets composed verse in the style of the *ukiyo*; women dressed like the courtesans in the *ukiyo*; a whole economy developed around the life of the *ukiyo*.

The shogun's policy in Edo proved so effective that it soon spread to other cities around the empire. The *daimyo* ruling Hiroshima moved the pleasure quarter out of the city proper to a literal island in the bay called Miyajima. Ironically (or perhaps not), Miyajima Island was also home to one of the area's most beautiful Shinto shrines: Itsukushima. Widely admired for its massive, red *torii* entrance gate which sat just off-shore of the island and appeared to float on the water, the shrine drew visitors from all over the region.

With a mixture of excitement and curiosity, Kinko and Harushige made their way to the ferry-landing on the south-west side of the city's harbor. It was late afternoon on a warm autumn day, and ferry traffic was heavy. It was too early for the regular clientele of the pleasure quarter, but boats plied back and forth from the island carrying merchants and comestibles, along with performers such as Kurosawa. Other boats carried the many pilgrims returning home from the Itsukushima shrine.

It did not take them long to find Taka, who sat in a cluster of musicians: another *shamisen* player, two *biwa* players, and a *shinobue* player. The last member of the group, who arrived at the same time as Kinko, carried no instrument and turned out to be a *koto* player. Because her instrument was so long and awkward to carry, she would borrow a *koto* from the "tea house" in the pleasure quarter where she worked.

They were a lively group, and Harushige immediately engaged Taka with a barrage of comments and questions about her performance the previous night. Again, Kinko found himself surprised by his friend's depth of musical knowledge. They all made their way over to a ferry and boarded for the short trip.

Kurosawa gasped in amazement at the beauty of the Itsukushima Shrine from the water, whose red vermillion buildings appeared on fire in the glow of the setting sun. The island landing was a chaos of ferrymen and merchants unloading packages from boats and reloading them onto carts going to different houses in the quarter. As the little musical troop arrived at the quarter's entrance gate, they joined a line of people whom the guards checked for hidden weapons.

Samurai, of course, ignored the line and entered a small building immediately to the right inside the gate. As Kurosawa passed it, he saw two armed guards flanking a grizzled old warrior with a scar down his cheek who sat in front. The shed contained the deposited swords of the samurai, who each received a ticket which allowed them to reclaim their weapons when their evening revelry was over.

Reflecting the rigid social hierarchy of Tokugawa Japan, the pleasure quarter had its own—equally rigid—ranking system. Immediately inside the entrance gates were the lower-class brothels, where simple prostitutes—called *yujo* or *hashi*—conducted their trade. For the *hashi*, business was a simple exchange of money for sex, and the girls took turns for the shared rooms in the brothel. As Kinko and the musicians passed by, half-clad girls hung out of the windows, waving and beckoning.

Deeper in the pleasure quarter were the more respectable establishments, with the more costly entertainment. On the ground floor of these "houses of assignation" sitting by the windows, or looking through latticed partitions that reminded Kinko uncomfortably of cages, were the third-ranked courtesans—*tsubone*—who at least benefitted from their own rooms for entertaining. The first and second-ranked courtesans resided on the upper floors, where a more subtle game was played.

This game began in the nearby "tea houses," which acted as the intermediaries for these higher-ranked courtesans. At a tea house, a patron needed to ingratiate himself with the proprietor, who would then introduce the client to the "entertainer." If the client reached an arrangement with the courtesan, she invited him to join her at her nearby house of assignation. If the woman in question were a *koshi*—second-ranked courtesan— she would entertain her client with singing, dancing, and witty banter once they got to the house. Sex was the assumed culmination of this delicate dance, but the foreplay was a sophisticated game. And—although it was unusual—the *koshi* could deny her client her sexual favors.

The *tayu*—the courtesans of the first rank—perched atop the pinnacle of this hierarchy. These women honed their artistry to the highest level and could sing, dance, recite poetry, and discuss philosophy and current affairs. Their cost was staggering, and engaging one was a process of wooing. A prospective client needed to meet with the *tayu* and her entourage at least three times at the tea house, and each visit required a significant financial outlay. And if the *tayu* accepted the client, and the evening of entertainment ensued at the house of assignation, any physical intimacy was entirely at the discretion of the *tayu*.

As the troop of musicians made their way deeper into the pleasure quarter, members of the party broke off to find their way to the different houses of assignation employing them. Kinko, Harushige, Taka, and the *koto* player made their way to an imposing establishment with the hopeful name of "The Scent of Cherry Blossoms." Kinko left Harushige on the first floor, flirting with the third-ranked courtesans, while he climbed the stairs with the other musicians.

At the top of the first landing sat an enormous man, with a large oaken club by his side. "Who's your friend, Taka?" he asked suspiciously.

"A *shakuhachi* player I met. He'll be a wonderful addition to the entertainment."

"Orochi ain't gonna be happy about paying another musician," grunted the enormous man. "But go ahead."

Taka led them down the hall to the right and slid open the door to a small room occupied by an equally small man with beady, close-set eyes. He looked up, flustered by the unknown face. "What's this about?" he asked in a querulous voice.

"An addition to the music," responded Taka. "The clients are going to love it. Trust me."

"They won't miss what they don't know, and we don't have money to throw at random musicians."

"Listen, Orochi, you buffoon, what you know about music wouldn't fill a sake glass. I'm telling you, he's gonna be great. There's more work than the two of us can handle, and you've got plenty of money; so give me the OK, or I'm going to go to Madam Usagi, and you're going to look like the moron you are." The small man looked down at the papers in front of him as if searching for something that would answer this challenge.

"Fine," he eventually agreed, without looking up. "But he

only gets half pay until we see how he works out." Kinko opened his mouth to agree, but Taka stepped on his foot.

"Nope," she continued. "I was only able to steal him away from the Clouds of Heaven house by telling him what we paid. And I told him that he'd get a onetime bonus for joining on as well."

"You impertinent trollop!" Orochi erupted. "You have no authority to make those kinds of promises!" Then turning to Kurosawa, he continued, "I will give you the standard rate; but no bonus!"

Trying his best to look disappointed, Kinko replied, "I agree."

"Fine, then. You and this huckster can go down to your room and prepare for tonight."

The musicians retreated to a small room on the second floor where they could store their belongings, dress, and—if they remained past the *yukaku* closing hours—spend the night. There, the three changed into the elegant kimonos that the house loaned musicians to maintain its standards of excellence. After getting food from the kitchen, the musicians assembled in one of the many large rooms used for group entertainment. There was a *koto*, and the three spent some time playing together to get a sense of each other's style.

The two more experienced performers instructed Kurosawa on what he should expect from the evening. All the first and second rank courtesans were skilled musicians—generally on the *koto* or *shamisen*, or sometimes both—and they would usually accompany themselves when they sang. But occasionally, they needed a musician if they danced or wanted to play a duet. And sometimes a room needed musicians while the courtesans ate and gossiped with their clients. Consequently, musicians rotated among the various rooms as needed—as a soloist, or accompanying a courtesan, or with the other hired musicians.

Awaiting the night's festivities, Kinko gazed out from a third-floor window and watched the pleasure quarter transform. When he arrived a couple of hours earlier, it looked much the same as any other urban commercial district. But after the sun set, strings of huge lanterns were hung from ropes across the streets. Meticulously painted and elaborately clad, *koshi* and *tayu* roamed the streets, followed by the servants of their houses. Vendors sold every kind of delicacy; itinerant street musicians played for donations.

And everywhere all manner of men prowled and strutted: proud samurai, wealthy merchants, greater and lesser lords followed by their servants. All on the hunt. Kurosawa watched with a fascinated detachment. It all looked like theater. Soon, however, his services were needed. He turned from the magical night outside to the raucous celebrations within the Scent of Cherry Blossoms.

The evening was a whirlwind of activity as Kurosawa moved from one room to another: performing while a beautiful *tayu* danced before a minor lord and his retinue; accompanying an elegant *koshi* as she sang and played her *shamisen* in front of a table of drunken samurai; resting downstairs and watching a wealthy merchant tossing coins to a group of third rank courtesans to entice them to remove pieces of clothing.

In a small upstairs room, Kinko and Taka joined a delicate *tayu* as she performed for a small group of minor officials. The musicians set up in the furthest corner of the room, while the courtesan chatted with her clients. She began singing without any accompaniment, and Kinko and Taka quickly joined her. All eyes were riveted on the porcelain face of the singer, while the instrumentalists became an unimportant part of the background, akin to a wall-hanging that has ceased to be noticed.

Kinko's music was generally the focus of wherever he was, so it was a new experience for him to be completely overlooked while playing. Initially, he frowned at his audience's disregard, but he soon found that the freedom from worrying about his performance liberated him musically. It also provided an unusual opportunity to watch and observe.

As an observer—and a hireling—Kurosawa could also scrutinize the world of the servants—a new perspective for him as a samurai. He watched their easy camaraderie, their mutual support in the face of frequent abuse and demeaning behavior from the house's patrons. It was like being backstage at a theater among all the technicians who enabled the magic on the stage.

Taka was a much-loved member of this community and engaged all the members with laughter and elan. Kinko envied her easy way of moving among the different classes of this tightly ordered society, as comfortable chatting with a first-ranked *tayu* as with the girl washing the sake bottles. And once, when she pinned back her kimono and humorously imitated the mincing steps of a courtesan, he could not help noticing her unexpectedly attractive figure.

Sometime later, as the pleasure quarter prepared for closing, Orochi summoned the three musicians to his office, and the little man placed a pile of silver coins in front of each. "I heard good things about your friend," Orochi said to Taka. Then, turning to Kurosawa, he added, "You're welcome back, if you'd like to come." The three performers bowed and backed out of the office.

"Nice job, monk," Taka said, smiling. Kinko, also smiling, bowed.

"Thank you! This is more money than I could have made in a week of begging. Can I join you again?"

"It was great having another player tonight. Come back tomorrow."

The three made their way to the musician's room and changed. Kinko thrust his *shakuhachi* into his *obi* and waited for his companions. The *koto* player followed him, but Taka rolled out a thin futon from a cupboard against the wall.

"It's too late for me," she said, yawning. "I'm going to sack out here. I'll see you tomorrow evening." Kinko felt an unexpected pang of disappointment, but smiled, bowed, and closed the door behind him.

Down on the first floor, Kinko found Harushige waiting for him by the fire, still flirting with the third-ranked courtesans, and thoroughly enjoying himself.

"Sorry to tear you away from your admirers," Kinko laughed, grabbing his friend by the sleeve. Harushige laughed as well, and the two men walked out into the night.

For the next several nights, Kurosawa found his way down to the ferry to Miyajima. It was an easy rhythm to fall into; and, while dramatically different from the rhythm of a temple, it also quickly became comfortable. He learned the flow of the evenings at the Scent of Cherry Blossoms and became acquainted with its cast of characters, each—like in a temple— with their own set of talents, quirks, and history.

During slower moments, he and Taka kept company with the workers on the first floor. They drank sake by the cooking hearth and chatted with the courtesans as they laughed about the customers of the day. It was easy, casual conversation; but as he got to know the women better, Kinko detected an undercurrent of sadness from them. Night after night, he would watch as they left rooms laughing with the customers inside, only to see their smiles fade as they turned away, and their faces take on a world-weary look.

As a samurai and a man, Kurosawa rarely questioned the rightness of his position at the top of the social order. But as he watched these evenings unfold, he was frequently disappointed — sometimes disgusted—by the behavior of his peers. They were often boorish, drunken, and disrespectful to the workers at the house. More than once, he noticed Taka with her arm around one of the courtesans to comfort her after some humiliation inflicted by a brutish samurai.

Among themselves, the women made little secret of their disdain for their patrons, laughing and mocking them behind their backs. Some of these women were themselves from samurai households, and many were unusually talented musicians. Some were exceptionally intelligent and sophisticated—imaginative poets and thoughtful observers. To his surprise, Kinko found himself feeling more empathy for the courtesans than he did for his samurai peers.

One evening, when the house was quieter than usual, he and Taka were sharing a bottle of sake by themselves. Chatting about the evening, Kinko observed, "It sometimes feels as though the dynamic between the patrons and the courtesans is more about power than sex."

Taka tilted her head and looked at him curiously for a moment. Then—much to his consternation—she burst out laughing.

"Kurosawa, my sweet, sweet friend. You are so smart and accomplished that I sometimes forget how charmingly naïve you are. Of course, it's about power. It's about samurai being samurai and making sure that everyone knows their superior status. It's about wealthy merchants showing that their money gives them the power to be as loutish, inconsiderate, and arrogant as the samurai. These women aren't here by choice; almost every one of them ended up here because of poverty. They are sold here—often by their own families—and are not free to leave before their contracts are purchased, either by themselves after saving money for years or by a wealthy patron who will make them a wife or concubine."

The surrounding room was silent except for the crackling of the fire. Two women at a nearby table listened carefully to the dialogue while they stared fixedly into their sake glasses.

"In fairness," Taka continued, "the women are playing power games as well. How long can they string a man along before his interest turns elsewhere? How much money can they squeeze out of a client before finally having to give him what he wants? Can they get a man drunk enough that he will fall asleep without ever getting what he came for? This is not a place that brings out anyone's best. The women are depressed and degraded; the men are desperate and pathetic."

The two sat in silence for a while. "Well, that's fairly dismal," Kinko finally concluded.

"Don't let it depress you too much, my friend. Everyone is doing the best they can in their own hard circumstances."

After the two sat in silence for a time, Taka rose. "We might as well get paid for our work; let's go see Orochi." As he stood up beside her, Kinko stumbled against her. Was it his imagination, or did she lean into him? Once they collected their fees, Kinko packed up to return to the Asano home, while watching Taka change from her formal kimono into her regular clothes. As she straightened up, Kinko cupped his hand gently behind her neck and drew her face to his. The kiss was delicate, furtive. Kinko trembled at the touch, surprising himself at his unplanned advance. Taka seemed caught off guard as well. But she smiled and said, "Well, it is quite late and by the time we get home, the night will be half gone." And without another word, she took his hand and blew out the lantern.

The next morning, Kinko awoke with the sun and found his arms wrapped tightly around Taka, whose back was snuggled into his chest. He had never spent a night with Matsu, so this was a new experience for him. He thought of the poet Basho's lines:

> Under one roof,
> Courtesans and monks asleep —
> Moon and bush clover

He did not move, wanting her to sleep, and wanting the moment to last. She was so warm and soft, and the scent of her hair in his nostrils was still intoxicating. "Is this what married couples feel like in the morning?" he wondered. "It's magical." Almost involuntarily, he drew her in closer to himself, causing her to stir and turn to him with a smile.

"Not bad for a monk," she said, kissing him delicately on the corner of his mouth.

"It does make me think that there are other viable alternatives to temple life," he returned, smiling back.

"There are indeed," she said. "You and I could make enough here in a short while to set up a teaching studio in the city. Not a bad option." She slipped out of bed and put on her *yukata*. Kinko could not take his eyes off of her, mesmerized by the curve of her hips and the graceful movement of her body.

"Now, Kinko, you are going to embarrass me if you keep staring."

They both quickly dressed and wandered out into the streets of the *yukaku*. The morning's aftermath of the night's festivities was a dismal sight. The entire quarter appeared to be waking up with a head-splitting hangover. Bleary-eyed madams hauled in burnt-out lanterns. Morning workers carted off debris from the streets. Intoxicated revelers lay sleeping in random corners between houses.

There was not much by way of food at this early hour, and Taka asked, "Where would you like to go and eat?"

"If you would humor me, I would really love to visit the Itsukushima Shrine."

She laughed. "Will this be a business trip, then?"

"No. All pleasure."

For over a thousand years, the Itsukushima Shrine was a center for pilgrimage throughout western Japan. It was a huge complex with four main sanctuary halls and a scattering of smaller shrines. The largest of the main shrines was dedicated to the goddesses of the sea, fortune, and the arts.

In stark contrast to the pleasure quarter, the shrine was dazzlingly immaculate. The lacquered, vermillion roofs gleamed in the early morning brightness, celebrating the new day. Sunlight danced on the water as a gentle breeze toyed with the waves between the island and the shore. The buildings were in an architectural style known as "Chinese gable," and imparted the complex with an echo of the refined elegance of a bygone era.

Even at this early hour, pilgrims made the trip across the water to visit the shrine. Along with them arrived the owners of food carts, setting up outside the main entrance. Kinko and Taka bought some breakfast from a vendor, and wandered into the shrine, exploring whatever caught their interest. The front of the main sanctuary extended out over the water, with striking views of the bay. They also stumbled upon a beautiful Noh stage, likewise built out over the water. Kinko discovered from one of the shrine attendants that in recent years the stage had been renovated by the Asano *daimyo* clan. He made a mental note to tell his friend Harushige about his extended family's generosity.

Throughout the morning and early afternoon, they explored the shrine. Beautiful gardens lay behind the main buildings, and the two lovers strolled down the flagstone walkways, amidst broad lawns of moss dotted with hoary, aged stone lanterns. They stopped to appreciate a delicately sculpted weeping plum tree draped protectively over a small pool. As Taka leaned discretely against him, he enjoyed the weight of her body pressed against his.

Kinko spent the next week with Taka. During the day, she showed him around Hiroshima, sometimes exploring, sometimes sharing small domestic tasks. She took him to the studio where she taught *shamisen* and the small room above the studio that she shared with the two other instructors. She introduced him to the best businesses for buying gifts for the Asano family; his rapidly expanding finances contributing to his growing generosity. In the evenings, they would play at the Scent of Cherry Blossoms and spend the night together in the musicians' room.

One night, when they both needed a break from the pleasure quarter, they parted ways and Kinko joined the family dinner at the Asano house. He and Harushige walked to a nearby tavern for some sake afterward and talked until late in the evening.

"I've missed your company these last few days, Kurosawa," his friend said, smiling. "I didn't realize how used to your presence I had become. And don't bother telling me that you missed mine as well; you found a better option." Harushige laughed at his own joke. "I'll be here in Hiroshima for the next couple of days, but I'll head back to Hakata soon with a load of lovely cloth for my brother-in-law to sew into *yukata*."

Kinko knew that he should move on as well. He had not intended to stay in Hiroshima for nearly this amount of time, but he was more relaxed and joyful than he could remember. So, with a heavy heart, he boarded the ferry the following afternoon for the pleasure quarter. The night went as usual, and as the evening drew to a close, he found himself sipping sake again with Taka in front of the cooking fire.

"Taka," he started, tentatively. "I think it's time I continue my journey."

She stared at him blankly for a moment, before seeming to jolt to awareness. "Oh," she laughed hesitantly, "I was hoping I could tempt you into starting that music school with me."

Even though he knew she said it half-jokingly, he responded, "It is a beautiful idea, and I'm tempted. But I'm not ready to abandon what the abbot at Ichigetsu Temple has invited me to do." He watched as various arguments formed themselves in her head, without ever making their way past her lips. Eventually, she seemed to make a decision and sighed.

"Well then, I guess this is our last night." They both made some modest attempts to navigate the conversation into less fraught waters, but eventually gave up and just sat together in silence.

There was a tentativeness about their coming together that night, an awkwardness, as though they had not touched before. Afterward, he lay towards the open window with her wrapped in his arms. Moonlight crawled across the wall through the slatted shades. Why did he feel compelled to go? Although not the life he imagined for himself, it was not a bad life. It would horrify his father, of course, and that was appealing. How was he in love so soon? He seemed to have a propensity to fall in love too easily, and he doubted that it was a helpful character trait for an ambitious monk. But that also felt like a trivial and abstract goal as he lay next to this living woman, feeling her rhythmic breathing against his chest.

He lay there for hours, reflective and uncertain. Gazing at her sleeping face, he marveled at her beauty by moonlight. Her soft, gentle breathing was the only meaningful measure of the passing time. His left arm, which lay under her neck, was losing feeling, so he shifted it, careful not to wake her. As his hand lay on a different part of her pillow, he noticed that it felt wet—wet, he realized suddenly, with her silent tears.

Kinko was not aware of falling asleep, but when he opened his eyes, Taka was already dressed and sitting by the open window, observing the ripening morning. Without speaking, he drew on his clothes.

"I happened upon this in a print shop the other day." He reached into his pack, "...and thought you might like it." He handed her a small wood-block, *ukiyo-e* print of a *shamisen* player sitting by an open first-floor window and looking out into the street where a komusō monk was playing his *shakuhachi.*

Pensively, she turned her head to look at the print in his offered hand and reached out for it. "I didn't know that I would need a gift," she said slowly, "but I would be grateful if you would take this and think of me when you pray." She handed him a short circlet of wooden prayer beads, called *o-juzu*— "counting beads." They were beautifully shaped of rosewood, and at the point where the circle met, there was an elegant jade bead, out of which ran the tassel of strings.

"I bought this at the Itsukushima Shrine when we visited. I will get another set when I visit later today."

Kinko bowed to her. "I will keep these with me always, and remember you in my prayers, always." And he did.

LIGHTNING FROM A CLEAR SKY

The night before they left Hiroshima, Kinko and Harushige were fêted to a wonderful farewell dinner by the extended Asano family. Kinko presented gifts to everyone, including the numerous children. At the dinner, Kinko discovered that while Harushige planned to return to Kyushu, his cousin Masahiko (whom he met at the tavern his first night in Hiroshima) intended to travel east. The young man was to transport a load of cloth to Kurashiki, further east along the coast. He planned to travel the San'yōdō with a small group of merchants and invited Kurosawa to join them. Having traveled some distance with merchants already, Kinko relished the company, which felt like a continuation of his time with Harushige.

Early the following morning, the two cousins and Kinko bade farewell to the Asano family and headed back to the San'yōdō. Upon arrival, Kinko lept lightly out of Harushige's cart, and the two friends bowed deeply to each other. "Take care of my little cousin," Harushige told him. And with a smile and a wave, he headed back towards the western tip of Honshu.

Kinko climbed into the cart driven by Masahiko, and the two waited for the other merchants in the party to arrive. The morning was surprisingly brisk, the bright sun reluctant to warm the autumn ground. By mid-morning, the other members of the party joined them, and the little troop set out eastward. Kurashiki was about 90 miles away, and the trip would take roughly a week.

Images of meeting Taka in the tavern flooded Kinko's mind as he renewed the conversation that he had broken off with Masahiko earlier that night. Trying to keep focused on his new friend, he found Masahiko just as delightful a companion as he remembered. Much younger than his cousin Harushige, Masahiko was also far more open and talkative. Their conversation picked up right where they had stopped that first night, with Masahiko reporting excitedly on his upcoming marriage plans. His betrothed was a young woman named Yuzu, who grew up in the same neighborhood as the Asano family.

"Her family runs the miso shop three streets over from us," he told Kinko, as they rode together. "I remember the first time I saw her when I accompanied my mother to go buy miso for the house. I thought she was the most beautiful girl there ever was! Our families have been friends now for many years."

"Did your parents allow you to be part of the process of selecting your bride?" Kinko inquired, surprised.

Masahiko was equally surprised. "Of course, I was 'part of the process,'" he responded, almost affronted. "It's my marriage!"

Kurosawa laughed, "Well, in a samurai family, the children aren't involved in selecting a marriage partner at all; in fact, parents actively discourage their opinions. Many husbands and wives have never met before they become betrothed."

"But how do they know if they will like each other?" the young man asked, appalled.

"I don't think that anyone cares if they like each other. Marriage is an alliance between families, and the children know that they have a responsibility to work for the strengthening of their family. The right marriage is part of that responsibility."

After pondering this for a few moments, Masahiko admitted, "I'm not sure that I could do that."

The two men sat in silence for some time, each following his own thoughts. As Kinko reflected on the samurai marriages that he knew, he acknowledged that the merchant's model provided some advantages. In his own family, Kinko's parents rarely expressed much mutual affection (or seemed to experience much joy) in their relationship. They bore children—a social and familial obligation—but their relationship always felt to Kinko more like a business arrangement. Masahiko was clearly in love with his betrothed and excited about the life they would build together. It was hard for Kinko not to feel a little envious of the young man, thinking of Taka and his brief fantasy of a new life.

The idyllic autumn weather continued for the next several days, and the traveling was easy and pleasant. The merchants were agreeable company and disinclined to push the pace of their journey, generally halting their progress in the late afternoon. To save money, they would share rooms at the local inns along the way, although they spent any savings on their nightly sake drinking.

The days quickly passed; and by late afternoon on the sixth day from Hiroshima, they entered Kurashiki. Located where the Takahashi River flowed into the Inland Sea, the town was an important port for cotton, oil, and rice. It was important enough that the government in Edo maintained direct control over the city, rather than assign it to a regional *daimyo*. Approaching the town, the San'yōdō veered sharply north to cross the Takahashi at a point where travelers could ford the river. As the merchants arrived, they found a crowd on both sides. Ferrymen pulled low flat barges across for those pedestrians unwilling to get wet, though the river was shallow enough for the merchants' oxen to pull their carts.

After crossing the river, the group turned south towards the port quarter of the city. Kurosawa was loath to part from his new friend, so rather than continue his journey eastward, he rode south with the merchants into the city. The road was thick with carts ferrying goods to and from the harbor. As they got closer, the road joined a canal that ran north and south parallel to the river, carrying small barges to the port. The canal lay on their right hand, while whitewashed warehouses with unusual black-tiled roofs lined the left side of the street.

Merchants in their party soon broke off from the group at the different storehouses, while at each location, workers rushed out to unload the carts. The group planned to spend two days in Kurashiki, purchasing merchandise for the return journey to Hiroshima. They agreed to meet at an inn near the port for dinner that night.

Masahiko was selling his dyed cloth to a wholesale merchant who resold it to clothing makers around the city. Since his family already partnered with a cloth supplier in Hiroshima, Masahiko had no need to purchase anything for the family business in Kurashiki and therefore contracted with an oil merchant in Hiroshima to bring back a cartload of oil casks.

Kurosawa helped him unload his bolts of cloth at a small warehouse facing the canal. Only a single worker emerged when they arrived, but it did not take the three men long to empty the cart. Since there was nowhere to keep a cart overnight in the crowded port center, Masahiko left it at the warehouse where he would collect it the next morning. Tired and sore, the two men walked down the canal to the port quarter and found the inn—The Wandering Albatross—where their friends gathered for the night's revelries.

It being his last night with a member of the Asano family, Kinko sat with his friend long into the evening as the sake flowed freely. "Growing up in a small family," Kinko admitted to him, "it was a wonderful surprise to spend time with your extended clan."

Masahiko shook his head and laughed, "We are a handful, if you're not used to a lot of activity. I hope the farewell dinner wasn't overwhelming."

"No! Quite the contrary. It was enormously enjoyable and oddly freeing—so different from the rigid protocols of my own family dinners."

"When Yuzu and I grow old, I hope that our family home will have the same feel, with my children gathered around the table and grandchildren underfoot. Yuzu comes from a smaller, more subdued home, but she also enjoys the chaos of our family get-togethers." The two talked on until the party of merchants broke up, and everyone retired to their shared rooms.

In the morning, the party gathered for breakfast before the merchants headed out for their various activities. Masahiko planned to return to the cloth warehouse, collect his cart, and then travel over to the oil merchant's to pick up the load he would transport to Hiroshima. As long as he was already down in the busy port district, Kinko decided to do some *shakuhachi* playing (and alms collecting). The two men agreed to meet around midday at the oil merchant's, where Kinko could help with the loading.

The cool autumn morning air was heavy with the smell of

sea salt and fish. Even at this early hour, that morning's seafood market was largely over, with a few remaining fishermen haggling with buyers over prices for the last of their catch. Kinko found a square near the market to set down his bowl and play. *Shakuhachi* players being rare in this part of Japan, he quickly collected a crowd and passed his begging bowl. As the crowd thinned, Kurosawa continued playing, while passers-by dropped coins at his feet.

As the lovely morning waned, Kinko made his way north and east of the port to where Masahiko had described the oil merchant's warehouse. Not being in a particular hurry, he enjoyed taking in the sights, smells, and sounds of an unfamiliar city. He turned into the street where he expected to find his friend and began looking for the right warehouse.

Suddenly, halfway down the block, he heard a massive crashing sound, followed by a cloud of dust billowing from a large building. With a sinking feeling in his stomach, Kurosawa ran towards the structure. There, he watched a handful of men flee the doors, coughing and hacking up dust. Kinko grabbed one of the men and asked, "What happened?"

Trying to regain his breath, the man said, "They were shifting some oil barrels in an upper loft when the bracing beam collapsed, and the whole loft fell." When the man saw Kinko about to enter the building, he added, "Don't go in: there is spilled oil everywhere; if that catches fire, we'll lose this whole block."

Kinko nodded in acknowledgment while he rushed into the building. It was dark and clouded with dust, which made it nearly impossible to see anything. He helped several men towards the door while frantically looking for his friend. Finally, he found an old man doubled over with coughing. "Come, father," he urged. And as they approached the door, he added, "I'm looking for a young friend of mine from Hiroshima; have you seen him?"

The man nodded. "Your friend saved my life, pushing me out from under the falling loft. But I'm afraid that he might have been caught."

Kinko rushed towards the epicenter of the disaster. He could barely see, and every surface seemed slick with oil. Keeping his head as low as he could and feeling his way among the rubble, Kinko searched among the chaos. "Asano, Asano, are you here?"

Eventually, he discovered Masahiko, pinned under a huge beam, surrounded by broken debris. When Kinko grasped him by the shoulders, his friend groaned. The beam was far too heavy for him to move on his own, so Kinko rushed to the front door. A crowd had gathered around those who escaped the building, but Kinko's eyes first lit on two samurai who slowly rode down the street. Appealing instinctively to his fellows, he called, "Come, quickly, I need help freeing a young man in here!"

The two men turned their haughty eyes to the dust-covered figure on their left; but with no acknowledgment, continued down the road. Kinko's anger welled up in his chest, spilling from his lips, "Heartless cowards!" The samurai paused, word-lessly debating whether they chose to hear this provocation. Deciding to ignore him, they continued down the street.

Desperately, Kinko turned to the crowd around the door and called with wild urgency, "I need some strong men to help save the young man inside!"

Those gathered looked shamefaced at one another, fearful of the imminent risk of a fiery explosion. Three men slowly shuffled forward, and Kurosawa led them into the chaos of the building. He rushed to the back of the room where Masahiko lay trapped. Pointing to a heavy fallen plank, he said to one of the men, "Quick, wedge that end against the floor, under the beam. You two," he urged the other men, "when I give the signal, push up as hard as you can on the other end."

Without speaking, the men followed his instructions; and on Kurosawa's signal, the three men hoisted the huge beam up a few inches. It was not much, but enough for Kurosawa to drag out Masahiko's limp body. As they approached the front door, carrying Masahiko between them, Kinko saw a team of fire-fighters douse the building with water. Scanning the crowd, Kinko found the old man who had directed him to Masahiko. Assuming him to be the proprietor, he asked, "Where is the cart that my friend arrived in?"

The man hurried around the back of the building and returned shortly, driving the cart. Kinko thanked him and jumped into the driver's seat, while the other three men loaded Masahiko's body carefully in the back.

"I'm taking him back to the Wandering Albatross to find some medical help."

Without waiting for a response, Kinko hurried back to the inn with the cart. He paid for a single room for his friend and asked the innkeeper to find a physician as quickly as possible. While he waited, he cleaned the dirt and grime from Masahiko's face and body, keeping his fevered brow cool. Within the hour, the innkeeper returned with an old monk carrying a crate of elixirs and herbs.

Kinko stepped aside to let the monk examine Masahiko and anxiously watched as the man prodded the motionless body and shifted the positions of his limbs. Occasionally, Masahiko would moan, but otherwise, all was a hushed silence. Finally, the old monk straightened up and stretched his lower back.

"Well, the accident didn't break any of your friend's limbs. Several of his ribs seem cracked, but those generally heal by themselves. What I am most concerned about is internal bleeding and injuries to his organs. I can give him an elixir for pain, and some herb poultices for the bruising. Other than that, it's simply a matter of waiting to see how his body responds." He then gave Kinko specific instructions on how to administer the treatments.

Kinko thanked the monk for his services and began to tend to his friend. He was able to get a little soup down his throat, but nothing else. As the afternoon wore on, the other members of the troop from Hiroshima returned to the inn, and one by one joined Kinko's vigil in the room. One of the merchants found a Shinto priest who chanted healing prayers over their friend and left a small amulet for healing hanging above his head. Kinko did the only thing he could do and played some quiet *honkyoku* music on Ikkei's long *shakuhachi*.

Late in the evening, the old oil merchant visited. He was still visibly shaken by the events of the day and grateful to Masahiko, whom he credited with his life. Throughout the long night, Kinko knelt by his friend's futon, prayed and cooled his brow, while the other members of the party took shifts, so that there was always some company for Kinko. Twice during the night, Masahiko moved slightly. Once he called out something indistinct. Kinko tried not to read too much into these small gestures.

Morning brought no new developments. The troop of merchants delayed their departure for Hiroshima another day. They were able to get a little more soup in him, but he did not regain consciousness. Kinko spent the time playing for his friend and trying to stave off the sadness and despair of watching his shallow breathing and gray pallor.

In the afternoon, the monk returned with more medicine. He looked his patient over carefully, gravely shaking his head. "I am afraid that there's not much I can do other than alleviate the pain. It's all up to his body." Japanese medicine—based on

Chinese theory—aimed to support the body's natural processes of healing itself. As such, it was better suited to addressing sicknesses and diseases than injuries. Later that afternoon, Kinko discovered that the oil merchant had given the innkeeper enough money for the room and the cost of the medical assistance.

Exhausted, Kinko napped in the late afternoon, lying down next to his friend's futon. When he awoke, grey twilight suffused the room. The air was hot and stuffy. Two of the merchant troop knelt on the other side of Masahiko's futon, talking quietly to each other. Evening segued into night, and different friends rotated in and out of the quiet chamber.

Watching his friend by the flickering lamplight, Kinko began to spiral into despair with the weight of the impending loss. Both as a samurai and as a Buddhist, he trained to prepare for death. But he could not stop envisioning the extended Asano family and Yuzu back in Hiroshima, dreaming of a life filled with children and joy. His swirling thoughts seemed untamable and oppressive.

In the dark early hours of the morning, with all the city quiet around him, he noticed Masahiko's breath change, become more rapid and shallow. Kinko took his friend's hand, which was hot and clammy most of the day, and felt the heat draining away. He brushed aside the damp hair that had fallen into Masahiko's eyes and stroked the young man's forehead.

Gradually, his breath became more irregular, with a jagged quality. And then, without warning, his breathing stopped; the cradled hand became limp. Kinko sat in the darkness of the silent night with tears rolling down his cheeks.

UNEXPECTED COMPANY

Cool, misty autumn rain drifted down on the solemn group gathered in front of the Wandering Albatross two mornings later. A hastily performed cremation ceremony the previous day allowed the company to return with Masahiko's remains to his family. Kinko spent much of the sleepless night trying vainly to draft a letter to the Asano family, but every attempt seemed inadequate and trite. Finally, he simply wrote three lines:

> Brightly colored leaves
> Torn from unready branches
> Fall like lonely tears

Kinko rode with the company north to the San'yōdō, where he disembarked and bid the party farewell, giving them the haiku to bear west to Hiroshima.

He set off east, continuing his route to Kyoto. Trudging down the cold, lonely road, a deep sadness overwhelmed him. He grieved for the Asano family, as well as for his own accumulated losses of the past months: Matsu, his temple, Taka, his new friendships with Shizu and Harushige, and now Masahiko. It seemed as though every time something positive happened, fate tore it away. His body sagged under the emotional weight.

He passed through Okayama the following day, after which was a long stretch of road before the next castle town of Himeji. The weather cleared and the next several days passed without event. Desiring solitude, he avoided inns and slept in roadside shrines, and once out in the open air. This stretch of the San'yōdō ran close to the sea. The trees were a glorious palette of golds and deep reds on the mountainsides rising on his left, with the view to his right frequently punctuated by sweeping vistas overlooking the water.

One dull, grey morning, when he was about a day from Himeji, he played his *shakuhachi* as he walked. Cresting a low hill, he saw far down the road another *komusō* monk walking towards him. This was unexpected since there were no Fuke temples between the western tip of Honshu and the imperial city of Kyoto, so *komusō* were uncommon. However, monks—like Kurosawa himself—did travel between Kyoto and Kyushu Island.

As expected among *komusō*, Kurosawa stopped playing the piece he was practicing and began to play *yobitake-uketake,* "Calling bamboo, receiving bamboo." He played the first phrase of the piece, and oddly, the other *komusō* failed to respond. Even more oddly, he did not even take the flute out of his *obi.* Kurosawa started the piece again, though thinking that it was hardly possible that the other monk failed to hear him.

The two men were quite close now. As Kurosawa played for a third time, he became increasingly certain that he was facing a Tokugawa spy masquerading as a traveling *komusō.* While he played, he moved over to the other side of the road so that he was directly in the path of the other monk. The other man stopped as Kurosawa approached him, then tried to walk around him. Kurosawa moved back in front of him and stopped as well.

They were no more than five feet apart with no one else visible on the road in either direction. The stranger wore both swords, which—while lawful for a *komusō*—was unusual. Knowing that his life was at stake, the man dropped his right hand to the hilt of his *katana* and began to draw. Kurosawa, expecting exactly that response, stepped in close to his opponent's left side, and using his *shakuhachi* delivered a bone-shattering strike to the man's sword hand at the wrist. He smiled grimly at how ironic it was that this fake *komusō* failed to understand what a useful weapon his *shakuhachi* actually was.

Then, he took one more step, and placed his left leg behind his opponent's. Then he caught the stranger just under the throat with his left arm, and twisting his hips, hurled the man to the ground. He then swung his leg over his fallen opponent, sat on his chest, and brought the flute with both hands against the stranger's windpipe.

"Please don't kill me," the man croaked.

"That is the punishment for impersonating a *komusō*," replied Kurosawa, as he pushed slightly harder.

"Please."

Kinko did not intend to kill the man, but he did want to scare him badly. Was he retaliating for the two samurai who had ignored Masahiko's plight? He pushed just enough so that the man could not breathe. Before he lost consciousness, however, Kurosawa released the pressure. Standing up, while taking the man's two swords from his *obi*, he kicked the man's *tengai* basket across the road. Drawing the *katana*, he held it at the stranger's throat.

Keeping his own *tengai* firmly in place, so that the samurai could not see his face, Kurosawa said roughly, "Hand me your

157

bag." The stranger pulled the heavy cotton bag over his head and held it out to his captor. Glancing briefly inside, Kinko made out several sealed letters, the man's travel permit, and a string of coins. "I'll take this," he told the stranger, as he swung the bag over his shoulder.

"Then you might as well kill me; without'em, I'm good as dead."

"Well, that will be someone else's decision; I don't happen to be in a killing mood today. Listen to me carefully, however: I am going to Himeji to catch a ship, and if I catch sight of you in town, I will know that you are following me and will most definitely kill you. Keep walking towards Okayama and thank the Buddha that I am in a gentle frame of mind." It was a feeble lie, but all Kinko could come up with on the spur of the moment.

With that, he launched a kick at the stranger, who scurried off westward down the San'yōdō. Kinko watched him until he crested the hill and disappeared. He was no longer worried about retainers of the Ekken family following him, and he was well within his rights to have punished the spy, but the whole experience left him unsettled. It was likely that the spy was part of the Tokugawa network of informants, which could be problematic, but only if the spy did not get caught and killed first. All the same, Kurosawa stuck the man's two swords in his *obi*, grateful for the added protection.

Anxious to avoid any potential trouble from the *bakufu* spy, Kinko passed straight through Himeji. As evening approached on the following day, he reached the small castle town of Akashi on the coast of the Inland Sea, opposite the northern tip of Awaji Island. The castle had been constructed in just a year, with design help from the swordsman Miyamoto Musashi. It was situated to protect Osaka from attacks by any of the western *daimyo*. Other than the castle itself, there was not much else to distinguish Akashi from any other coastal fishing town.

The check-point guard admitted Kurosawa just as evening fell. He asked the soldier where he might find a reputable inn, and the guard suggested a place called the Gatehouse in the center of town. Kinko easily found the inn and entered a well-tended common room, with a cozy hearth fire blazing and a roomful of patrons. Kinko took an empty table in a corner, as he usually did, in a place that provided a good view of the whole room as well as the entrance door. A young man took his order for a bottle of sake and recommended a regional specialty for dinner called *akashiyaki*, which were bits of local octopus fried in a flour ball.

As they roamed the room, Kinko's eyes briefly rested on a young woman of uncommon beauty at a small table in the far corner, opposite him. She was well-dressed in the traveling attire of an affluent woman with a long, blue cloak fastened by a silver broach covering a slate grey kimono of the highest grade of silk. The simplicity of the colors and lack of pattern on the kimono and cloak highlighted her lustrous jet-black hair and the startling color of her unusual grey eyes. Besides her beauty, she stood out by having no male escort, although she was joined shortly by an older woman who appeared to be her attendant. The two women ate without much conversation, as the young traveler regularly glanced about the room uneasily.

The dinner hour ended and many of the inn's local customers returned to their homes, leaving the common room emptier and quieter. So there was no missing the two men who entered the front door of the inn, looked around, and spotted the two women in the far corner. The young woman also noticed them and visibly blanched as they approached her. They stood menacingly over her table and began a heated— though hushed—argument.

Amid this altercation, one of the men grabbed the young woman by the arm and started to drag her from her seat. Kurosawa arose from his table and walked over to the antagonists.

"Might I be of any assistance?" he asked as gently as his rising blood allowed.

"You *might* mind your own bloody business," said the larger of the two, eyeing the two swords at Kurosawa's hip.

"When women travelers are being accosted by random thugs, it is the business of a samurai to offer aid."

The smaller man responded, "These ladies are acquaintances of ours, and our business is between us."

"Ladies, I am happy to retire if you do not require any assistance."

"It would be lovely to have you join us, kind sir," replied the beautiful young woman. "Perhaps you would share a bottle of sake?"

The two men looked frustrated and flummoxed. "This matter is not over, Minami," growled the smaller man. "We'll meet soon enough." And sneering at Kurosawa, the two men withdrew and left the inn.

"We are very grateful for your support, Sir," said the young woman as she offered Kinko a seat. "Those two have been bothering us on the road with very inappropriate proposals." She blushed becomingly, but Kinko did not miss the quick silencing look that she threw at her maid. "My name is Rokujo Minami. My maid Jun and I are traveling to Kyoto. May I ask the name of our gallant samurai?"

"Kinko Kurosawa. I am from Kyushu, also traveling to Kyoto." The young woman smiled and her tension visibly eased.

"What a wonderful coincidence! Perhaps we can share some of our journey." Kinko was not so naïve as to flatter himself that she flirted with him. He was convenient protection on a dangerous road. But he was also content to have the company of a beautiful and—he hoped—charming young woman on the journey. For the first time on his trip, he was happy to have a sword.

Before retiring to his room for the night, Kurosawa strolled out on the veranda in front of the inn. Glancing up and down the street, he caught the glimpse of a familiar figure retreat around a corner at the end of the block; he looked much like the man who had accosted Rokujo earlier. Kinko hoped that there would be no further trouble, but he was not counting on it.

The next morning, he met Rokujo and Jun in the common room, where they all shared breakfast before getting on their way. Rokujo rode a small, but smartly appointed horse, while Jun rode a mule. The pace of the mule would not exceed a comfortable walk, so traveling together would be an easy process. Bearing in mind the threats from the previous night, Kurosawa decided not to wear his *tengai* basket, except when approaching a checkpoint. And he carried the two swords.

It was a clear, crisp morning as the three of them departed the Gatehouse Inn and made their way out of Akashi. As soon as they crossed through the checkpoint at the eastern edge of the city, Kinko asked, "Might we pause for a moment in the tea shop over there?"

"We just ate breakfast, Kurosawa. You can't possibly be hungry already!"

"Just a brief stop. I promise."

The two women looked at each other as though wondering if they had made a mistake in their choice of a traveling companion. But shaking their heads, they followed Kinko into the tea shop. He ushered them to a table next to the front window, looking out on the checkpoint station. He ordered tea and waited.

As he suspected, within ten minutes of their crossing, the two men from the previous night's encounter showed up with two additional thuggish-looking companions. While the guards checked their travel papers, Kinko approached from the tea house.

"Excuse me, honorable sirs," he said to the guards. "These men accosted a young noblewoman of my acquaintance last night at the Gatehouse Inn. I guess that they are here now to follow her and continue that effort."

"That's a lie," growled the smaller man. "We are on our own business."

Ignoring the man, Kinko addressed the guards directly: "Please go and check with the proprietor of the Gatehouse Inn, should you doubt my story."

"If you will all follow me to the guardhouse," one of the guards said. "Our shift officer will sort this out." The four men looked as though they wanted to bolt, but to do so would be an admission of guilt and likely lead to arrest. So, they all walked to the guardhouse. There, Kurosawa told his story in some detail to the officer in charge, and then excused himself, rejoining his two companions at the tea shop.

"I think now would be a good time to be on our way," he told them.

After traveling by himself, Kinko was happy to have company and found Rokujo a delightful comrade, well-educated and witty. Jun—while quiet—was a pleasant presence. The little party made steady progress, although the clear sky soon became overcast. After midday, the clouds made good on their impending threat, and a cold steady rain began to fall, washing away the cheerful banter of the morning.

The trio did not encounter another village until late that

afternoon. Thoroughly drenched in body and spirit, they found an inn and stopped for the night. Their lodging had only two baths and etiquette demanded that Kinko, being the man, bathe first. However, as the women were soaked to the bone, Kinko ordered himself some tea in the common room, and allowed the two women to wash. "There's probably room for two in my bath," laughed Rokujo coyly. Kinko smiled, bowed, and turned to his tea.

Clean, warm, and dry, the three reassembled in the common room for dinner, where the conversation of that morning, cut off by the rain, continued. Kinko learned that Rokujo was from Fukuyama—a castle town to the east of Hiroshima— and on her way to visit relatives in Kyoto. She was a little vague about the purpose of the visit, and why they were traveling without accompaniment—a dangerous enterprise for two women, even in Tokugawa Japan. But Kinko decided not to push a question that she did not feel comfortable addressing.

As the dinner broke up for the night, and the women excused themselves, Rokujo gave Kinko a very flirtatious smile behind her fan and retired. Kurosawa, who was anxious about being overtaken by the four men from Akashi, stayed behind to keep an eye on the door while he finished his sake. While he sat, he ruminated on his new acquaintance. She was delightful and charming, and unsettlingly beautiful, but there was a guardedness about her that left Kinko feeling cautious.

Finally, he shook his head and laughed at himself. "After all the intrigue that I've encountered over the past few months, I'm seeing dangers everywhere." And with that, he took himself to bed.

By the next morning, the rain stopped, and the little troop continued on their way. The roads were muddy, and the progress was slow. Kurosawa would have made much faster headway on his own, but enjoyed being a support to the women. And he was not comfortable leaving them by themselves, knowing that the men they left in Akashi might be behind them.

The next days progressed slowly, with intermittent rain keeping the roads difficult. After four days, the little party finally reached Osaka, which was by far the largest city that Kurosawa had ever seen. Strategically located where the Yodogawa River emptied itself into Osaka Bay, the city had been the largest commercial hub in Japan for centuries. From here, the San'yōdō made a sharp turn to the north for its final segment to Kyoto, a three or four-day trip from Osaka. Having seen no sign of danger for the past several days, Kurosawa was beginning to breathe a little easier.

The travelers found space in a comfortable inn north of the harbor. Relieved to have reached the city without mishap and excited to begin the last leg of their trek, the party indulged in a celebratory dinner. The mood was festive and exuberant; the sake flowed freely, and Kurosawa could feel the tension in his body begin to dissolve. After Jun left to go and lay out her mistress's bed, Rokujo leaned very close so that the scent of the incense permeating her kimono was intoxicating.

"I am so grateful for your protection for these days," she whispered. "Could I thank you properly for your service?"

Though flattered by the surprising proposal, Kinko still felt very raw emotionally from his parting from Taka. But the sake and the unusual beauty of his companion overcame his qualms, and he let her lead him by the hand to her room.

Whether instructed by her mistress, Jun clearly anticipated this ending to the evening, and left the room delicately lit with tapers and scented with incense. Kinko let Rokujo disrobe him and rub some oil on his body. When her kimono slipped away, he knew that he had never seen such feminine perfection.

He was surprised to see that her pubic hair was entirely

shaved. And then, in an instant, all the missing pieces fell into place: shaved pubic hair was common among first and second-ranked courtesans. If Rokujo had been sold to a house of assignation in some city's pleasure quarter and then fled, of course there would be agents trying to find her and bring her back. She would need protection and would pay with her body. To ask Rokujo about this now would frighten her; and disinclined to engage in conversation at the moment, he simply took her in his arms.

Rokujo's expertise as a lover confirmed Kinko's suspicion; but while pleasurable, the experience left Kinko emotionally hollow. Rather than feeling more closely bonded with her, Kinko felt as though they were disconnected performers, going through the motions of a play. As he held her against his body and drifted off to sleep, he missed Taka fiercely.

He awoke with a start in the middle of the night to find Rokujo gone. When he rolled over, he saw her silhouetted against the window, looking in his pack. "Can I get you something, Rokujo?" he asked.

She jumped, but then turned to him and replied, "I couldn't sleep, and I remembered you telling me that you carried a booklet in your pack that described the origins of the Fuke order. I thought that I might be able to read it here by the window, where the moonlight is so bright."

This struck Kurosawa as an unlikely explanation, but he laughed and replied, "Well, that would certainly put you to sleep. But I'm happy to tell you the story tomorrow while we travel. In the meantime, you will probably sleep better if I retire to my room."

She made some small protest, but Kurosawa smiled and returned to his room. Once there, he lit a taper and checked through his pack. Nothing was missing. What could she possibly have wanted? All the simple things that she might need in the middle of the night—a paper handkerchief, a drink of water—were in her room. She did not appear to need money, but that was hard to determine. In any case, feeling flush with resources, Kinko determined to at least pay the bill for the two women the next morning.

The three travelers got off to an early start the next day, under a low, grey sky. Much of the morning was a slow process through the crowded streets of Osaka. As they moved north with the Yodogawa River on their left, they rounded a corner to see the massive Osaka Castle. Hideyori Toyotomi built this enormous fortress to rebuff the attack by Ieyasu Tokugawa in 1614, though the castle was finally sacked the following year. Tokugawa rebuilt it soon afterward, with its distinguishing central tower now overlooking the city.

It was not until early afternoon that the little band finally passed the checkpoint on the north end of the city and began to make good progress. The traffic between Osaka and Kyoto was much heavier than at other points on the San'yōdō, so there was little risk of an ambush by anyone following from Akashi. Given some of the awkwardness of the previous night and the dreariness of the threatening sky, their conversation was minimal.

They stopped in the early evening at a roadside inn. At dinner, to Kinko's relief, Rokujo made an effort to engage in some light conversation. A *biwa* musician provided entertainment, and dinner was quite good. Everyone's spirits rose as the evening progressed until it was time to turn in for the night. Rokujo again took Kinko's hand to lead him to her room. When he demurred, pleading fatigue from the journey, she snapped at him, "You needn't worry about paying for our rooms again; I wasn't selling my favors." And she stormed off to her chamber.

Kinko sat at the table for some time and sipped the last of the sake, reflecting. Relief was his overwhelming emotion. Something about Rokujo was so intense and insistent that it exhausted him. The intimacy was lovely, but hollow. He was on the edge of a precipice, and had been able to step back. He was close enough to feel the danger, but was no longer in immediate peril.

In the morning, Rokujo showed no sign of remembering the previous night's spat. The day was brighter, though still cool. Kinko, eager to keep Rokujo in a good mood, said, "The other night you were curious about the booklet I carry. We call it the *honsoku*, and every *komusō* monk carries a copy. It tells a little of the history of our order—taken from a much larger work called the *Kyotaku Denki*—and explains our practices and why we dress the way we do."

Rokujo appeared less enthusiastic about hearing the story than he expected, but seemed willing to play along. "So tell me the story," she responded.

"Well, according to our official documents, a Chinese monk named Pu'hua—which we pronounce "Fuke" in Japanese—founded our order. He lived nearly a thousand years ago and was a friend of his more famous contemporary, the Zen monk Rinzai. He was deeply cynical about power structures of any sort—religious or political—and preferred to spend his time with the farmers in his rural community, who were trapped in poverty and ignorance.

"An eccentric man, he was prone to shouting paradoxical aphorisms at whoever would listen. He preached that no one could attain Buddha-hood through reason, and the aphorisms were his attempt to jolt people into enlightenment. Ironically—in terms of *komusō* history—he never actually played the *shakuhachi*. He did carry a bell, ringing it to recall people to their quest for Buddha-hood.

"Sensing his death approaching, he made a coffin and told all the peasants in his village that he was going to die the next day. So they all gathered around the coffin, only to have him say, 'Not today!' The same thing happened the next two days, and by the fourth day, no one believed him. So he asked a random stranger to nail him in his coffin and he died. When the villagers came and opened up the coffin, they found his body gone, but heard his bell ringing from the empty sky.

"As the story goes, sometime later, one of Fuke's disciples was walking through a bamboo grove and heard Fuke's bell ringing. He followed the sound into the grove, eventually finding a tall stalk of broken bamboo. He noticed that as the breeze blew across the broken stalk, it made a sound that mimicked the sound of Fuke's bell. So he cut a piece of bamboo and fashioned the first *shakuhachi*. He supposedly composed the earliest piece of *shakuhachi* music: *Kyorei* ("Hollow Bell"). It is an unlikely story, but that is what the document claims."

Jun was listening carefully and asked, "And how did this tradition make its way to Japan?"

"Well, for several hundred years, the order grew in China before a Japanese priest named Gakushin visited China to study Buddhism. He fell in love with the sound of the *shakuhachi*, which he then studied for some time. Returning to Japan in Kenchō 6 (1254), he acquired many disciples, eventually founding a temple south of Kyoto on the Kii peninsula called Kokoku-*ji*.

"Gakushin's most senior disciple was a man named Kichiku. The story goes that Kichiku was on a pilgrimage to the shrine at Ise. On his way, during his evening meditation, he drifted off to sleep and the Buddha granted him a dream-vision in which he heard two beautiful pieces of music. When he awoke, he tried his best to imitate them and composed the next two oldest *honkyoku*: *Kokû* ("Empty Sky") and *Mukaiji* ("Flute on a Misty Sea"). Kichiku went on to establish the Myoan-*ji*—the 'Temple of Light and Darkness'—in Kyoto. That is where I am bound on this journey. It is the most revered temple in our tradition."

The rest of the day passed amiably, with conversation veering from one topic to another until they stopped for the evening at an inn. Again, at the end of dinner, Rokujo held out her hand, inviting Kinko to join her. And again, Kinko demurred. She sat down, cold fury in her eyes. "This is not my usual experience: I am generally the one being pursued, not doing the pursuing. Is there something I have done wrong? Did you not enjoy our night together?"

As she spat out the question, Kurosawa realized for the first time that this woman would be a formidable enemy. Before he could even frame an answer, she spun on her heel and hissed, "You are not worth my effort." But instead of storming to her room, she took a table at the far end of the common room, near a boisterous table of merchants. Kurosawa watched as one by one they began buying her drinks. Soon three of them joined her, vying for her attention. She chatted and flirted and toyed, all the while keenly aware that Kinko watched.

Kinko, however, soon tired of the game and was quite certain that he did not want to see how it ended. He was grateful that he had decided to economize and share a room with several other travelers, and would not be subject to any late-night confrontation. So, finishing his sake, he retired to his room to sleep.

He tossed and turned for much of the night, and finally, hours before dawn, he made a decision. Quietly packing his belongings, he crept downstairs and found the innkeeper and his wife in the kitchen getting ready for the morning breakfast. He borrowed paper, ink, and a brush, writing:

"Dearest Rokujo, I am sorry for having offended you last night and beg your forgiveness. Given that you and Jun appear safe from your pursuers, and that I keep offending you, I think it is best that I continue my journey alone. Thank you for your company over these past days. Travel safely to your family."

"Please give this to my dinner companion from last night," he said to the proprietor, adding a few extra coppers to his bill. And feeling a great weight lifted, he set out into the pre-dawn darkness for the last stage of his journey.

TEMPLE OF LIGHT AND
DARKNESS

The last two days of the trip to Kyoto passed quickly. Kinko kept a vigorous pace, taking little time for breaks. Wishing to avoid inns, he spent the first night with a farmer whom he met along the road and the second night in a small shrine set off from the San'yōdō.

He arrived in Kyoto by mid-morning on the third day, dazzled by the size and activity of the city. Food stalls crowded the streets, and shops sold every imaginable ware. Countless temples and shrines littered every neighborhood, in addition to the multitude of small parks scattered throughout. For nearly a thousand years, Kyoto had been the capital of Japan and the home of the emperor. Even though the center of political power had moved east to Edo—the home of the Tokugawa—Kyoto remained the formal capital and the cultural heart of the empire. Similarly, the temple of Myoan-*ji* was the spiritual heart of the Fuke sect.

Kurosawa wandered the city for a while getting his bearings, until he found someone who could give him directions to Myoan-*ji*, still a minor temple by the standards of the capital city. On the way, he found a sword shop and—feeling no more need of them—sold off the two swords taken from the false *komusō*. He spent some of the money on a finely forged *tanto* dagger that he slid into the back of his *obi*. He finally reached Myoan-*ji* on the southern side of the city, arriving in the early evening. The doorkeeper pointed Kurosawa towards the main administrative building. There, he bowed to the attendant, offered his *komusō* identification papers and said, "This humble traveler from Kuzaki-*ji* begs the favor of an audience with the abbot to convey greetings from his abbot."

"Sadly, the abbot is busy just now," the monk replied. "He would be happy to see you tomorrow morning after meditation, however."

Kurosawa bowed and left, having been shown the building for visiting lay monks. While Myoan-*ji* was not a huge temple, it received more pilgrim monks than any other Fuke temple, so the guest quarters were large and well maintained. He left his pack in these quarters and joined the monks for evening meditation and then dinner.

The meditation was preceded by some *shakuhachi* playing by the head teacher. Kurosawa enjoyed the music, but found it a little rustic sounding for his taste. Still, it was a lovely experience to be anonymous in a group of *shakuhachi* players and simply to sit and listen. He spent the evening sitting on the porch of the guest quarters chatting with itinerant monks from all over the country and enjoying the combination of gossip and edification.

The following morning, he again found his way to the temple's main administrative building and the attendant admitted him to the abbot's presence. The abbot was meeting with several of his advisors in a large room on the second floor, but there was no doubt about who the abbot was. He was a massive, mountainous man, with a stomach that made him look like some of the Buddha statues Kinko knew. The tatami mats were well worn, but clean, and the abbot bore a broad smile on a weathered face. "Good morning, brother Kurosawa," he exclaimed as Kinko entered the room, his face to the floor.

"Good morning, honorable Abbot," he returned. "I bring you greetings from the abbot of Kuzaki Temple in Nagasaki." There seemed little more to say on that particular subject. "I also was favored with an extended visit to Itchōken-*ji* in Hakata, whose abbot also sends his greetings and asked that your unworthy servant bring you these papers." Kurosawa handed the abbot the parcel from Itchōken.

The abbot set them aside for later reading. "My name is Minzan Zenji," he said. "Your name and reputation have preceded you, Kurosawa. Congratulations on your invitation to teach at Ichigetsu-*ji*; that is a great honor for you. And I understand that they are profoundly in need of a good teacher." This comment elicited low laughter from the room. "Perhaps you would honor us with a piece of music."

Expecting this request, Kurosawa pulled his 1.8 teaching *shakuhachi* from his *obi* and played one of the pieces from his home temple called *Namima Reibo*. The abbot and his colleagues listened appreciatively and, at the end, thanked him for his playing.

"You are welcome to remain here at Myoan-*ji* as long as you like, Kurosawa," the abbot continued. "You are our honored guest."

"With your permission, *Oshō*, I would be grateful if I could stay for enough time to learn the *honkyoku* that are part of Myoan-*ji*'s tradition. I have collected a few pieces from other temples on my way here, and to learn some of your music would be an enormous gift."

"Of course. Please introduce yourself to Gendo Kanmyo, our senior instructor, and tell him that I have requested that he work with you." Understanding this as a dismissal, Kurosawa bowed and retired from the room. He had played well, and yet the abbot failed to request that he do any teaching, which seemed strange. And while Zenji extended the hospitality of the temple, he did not offer Kurosawa lodgings in the *jūshoku* priest quarters, which left him feeling slighted.

Kinko spent the rest of the morning exploring the temple grounds and listening to *shakuhachi* practice. When the head teacher was between students, Kurosawa approached him and introduced himself, adding, "the abbot suggested that you might help me learn some of the temple's pieces." Gendo Kanmyo did not look particularly pleased with having been volunteered for this duty, but was gracious.

"I generally work on our Myoan-*ji* pieces in individual lessons with my senior students in the afternoon. Would it be satisfactory to you if you sat in on some of those to begin learning the pieces?" The two agreed on a time later that day.

At the appointed hour, Kurosawa joined Kanmyo, who introduced one of his students. They began working on *Kyo Reibo*, a begging piece using an older name of the capital. It was quite beautiful, and Kurosawa appreciated how Kanmyo engaged in his teaching with a mixture of grace and discipline. Kanmyo, on his part, seemed to gain in his appreciation for Kinko as well—particularly the latter's technical expertise—and soon included him in the lessons as a co-teacher.

Learning new music was one of Kinko's favorite activities. Over the following weeks, he mastered *Kyo Reibo, Shizo no Kyoku,* and an unusual piece called *Yoshiya Reibo.* He also learned several interesting variations on some of the standard pieces that all temples shared. Kurosawa added all of this material to the written notes he had started in Itchōken-*ji.* Gendo Kanmyo was a gifted player and teacher, and he and Kurosawa soon became friends.

The days passed swiftly and pleasantly, with Kurosawa easily falling into the rhythm of temple life. Most mornings, he left the temple to beg alms and explore the city. He was deeply struck by its ancient beauty and the staggering number of temples and gardens. He was aware of the number of Buddhist denominations, but seeing them all pressed up against one another was fascinating. The Emperor's palace was a massive structure, with a close-fitted stone outer wall rising up from a wide moat to terraced towers defending every corner. The shogun's castle—built to keep an eye on the Emperor—looked dark and forbidding. Returning to the temple in the early afternoons, he turned over his earnings to the temple treasurer, contributing in a small way to the life of the community.

One evening, about two weeks into his visit, Kurosawa joined the other monks entering the *zendo* for meditation when he heard a familiar voice call his name. Turning, he saw Rokujo standing under a brilliant red maple close by the *zendo* entrance. In the weeks since he had seen her last, his memory had faded; catching his breath, Kinko was struck again by how beautiful she was. Approaching her, he bowed.

"It is good to see you, Rokujo. I am very glad that you and Jun made it safely to the capital."

"I have missed you, *Anata*. I see that you are about to have service, but I hoped we could speak afterward." Kinko began to search for an excuse, when she added, "Please, I owe you some explanation, and you owe me a hearing."

"I would be delighted to speak with you, Rokujo."

"There is a tavern down the street from the temple called the Wisteria House. Please, join me there after your meditation." And, without waiting for a reply, she turned and left.

Trying to meditate after that exchange was a useless

endeavor. His mind was a whirlwind, and all he could do was make his body sit still. And barely that. He knew that seeing her was not going to do either of them any good. And yet, he could not keep himself from it. Just this once, he told himself, and then we're done.

He found Rokujo in a quiet back corner of the Wisteria House. The tavern was largely empty at this time of day, and the two could talk unobserved. Sitting down, he looked at her for a long moment before speaking. Dressed plainly but elegantly, her make-up delicately accentuated her high cheekbones, the perfect contour of her lips, and the arc of her eyebrows. The balance was just a little too perfect.

Enjoying his careful appreciation, she smiled coyly, ordering a pot of tea from the nearby waiter. "Thank you for agreeing to meet with me."

"Well, you were right to say that I owed you as much."

"I behaved badly on the road, and I apologize. I felt vulnerable and insecure, and I took that out on you."

"You have nothing to apologize for, Rokujo. I also felt conflicted and unsure. Please forgive me."

"Must we be so formal with one another, Kinko?" she said and laid her hand on his. "We have shared much together."

"Yes, we have," he agreed, accepting her hand in his.

With the forefinger of her other hand, she traced the vein that ran across the back of his. "I have always loved how strong these hands are," she said. "And how delicately they can touch." She bent low and kissed it. They were moving into dangerous territory.

"I should have been more honest with you when we first met," she continued. "Some years ago, my family sold me to a house of assignation in the pleasure quarter of Fukuyama. I rose through the courtesan ranks quickly and saved as much money as I could. I had almost saved enough to buy my freedom when a local lord offered to buy my contract and make me his third wife."

Rokujo paused, eyes cast down on the table, and collected herself. After a moment, she took a deep breath and continued.

"He was a vile and violent man, and I decided to die rather than be bound to him. So I left my savings with the house's proprietor and fled, hoping that the owner would take a small loss and grant me my freedom. Unfortunately, he did not want to take a small loss—nor offend the lord—and sent two servants after me: the two men you encountered the night we met. I was trying to persuade them that I could pay the balance of what I owed if I could get to my cousins in Kyoto, who would make up the difference."

Raising her face, Rokujo looked directly into Kinko's eyes and edged closer, her knee touching his below the table.

"You made it possible for me to do that. But now I find that my cousins do not have the financial resources to help me. They have sent me to another branch of the family, who live in Edo, which is my new destination.

"I came to you today, because—since you are also going to Edo—I hoped that perhaps you could provide me with some protection on the road. And I also hoped that you and I could get greater clarity on the nature of our relationship." She squeezed his hand tighter.

"Rokujo, I am sorry for your dilemma, but I don't think I can help. I am not sure how long I will be here in Kyoto. I am in the midst of learning music that I hope to carry to Edo, but I'm not finished yet. And while I am attracted to you, my life is committed to the Fuke order, and I can take no wife."

"There are many Fuke monks who marry, Kinko," she retorted.

"There are lay monks who marry, not priests who live in

the temple. There are no *shakuhachi* instructors who are not resident priests of a temple."

"It feels to me as though you are making up excuses to avoid hard choices," she said petulantly. Then, after a pause and a deep breath, she continued, "I don't want to fight about this. I just thought that a little time traveling together might help clarify our feelings."

Or confuse them, Kinko thought to himself. "Rokujo, all this is speculative right now. I am in residence at Myoan-*ji* and will stay here until I have mastered this music. After that, I may be free to travel; but I don't know when that will be."

"Well, I would like to continue this conversation," she said.

"Do you want me to let you know when I am planning to leave for Edo? Where is your family's house?"

"I'll be in touch with you," she said, abruptly rising. "I must be going. Goodbye, Kinko." Kinko watched her exit, sipping the cool tea. As she vanished down the street, his heart lightened and his breath deepened. His natural instinct was to be helpful, and he wanted her to be safe, but he was wary of becoming emotionally entangled with her. Her final burst of frustration and anger had freed him from any residual guilt that he felt. Paying for their tea, he slowly returned to the temple, his heart peaceful.

A few days after their meeting, while he practiced with Gendo Kanmyo, the latter said to him, "While you are here at Myoan-*ji*, I think that you should spend a little time practicing with the abbot." This suggestion took Kurosawa by surprise, since abbots —in his experience—were typically chosen for their administrative gifts rather than their musical ones. As though aware of his thoughts, Kanmyo added, "You both might enjoy the time together. I will set up an appointment for you."

Two days later, Kurosawa found himself sitting alone with the abbot in the second-floor meeting space of the administrative building. He had seen the abbot often since their initial meeting, but only during the daily *zazen* sessions. Sitting opposite him on a low cushion, Kinko was again struck by the man's size, as well as his demeanor. He possessed an ability to appear completely absorbed in the present moment.

"May I hear some of the pieces you have learned from Kanmyo?" he politely asked. Kurosawa picked up his *shakuhachi* and began playing *Kyo Reibo*. It was a piece that the monks of Myoan-ji often used for begging, and Kinko played it many times while begging in the city. He played it well for Minzan Zenji, who sat for a few moments with his eyes closed as if he savored the sound.

Finally, he took a deep breath, expanding his vast belly. "You are very smart, Kurosawa." Silence. What did that mean? Somehow, from the way the abbot uttered the words, it did not feel like the compliment it was on the surface. Kurosawa sat silently, and waited for more feedback. Eventually, the abbot picked up his own flute and said, "Let me play it for you the way my teacher taught it to me."

As soon as he began, Kinko realized, to his great surprise and delight, that the abbot was a brilliant musician. He had seen abbots as administrators for so long, he stopped thinking about them as musicians at all. Minzan Zenji was a different matter entirely. His tone was unlike Kurosawa's: "roughhewn" was the expression that came to Kinko's mind. His technique was subtle and accomplished, and the range of his sound was staggering, like meeting a headwind as one summited a mountain.

When he finished, it was Kinko's turn to sit in silence. Finally, he spoke. "That was amazing, *Shishō*. Could you work on this piece with me a little more?" The older man's weathered face broke out into a smile.

"That would give me great pleasure." The two spent the next hour going over some of the phrases that the abbot played differently from Kinko. The latter realized that the raw sound of the abbot's playing was not from a lack of embouchure control, but an intentional technique. This intrigued Kinko, who tried—with limited success—to imitate it. And, oddly, the abbot was just as stymied in trying to explain it. Ultimately, he waved his hand and said, "You just have to practice."

"If you can afford the time," Kurosawa hesitantly said, "I would be grateful to continue this practice with you."

"Yes, let's meet in two days at the same time," said the abbot.

On leaving the abbot, Kurosawa sought out his friend Kanmyo. "Your abbot is amazing," he enthused. "I have rarely heard *anyone* play like that, much less an abbot!"

"Did I fail to mention that before becoming abbot, he was our senior *shakuhachi* instructor?" Kanmyo asked playfully. And then, on a more serious note, he added, "I'm not sure that there are many temples in Japan who take their music as seriously as here in Myoan-*ji*. We honor great players and trust that they will shape how our temple evolves." Kinko recounted his experience with the abbot and was disconcerted when his friend laughed.

"Well, to begin with, if he invited you to come back to learn, he thinks very highly of you; he does not teach anymore. Congratulations. His comment about your intelligence may have been a suggestion to focus less on the precision of your technique and more on experiencing the music spiritually. But you may want to ask him when you see him next.

When he met with the abbot two days later, Kinko did just

that. It was a wet day, and Kinko could hear the calming rain drum on the roof as Minzan Zenji sat in silence, framing his response. "Kurosawa, my friend," he finally started, "the wise sages of our tradition used the *shakuhachi* as a *hoki*—a spiritual tool—rather than just a musical instrument. They did so, believing that making sound with this instrument—ironically—drew one deeper into silence. They developed this music over the centuries as a way to take us deeper into ourselves, to lead us to enlightenment."

As the abbot spoke, Kurosawa felt his anxiety rise. This conversation sounded like his old teacher Ikkei and provoked an unaccustomed insecurity in him. He heard the solemn sound of a temple bell ring in the distance.

"But there is nothing about simply playing the instrument itself that takes us to that place. Like all spiritual disciplines, one can go through the motions of practice and never let them take you deeper. We can sit *zazen* our whole lives and not be one step closer to enlightenment. We can read the words of the Buddha and never open ourselves to be transformed by them. And, in all honesty, that deeper place is frightening: we see ourselves exposed and bare; we have to acknowledge the unattractive parts of our character. Going deeper—becoming enlightened—involves releasing control, opening up, being vulnerable. That is not easy for anyone. And it is particularly difficult for samurai."

Kinko thought of his father, and the vast lengths to which he would go to avoid being vulnerable, and of how he had learned that himself.

"Our intellects can trap us, defend us from the vulnerability of self-knowledge. You play the *shakuhachi* with enormous technical sophistication, but I'm not sure that you are opening yourself to the music. I don't have a sense that you are letting it center you, quiet you, lead you to know yourself better. But I could also be wrong, so let's work together and see what we learn."

Walking back to the visiting monks' quarters, Kurosawa reflected on the abbot's words. They echoed what both his teacher Ikkei had suggested, as well as the sage observations of his friend Harushige Asano. He was always performing, always keeping himself apart, untouched. He minimized the empty spaces in the music–the *ma*–because that is where he felt vulnerable, unprotected. He used technique and sophistication to avoid letting the music shape him. He vowed to bring a "beginners' heart" to his lessons with the abbot.

Over the next weeks, Kurosawa practiced regularly with Minzan Zenji every couple of days. They continued working on *Kyo Reibo*, but also spent time on the other Myoan-*ji* pieces, as well as the three classics. Kurosawa could not remember a time—other than first encountering the *shakuhachi*—when he learned so much or grew more as a musician. He also came to have a deep affection for the old abbot, appreciating his wisdom as well as his musicianship.

He eventually mastered the breathy, "rough-hewn" sound of the abbot, but Minzan Zenji did not react as enthusiastically as Kurosawa hoped. The depth of his desire to please the older man surprised Kinko. At the same time, he felt Minzan push him in ways that were profoundly uncomfortable, and which he was not even sure that he could learn. He often ended these sessions emotionally raw and fragile.

One morning, finishing with his lesson, the abbot said, "Kurosawa, I would like to make a suggestion that will not make you happy. I know that you are eager to begin your new life at Ichigetsu-*ji*, and I am grateful that you have taken the time to work with me so hard. But I feel as though your sense of urgency is competing with your ability to learn. Some processes cannot be hurried.

"So here is my suggestion: I would like you to take a letter from me down south to our oldest Fuke temple: Kokoku-*ji* in southern Kii province. It is a temple with a rich history in our sect. And then, I would like you to stop at nearby Kōya-san, the holy mountain. Kukai, the founder of Shingon Buddhism, established Mt. Kōya as a religious center some nine hundred years ago. The mountain now has hundreds of temples, most dating back centuries. Our order built no Fuke temples there, but you will find a very holy monk, who is an exceptional *shakuhachi* player. I think that you could learn much from him. And staying on Mt. Kōya is itself a remarkable experience."

"But *Shishō*," Kurosawa objected, "Kōya-san is in the exact opposite direction from Edo. It would take many days of travel even to get there, much less spend time with this monk you suggest. There must be an easier way."

"Kurosawa, my friend, you are a brilliant musician," said Minzan Zenji, "one of the most talented I have ever heard. But you haven't learned what the *shakuhachi* has to teach you. Perhaps you never will. But you will certainly never learn it in Edo. This is your best opportunity."

Kinko felt as though he were a child again, fruitlessly flailing in the arms of his mother when she reprimanded him. He wanted to run; he wanted to get on with his life. And he also wanted Minzan Zenji's approval. The abbot looked at Kinko with great compassion, seeing the conflict in his heart.

"Do me at least this one small favor. Before you make a decision, spend the night meditating on it. And, if you will take one more small piece of advice from an old man, take a trip south of us a couple of hours and visit the Shrine of Fushimi-Inari. It is a remarkable, holy place, a good site to spend the night in contemplation."

A NIGHT AMONG FOXES

Fushimi-Inari: Kurosawa was familiar with the name, but little more. Following the directions of the temple gate-keeper, he walked to the southeast edge of the city and then proceeded directly south. As soon as he left the city proper, the traffic on the roads became less busy, and his progress was swift. As he walked, he tried to remember what he could of the ancient Shinto shrine. It was founded over a thousand years earlier when—legend claimed—a nobleman named Irogu no Hatanokimi used a rice cake as an archery target. Throwing the rice cake in the air, it suddenly transformed into a swan and flew to a mountain where rice began to grow. The nobleman followed the flight of the swan and built a shrine to Inari, the Shinto god of rice and sake. Thousands of Shinto shrines were dedicated to Inari across the empire where merchants prayed for success and prosperity, but Fushimi Inari was the most magnificent.

As Kinko walked, the abbot's words from that morning echoed in his ears. He was particularly stung by the phrase "you haven't learned what the *shakuhachi* has to teach you.

Maybe you never will." Accustomed as he was to criticism—he certainly got enough of it from his father—he had never before had his musicianship criticized. The abbot's doubt that Kurosawa could grow in Edo also struck him as unnecessarily harsh. To avoid obsessing over the perceived slight, he began to attend to the splendor of his route.

It was a beautiful day for a walk. The crisp, late-autumn sunlight poured through the red and golden leaves of the trees; birds sang with abandon beneath the broad canopy, and the earth smelled rich and verdant. By late afternoon, Kurosawa walked under the towering vermillion *torii* gate that marked the threshold to the shrine. He walked up the incline to the entrance building, where he bowed, prayed, and made an offering of copper coins. The steps of the building were flanked by two massive stone foxes, each holding a key in its mouth. People had long believed foxes to be the messengers of the god Inari, and their keys symbolized access to the granaries of rice that Inari controlled. The statues possessed a hard, fierce look. They were not intended to welcome.

When he asked a nearby priest for directions to the main shrine, the man pointed wordlessly towards the mountain rising behind the building. Walking behind the entrance shrine, Kinko met a series of bright *torii* gates which ranged in color from burnt-orange to Chinese-red. The flagstone path that ran through them led up the side of the mountain, at the top of which—he assumed—he would find the main shrine where he hoped to spend the night in meditation.

Although each gate was free-standing and independent from its neighbors, they were positioned so closely together that they appeared to form an endless crimson tunnel. Clouds scattered the twilight rays, momentarily shining a red-orange light that intensified the colors of the gates. Kinko felt as though he had crossed an invisible boundary into another world. A gentle wind rustled the golden leaves, and Kurasawa felt his breath slow with the breeze and his spirit quiet—a little.

Why was he here? To gain the approval of an idiosyncratic old man he would never see again? Ridiculous. He should be on his way to take up a post as the senior instructor of the pre-eminent Fuke temple in the empire, a temple that would give him access to the highest levels of the Japanese aristocracy. He could undo all the damage brought on through his disastrous affair and regain his status and prestige. He was going to make his father proud.

His father? Was that the reason for his urgent need to succeed in Edo? To somehow prove to his father that he was worthy? To raise the reputation of the family? Foolishness and vanity. As Kurosawa walked through the endless ranks of *torii*, in the waning daylight, he could just make out the inscriptions on each donated gate: dedications that celebrated family successes, prosperous business ventures, and fortuitous wedding matches. Is this what achievement and advancement looked like: the ability to sponsor one of several thousand *torii* gates lining the paths on the way to a Shinto shrine?

The pathway led him up for a long time. The mountain was high, and the route quite steep in places. As he pondered and walked, Kinko began to worry that he was lost. With no specific idea where the main shrine lay, all he could do was follow the path of *torii* gates. Already he passed several places where the path branched and simply assumed that the divergent paths would provide different scenic routes to the same shrine. But they did not appear to come together, nor was their final destination any clearer.

Kinko's anxiety rose as his surroundings darkened. The path climbed through swaths of deep forest, the passage of *torii* gates surrounded by monumental, soaring cedars. Occasionally the tunnel would end, and Kinko found himself walking through rows of ancient stone lanterns, their rounded edges covered in moss. Some were lit with candles left by devotees earlier in the day. Twice he passed through small graveyards, whose burial monuments vanished into the darkness up the slopes of the mountain. In the near-darkness, they seemed to loom up and catch him by surprise. Kurosawa was not a superstitious or timid man, but in the gathering darkness, he hurried quickly through these monuments.

The path's ongoing ascent provided some hope he would eventually find the central shrine. Over and over again, he spied lights ahead of him and breathed a sigh of relief that his goal was close, only to find that the light was from a cluster of stone lanterns, or a small shrine by the side of the path, invariably flanked by fox statues.

Full night fell, with Kinko still lacking any sense of direction, other than the rising path. He passed the last visitor over an hour before and now seemed to be completely alone. Picking up his pace, he walked as quickly as the darkness allowed, looking for some sign of the shrine. His impatience and frustration grew: the sole purpose of this trip was to spend the night meditating in that holy place, and instead he was lost in a darkened wood with no sense of where he needed to go.

Frustrated and angry that his plans for the night were being thwarted, he sunk down in despair at one of the small roadside shrines. He ate a little of the remaining food that he brought with him and listened to the rustle of unseen animals in the dark forest. After a time, he got up to stretch his legs and walked around the small shrine area. It was bigger than he initially realized: consisting of several small shrines and gravesites thrown together along the hillside.

It was an interesting hodgepodge of structures, with two of the *torii* gates slightly askew, faded banners tied to poles, red bibs tied around the necks of the fox statues (a near-universal gesture of protection), and the tall wooden *sotōba* slats attached to the grave markers. Since the mountain slope was particularly steep here, a series of short flights of stairs led from one structure to another. Kinko lit two guttered shrine candles as an act of reverence, and also to better see what was around him. Although it was still too dark to make out any of the writing, the candles cast eerie shadows against the massive trees beyond.

He gave up trying to find the main shrine and decided simply to spend the night where he was, sitting down and quietly meditating with his back against one of the shrine altars. The high mountain air was cold, and he wrapped his cloak closely about him as he pulled out his *shakuhachi* and began to play. In honor of Minzan Zenji, he first played *Kyo Reibo*, and then several of the other pieces that the two had practiced together. The darkness on the mountain was profound, as was the silence. Once or twice, Kurosawa thought that he heard the cry of a remote fox calling for its mate. Finally, he wrapped his thin travel cloak closely about himself, leaned back against the altar of the shrine, and fell asleep.

A cold, lifeless sun gave light to the morning, but no warmth. Kurosawa arose, stamped his feet to get the blood moving through his frigid limbs, and ate a rice ball for breakfast. He was still frustrated by his failure the previous night; nevertheless, he wanted to find the main shrine and spend some time there before returning to Myoan-*ji*. As he made his way through the seemingly endless maze of *torii* gates, he crested a small incline overlooking the valley to the west, which—at this hour—still lay in the shadow of the sacred mountain. He realized with some surprise how high he came the previous evening and knew that he must be near the mountain's summit. He climbed a large rock and craned his neck, as he tried to get a sense of where the main shrine might be. He saw nothing.

And then, in a flash of insight, he understood what he missed the night before: there was no main shrine at Fushimi-Inari. The mountain was the shrine. The whole mountain. The mountain itself was sacred and holy, and the endless paths of *torii* gates were simply opportunities to commune with the mountain itself. Just as any major temple or shrine would have an abundance of small sub-shrines and a graveyard within its precincts, this mountain was littered with small shrines and graveyards as well. He had spent his night in the very place that he sought the whole time.

It was all so obvious that Kinko laughed out loud. He felt light and carefree. Unbidden, the words of the poet Basho came to his mind:

I still want to see
in blossoms at dawn, the face
of the mountain god

Despite his perceived failure, he had spent the night in the shrine of Fushimi Inari and honored the god with his music. And so, unhurried, unburdened, and unscheduled, he spent the morning wandering through the passages of *torii* gates and worshipping the mountain god. As he walked, the mood of the sun also improved and finally warmed the cold autumn morning. Kurosawa ambled among the shrines and graveyards, reading the snippets of stories contained in their inscriptions, and the prayers of hope and celebration written on the *torii* gates.

Later that morning, while sitting and playing his *shakuhachi,* perched on a high rock overlooking the valley, he reflected on his early morning revelation: how a simple shift in perspective allowed him to see everything in a new way; how his stubborn search for the "main shrine" kept him from attending to the beauty and sacredness all around him. How easily he might have returned to Myoan-*ji* frustrated and empty, thwarted by his own preconceptions and assumptions!

And then he received his second epiphany of the morning: perhaps this was exactly why Minzan Zenji wanted him to travel to Kōya-san. Perhaps his narrow focus on the next step in his career blinded him to the bigger picture of what lay before him—blinded him to where his music might lead him. Maybe the mission to Kōya-san was an invitation to step back and get a broader perspective on his life and vocation. Kōya-san was a good place to do just that.

He knew what he needed to do. His decision caused him some anxiety, but it also brought a sense of peace, of "rightness." Conveniently, it also allowed him to avoid having to escort Rokujo to Edo, precluding all the complications of traveling with her. So, with a lightness in his step and spirit, he began to make his way down the mountain. On his way, he blew his *shakuhachi* with abandon and power. No one was listening; there was no need to perform. The sound itself was all that was important.

The return journey to Kyoto was glorious. The elms, cedars, and maples—sensing the coming winter—celebrated with a final orgy of color before they fell into their long snowy slumber. As if trying vainly to generate their own heat, the travelers along the road moved with a greater sense of urgency, ferrying commodities and goods into the city. Once he arrived, rather than returning immediately to the temple, Kurosawa took some time to wander through the city, soaking up the sights and sounds of the ancient capital.

He arrived at the temple in time for the evening meal and *zazen* session and was granted permission to see the abbot the following morning. When he arrived at the abbot's meeting room the next day, he found Minzan Zenji in high spirits. "Tell me about your visit to the shrine, Kurosawa."

"I thank you for your suggestions, *Shishō*. It was very helpful, and I have decided to take your letter to Kokoku-*ji* and visit your friend on Kōya-san."

"Excellent," the abbot returned, "but you did not answer my question: tell me about your visit to Fushimi-Inari." So Kinko told the abbot about his trip, the night in the small shrine, and his revelation the next morning. And talked about how that all contributed to his decision to make the trip south.

"Excellent," the abbot repeated, this time more thoughtfully. "That sounds like both a good decision and one well-made. I am grateful for your willingness to be open."

"And I am grateful for your push. And your honesty."

"Certainly. Please give me a couple of days to pull together the material that I'm sending to Kokoku-*ji*. I will let you know when I am ready." With those words of dismissal, Kurosawa left the abbot's presence.

For the next few days, Kinko continued in the daily routine of the temple, including studying with Gendo Kanmyo. He spent one day outside the temple in Kyoto, stopping at several shops to purchase straw sandals, paper handkerchiefs, and other necessities for the road. With his money from Hiroshima and the sale of the swords, he was able to buy himself a heavy, padded travel cloak, as well as several small gifts of food for his friends at Myoan-*ji*: delicacies on which they would not ordinarily splurge. He was delighted to find just the right items for the abbot and Gendo.

After *zazen* one night, Kurosawa was summoned to the abbot's quarters. "Kurosawa," said the abbot, "it has been a pleasure to have you in our temple. I appreciate your hard work and your receptiveness. Those traits will take you far."

"Thank you for your kind hospitality, *Shishō*. Please accept this small gift from an unworthy pupil." The abbot smiled at receiving the sweets, his one obvious weakness.

"Keep in mind, my friend, that Kōya-san is a special place. Shingon Buddhism is very different from our own Rinzai tradition, but its founder—Kukai—was a wise and powerful teacher. Also, our great Fuke founder Gakushin resided on Kōya-san for a time after he returned to Japan from China. And it is said that his disciple, Kichiku, was on his way from Kōya-san to the Ise Shrine when he received the vision in which he was given the two pieces *Empty Sky* (*Kokû*) and *Flute on a Misty Sea* (*Mukai-ji*). So Kōya-san is important in our tradition as well.

"Go there with a 'beginner's mind,' open and ready to learn from everyone. The older we are—and the more accomplished we are—the harder that is for most of us. But try not to judge; always seek to understand."

"I will do my best, *Shishō*. Thank you again." Minzan Zenji smiled and gave Kurosawa a bundle of documents wrapped in waxed rice paper for the abbot of Kokoku-*ji*. Kinko bowed low and left.

He slept deeply that night and arose at dawn. Having said his goodbyes the night before, he was ready to be on the road for the next chapter on his pilgrimage. Hoisting his pack on his back, staff in hand, he walked out from under the entrance gate and set off down the road. It was a cold morning, and a light frost covered the needles of the fir tree at the temple gate. Winter had arrived at last.

SNOW ON A DISTANT PEAK

THE ROAD SOUTH

I n a reflective mood, Kurosawa chose not to return south through the chaos of Osaka, following instead a smaller, southeastern road from Kyoto towards the ancient Japanese capital of Nara. This would involve a longer—but much more scenic—journey. Having heard about Nara all his life, he was eager to see this ancient and historic city. For most of the eighth century, Nara served as the first permanent capital of the empire, before a new emperor had moved the capital to Kyoto. Since Buddhism established itself in Japan at that time, all the major Buddhist schools founded their headquarters temples in Nara to reap the benefits of proximity to political power.

Arriving in Nara on his second day, Kinko was immediately struck by the beauty of the ancient city, as well as its foreign feel. In most Japanese cities, roads meandered haphazardly and often respectfully detoured around sacred trees or rock outcroppings. However, Nara—like Kyoto—was modeled after an old Chinese capital and laid out in a clear grid pattern, filled with temples and parks. It was a clear, cool day, with red and golden leaves carpeting the ground. Kurosawa immediately embarked on a tour of the city's grand, old temples. He was particularly struck by the magnificent Todai-*ji* temple, the scale of which took his breath away.

Tearing himself away after two days, Kurosawa continued south down the Kii Peninsula towards Wakayama, the closest city to Kokoku Temple. Whereas most of his journey thus far had been through open land, littered with rice fields, Kii was an alpine province full of dense forests. Both wetter and more mountainous than other parts of the country, the peninsula's economy relied on fishing and lumber production.

Soon after leaving Nara behind him, Kurosawa entered a dense, humid cedar forest. Other than an occasional woodcutter, Kinko found the mountainous roads deserted and harder to navigate than the flat, smooth thoroughfares to the west. He did not play his *shakuhachi*, but reflected much on his brief stay at Myoan-*ji* and the wisdom of its unusual abbot. Though still resistant to the detour from Edo, he was also excited about the prospect of spending time on Kōya-san, which loomed large in the history of Japanese Buddhism.

On his first night out, Kurosawa met a woodcutter near twilight, who was happy to share his family's small hut with the traveler. The second night, he was able to stay in a roadside tavern. The third night only offered a small shrine porch on which to lay out his mat. In the cold mountains, he was grateful for the padded travel cloak he bought in Kyoto. Towards the end of the fourth day, the road descended from the mountains, down to the port city of Wakayama.

Wakayama Castle was home to the branch of the Tokugawa clan that had produced the last several shoguns and took great pride in that fact. Ships departed its busy port carrying the province's lumber, while rice and vegetables arrived from the agricultural north. Kinko found a comfortable inn and was grateful for the opportunity of a hot bath and a good meal.

The following morning, he got an early start for Yura, the small seaside town south of Wakayama, home to Kokoku-*ji*. The day was cold and overcast, the clouds heavy with impending snow. Wet, heavy flakes fell in the early afternoon, making the steep, mountain roads slippery and difficult. It was dark before Kinko arrived in Yura. He stopped at a tavern for dinner, whose owner gave him directions to the temple, two miles from the harbor, on the northeast edge of town. To Kinko's great frustration, he had very nearly passed it on his way from Wakayama.

Retracing his steps, he arrived at the temple quite late and knocked on the large double wooden door for some time before a monk—none too happily—answered his call. Grudgingly, his host showed Kurosawa to the quarters for itinerant monks and left him without a word of welcome. There were only two other men in the large dormitory, and they were already settled in for the night. After hanging up his wet clothes, Kinko wrapped himself in a borrowed blanket and did the same.

The bell summoning the monks to morning meditation awoke Kurosawa in the slate-gray light of dawn. In the *zendo*, as he glanced around at the gathered monastic community, Kurosawa observed that Kokoku-*ji* was a modest-sized temple, though larger than he expected, given its remote location. The temple complex itself was unusually large to accommodate the numbers of monks making pilgrimage due to its enormous historical significance: it was here that the great monk Gakushin settled, after he returned from China and introduced the *shakuhachi* to Japan. So while Myoan-*ji* in Kyoto was the spiritual center of the Fuke sect, this temple was the earliest.

Following *zazen* and breakfast, Kurosawa made his way to the administrative building to greet the temple's abbot, a narrow-faced man with a perpetual grimace below a high fore-head. With apparent reluctance, he accepted Kurosawa's greet-ings and the papers that he bore from Minzan Zenji in Kyoto and extended the welcome of the temple.

On leaving the building, Kurosawa recognized one of the monks from the guest quarters the previous night. Approaching him, Kurosawa greeted the visitor and introduced himself. "Good morning, brother. My name is Kinko Kurosawa, and I come from Kuzaki-*ji* in Nagasaki. I assume that you are also a visitor here?"

"Good morning, Kurosawa," his comrade answered brightly. "My name is Nagate Chikuzen, and I am from Reihō-*ji* in Edo. My abbot sent me here to do some historical research in Kokoku-*ji*'s library." Chikuzen possessed a youthful face—though Kinko estimated that he was nearly Kinko's own age—set atop a rotund body. Inadvertently, Kinko found himself wondering how the young man had traveled here all the way from Edo: he hardly seemed capable of walking such a distance.

"Then we will be neighbors," responded Kinko. "I am trav-eling to Ichigetsu-*ji* to take on *shakuhachi* teaching responsibili-ties there."

"Oh, wonderful!" exclaimed Chikuzen, clapping. "We will be more than neighbors. Ichigetsu-*ji* and Reihō-*ji*—though located in different parts of the city—operate very closely, with many of the priestly staff serving both communities. Perhaps you and I might travel together back to Edo," he added hopefully.

"As delightful as it would be to travel with some company, Chikuzen, when I leave here, I'm going to spend some time on Kōya-san."

"At the risk of beginning our relationship with you thinking ill of me, I can't imagine anything less enticing than climbing the holy mountain in winter to spend time with some ascetic Shingon monks." Chikuzen visibly shuddered at the idea.

"Since you have been here longer than I," Kinko asked, changing the subject, "perhaps you could show me around the temple complex?"

"Of course!"

"And I'm curious to see this library. Fuke temples are not known for their libraries, and you have traveled a long way to see this one."

Chikuzen lit up at the invitation to discuss the library; his face beamed like a child offered candy. "I would love to! But first, let me show you around this beautiful old temple." With that, the two set off.

Kokoku-*ji*'s beauty was indeed notable. Built in Karoku 3 (1227), it honored the memory of Emperor Minamoto no Sane-tomo, murdered by his nephew. The whitewashed walls of its buildings were edged with the ancient, dark, bare wood, exuding an elegant simplicity. Nestled amidst a cedar forest, surrounded by high mountain peaks, the temple's setting enhanced its feeling of quiet steadfastness. When the original structure was nearly complete, Chikuzen told Kinko, a fire destroyed many of its buildings. The annals of the temple reported that a *tengu*—a mountain spirit—rebuilt the structures in a single night, as a sign of respect for the monks.

Chikuzen strategically ended the tour at the temple's library, which he entered with the kind of reverence usually reserved for the main sanctuary. And, indeed, it was a remarkable building. It seemed somehow larger on the inside than it did from the outside. Upon walking through the doorway, they entered a large open room with high shelves lining the walls. A narrow plank walkway in front of the shelves was bounded on its remaining side by a balustrade, which encircled a large opening in the floor that, in the dim light, appeared to be a black abyss. High windows above the shelving provided a diffuse natural light for the space.

Kinko had never seen such a huge room full of scrolls and texts, but Chikuzen hastened around the walkway to the back of the room with barely a glance. In the middle of the walkway opposite the main entrance was a small door opening into a corridor, branching left and right.

Turning to their left, they followed the long corridor to its end and turned right, deeper into the building. Following this passage, they came to an intersecting corridor and climbed down a set of stairs to their right. These ended in another passage, with a door directly in front of them. Chikuzen pulled a key from his robe and thrust it into the keyhole.

The door opened upon a cavernous room filled with rows of shelves which held countless numbers of scrolls. Light filtered down through the massive hole in the floor of the first room, far above their heads. Rows of shelves funneled the visitor towards a central reading area, lined with broad, heavy oak tables. The light from the windows far above gave enough illumination to see, though not enough to read by, necessitating lamps on all the reading tables. It was a beautiful space and the finest library that Kurosawa could imagine. Chikuzen noted appreciatively the awe on his new friend's face.

After taking in the magnificence of the structure, Kinko turned back to his new acquaintance and asked, "What have you been researching?"

"Our abbot sent me here to find any documents I could about the origins of our Reiho temple in Edo. To tell you the truth," he added, lowering his voice, "I think the abbot hopes I will find something that would be useful in building the case that our temple should be superior in status to your new home of Ichigetsu-*ji*, which has always maintained its pre-eminence."

Kinko laughed. "Given the multitude of teachings on

humility in Buddhism, it is endlessly amusing to me how desperately we seek status. 'My temple is the oldest, biggest, richest, most important...' It feels like we've missed something important along the way." He shook his head. "And have you discovered anything that will help in this matter?"

It was difficult to tell in this light, but it seemed to Kinko that Chikuzen flushed slightly and hesitated in answering. "Oh, nothing worth mentioning." If he had known Chikuzen longer, Kurosawa might have pressed his question, but instead, he simply let it drop.

The two men spent the rest of the day together wandering around the temple precincts and the surrounding neighborhood. Kinko found that he greatly enjoyed the younger man's company. He was smart, educated, and studious, and clearly loved the journey of learning. They sat next to each other during the afternoon *sui-zen* session, and Kurosawa found him to be a competent *shakuhachi* player as well.

Over the next few days, the two friends became inseparable. Given the brevity of their acquaintance, Kinko was surprised at how quickly he came to trust his friend, enough to share the outlines of his embarrassing story. In return, Chikuzen shared his own story of being the oldest son in his samurai family, but sent away to become a *komusō* because his father preferred that his younger—and more martial—brother inherit the family title.

Although he lacked prowess as a warrior, Chikuzen possessed a gift for words and calligraphy. He loved to quote poetry and often scattered memorized haiku into his conversation. As they returned from a trip to Yura one cold day, Chikuzen stopped to appreciate a beautiful, snow-covered glade. Kinko also suspected that he paused to catch his breath. After a moment Chikuzen said:

Barren, blanketed,
Lonely cedars awaiting
The friendship of Spring

"That was beautiful," Kinko commented. "Who wrote it?"

"Oh, it just came to me now," his friend blushed.

"It makes me think of Basho's words," Kinko said: "'This is haiku country, seeds from old days blooming like forgotten flowers, the sound of a bamboo flute moving the heart.'"

A day or two later, upon meeting Chikuzen as he walked to the old library, Kinko remembered his earlier question. "Chikuzen, I have been wondering: a few days ago, when I asked whether you had discovered anything interesting in the library, you seemed a bit hesitant in your answer. *Have* you discovered something?"

To his great surprise, Chikuzen stopped dead in his tracks and glanced around them, as though ensuring that no one else might be listening. Nodding to the library, he motioned for Kurosawa to follow him. For no reason that he understood, Kinko found himself also checking to make sure that no one watched as they walked over to the library. Again, they walked down the dimly lit corridors and descended the steps to the main hall of the vast collection.

On this visit, Chikuzen wordlessly motioned for Kinko to take a seat at one of the tables. He lit a lamp and scurried off along a darkened aisle of shelves. Kinko felt as though he was being initiated into some sort of occult sodality, whose members concealed themselves in the shadows of the vast chamber. He waited, increasingly unnerved by the capacious silence of the space.

Finally, Chikuzen appeared, with his arms full of manuscripts. He dropped them on the table, and turning to Kinko, said—in a hushed voice— "You probably know, Kurosawa, that the founders of our Fuke order held their first meeting in this very temple in the early spring of Kan'ei 5 (1628). Monks gathered from all over the country to consult about the precarious position of our sect, worried that without official government sanction, local authorities could disband us. Many of our initial members were *rōnin*, whose lords were on the losing side against the Tokugawa, leaving their retainers mistrusted, jobless, and destitute. The retainers' lives as *komusō* had saved them.

"What emerged from those discussions was the document which every Fuke temple possesses: the *Kyotaku Denki*—the founding credentials of our order. We carry excerpts of this document in our *honsoku* wherever we go. The *Kyotaku Denki* outlines every part of our practice and beliefs, the stories that define us. It was this document that the shogunate approved later that year, officially authorizing our order.

"The *Kyotaku Denki* attests to our origin in the work and teachings of the Chinese monk Pu'hua or Fuke from the ninth century. The *Kyotaku Denki* recounts the travels of our great forebear Gakushin to China, returning to teach us the spiritual discipline of the *shakuhachi*. We all know the story.

"But as I have explored this library—which has many copies of the *Kyotaku Denki*—I have only found two copies that appear to date all the way back to the actual momentous meeting in Kan'ei 5 (1628). They are these," said Chikuzen as he gently unrolled two fragile manuscripts. Kinko held down one of the scrolls and looked at the ancient text.

"Look at the writing on both of these documents," Chikuzen observed, as he ran his finger down the lines of script. "Both of these are written in the 'mixed characters'—*kana maijiri*—typical of the time: a mingling of pure Chinese and colloquial Japanese. The early portions of the document tell of the Chinese monk Pu'hua. But after those stories, we encounter the passage about Gakushin. It states:

"'When Hotto Kukushi'—the formal title for Gakushin—'returned from China, his four primary disciples accompanied him: Kua Tsuo, Li Cheng, Tseng Shu, and Pau Pu.'

"As you can see, this text is written in just Chinese characters. And the brushwork is slightly different."

"What do you infer from this?"

Lowering his voice to a whisper, Chikuzen responded, "I believe that these words are a later addition to our founding document. I think that someone added them to give our order a richer historical lineage in Japan."

"Other than a slightly enhanced status, why would that be important?" Kinko wondered aloud.

"Well, in the first place, I wouldn't discount the importance of an enhanced status in the religious community. And in the second place, you must know—as a native of Kyushu—that when the shogun crushed your island's Christian rebellion in Kan'ei 15 (1638), fear of the Christians caused the shogun to closely scrutinize the beliefs of all religious organizations. I guess that our newly formed order felt vulnerable, and so added a richer Buddhist pedigree to its history to protect itself."

"So are you saying," Kinko asked with some amazement, "that Gakushin and Kichiku were not the originators of our Fuke order in Japan?... That all of those stories that we have been telling people—and ourselves—for all these years are fake?"

"Well..." hesitated Chikuzen, "they are certainly part of the oral tradition of our order and there are later writings that speak in detail about their role in our history and music. But these lines are their only mention in our founding documents; so, I'm just not sure that the written history supports our oral tradition."

Kinko's raucous laugh resounded in the quiet of the old library. "Well, I'm pretty sure that this information is not going to please the people who sent you down here, Chikuzen. They were looking for evidence that would improve their status, and all you have found is documentation that undercuts it." He laughed again.

"I know! Now you understand my quandary. What should I do?"

Still chuckling, Kinko answered, "My friend, I am the worst possible person to advise you on navigating temple politics. My suggestion is that you mention none of this in your written report to the abbot. Disclose it verbally to one of the abbot's inner council whom you trust and let him decide what to do with the information."

His answer seemed to please the young monk, who breathed a small sigh of relief. Pensive, Chikuzen speculated aloud, "I wonder how much of our self-image—both corporate and personal—is built on stories we have heard that are just not true? Stories that reflect the way our forebears wanted things to be, rather than the way they were. And those stories get repeated over and over again through the cascading years, until the reality has been washed away, and all we know are the stories. Eventually, those stories become who we are, and how we see ourselves."

Chikuzen paused, reflecting for a moment before continuing.

"My father thinks that we are a family of great warriors because one of his forebears fought bravely at the Battle of Sekigahara and helped establish the Tokugawa shogunate. But did he? Who knows? Maybe the man hid behind a tree during the whole battle or lay with a pile of bodies pretending to be dead.

"Our Fuke sect believes that Gakushin brought over the

first *honkyoku*—*Kyorei* (Empty Bell)—from China, where it had been handed down from one monk to the next for centuries from the time of Fuke. Did he? Or did some random *komusō* make it up a hundred years ago and teach it to another, attached to a picturesque story? It's all very disconcerting."

"It is," agreed Kinko. "And yet, there are some hopeful elements to it as well. Maybe we play *Kyorei* with more reverence and power, imagining it to harken back to Fuke's disciple. Maybe your father holds himself to a higher standard, imagining that his ancestor was a great warrior."

"Perhaps. And perhaps it just means that he disinherits a worthy son," noted Nagate Chikuzen, sadly.

Over the next few days, the snow fell heavily on the small temple, leaving Kurosawa little inclined to continue his journey to Kōya-san. He enjoyed the quiet temple and made a few other friends among the monks. But the snow came to an end, as did his sojourn. So on a bright, cold morning, Kinko packed up his belongings and prepared to travel. He took his leave of the officious abbot and then set out to find his friend Chikuzen. Not surprisingly, he was buried deep in the library.

"Well, Chikuzen, I'm afraid that our paths are parting for a period. I wish you joy in your studies and a safe passage back to Edo when you are through."

"May the Buddha's blessings rest on you also, Kurosawa. It has been a joy meeting you, and I look forward to renewing the friendship when you take up your post in Edo."

"As do I." The two friends bowed deeply to one another and Kinko left the library and the temple to continue on to the holy mountain.

HOUSE OF A THOUSAND LAMPS

The road to Kōya-san rapidly rose into the mountainous interior of the Kii Peninsula. It would be at least four days of hard walking to get to the holy mountain. Winter advanced more rapidly as Kinko's path climbed to higher altitudes. As night fell on his third day, he reached the village of Kudoyama at the foot of Mt. Kōya. He spent the night at Jison-in, a small Shingon shrine in the village, from which commenced the path up the temple complex.

He arose early to share prayer and breakfast with the monks before setting out. The path up the mountain's side— known as the *Kōyasan chōishi-michi* was a steep sixteen-mile hike, marked by one hundred and eighty stone pillars. Each of the tall markers was numbered and decorated with a different Sanskrit syllable for pilgrims to chant while walking. The morning was clear and cold, and the frost continued to cling to the ground long after the sun was up.

The route through the forest was narrow, and as Kurosawa made his way higher up the mountainside, he found himself walking through dense clouds. A thin blanket of snow lay upon the ground, crisp and hard. The stone markers suddenly emerged from the mist, like sentinels guarding the pathway. Kinko felt as though he had left the ordinary world behind him and journeyed into a sacred, hidden realm.

He cleared the clouds by mid-day and passed under the massive Daimon Gate by early afternoon. The main temple settlement—called *Danjō Garan*—contained hundreds of small temples and thousands of monks. A quiet snow lay on the rooftops of the multitude of temples and shrines, although churned into mud by many feet on the streets.

Minzan Zenji had told Kurosawa to find a monk named Akira Kendo, who lived in a small sub-temple called Eko-*in*. After he asked several passing monks, one directed Kurosawa to the temple. On entering the gate, the simple beauty of the place overwhelmed Kinko. Its precincts—as all the temple compounds in Kōya-san—were enclosed within a wall of moderate height, perhaps ten feet. A broad double lintel crowned the main entrance doors, topped by a gracefully curved roof that resembled a flattened bell, the peak just above the door.

Inside the main gate, he found a small but immaculate rock garden. Most of the buildings were built from dark, ancient cedar, left plain and weathered. Seeing no monks, he walked to the door of the first building and knocked. After a few minutes, an old monk with a long, white beard opened the door. "Greetings, holy father," Kinko bowed. "I am seeking one of your brothers by the name of Akira Kendo. I believe he is in residence here."

"He is indeed, my young friend; but he is in study now. Please follow me."

Kurosawa followed the old man down a corridor to a small

sitting area, where the man offered Kinko a *zafu* cushion on which to sit. A few minutes later, a young novice monk brought in some green tea, leaving immediately. Kurosawa sat for what felt like a very long time—wondering if they had forgotten him —when an older monk walked through the door. He was of modest height—just shorter than Kinko—and slight build. Sitting down with a smile on a *zafu*, he took a deep breath and closed his eyes as though he prepared for meditation. But then he opened them and said, "I take it from your *komusō* garb that my friend Minzan Zenji has sent you here?"

"Yes, *Shishō*. He told me that you were a gifted *shakuhachi* player and that I might learn something from you."

Kendo smiled. "I am not sure that brother Minzan's confidence in me is well-placed, but you are welcome here. I would love to have the chance to work with another of his students."

Kinko was nettled at being lumped in with the abbot's other students, feeling his own circumstances were unique. Eager to clarify, he said, "Actually, I was only a student of Minzan Zenji very briefly while passing through Kyoto on my way to teach in Edo. I stayed in Myoan-*ji* to learn some of their music and Zenji thought that a brief side trip to Mt. Kōya might prove helpful."

As he spoke, Kendo closed his eyes, as though listening very carefully. When Kurosawa finished, Kendo took another deep breath and simply said, "I see." There was a long pause. Long enough for Kinko to feel uncomfortable.

"Well," he finally responded. "Let us spend some time together and see where it leads. I will speak to the abbot about having you stay in our guest quarters as a temporary member of our community. Please make yourself at home, and I will see you at dinner."

With that, Akira Kendo smiled, arose, and departed,

leaving Kinko unsure of both what just happened and what to expect. He sat for a few minutes deciding what to do. Finally rising to go in search of someone, Kinko met a young novice at the door who said, "Please follow me, brother Kurosawa. The abbot has asked me to take you to your room."

Escorting his guest down the hallways, the young man talked about the rooms they passed. He noted, with evident pride, that their temple was one of the oldest on the mountain— nearly a thousand years old—and founded by Dosho, a disciple of Kobo Daishi himself. The young man led his guest down several hallways, finally ushering him into a small monastic cell, with a futon folded in one corner, a *zafu* for sitting, and a low writing bench. A window in the room looked out over a lovely garden at the back of the temple.

"You are free to rest or use the library until dinner," the young man told him. Kinko set down his pack and asked, "Would it interrupt the routine of the temple if I played my *shakuhachi?*"

"Not at all. With Brother Kendo here, we have all come to appreciate the beauty of your instrument."

The novice left Kinko in the room. A gentle snow began to fall in the garden, dampening what little sound there was. Feeling restless and unaccountably agitated, Kinko pulled out his *shakuhachi* to play.

Dinner arrived early in the little temple. When the full community gathered, there were only 23 monks total. After they assembled, the abbot—who was surprisingly young—introduced Kurosawa as a colleague from their Rinzai brothers. Then, addressing Kinko directly, he said, "Brother Kurosawa, you are welcome here for as long as you would like and will be treated as a member of our community. As such we will expect you at morning and evening prayer service and meals, and I will list your daily work assignments along with the other monks. If you have questions, any of your brothers here will be happy to help."

This was not exactly what Kurosawa expected, but he smiled, bowed, and thanked the abbot for his hospitality. He joined the rest of the community for evening service. The temple boasted a beautifully constructed *butsuden*, with a statue of a serene Buddha on the altar flanked by the two sections of the Mandala of the Two Realms. They chanted sections of the *Mahavairocana Sutra*, after which there was a brief talk by the abbot, followed by more chanting. Sutra chanting was not a significant part of Zen practice, but since much *shakuhachi* music developed from sutra chanting, they echoed the cadences of each other, and Kurosawa followed along easily.

The following morning began with prayer and breakfast, and then the monks built a large fire in the main *butsuden* for the Goma Fire Ritual, invoking the name of the great Wisdom King Fudo Myōō to cleanse themselves spiritually. Afterward, members of the community broke off into their own tasks or study. Kurosawa's task was to dust and polish two of the small sub-shrines of the complex.

Kurosawa saw Akira Kendo at several points throughout the day and was surprised when Kendo never approached him about practicing together. On the second day, Kinko actually heard Kendo playing in another part of the temple, without ever extending an invitation to Kinko to join him. By the third day, Kurosawa's frustration was rising, and when he happened to pass Kendo in a hall, he stopped and asked, "Excuse me, *Shishō*. I was wondering when we might begin our practice together?"

Kendo looked at him curiously and paused, as though the

question caught him by surprise. Finally, he replied, "I expected you might want to settle into temple life for a while. I wasn't aware that you had time constraints."

Flustered, Kurosawa replied, "Well, I don't know if I would call them 'constraints'; it's just that I am expected in Edo to take up a teaching position at Ichigetsu-*ji*, and I did not originally plan on making the trip here to Mt. Kōya."

"I see," said Kendo, followed by an extended silence. "Perhaps we should meet tomorrow and plan our time together." Kurosawa felt some relief at this, but the conversation as a whole unsettled him.

The following afternoon, Kinko knocked at the door of Kendo's room and slid it open at the latter's invitation. The room was as simple and austere as his own, showing little sign that its occupant was a long-term resident of the temple. Akira Kendo sat on a *zafu* cushion with his *shakuhachi* beside him, facing an empty *zafu*. Kinko knelt *seiza* facing him, flute in hand.

"Tell me about yourself, Kurosawa," Kendo began. As Kinko spoke, Kendo closed his eyes as if to intensify his listening. Kinko talked about his family, and his growing up in Kuroda. He talked about his father sending him to Nagasaki and life in the temple there. He recounted his swift rise to the position of senior instructor and ended with a highly-sanitized version of the story of his invitation to teach in Edo.

Kendo sat silently with his eyes closed, as he sifted through this information. "It is unusual for an abbot to let go of a gifted teacher," he reflected. "They are notoriously hard to find."

"Well, to tell the truth, my abbot and I had some frustrations with each other," Kinko replied, uncomfortable with the turn of conversation.

"Oh? What was that frustration about?"

"It's a little embarrassing," Kinko responded vaguely, feeling his stomach start to tighten.

"Good. Let's hear about it."

Now Kinko felt defensive. "Well, it's rather personal, and I'm not sure how it bears on our playing *shakuhachi* together."

At this, Akira Kendo's eyes snapped open with a look of surprise. "Really?" he said incredulously. "You are not 'sure how it bears on our playing *shakuhachi*'?" Kendo picked up his instrument.

"You understand that this is a spiritual tool, correct?" Kinko bit back his sarcastic reply. "How is it possible to share who you are as a *shakuhachi* player if you are unprepared to share who you are as a person, even an embarrassing incident from your past? An incident that may well have an impact on your playing."

Kinko's face was hot, his body as tense as an over-tightened *koto* string. His every impulse was to rise, leave Kendo, and forsake Mt. Kōya; it had been a waste of time to come here in the first place. He was wasting precious time when he should be on his way to Edo to rebuild his career. But Minzan Zenji's face floated to mind, and—mirroring Kendo's mannerisms—Kinko closed his eyes, took a deep breath, and sat for a moment. When he was calm, he opened his eyes and saw Akira Kendo staring at him with eyes that somehow conveyed great sympathy. Kinko breathed again and told Kendo the whole story.

It poured out of him like a torrent, too long dammed up, full of anger and spite and guilt and sorrow. In the end, he just sat. Kendo sat also, his eyes cast down on the ground in front of him. "Thank you, Kurosawa. I am grateful for your trust. And I am grateful for your willingness to be vulnerable." Kinko noted how similar Kendo sounded to Minzan Zenji in that moment.

Still feeling a little raw and petulant, Kinko asked, "so how does that impact our *shakuhachi* playing?"

"To play the *shakuhachi* is to seek enlightenment. Enlightenment depends on self-understanding. You can not seek enlightenment if you are clinging to hurt and shame; you need to gaze directly into yourself and reflect on those pivotal moments. Why did you do this? What emptiness were you seeking to fill? What wound were you seeking to heal? These are the questions that lead to enlightenment.

"Although I am not a *komusō*, Kurosawa, there are many of us here on Mt. Kōya who appreciate your tradition. Remember the words of your *Kyotaku Denki*: 'The *shakuhachi* is an instrument of the Dharma and there are numerous meanings to be found in it... Taken as a whole, the *shakuhachi* is the profound wellspring of all phenomenal things. If a man plays the *shakuhachi*, all things will come to him. His mind and the realm of light and dark will become one.'"

A bird sang in the garden beyond the window. Kendo closed his eyes again, taking a deep breath before continuing.

"Bear in mind also that the first of Buddhism's 'Noble Truths' is that all life involves suffering. We cannot escape that reality. And the second truth is that this suffering originates in our 'attachments.' Isolated in our temples, we can easily see the attachments that laypeople have in the outside world: desires for wealth, dreams of status, bodily lusts. But we do not always pay as close attention to our more subtle, monastic attachments: the sense of spiritual accomplishment, our status in the community, even the desire to triumph over one's self can be an 'attachment.'

"You cannot undo what you have done. You cannot escape from your actions. The damage from your affair is part of your karma; it is part of Matsu's karma; it is even part of the karma of your temple. But it is also true that even in that debacle, you—

and she—were seeking some sort of wholeness, filling some emptiness within you. And that, too, is part of the karma and may provide the space for some sort of healing. The question right now is how do you move forward in a way that seeks wholeness, Buddha-nature?"

Kinko reflected, surprised and embarrassed that he had not asked himself those questions; that he needed the prodding of a near-stranger to see the obvious.

Kendo took a deep breath and said, "This has been a good *shakuhachi* lesson."

Akira Kendo's words unexpectedly shook Kurosawa and left him less eager to seek out more time with him. He decided not to ask for the next lesson; he would wait for the invitation. He spent the next couple of days focused on learning the rhythm of the Eko-*in* temple, while he reflected on Kendo's questions.

When Kendo invited him to a lesson, Kurosawa undertook to follow Minzan Zenji's advice and engaged the lesson with a beginner's mind. He entered Kendo's room, sat on the empty *zafu,* and waited. Kendo sat too, with his eyes closed and took deep, measured breaths. Kinko emulated him. After what felt to Kinko like a very long time, Kendo vigorously rubbed his prayer beads together in his hands and then bowed.

"Welcome, Kurosawa. It is good to have this time with you. How are you settling into temple life here?"

"I enjoy it very much, *Shishō.*"

"Have you reflected on the questions I asked you when we last met?"

"I have, *Shishō.*"

"And what insights did you uncover?"

"I recalled how lonely I felt at Kuzaki-*ji,* which is odd to say, living in a large community full of monks and priests. But I realized that I have always kept myself apart. I wanted—I want —people to see only the image of confidence and accomplishment that I project. I don't want them to see my fears and insecurities. Matsu gave me a place to let those go, and to be myself. She allowed me to be vulnerable."

"A helpful insight. What does that reveal about your playing?"

"I guess it means that I also play in a way that projects polish and confidence."

"Also helpful. Will you play me something?"

Kinko picked up his *shakuhachi* and played *Kyo Reibo* from Myoan-*ji* in Kyoto. When he finished, Kendo said, "Very beautiful. And very controlled. It feels like you are walking a dog on a tight leash; as though you are afraid of what might happen if you let the music go.

"I think that while you are here, I would like to practice *Mukaiji* (Flute on a Misty Sea). This feels like an appropriate choice for a couple of reasons. First, *Mukaiji* has a strong connection with Kōya-san. You may know that when the founder of the Fuke sect—Gakushin—returned to Japan from China in the year *Kenshō* 6 (1254), he initially came to Mt. Kōya to live. It was only later that he went to Kokoku-*ji*, where you just visited. And it was later still, after he became abbot of Kokoku-*ji*, that he broke off relations with the Shingon Buddhist order and turned Kokoku-*ji* into a Rinzai temple. We're still somewhat bitter about that here on Mt. Kōya," he added, smiling.

"According to our tradition, Gakushin was still on Kōya-san when he sent his disciple Kichiku on a pilgrimage to the Ise Shrine, on the eastern side of the Kii Peninsula. On that pilgrimage, Kichiku—while falling in and out of sleep during a prayer vigil—received a vision in which he was floating in a boat on a calm sea. Sitting awestruck by the beauty of the full moon, a heavy fog rolled across the water, cutting off the sight of the sky and everything else. In the midst of this impenetrable mist, he heard a *shakuhachi* playing music of unearthly beauty. When he awoke, he tried his best to recreate the music on his *shakuhachi*, and immediately returned here to Kōya-san to tell Gakushin about his experience. When he heard the piece, Gakushin told Kichiku that the music was a gift from the Buddha, and he named it 'Flute on a Misty Sea.'

"The second reason *Mukaiji* feels like the right piece for us is that it is about losing sight of a clear moon but discovering beauty amid a disorienting fog. That's not a bad description of where you are, my friend, is it not?" He sat smiling.

Kurosawa responded, "*Shishō, Mukaiji* is certainly a beautiful piece, and I have always enjoyed it. But as one of the three classic pieces of the Fuke sect, I learned it many years ago, and have played it often. I was hoping that while I was here that you might teach me a piece that I do not know."

As soon as the words came out of his mouth, Kurosawa realized his misstep. Akira Kendo fixed him with the piercing gaze with which Kinko was already becoming familiar, and asked, "What does it mean, I wonder, to *know* a piece of music?"

He paused as if considering and closed his eyes. "Does it mean that you know all the notes? Does it mean that you have it memorized? When we read the words of the Buddha, do we 'know' them? Once we have read them, do we simply store them away in our memory and go on to the next teaching?

"No. We meditate on them; we ruminate on them; we turn them over in our minds. Their wisdom is eternal, and what they say to us today may be different from what they say to us tomorrow. You must treat *honkyoku* music like Buddhist scripture. A piece of music engages us in a particular way when we first encounter it, and in a different way when we encounter it later. The purpose of *honkyoku* is for the music to be a partner in our living, a partner with whom we are in dialogue over the years. We never 'know' it. We keep 'knowing' it, as it keeps knowing us at a deeper and deeper level. That is why many monks only learn a piece or two over a lifetime. That is how mastery happens."

"I understand, *Shishō*. Forgive my impertinence."

"I know that you 'understand,'" responded Kendo as he tapped Kinko's head with his finger. "What I want is for you to "*understand*," tapping the center of his chest. "You need to embody what your intellect has learned. So let's practice."

Kendo picked up his *shakuhachi* and the two men began to play. As opposed to Minzan Zenji, Kendo was not a brilliant musician. He was a solid player and played with great feeling, but no brilliance. But Kurosawa noted with surprise how much space he gave between the musical phrases. This empty space —*ma*—was part of all *honkyoku*, inviting the listener into a quiet, contemplative place. Kinko always minimized it, however, thinking that it would be uninteresting to a casual listener. He was surprised at how it changed the feeling of the music, giving it a far more meditative quality. He tried to give himself permission to take that space and expand the sense of quiet.

The following day, after the Goma Fire Ritual, Kinko decided to walk around Kōya-san and explore the heart of its temple ward, the *Danjō Garan*. Beginning at the Grand Stupa, a beautiful two-story shrine that stood over 150 feet tall with two sets of vibrant red roofs, he meandered through the maze of historic structures. After visiting the massive "Golden Hall," one of the original buildings on the mountain, he asked a passing monk about other landmarks that he should see.

"Ah, brother! Follow me to the mausoleum where the

Grand Master Kobo Daishi rests! It is a very holy spot here on the mountain. Are you familiar with Kobo Daishi?" Kurosawa told his companion that he knew little more than the name.

"Let me tell you a little of his story while we walk," his companion said. "Kukai—the birth name of Kobo Daishi—was a member of a powerful family who sent their son to the capital at Nara to study, with an eye towards his joining the emperor's court. Instead, he encountered Buddhism and found his life transformed. Buddhism was only beginning to make its way into Japan at the time, so Kukai left to study in China, where his instructor said that teaching him was like pouring water into an open vessel. He attained the status of master teacher in a very short time before returning to Japan.

"After teaching for some time in Nara, he realized that Buddhism needed a teaching center far from the corrupting influences of the imperial court. He petitioned Emperor Saga, who gave Kukai permission to found the center of Shingon Buddhism on Mt. Kōya, in the year *Konin* 7 (816). Kukai's ambitious dream was to build a series of temples around this plateau on the mountain whose configuration would mirror the design of the Mandala of the Two Realms. A scholar, poet, translator, engineer, and calligrapher, he supposedly died twenty years after founding Kōya-san. But because his body never decomposed, we believe that he did not die at all, but rather entered a state of perfect and eternal meditative bliss. His body resides in a mausoleum—the *Okuno-in*—just down this path."

Kinko and his companion arrived at a bridge at which Kinko's guide stopped and bowed. Kinko did the same. On the other side was a stately path covered in broad, even flagstones, and lined with ancient, regal-looking stone lanterns. Colossal pines and cedar trees towered above these lanterns, their crowns indistinguishable in the mass of foliage scores of feet above their heads. Even in the day's bright sun, the diffuse light making its way through the dense umbrage gave the path the feeling of a massive temple. Behind the lanterns, scattered amidst the vast trunks of the forest, were hundreds upon hundreds of gravestones and monuments, commemorating the leaders of great *daimyo* families, monks, and religious leaders.

Gesturing towards the multitude of gravestones, Kurosawa's companion said, "Many people over the centuries have believed they would rest more peacefully while lying near the great teacher."

"I'm sure they're right," agreed Kurosawa.

The two men strolled companionably a little over a mile until they arrived at a second bridge, leading to a small inner graveyard around the shrine. Again, both men bowed and walked through the handful of graves in the central courtyard. They climbed a steep flight of twenty-four flagstone steps, entering a building of wondrous luminosity.

Thousands of lanterns glowed dull red in rows upon rows lining every wall of the mausoleum, as though one were inside the glowing embers of a fire. Walking in from the cold winter afternoon, the heat was welcoming, though nearly overwhelming as well. With evident pride, his host pointed out one nondescript lantern. "That lantern has burnt continuously since the day of Kobo Daishi's internment here."

Knowing that every monk occasionally fails in his duty at some point, Kinko doubted that this was actually the case, but he loved the idea of a flame unbroken for over 900 years. He stood in awe at the centuries of prayer that this building—and Kōya-san itself—embodied. His new acquaintance left him at the mausoleum, while Kinko tarried for some time, praying and reflecting. As dusk fell, he made his way back to Eko-*in*, passing monks returning for the night to their various temples and shrines, just as they had done for centuries.

. . .

Over the next weeks, Kurosawa continued meeting Kendo for practice. He learned to pay attention to where he held tension in his body. He worked on making sure that he was not gripping the instrument too tightly, and that his facial muscles were not clenched. When the quality of his sound frustrated him— the *shakuhachi* was a notoriously temperamental instrument— he began to look at his emotional state and to identify places of psychological tension. It was a period of great growth and joy. He began to see the instrument as an insightful partner, rather than a cherished object.

He also easily fell into the brotherhood of monks residing at the Eko-*in*, and learned the idiosyncrasies of the various members: what got somebody angry, who was reliable, who were lovers—*Kōya-san* was notable for the level of sexual activity among its monks. He enjoyed the prayer services, as well as the work. During his stay, he was assigned several tasks and engaged in them with deliberateness. One day, he looked at the list to find his name next to a new assignment which read: "Provisions to the hermitage."

When he asked Akira Kendo about this, his teacher smiled. "Well, to be honest, I suggested to the abbot that he give you that duty. We have a member of the temple who took up residence in a cave further up Mt. Kōya several years ago, and who lives and prays there in solitude. He has a meager vegetable plot next to his cave, but every few weeks we send him a supply of rice and other necessities; more during the winter months.

"I thought that you would benefit from meeting him because he is the other member of our community who plays the *shakuhachi*—instruments that he makes himself. I thought you might spend some time with him; he has much to teach." Kurosawa was crestfallen at hearing this. He believed he might be near the time to continue his journey, and going to learn from this new monk felt like a delay of indeterminate duration.

"*Shishō*, I appreciate your desire to help me, but starting to study with yet another teacher feels like a setback. I've lost so much time already because of this detour; and each day longer I take on my journey, the further behind I get." Kendo—his eyes closed again—sat thinking.

Without opening his eyes, he finally replied, "I wonder how one 'loses time?' It's not as though it disappears. Or at least, no more so than it disappears for all of us, endlessly slipping through our hands. There is a *koan* that asks 'How do you stop the sound of a temple bell?' You should meditate on that for a time.

"I can hear your frustration, Kurosawa, and understand your reticence to start something new. But that is the same struggle that you have had since you arrived here. You want to hurry, hurry, hurry: hurry to Kyoto, then hurry to Kōya, so you can hurry to Edo and set everything right. You will never get to where you need to go by hurrying. Impatience, my friend, is an expression of anger."

Kinko, too, closed his eyes and thought about this. Was he angry?

"*Mukaiji* teaches exactly this lesson. You will never learn this piece in a hurry. You are not acquiring a 'thing.' You are not even learning a piece of music. You are learning *from* a piece of music. Until you stop and listen, you will not hear what it has to say." Kinko hung his head.

"How long did you want me to stay with this hermit?" he asked, defeated.

Kendo laughed. "I am not imprisoning you there. Take him his provisions, ask him to help you with *Mukaiji,* and stay as long as you are learning."

It was hard to argue with that, and Kurosawa left feeling

thwarted and frustrated. As he was leaving, Kendo called, "Oh, and brother Kurosawa, when you pick up the supplies, please pick up a set of work robes for you to wear. Tell the monk in charge of supplies that you will be spending time with Brother Tanaka. He will understand."

MISOGI

When Kurosawa spoke with the monk in charge of provisioning about staying with Brother Tanaka, he thought that he saw a slight smile flit over the man's face. The brother gave him a heavy bag with rice, jars of pickled vegetables, and several pairs of straw sandals. He also gave Kinko two worn sets of *samue*—monk's work clothing—and said, "These will be better suited to staying with Brother Tanaka than the robes you are wearing. You might want to leave those here at the temple with your other belongings."

Soon thereafter, his heavy traveling cloak covered the worn *samue* as Kinko set off up the mountain. Brother Fumon Tanaka did not live on a well-traveled path, so the directions provided to Kurosawa were a bit vague. Kobo Daishi built the temple complex on Kōya-san atop a plateau on the side of the mountain, surrounded by eight taller peaks. It was on one of these peaks that Fumon Tanaka lived.

A light but constant snow had fallen on the mountain over the previous several days. As Kurosawa followed the unfrequented roads, accumulated snow compelled a slower pace and made the path difficult to find. By late morning, the snow began to fall heavily in large, wet flakes. With some difficulty, he found the marking for the small path that led off the main road. The path markings were very hard to see in the snow, and the path itself was steep and slippery.

By mid-afternoon, he was tired and soaked. The wet snow blew harder now. He pulled his cloak more tightly about his shoulders and leaned into the wind, the bitter taste of snowflakes on his lips. He was grateful once again for the solid staff from his mother. Finding the last turn to the monk's cave, Kurosawa trudged up the final slope, after which the cave should have been in the woods off to his right.

He walked a little while further and worried about losing his way in the storm when he heard the familiar sound of *shakuhachi* playing. He followed the sound as the storm made its last attempt to thwart his progress. Cresting a low ridge, he looked down into a snow-covered dell and saw an old monk in nothing but a thin *samue* kneeling *seiza* in the snow while playing an enormously long *shakuhachi*. He knelt in front of the mouth of a cave which was covered by a curtain of rough hemp cloth.

Spying Kurosawa, the monk arose and met him as he slipped down the snowy decline, steadying him with an arm of surprising strength. Without speaking, he took the heavy bag from Kinko's shoulder and led him into the cave. Pushing through the curtain, Kinko saw a small but dry den, with the coals of a fire in a central pit, a heavy iron pot hanging above. Behind the fire pit was a bed role above which was some primitive shelving that held several personal items. In a far corner, Kinko saw a small pile of bamboo stalks that he assumed would become *shakuhachi*.

Tanaka laid the bag in a corner of the cave and from one of the shelves took two small teacups. He then poured tea from the cast-iron pot into the two cups and offered one to Kuro-sawa. Shaking off the snow near the mouth of the cave, Kinko gratefully accepted the cup of tea. "You must be new," his host observed. "I am Fumon Tanaka. Please sit."

Kinko sat on a stump positioned near the fire pit and held his frozen hands to the heat. Fumon Tanaka squatted on the opposite side of the fire, while drinking his cup of tea, and watched his guest in silence. He appeared to be in his sixties, his head covered with a short bristle of iron-gray hair. He was of average height; lean, though his arms were well-muscled. His *samue* was frayed and patched, but clean. Kinko noticed that he wore nothing on his feet at all.

Uncomfortable with the silent staring, Kinko introduced himself. "I am Kinko Kurosawa from Nagasaki on my way to Edo to join the Fuke temple there. I was practicing with Akira Kendo at Eko-*in*, and he suggested that I might come to prac-tice with you. So I brought your provisions and hoped that I could stay for a short while to study."

Fumon Tanaka continued to sit in silence for some time. Finally, he said, "Stay if you like. It's no matter to me." And with that, he arose and left, walking barefoot out into the late afternoon snow.

Tanaka returned about an hour later, as dusk began to fall. Without a word to Kurosawa, he put some snow in the cast-iron pot, and two handfuls of rice, and hung it above the coals on which he began to blow as he added wood. Soon, the pot boiled merrily as Tanaka opened up one of the large jars of pickled vegetables and put a few on two plates.

Once the rice was cooked and added to the dinner plates, the old monk went back outside, discarded the rice water, and returned with a fresh pot of snow for tea. Each man placed his hands together and bowed, muttering *"Itadakimasu"* in gratitude over the food, after which the two men ate in silence.

For Kurosawa, unsure how to engage this strange hermit, it was an awkward silence. He knew that many temples—primarily in the countryside—supported hermits, but he had never met one. He assumed that it would be a peculiar type of person who would seek out this sort of life. And it was certainly a lifestyle that would exacerbate any peculiarities.

"How long have you lived out here, apart from the temple?" he finally asked, when the silence became too uncomfortable for him. The old man shrugged.

"Don't remember."

"What drew you out from the temple to this life?"

"Seeking Buddha. I tired of the triviality of the temple."

Kinko found himself feeling defensive on behalf of the temple, whose life he barely knew. Even so, "triviality" was not a word that sprung to his mind to describe life on Kōya-san. However, he kept his thoughts to himself.

"So play something," Tanaka said. Kinko, who anticipated this request, brought out his teaching *shakuhachi* and said:

"I have been working on *Mukaiji* with Kendo." And taking up his flute, he began to play. He had barely begun when Tanaka's face broke into a broad grin. By halfway through, Tanaka burst out into a course laugh, almost rolling over in amusement.

Kinko stopped playing, angry and offended by Tanaka's merriment. The old hermit got up—still laughing—and said, "It's so pretty! Like a little dancing girl." Mimicking the mincing steps of a courtesan, he sashayed around the cave. "Is that what *shakuhachi* is about in your fancy temple in Nagasaki?" he asked laughing. Then, stopping, he became deadly serious. Spitting on the ground, he growled, "The Fuke have forgotten what they are about, debasing their once-noble tradition. Your temples—all temples—are filled with soft, effeminate men pampering themselves and fucking each other."

Stunned, Kurosawa sat silent, with no idea how to address this diatribe from a crazy man. He stared at the man's grotesquely gyrating hips and mocking mouth, unable to respond.

"Have I offended you, dancing girl?" Tanaka continued, bringing his face so close that Kurosawa felt his spittle. "I don't care. If you want to learn, you can stay here. But you will do as I do. I will not coddle you. Do you understand?" Tanaka's anger was palpable. Kinko realized that he needed to answer, and answer immediately. He bit back his own anger and hurt, responding, "I am sorry that I have disappointed you, *Shishō*. I humbly request that you teach me." He arose and bowed deeply.

Tanaka stood there for a long time and appraised Kurosawa. After a protracted interlude, he seemed to gather himself, and replied, "Fine, we begin tomorrow morning." And with that, he walked out of the cave into the night. He did not return by the time that Kinko—physically and emotionally exhausted—rolled out his sleeping mat on the floor near the fire pit, wrapped himself in his traveling cloak, and fell asleep.

A toe jabbed his ribs and awakened Kinko from a deep and dreamless sleep. "Get up, dancing girl!" spat Tanaka. "It's time to work." When Kurosawa opened his eyes, it was as dark as when he had them closed. It took him a few moments to orient himself, and remember where he was and the events of the previous night. The fire pit was cold, and the cave bone-chilling. Gradually, his eyes became accustomed to the dark, and he made out Tanaka standing in the mouth of the cave waiting for him.

He climbed up, shivering, from his mat in the pitch darkness and followed the old man outside. If possible, the cold was even deeper out there. Several hours before dawn, a waning quarter moon hung low in the sky. Without saying a word, Tanaka tossed Kinko a five-foot *jo* staff and began to make high cutting motions; his bare feet shuffled forward and back in the snow with each strike. Kinko knew these *suburi* exercises from the weapons practice at Kuzuki-*ji* and fell in quickly with the old man, watching his breath as clouds formed in front of his eyes.

After they practiced these *shomen* strikes for some time, Kurosawa's body began to ache. He knew that aching was a sign that he relied too much on his arm and back muscles and tried to focus on using his core. Even in the freezing cold, by this time Kurosawa felt the sweat start to roll down his back. At the point when he felt he could not raise the staff one more time, Tanaka changed the technique to a *tsuki* thrust, which he executed moving forward, followed by retreating with a head block. They practiced this pattern over and over again until Kinko felt that he could not make one more move, and then Tanaka changed the technique a third time.

They repeated these patterns for close to two hours while the sun began to rise. When there was enough light to see each other comfortably, Tanaka changed to paired *jo* exercises, with the two of them alternating offensive and defensive roles. The staff had always been Kurosawa's weapon of choice, and he felt confident in his use of it. Tanaka, however, was superlative, and the power of his strike was devastating.

After they did this for about an hour more, Tanaka finally put down his staff. "Good," he said approvingly. "You are less hopeless than I feared. Now come." And laying his *jo* against the entrance to the cave, he grabbed a bucket from just inside and strode off around the hill. Kinko followed.

They walked in silence for about 10 minutes when they encountered a stream. Tanaka turned right and followed the stream for a few minutes until it broadened into a lovely, small lake, covered by a thin sheet of ice in the early morning cold. With barely a pause, Tanaka set down the large wooden bucket that he carried and stripped off his clothes down to his loin-cloth. Clasping his left hand over his right hand, he shook them vigorously in front of his *hara*—the point in the lower abdomen that is the center of *ki* or life energy. Kurosawa knew that this practice—called *furitama* or "soul-shaking"—aimed at centering the body and spirit and building up internal energy. Kurosawa joined him. Then, taking from the bucket a large, heavy, club-like *shakuhachi*, Tanaka struck the ice and shattered it for several feet around him. Marching into the freezing water, he continued to break the ice before him with the bamboo.

Kinko watched this performance aghast, with a disheart-ening presentiment of what was to come. As he feared, Tanaka turned and pointed to the bucket—in which Kinko saw another long *shakuhachi*—and motioned for him to follow. Turning back to the lake, Tanaka placed the flute to his lips and began to play *ro*—the lowest note on the instrument—as he waded further into the frigid water.

Tanaka was engaged in a ritual called *misogi*, practiced by both monks and warriors as a rite of purification, intended to cleanse the spirit and prepare one for a spiritual endeavor of some sort. Often, *misogi* was performed under a flowing water-fall, but when waterfalls were unavailable, any body of water would do. Resignedly, Kinko also took off his *samue* and hung it from the branch of a fallen tree. The cold air painfully struck his sweaty body; every hair prickled.

Leaning over the bucket, he saw that the *shakuhachi* was quite long and heavy. Picking it up, he also saw that it was very roughly formed. Most *komusō* monks refined the inside bore of the *shakuhachi* and made it as smooth as possible to give the instrument a clearer tone. Many also spread a thin coating of lacquer on the inside bore to make the tone brighter and to protect the instrument from the moisture of the breath. This flute showed no signs of that sort of work at all. Tanaka had broken through the nodes of the bamboo, but otherwise, the inside bore looked raw and unfinished.

Shrugging at the inevitable, Kinko picked up the *shakuhachi* and followed Tanaka into the lake. His entire body seized up at the staggering cold. He paused, thigh-deep in the frigid water and tried desperately to acclimate. The mud on the lake bottom squished between his toes and around his feet. Tanaka, in front of him, was already waist deep and blowing strong, deep notes. Kinko drew in his breath as deeply as possible and attempted to relax his clenched muscles. He could barely manage a ragged, breathy tone from the *shakuhachi*.

Gradually, his body began to unclench, and his breathing became deeper. The flute responded with a more robust sound, though still with a shredded, fragmented quality to it. He too was over his waist in the freezing water now, his lower legs and feet rapidly becoming numb. Tanaka stopped ahead of him about chest-deep in the water, his head tilted up to keep the *shakuhachi* from getting wet.

Forcing each foot in front of the other—though he could not feel them anymore—Kinko moved out until he was as far as Tanaka, chest-deep in the frozen lake. They stood there for a few minutes blowing *ro,* Kinko grateful they did not attempt any actual music. The feeling in his lower body had disappeared, but Kinko was determined to stay in place as long as Tanaka—a sentiment that he recognized lacked in spiritual depth, but was all he possessed at the moment.

His relief was beyond expressing when Tanaka turned to head back for shore. As they left the water, Tanaka took two towels from the bucket and tossed one to Kinko. After drying off, he took his *samue* and washed it in the cold water, Kinko doing likewise. Wrapped in their towels, they trudged through the snow back to the cave, where Tanaka started the fire back up to boil some water for tea. Kinko laid his wet *samue* near the fire to dry while dressing in the second set, silently blessing the monk at Eko-*in* for providing him with two.

Huddled by the fire, he desperately tried to warm his aching body. Kinko looked at Tanaka, silent since the end of their *suburi* practice. Finally, Kinko turned to Tanaka and said, "Shishō, is something special happening today? Where I come from, we practice *misogi* in preparation for some endeavor of spiritual significance."

Tanaka tilted his head and looked at Kinko curiously, as though trying to figure out a puzzle by viewing it from a different perspective. Finally, he simply said, "Every day is an endeavor of spiritual significance."

Another surprise awaited Kurosawa later that day when he heard Tanaka play his *shakuhachi* for the first time.

"Time for meditation," Tanaka said as he picked up the rough, heavy instrument from that morning. When Kinko reached for his own *shakuhachi*, Tanaka waved him off, and pointed instead to the long, unfinished flute that Kinko had played in the lake that morning. Together they knelt outside the cave in the snow and blew the note *ro* for a long time. Only then did Tanaka say, "This is how one plays *Mukaiji*."

With that, he launched into the music as though engaged in a battle with his *shakuhachi*. *Honkyoku*, by its nature, was less melodic than either folk music or traditional classical music. In this case, however, so hard and aggressively did Tanaka attack his playing that Kinko could hardly discern the musical motifs at all. Finishing, Tanaka set his flute down and immediately began to sit in meditation. Kinko joined him in *zazen*, never having picked up his *shakuhachi*.

Every day, Tanaka's routine was the same: awaken two hours before dawn, practice intensely with the *jo* for three hours, *misogi* in the frozen lake, and then tea at the cave. Afterward, a variety of tasks filled the day: cleaning out the debris from the dormant vegetable garden, washing anything made of cloth, collecting firewood, and repairing the frames, tables, and shelves he used. He interspersed these tasks with periods of *shakuhachi* playing and meditation.

After the first day, Kinko—without waiting for an invitation that probably would never come—picked up his *shakuhachi* and joined Tanaka in this pre-*zazen* playing. He did not ask any questions, but tried his best to imitate what he heard. Likewise, the old hermit never said anything while the two played, although sometimes he would re-emphasize a phrase, giving Kinko the chance to go over it again.

Kinko often imagined how to describe Tanaka's playing. There was a wild, frantic air about it, as though he was on the edge of reason (although the old man often seemed to have abandoned reason—or at least taken an extended holiday from it). It also fascinated the younger monk how the old man used his entire body in the *shakuhachi* playing. Kinko knew that all good breathing—for music, for martial arts, for meditation—came from the *hara*, the lower abdomen. As Tanaka played, one could see the explosion of energy from his lower body. It looked as though he were practicing a martial art, rather than playing a piece of music.

Their practice was always outdoors, generally in the small circular dell in front of the cave's mouth. One morning, as they knelt seiza and played, a light snow began to fall. This did not bother Tanaka at all, who continued playing as before. Kinko, however, stopped to watch the snow and breathe in the cold air. By chance, he looked over at the old monk—eyes closed in concentration—and noticed the surrounding ground was wet, but not covered in snow. Without being obvious, he looked more carefully and realized that when the new snowflakes fell close to him, they melted into water. Kinko watched in amazement at the growing puddle around the old man.

After their practice, Kinko pointed to the water pooled around Tanaka compared to the packed snow where Kinko sat. "*Shishō*, what causes that?"

Tanaka rolled his eyes. "You must play the *shakuhachi* with great energy; like *jo* practice." He pointed to his *hara*, about two inches below his navel. "Your energy must radiate from here out. If you are cold, you are not producing enough energy. Focus. Concentrate. Pour every bit of yourself into the music. Understand this."

Over time, the actual martial arts practice, in which the two men engaged every morning, also took on a fiercer, more combative quality. Tanaka pushed harder as he gained trust in his guest's competence with the staff. Kinko was never pushed so hard as he was by this hermit. He sometimes laughed to himself at the fact that he came here to become a better musician and would leave as a worse musician, but a better warrior.

One morning, shortly after sunrise, the two men sparred harder than ever. The *jos* whirled in the delicate light of the new day, while sweat poured off of them. Tanaka parried a blow and raised his staff to strike Kinko's head. As he did so, he drew his staff back slightly too high and left an opening for an attack. Kinko, eager to discomfit his teacher, quickly moved forward for a *tsuki* strike to his torso.

As Kinko thrust the *jo* at Tanaka's chest, the latter stepped into the thrust, turned just before the weapon landed and allowed it to slip by him. Then, pivoting his *jo*, he drew it up against his shoulder like a shield, without ever losing contact with Kinko's weapon. Helpless to resist, Kinko felt the movement draw him forward and slightly off balance. Then, with a movement so fast it was a blur, Tanaka swung the *jo* around his head and down in a diagonal strike at Kinko's head.

Kinko knew that in an actual fight, the blow would kill him or at least knock him unconscious. He tried to parry with his own staff and realized too late that the full weight of the blow threatened the hand holding his *jo*. A fraction of an inch before shattering Kinko's hand, Tanaka's strike froze. As if speaking to himself, he said, "No, he needs his fingers." And he dropped his *jo* to a walking *kamae*, turned abruptly, and strode away.

Kinko could barely imagine the staggering degree of control required to stop a blow with that much momentum. He generally thought of Tanaka as being marginally out-of-control; his *shakuhachi* playing certainly seemed to be. And then Kinko wondered: was it possible that Tanaka's playing—as wild and erratic as it seemed—was as tightly controlled as the blow from his staff? Was it all as carefully—thoughtfully—disciplined?

Kinko had been at the cave about three weeks when another monk from Eko-*in* brought provisions for the two of them. He was a young novice who Kinko knew by sight, but no more. The young man was visibly unsettled in Tanaka's presence; and although he accepted the hermit's offer of tea, he left as quickly as he could without giving offense.

Having become acclimated to Tanaka's odd behavior, the novice's discomfort amused Kinko. After the young man left, Kinko and Tanaka sat silently in the cave and sipped the tea, providing Kinko a chance to ask a question on his mind since his arrival. "*Shishō*, I'm curious: why does the temple send you provisions every few weeks? What benefit do they get from it?"

Tanaka was silent for a while and pondered the question. Finally, he said, "I protect them from attack. I stand sentry."

Kinko was confused. "I know you are a powerful warrior and that we are far from the protection of the shogunate here on Mt. Kōya; but if you are standing sentry, shouldn't you be lower down the mountain from the temple? Any attackers would come from below."

"Idiot!" Tanaka exploded. "Not from human beings! You're a monk, aren't you? You know that we live in a world of spirit, don't you? A temple is in far more danger from spiritual attack than from any group of bandits. Spiritual attacks bring pride, anger, lust, disunity—these are the dangers against which I guard."

"But why up here on the mountain? Wouldn't you be more helpful fighting those forces in the temple itself—praying, teaching, and guiding monks like the young man who was just here?"

"It is hard to see spiritual attacks in the midst of the temple. One is too close there. Up here, everything is clearer. For many, many centuries has Mount Kōya been a holy place. It was a holy place long before Kobo Daishi came here. Kobo Daishi chose this place for his temple *because* of the sacredness already here. There are places like this all over the world, places that are closer to the world of the spirit.

"But that does not mean that those places are 'good' or 'holy.' They can be more dangerous than the most corrupt city. Wherever there are forces seeking good, there will be forces in opposition. Only a fool ignores them or underestimates them. The monks of Kōya-san are not fools; and they support me here with provisions, as I support them in their spiritual battle."

This was more conversation from Tanaka than Kinko had heard in the entirety of his visit, but he couldn't keep from asking, "If it is a spiritual battle, why do we practice with the staff so relentlessly every morning?"

Tanaka looked at him with a mixture of pity and exasperation. "How can you not understand? A warrior—and a monk—spends his life in training for spiritual battle. It is who we are. Our minds must be sharp and awake; our bodies must be fit and strong, our spirits must be calm, deep, and steady. Everything we do impacts every other thing. We cannot sit *zazen* without being powerful. We cannot see clearly without being pure. We cannot fight without being centered. As the great Zen master Dōgen taught: 'to master one dharma is to master all dharmas.'"

He stopped again. Kinko thought for a moment and then continued, "But *Shishō*..."

"Enough! Speak to me no more. You weary me with your foolish questions. You will never understand. You must do." And with that, he picked up his *shakuhachi* and began to play.

THE TENGU

Kinko could not remember how long he had originally anticipated staying with Fumon Tanaka, but his first several weeks flew by like a hard wind coming down off a snow-capped mountain. In part, this was because of the relentlessness of Tanaka's training regimen, which never stopped. But every day, Kinko could feel his body become stronger and his spirit less tattered, re-woven by the physical exhaustion and gentle silence.

So it was a surprise, one morning—as they drank tea and warmed themselves by the fire after the morning's *misogi*—that Tanaka varied his usual schedule. Putting on heavy socks, he laced up a set of sandals, and packed several rice balls and a bamboo flask of water in a bag. The old man then turned to Kinko. "Come; today we walk. Bring a *shakuhachi*." The young man hurriedly dressed, grabbed a flute, and followed the old hermit out of the cave.

With his now-familiar purposefulness, Tanaka strode out; Kinko hastened to keep up. Tanaka turned to his left and began to make his way up a steep, snow-covered incline, following no discernible path. As they crested the top of the slope, Tanaka eased his pace, and walked along a ridge through the mountain forest. The pristine trees were covered in new-fallen snow, and the woods were silent, except for the cry of a distant hawk, hovering off to their left. Kinko caught up to the hermit, walked side by side, and watched as Tanaka's breath became slower.

While they walked, Kinko turned to Tanaka and started to speak, "*Shishō*..."

Tanaka held up his hand. "Too much talking. Listen for the music."

Kinko was silent, listening. Eventually—tentatively—he said, "*Shishō*, I don't hear any music."

Tanaka threw him a despairing look. "There is music in everything—wind, water, birds—everything. You must learn to listen."

The two men walked for some time in silence. Occasionally, Tanaka pointed wordlessly at some interesting feature of the landscape: a particularly beautiful tree or a striking cliff-face. They walked for several hours like this, without Tanaka giving any particular sense of their destination. Finally, around mid-day, they arrived at a bluff towards the peak of the mountain, overlooking a valley spread at their feet in crystalline elegance.

Tanaka pointed over to their right, where Kinko could catch a glimpse of smoke rising above the trees far below them. "There lies the *Danjō Garan*, the heart of the temples of Kōya-san. Let us play for them." He raised his *shakuhachi* to his lips and began to play *Mukaiji*, though this time very slowly, with great elegance. Kinko joined him.

When they finished, Tanaka sat on a fallen log, looking over the snow-blanketed countryside. Kinko sat next to him in silence. "Is this where you were bringing me, *Shishō*?"

"Not all journeys need a destination." They sat for some

time more before he added, "I thought it would be good to walk; good to connect with our mountain."

They sat for some time more, and Tanaka pulled out the rice ball from his bag. After eating, Kinko reached over and picked up his flute, and looking at it, asked a question that had been nagging at him for weeks: "*Shishō*, why do you not finish these instruments, so that the sound is more pleasing?"

Tanaka looked at him again with that quizzical expression now so familiar to Kinko and sighed, shaking his head. "Because they make us work harder this way; and the discipline of *shakuhachi* is about cultivating our spirits, not producing pleasing sounds. If the sound comes too easily, we have not worked; and we are, therefore, unprepared for the work of meditation—unprepared for the work of spiritual warfare. Besides, the rough, breathy sound of the unfinished bore is more natural. Like sitting on this mountainside, it grounds us in nature. *Honkyoku* imitates the sounds in nature—bird calls, the wind. Always remember that legend tells us that one of Fuke's disciples crafted the first *shakuhachi* when he heard the wind blowing over a broken bamboo stalk and it reminded him of the sound of Fuke's bell."

Kinko sat and thought about this for some minutes. "Thank you, *Shishō*. I begin to understand."

If the brief interlude of walking provided any hope that Tanaka's regimen was going to change, that hope was dashed in the darkness of the following morning, when the hermit jabbed Kinko in the ribs to wake him for their *suburi* practice in the pre-dawn hours. The next few days were the same as the previous weeks; but, feeling as though Tanaka was becoming slightly more communicative, one afternoon, Kinko ventured another question.

"*Shishō*, we have been practicing together for some time now, and I am still not approaching the level of power that you get when you blow your *shakuhachi*. Can you give me any guidance?"

"*Ro-buki.*"

"*Shishō?*"

"You need to spend time every day blowing *ro*." *Ro* was the lowest note on the instrument, played by covering all five of the *shakuhachi's* holes. "Enlightenment can come with the blowing of one perfect sound. You do not need to play a whole piece of music. Your goal should be to play a single note with such perfection that you attain Buddha-hood. Please, remember: Enlightenment through one sound."

"*Shishō*, how will that change my playing?"

Exasperated, Tanaka snapped, "In my youth, a student never questioned a teacher! All you do is question! As if by '*understanding*' you will unlock the '*secret.*' Stop trying to understand; simply practice. Practice, practice, practice, and maybe—just maybe—understanding will follow."

This was an unsatisfying response, but Kinko did not argue. Instead, he began blowing *ro-buki* every day—simply blowing the single note. It seemed odd and monotonous, and pointless. But he kept doing it day after day for long periods. Some days, it felt like he was getting more volume or a better tone, but usually it was hard to tell. After practicing it for several days, he finally approached Tanaka and said, "I'm not sure if I am making the progress I hoped; will you listen?"

Tanaka, exasperated with his young apprentice, closed his eyes and nodded his head. Kinko began to blow *ro*, with as much energy and volume as he could. He blew and blew, looking at the older man for some reaction.

Finally, Tanaka snapped at him: "Blow! you pathetic little girl. Blow with all your life, all your soul! Blow as if no one can hear you. Blow so that you would shatter that boulder before you. Blow like that ten minutes every day, and you will become the master you already think you are." And with that, he stomped off.

From that day, Kinko began blowing as if no one could hear him. He experimented with different embrasures and angles, producing different sounds from the instrument. Slowly, over the days and weeks that followed, he could see the change in his tone, as well as the greater power and variety of tone he was developing. It was akin to the process of building muscles that they did every morning.

The shift in his attitude was slower, but he began to realize that playing as though no one could hear—and up here on this mountain, no one could—allowed him a sense of freedom that he had rarely experienced in his playing before. He recognized that even while playing in a temple, he was always acutely conscious that there were people within earshot, and therefore, there was always an element of performance. This awareness became more pronounced after he had become an instructor in Nagasaki.

One afternoon, when the two of them played through *Mukaiji* again, Tanaka looked at him and sighed. "You keep trying to play beautifully. Give up being a great musician. That is the wrong goal. The goal is enlightenment. If it sounds like music, you are doing it wrong."

Yet again, Tanaka's words stunned Kinko. "*Shishō*, I am a musician. Why in the world would I play and not try to have it sound like music? That makes no sense!"

"Idiot!" Tanaka barked, slapping him hard on the side of the head. "How long will it take for you to learn that you are not playing a musical instrument (*gakki*)? You are playing a spiritual instrument (*hoki*). You may be a musician; I don't care.

Here you are a monk." And with that, (as Kinko had come to expect) he stormed off.

A week later, after their usual morning regimen, Tanaka said, "Time for you to help with my *shakuhachi* making." The two left the cave with a handful of tools in a bag and walked for an hour or so to a deep grove of bamboo on a hillside. The *madake* bamboo trees were extraordinarily tall and thick. The two men slid down the incline into the grove, and Tanaka began looking around. Earlier in the year, he explained, he had identified trees that would make good flutes and marked them with string. Now, in the winter, with the sap at its lowest point, the trees were ready for harvesting.

"Take the bamboo from the hillside," he instructed. "It grows out at an angle and then straight up seeking the light, developing a curve at the root end. This makes *shakuhachi* beautiful and interesting."

Kurosawa had made *shakuhachi* before—it was a traditional part of *komusō* training—but never with bamboo as large as these. They found the six trees with Tanaka's string, and with a sharp hand saw, they cut the trees about six feet from the ground. Then, with a heavy, sharpened cutting spade, they chopped the root-balls loose from their web of rhizomes. "Under our feet, this whole grove is one being—connected, communicating," Tanaka said. "It is giving us these trees to make way for new growth."

Carrying the shafts with their root ends back to the cave, Tanaka spent the rest of the day heating the culm gently over the fire, a process that expelled the remaining sap from the stem. After that, the bamboo was set on a shelf out in the sun, to continue the process of drying. Tanaka told Kurosawa that he would leave the bamboo culms out in the sun drying every day for the next two months, after which he would store them in the back of the cave to continue drying for the next year.

The next day, they took some of the culms harvested the previous year and began turning them into *shakuhachi*. They first sawed off the small roots from the root ball and delicately opened up the hole at the bottom of the root. Then, from the other end, they knocked through the nodes with an iron rod that ended in a file, opening up the bore. With a fine saw, they cut the angled blowing edge of the *shakuhachi*—called the *utaguchi*—making it playable.

In the days that followed, they continued the process by drilling the finger holes, and then adjusting the inside of the bore with the long file for pitch. It was delicate and painstaking work. Crafting several *shakuhachi* at the same time gave Kurosawa a more thorough understanding of the whole process than his previous experience at the temple.

Throughout the process, Tanaka took different individual *shakuhachi* out with him during his meditation sessions and sat *zazen* with the flute laying in front of him. It brought to Kinko's mind the story in *The Tale of the Heike* when Emperor Toba set his flute on an altar for seven days before he allowed the finger holes to be cut. When queried about this practice, Tanaka simply shrugged and said, "Checking if they are spiritually healthy."

Kinko also noticed that twice after meditating with a particular *shakuhachi*—not playing or listening to it—he cracked it against a rock and hurled the fragments out into the woods. Kinko assumed that those two were "not healthy" instruments. One day, after Tanaka meditated with one of the flutes on which Kurosawa had worked, he brought it back to Kurosawa and said, "This is your new *shakuhachi*. Treat it with respect. It will be a good partner." The flute was over two and a half feet long and heavy. Its length necessitated offsetting the holes from the central line of the flute so that his fingers could more easily reach them.

In the weeks that followed, Kinko practiced hard with his new flute and tried to understand Tanaka's idea that playing music was a "mistake." He blew *ro-buki* for long periods, experimenting with different sounds, different embrasures. What did enlightenment sound like? Truthfully, it made little sense to him; but he resolved to ask no more questions. He decided to treat Tanaka's words as a kind of *koan* on which to ruminate, rather than a puzzle he could solve. While the *koan* itself remained a mystery, Kinko noticed that his playing left him in a more meditative mindset. More and more he felt led to set the *shakuhachi* down and move into a time of *zazen*.

He also realized that his playing acquired a diagnostic dimension: when the sound of his playing was poor, he reflected on what was going on in his emotional life that could impact his playing, rather than look for some technique that he did wrong. And he discovered that his emotional state often impacted the instrument's sound as much as any of the technical details of his playing.

One afternoon, he practiced down by the lake where they did *misogi* in the morning. He sat on a log and looked out over the lake, the late afternoon sun cast deep shadows from the bare trees on the snow. The previous several days had been hard, and he was increasingly frustrated at the extended time that he spent here with Fumon Tanaka. He knew he could return to Eko-*in* any time he desired—and he was certainly learning from the old hermit—but the process felt endless. Already his sojourn here on Mt. Kōya had been far longer than he anticipated, and he was anxious about what awaited him in Edo.

He played for a few minutes by the frozen lake, and could not get a decent sound. He knew that Tanaka's raw unfinished *shakuhachi* was part of the problem. But no matter what he did, his tone was thin and reedy. Why did the flute sound that way? He became so frustrated that he wept. And then he kept weeping.

For some reason that he did not fully understand, a wellspring of grief opened up in him that he could not stop. Grief at his failure as a musician, at his loss of status, at his challenging relationship with his father, at his loss of Matsu—of Taka. Deeper, there was grief at his isolation and at the silent emptiness that met him when he meditated. It was all so hard. He found himself sobbing uncontrollably.

After some time, the sobbing gave way to a deep sense of tired emptiness. He sat on the cold log, breathing in the brisk air of the winter afternoon. The hard, cold light cast sharp, intricate shadows from the empty tree branches, and he watched them advance slowly across the forest floor with the afternoon sun. He watched the empty lake—no, not empty, he reflected: hibernating, sleeping. In truth, the lake was full of life, but it slept now, awaiting the time when it would spring forth in all its wondrous potency. It was not dead; merely awaiting rebirth.

Later that evening, Kinko gratefully accepted the cup of green tea that Tanaka proffered, while he warmed himself at the fire. Neither man spoke. Then, without any prompting, Tanaka said, "Remember the words of the poet, 'It is easier to subdue a bandit in the mountains than to subdue the turmoil in your heart. But the compassion of the Buddha reaches across all worlds.'"

Kinko began to remember his dreams. He knew that he dreamed, because he often awoke with a vague sense of their presence, clinging to the frayed edges of his consciousness; but they disappeared as quickly as his awareness of them. He envied those who recalled their dreams, and he knew that the Buddha often spoke to people through their dreams. *Mukaiji*— the piece of music with which he was living—was the gift of a dream.

But here on the mountain, those hidden remnants of his dream life began intruding into his memory. Perhaps it was the fact that he was often in the midst of a rich dream when Tanaka awoke him in the pre-dawn hours. Perhaps it was that the quiet—almost meditative—quality of his *suburi* practice gave him the space to pay attention to them soon after he awoke. And perhaps something in his soul invited his attention.

Often these dreams were erotic, although—surprisingly— the erotic element rarely involved an actual past sexual partner of his. More often, they involved women who he knew, but who were not romantic figures to him. Other dreams seemed quite random. One morning, a kick from Tanaka awoke him in a cold sweat. He went outside to practice with the *jo* and tried hard to remember the details and fix them in his mind. *Suburi* practice was always silent, which gave him the time to reflect.

Later that morning, while they shared tea by the fire, Kinko said, "*Shishō*, my dream last night was quite unsettling. I was sitting in a room in a high castle filled with powerful *daimyo*. I knew that they were waiting for me to play for them, but they were talking and laughing, and no one was paying attention. When they became silent, I put the *shakuhachi* to my lips, but could not blow a single sound. I blew harder and harder, and nothing came out. At first, a few of the *daimyo* chuckled, and then more and more. The whole room was awash in laughter when you woke me."

Then, much to his discomfiture, Tanaka himself began to laugh as well—a rapid, high-pitched laugh that was almost a giggle. "Forgive me, Kurosawa," he said, pulling himself together. "These are very common dreams for a performer of any type."

"I know, but why do you think they are happening now when I am doing no performing and should have none of those worries?"

"To practice Zen is to release the self; so our 'self' becomes anxious, and we see that anxiety in our dreams. Do not let your dreams worry you. Just watch them."

Some days later, Kinko continued the conversation: "Shishō, I dreamed again last night and can't get it out of my mind. It was night, and I was standing outside the vast wooden doors of a massive temple. It was not a temple that I recognized, but I was banging on the doors with my fist, trying to get in. I banged and banged for a long time; and finally, the door swung open, revealing a darkened interior. And suddenly, I couldn't remember why I was banging on the door or who I wanted to see. So, I walked away."

Tanaka said nothing and appeared lost in thought. "Interesting," he finally said. "Not all dreams bear interpreting. Just watch."

A toe in his ribs awakened Kinko from a deep sleep, and some inner clock told him that it was much earlier than usual. "Get up, dancing girl, grab your flute; an attack is underway." Kinko jumped up, *shakuhachi* in hand, and hurried out into the night. The moon had set, and the darkness was absolute. Far down the valley, he heard the roaring of a powerful wind as though a storm were brewing. Just ahead of him, he could barely make out Tanaka kneeling in *seiza*. Kinko followed suit and rested his hand on the *shakuhachi* by his side.

"Do you see it?" the old man earnestly asked.

"I can't see anything; not the hand in front of my face."

"Idiot! Not with your eyes. See with your whole body, your whole spirit. Feel. Reach out."

He deepened his breathing and tried to empty his mind. The atmosphere was heavy, ominous; the wind angry. It felt like a storm about to break—threatening, but not unusual.

"We must play *Kyorei*," Fumon Tanaka cried, as the wind whipped leaves and twigs around them. "You must keep your mind still and blow harder than the storm. Our playing brings peace to the chaos."

Kurosawa brought his *shakuhachi* to his lips and played this most ancient of pieces. He could hardly hear the sound he made as the wind tore the notes from the flute and cast them angrily to the ground. He played harder, thinking that two months earlier, he would have been unable to make any sound at all in this gale. Beside him, Fumon seemed to blow with the ferocity of a samurai in battle. Kurosawa tried to match the old hermit's breathing, playing the music in unison.

As they played, Kinko held his body as he practiced in *zazen*: back straight, eyes slightly downcast and narrowed and unfocused, giving him a broad range of vision to both sides of him. This was how swordsmen held their eyes, allowing them to see opponents on either side. He felt his body relax and center; he breathed deeply from his abdomen. He focused on the music and mentally projected the sound as a sphere expanding larger and larger as it moved away from him until it encompassed the mountain.

Once they finished with *Kyorei*, they began again, with vigor, but centered and calm. And again. And again. Scattered rain fell about them and then passed as quickly. And then—as suddenly as it began—the wind fell silent, and the stars emerged from the darkened sky. They continued to play. All was calm. Finally, Tanaka put his *shakuhachi* down.

"The attack has passed for tonight. Did you feel it? Do you

see now why we are here high up on the mountain? Do you believe me now, dancing girl?"

"I believe that *you* believe, *Shishō*," Kinko cautiously responded.

Tanaka laughed and slapped him on the back. "That will do for now."

The night of the "attack" was much on Kurosawa's mind over the next few days. Late one afternoon, when Tanaka seemed in a more talkative mood, Kinko risked a question. "*Shishō*, tell me how you discerned an attack coming to the mountain the other night."

Tanaka paused before responding, "*To* the mountain or *from* the mountain?"

"I don't know; you tell me. What is the difference?"

"Spiritual attacks come from different places. Some are from spiritual forces outside the mountain: ill-wishes coming from some human quarter, some anger or bitterness at one of our brethren or the community as a whole, jealousy over prestige, competition for power.

"Other attacks are from the mountain itself. I have already told you that in spiritually rich places, positive energy—energy coming from the liturgies chanted in the temples, the prayers and meditation of the monks, even *shakuhachi* practice—often provokes a negative reaction. This mountain is filled with ancient *kami*, not all of whom are benevolent.

"Some were once compassionate when local people worshipped them; but when their worshippers died out, they became neglected and grew angry. Some others have always been angry. And some others—like the *tengu*—are more mischievous than angry, but they can be very dangerous if one is not careful."

"I always heard of *tengu* referred to as demons, until recently," noted Kurosawa. "But when I stayed in Kokoku-*ji*—just before coming to Kōya-san—I learned that a *tengu* rebuilt the temple buildings there in one night following a fire. That seems quite compassionate."

"True, but also quite unusual. Generally, *tengu* are hostile towards Buddhism; and they are more likely to push a monk off the side of a cliff than to aid him. On the other hand, they are fond of warriors, particularly swordsmen. You are probably aware that the great twelfth-century warrior Minamoto no Yoshitsune received his training from a *tengu*."

"You have spoken of spiritual battle before, *Shishō*; but how did you discern the attack the other night?"

"You heard and felt the violence of the attack yourself, did you not?"

"I did, but it felt like many other storms that I have been in —storms that were purely natural."

Fumon Tanaka reflected for a few minutes. "I cannot describe it," he finally said. "To me, it felt different; malignant. This kind of discernment only comes when one has become accustomed to silence and more aware of the subtle changes of atmosphere here on the mountain. I can't explain. Just practice."

Over the weeks, Kurosawa began to develop his own rhythm to the day. He continued to arise with Tanaka, join in *jo* practice, followed by *misogi*, and ending with tea in the cave. But after that, the two men began going their own ways, and each would wander, sit *zazen*, and practice his *shakuhachi* as he chose. Tanaka preferred sitting in the cave after dark, while Kinko often enjoyed sitting outside, watching the bright, cold stars.

One night, as he sat under a frosty, cloudless sky meditating, he caught a movement out of the corner of his eye: it appeared to be the brief flutter of a white robe behind a tree, accompanied by the sound of a soft foot tread. It was far too late for a monk from the temple complex to be making his way to the hermit, and the furtiveness made Kurosawa anxious.

"Who is there?" he cried and rose from his knees. The flutter of a white robe moved past another tree, just out of sight. He arose, his flute gripped in his right hand, and cautiously moved forward into the darkness.

"Who are you?" he called again. "No harm will come to you here." The soft patter of feet moved away from him and drew him forward. "Show yourself!" he barked. He moved forward at a faster pace now, faster than was safe in the dark snow. But the steps were still ahead of him just out of his reach. He glimpsed the edge of the white robe around a tree several feet in front of him.

He ran faster. Whoever this was, he was not going to get away from Kinko. His feet slipped in the wet snow, and yet he ran faster. He sprinted at full speed as he rounded a tree, only to see a deep precipice open up under his feet. He plunged into its blacknes as a powerful hand grabbed the collar of his *samue* and pulled him back from the edge.

He fell to the ground, gasping for breath as he looked up into Fumon Tanaka's sweating face. "You must be more careful. I have warned you that we are engaged in a battle with spirits who are not benign; spirits who do not want to see you mature towards Buddha-hood. And in any case, it is good to see an imagined opponent before committing yourself to battle."

"What was I chasing? Was it a *tengu?*"

"I do not know; perhaps. It matters not what we call it. It did not intend you good."

. . .

A few days later, as they sat next to the fire pit drinking tea one morning, Tanaka said, "You have been in my thoughts during my prayer of late. You have been here for two months and have learned much. You must make a choice now: either you must decide to stay here and commit yourself to the work of a contemplative, or you must take what you have learned here and let it guide you on the next stage of your journey."

Tanaka's words surprised Kurosawa. He had not given much thought to living the kind of life that Tanaka led. But he also knew that it was not an invitation to be answered lightly. So he spent much of the next two days largely on his own, meditating and reflecting. Ultimately, he returned to the old hermit and said, "I am grateful for the time we have spent together and the invitation to continue here, but I believe that I should continue to my journey to Edo."

The hermit answered, "I think that is a good decision. Tomorrow you will return to Eko-*in*."

The next morning, Kinko was awakened just the same as the past two months, but there was a heaviness in his heart as he arose in the dark and practiced with the old hermit for the last time. After morning *misogi*, they sipped tea in the cave, while Kinko assembled his pack. Tanaka handed him several *shakuhachi*. "Please take these to Akira Kendo; have him choose one for himself and ask him to find a home for the others with monks among the temples."

"I am happy to do that," Kinko replied. Then, he added a thought that had nagged at him all morning. "*Shishō*, I am so grateful for all that you have shared with me during my stay. But even after all this time, I still have so many questions. I feel as though there is so much that we barely discussed: the beliefs that shape your practice."

"Don't you see," Tanaka said with uncharacteristic gentleness, "it matters not what I believe. It matters even less what I *say* I believe. All that matters is what I do. Temples are filled with monks and priests who love nothing more than to discuss what they believe; to argue about what Buddha taught or what he meant. Most of them have no idea what they *actually* believe; they barely know what they *think* they believe.

"Inside of a day, I could tell you what every one of them believes: by watching what they do—how hard they work, how intently they sit *zazen*, how gently they treat one another. That is the only measure of what they believe. Everything else is an intellectual game. None of it matters. Practice. Practice is all that matters.

"As soon as you begin to 'discuss,' you create a separation between your thinking and your action. Smart people—like yourself—love to do this, because it is easier to discuss ideas than to live those ideas. Don't get caught in that trap.

"The great Zen master Dōgen taught a great deal about 'intimacy.' And he was not talking about sex. He was talking about living in a way that holds nothing back; giving ourselves completely to every moment in which we find ourselves. That is how you know what you believe. That is the only way."

Tanaka paused and looked Kinko fiercely in the eye.

"One last thing, my friend: Edo in general, and Ichigetsu-*ji* in particular, will be a hard place to practice and live with integrity. The preeminent Fuke temple is rife with politics and intrigue. Your sect has benefitted from the patronage of the shogun with such advantages as the ability to traverse the country freely. But those benefits have come at a price—the loss of your independence. Your sect has become enmeshed in the machinations of politics—the shogun's spies masquerading as monks, *komusō* themselves acting as spies. It has polluted a once noble tradition. You must beware."

Kurosawa sat in silence for some time, thinking. "Thank

you, Tanaka. Those are wise and helpful words. I will meditate on them."

Having brought little, there was little to pack, and so in short order, Kurosawa was prepared to go. He shouldered the pack, much heavier with the new *shakuhachi*, and the two men walked out of the cave together. Turning to the old hermit, Kinko was surprised to see him bowing deeply; which Kinko returned. Then Tanaka held him at arm's length, with his hands on Kinko's shoulders and looked deeply into his eyes.

"May the blessings of the Buddha and all the bodhisattvas protect you, Kurosawa. Be prepared for the daily battle." And turning, he disappeared into the cave. Kinko slowly turned and with tears in his eyes made his way down the mountain.

CITY OF THE DEAD

Returning to the temple complex at Kōya-san by mid-day was like crossing back into a different world. The *Danjō Garan* felt like a metropolis after nearly two months alone on the mountain with Fumon Tanaka. The myriad sounds and smells overwhelmed Kurosawa as he made his way through the heart of the temple complex to the small Eko-*in*. Once arrived, he immediately sought out Akira Kendo.

As he anticipated, Kendo greeted him with his usual sincere warmth, eager to hear all about Kurosawa's time with the old hermit. He was also very excited to receive the new flutes. "I know just who should have these," he enthused. "Before you tell me anything, though, play *Mukaiji* for me!"

Kurosawa smiled and pulled out the new long *shakuhachi* that he made under Tanaka's watchful eye. Placing it to his lips, he played what he learned from Tanaka, while Kendo sat quietly with his eyes closed, an attenuated smile on his lips. He sat this way for several minutes after Kurosawa completed the piece, as though listening for the music's final, most delicate resonances to end. Eventually, he opened his eyes with a smile.

"Ah, there is nothing to tell me about your experience with brother Tanaka; I can hear it all. You have used your time well."

The duties of the day soon called Kendo away and left Kinko time to reintegrate into temple life. Seeing the smiling, familiar faces passing down the corridors gratified him unexpectedly; as did the smell of the hot dinner.

It was not until after dinner and the evening service that Kinko sat down again with Kendo to recount in detail his time with the old hermit. From Kendo's responses, Kinko inferred that the older man had also spent at least one extended period with the hermit, though not during the winter. Kendo laughed with recognition at Kinko's description of the early morning *suburi* and *misogi*, and he devoured the tales of harvesting the bamboo.

When Kinko spoke of the night of "the battle," however, Kendo became more reflective. After he finished, Kinko asked, "What do you think of all this?"

Kendo was silent for a long time. Taking a deep breath and closing his eyes, he said, "It would be easy to treat my friend Tanaka like an eccentric old man. And in many ways, he is." Kendo opened his eyes, smiling at this last phrase.

"But you have spent enough time with him, Kurosawa, to know his passionate commitment, as well as his deep spiritual insight. I do not pretend to have his level of awareness concerning spiritual warfare. But I have enough awareness to take him seriously. The Buddha taught that the spiritual warrior fights primarily against self-ignorance; hence meditation is our primary weapon. But our scriptures are so full of stories about demons and spirits that I do not discount their influence."

This opening in the conversation prompted Kurosawa to share his story of the night he chased the phantom *tengu*.

Kendo listened, in rapt attention. "How fascinating!" he said. "Tell me, what do you think it was?"

"Well," replied Kinko slowly, "I'm not sure what I believe about *tengu*, but what I chased felt very real in the moment."

"What an interesting phrase: 'very real in the moment.' And now that you are not 'in the moment,' what does it feel like?"

Now it was Kurosawa's turn to close his eyes, trying to envision that chase through the dark snow. "It feels symbolic, somehow. Not entirely of this world, but more real than a dream. Like I was chasing something I needed to catch but never would."

"And it nearly led to your death," added Kendo. "That bears reflection."

Later that night, in his room, Kinko tried to sleep. It seemed odd and luxurious to sleep in a warm room on a soft futon with a pillow. Then he laughed that this—relatively austere—temple life now felt luxurious. As he lay in the darkness, he asked himself, "What is it about talking with Akira Kendo that always leads to deeper questions? Is he that much smarter or more insightful? Perhaps.

"But his questions never feel unexpected: they're always the next logical step. And yet, one that I never take. If they're obvious questions, there must be some reason that I am not asking—what am I avoiding?"

The next day, when he spoke to Akira Kendo alone again, he asked, "*Shishō*, we were discussing yesterday the nature of the spiritual warrior, and you commented that the Buddha taught that the spiritual warrior sought to overcome self-ignorance." Kendo nodded, his eyes half-closed.

"But why should the fight against self-ignorance be so fierce? Should not everyone desire self-knowledge?"

"An interesting question. Do most of the people you know welcome insight about themselves?"

"No, perhaps not."

"Why is that, do you suppose?"

"I'm not sure."

Kendo paused and closed his eyes. "Doesn't self-knowledge —real self-knowledge—demand change? And isn't change always painful?"

Kinko paused for a long time. "I hope that I would be brave enough to face that."

"I hope you would, too," Kendo answered. "But not many are. That is the choice of the warrior. That is the journey of a Buddha."

During the next several days, Kurosawa reintegrated into the life of the temple and settled into the flow of meals, prayer, and work. While he enjoyed being back, he also found himself unsure of exactly what his purpose was there now. When he asked Akira Kendo, the latter nodded and asked. "What more do you believe you need to accomplish?"

Kurosawa always found himself momentarily frustrated when Kendo turned his questions back on him. It forced him to realize how quickly he sought out guidance rather than engage in self-reflection. Before he could respond, however, Kendo continued, "As you reflect on that question, why not take a little time to visit the wonderful graveyard surrounding Kobo Daishi's mausoleum? It is the largest cemetery on the islands of Japan and quite an extraordinary place."

"I have visited there already, shortly after I arrived here on Mt. Kōya."

Kendo again gave him one of his querying looks and

responded, "The great samurai Yuzan Daidōji wrote that 'a samurai must before all things keep constantly in mind the fact that he has to die. That is his chief business.' You may also remember from your *komusō* history that the great Chinese monk Fuke used to take his bell and wander the graveyards, ringing the sound of enlightenment. Maybe go for more than just a visit. Sit for a while and see what the cemetery has to teach you."

Feeling somewhat unsatisfied by the exchange—both at his part, as well as Kendo's—Kinko withdrew and left the small temple. It was a grey, cool day, threatening rain, or even a late-season snow. Retracing his way to the Okuno-*in*—the mausoleum of Kobo Daishi—Kurosawa came to the initial bridge to the shrine, which he now knew the monks called, simply and appropriately, *Ichi no Hashi*. He bowed with his hands together and offered a brief prayer for Kobo Daishi and all the souls resting in this place.

His mind quieter on this occasion than his first visit, Kurosawa was aware of the unseen curtain that he penetrated as he crossed the bridge and entered the sacred domain. As he experienced before, the staggeringly high cedar trees mimicked the pillars and roof of an enormous sanctuary; diffused light filtered down to the forest floor.

With no agenda, Kinko followed the main walkway as before, making his way back to the mausoleum of Kobo Daishi. The path was familiar now, and after stopping briefly at the mausoleum itself, he began to wander farther afield to better grasp the design of the graveyard.

As he explored, no discernible layout emerged. Nearest the mausoleum stood many of the oldest monuments. It was obvious that as the cemetery grew, different divisions expanded outward from the central core, with more recent graves occasionally filling in empty spaces throughout. The overall effect was rather a hodgepodge, but with its own charm as well.

Making his way further and further from the mausoleum, Kinko began to wander. He quickly realized that Kendo was not exaggerating the size of the necropolis. It was home to thousands upon thousands of graves, perhaps tens of thousands. But there was no order and no structure to the vast city.

Families often clustered in their own "neighborhoods," but other denizens joined later and mixed among them. In most of the cemeteries that Kinko knew, swathes of trees were cleared to allow neat rows of monuments. Here, the memorials followed the topology of the mountain and seemed to grow around and among the ancient trees which stood sentinel throughout the neighborhoods.

The fact that there was no organized layout made it easier for Kinko to release any semblance of a goal and to stroll aimlessly through the vast, silent city. He felt a sense of alien strangeness in this place that was so large and yet where nothing moved.

Passing by a more recent addition to the necropolis, he recognized the name of a major *daimyo* from the Settsu province near Osaka. The *daimyo* had grown so powerful that the shogun divided his territory and forced him to retire from his position to become a monk. All these thousands of people, at one point or another, were vibrant and full of life: filled with hopes and schemes and desires and failures. And now all were gone. Here they lay, silent and lost, trampled underfoot by a random stranger.

How much time and energy had his own dreams and ambitions consumed over the years, Kinko wondered? How much of his life had he spent worrying about the future and missing the preciousness of the present moment? How much worry and anger and hope had he frittered away on future ambitions, rather than paying attention to where he was, enjoying the people he was with, the work he was doing? Was not the essence of *zazen* paying attention to every minute aspect of your experience? Why was it so hard to carry that awareness from *zazen* into daily life?

As if a window opened, letting in the fresh morning sun, Kinko was suddenly and completely aware of everything around him. All at once, he heard the chattering of nearby birds, amazed that the moment before he had not noticed them at all. He watched each footstep treading on untouched snow. He drank in the beauty of the ancient, lichen-covered monuments surrounding him.

This was the secret of the graveyard: nothing mattered but the beauty of the present moment. True wisdom grew out of the joy contained in each moment of life. He need no longer regret the loss of his position in Nagasaki; he need not worry about what awaited him in Edo. There was joy enough in this present.

The following morning, after prayers, Kinko returned to the graveyard. Crossing the *Ichi no Hashi*, he again followed the broad flagstone path but soon wandered into the woods to his left. Many of the tombs here were ancient: their dark, hoary stone covered in moss and lichen, with etchings too worn to be read. Others were newer, with crisp edges to the stone, and detailed paeans to their occupants; powerful *daimyos* slept peacefully next to those who were deadly foes during life. The gentle, diffused sunlight fell on them all together, their antagonisms lost in the mists of time.

Kurosawa wandered aimlessly for most of the day, reading the epitaphs and occasionally stopped to play his new long *shakuhachi*. Evening fell, and as he worked his way back towards the main flagstone path he happened upon an unusual monument. A rectangle forty feet long and fifteen feet wide, its center consisted of a simple, narrow set of flagstones. Moss covered much of the floor, with clumps of grass thrusting their way between the timeworn slabs and the scattered snow.

Surrounding the perimeter of this flagstone floor ran a line of stone lanterns roughly five feet high, as erect as soldiers guarding a castle. Standing behind the lanterns—circling the entire outside perimeter—was a line of statues at least eight feet tall. At the base of each was a large square stone block, atop which sat a large stone sphere. Atop the sphere sat a crown-shaped block, squared with the corners upswept like the edge of a temple roof, and on top of that were two small orbs. These five shapes represented the *godai,* the five elements of reality: earth, water, fire, wind, and void. Though they were purely geometric in form, these sentinels conveyed an aura of watch-fulness, and in the deepening gloom, they felt ominous.

Kurosawa walked around the outside of these melancholy watchmen, noticing strange glyphs inscribed on their crowns, too worn for him to read in the dusky twilight. He looked up at the immense height of the cedars ringing the monument like the third row of watchers. Finally, he entered the center, sitting cross-legged on the cold flagstone. Placing his hands in his lap, he began sitting *zazen.*

Full darkness fell quickly, and the sound of monks returning to their temples along the unseen path nearby disap-peared as well. Having finished his *zazen,* Kurosawa continued to sit, watchful and listening. The air was thick with some unseen presence. He took up Tanaka's *shakuhachi* and began to play. He warmed the instrument up by playing *Choshi* and then transitioned to *Mukaiji.*

The expectant air seemed to press in upon him—listening, waiting.

After quietly sitting for a while, Kinko decided that it would be most fitting—he was sitting in a cemetery, after all—to play *Banshiki* as a prayer for all the souls in this immense necropolis. Pulling his heavy cloak tightly about him against the cold night air, he played. Breathing out the first notes of *Banshiki* usually produced a feeling of calm repose in his soul, and he hoped it did the same for any local spirits in turmoil.

While he played, he barely caught—at the edge of his hearing—the sound of the whispering voices of children. He did not want to stop playing to listen, but each time he paused between notes, he thought that he heard them. At the end of the piece, he set down his *shakuhachi* and paid attention. The voices were quiet, although every once in a while, he caught a hushed whisper outside the ring of stone. After the night on the mountain—his encounter with the *tengu*—he was not inclined to chase after whispering phantoms in the dark. Instead, he offered up prayers for the repose of any restless spirits.

As he prayed, a shadow passed overhead, as though a large bird momentarily blocked the light from the stars. A coldness seized him, like a blast of air through an open door. As he raised his eyes, the looming sentry stones felt ominous and hostile. Suddenly, he felt vulnerable there in the dark by himself, with no weapon but the *tanto* in the back of his *obi* and the flute gripped tightly in his hand. His every impulse impelled him to run, but he forced himself to sit.

A cold breeze blew across his face, bringing back the soft, barely audible children's voices. He dared not move, as though if he were motionless, whatever was out there in the dark beyond the stones would not see him. As he listened closely to the voices, he thought that he heard them say, "What do you fear?"

"What do I fear?" he nearly wondered aloud. "Not a robber or bandit, certainly; I have nothing to steal. Is it the restless spirits of the graveyard? I don't think so; how would they harm me? Is it the death that these stones represent and embody? What have I to fear in death?"

He must have closed his eyes for a moment, because without being aware of any movement, an old man stood before him, in front of the dark lanterns opposite. He carried a heavy staff, and a broad traveler's hat hid his face in shadow. Thin, attenuated fingers, with parchment-like skin, held the staff, and a string of prayer beads hung around the wrist, leaving Kurosawa with the impression that this must be an old monk.

"What brings you here, my son?" an ancient voice said from the shadow of the hat.

"I have come to reflect on death and pray for the repose of the spirits here."

"And what have you learned in your reflections?"

"Honestly, father, I am not sure," Kinko said, sincerely. His brief time there had not yielded any profound revelations; though, in the presence of this monk, he somehow felt guilty about his lack of insight. Finally, he added, "The great antiquity of this place humbles me, certainly."

Slowly, the old man turned and began walking along the edge of the flagstone floor; his empty hand ran over the moss-covered stone. "This place where you are sitting and playing and praying—whose tomb is it?"

"I do not know."

"Hmmm... Judging from the size and majesty of this monument, it must be the resting place of some great *daimyo*, don't you think?"

"Probably."

"Likely, it was someone who ruled the lives of many. Someone admired or feared. Perhaps someone who set an emperor on his throne, or ruled some vast province. Perhaps he achieved enlightenment. Perhaps he endowed one of the temples here on Mt. Kōya. Wives and children and households

gathered around these stones and wept at the great one's passing. Behind them, lovers stood hidden, grieving silently in the
shadows. Priests solemnly intoned sutra chants for the repose
of their souls."

"Perhaps, father," Kinko said, "but that is all speculation;
there is no way of telling who he—or she—was, and what he
might have done."

"That seems strange," said the old man, running his finger
down a line of faded etchings. "Certainly, these carved stones
hold a record of his accomplishments, meant to immortalize his
achievements?"

"Yes, father, but there is no way to read that now."

"So all of those accomplishments are lost to us."

"All lost," repeated Kinko.

"Will you ever have such a grave, my son?"

"No, father," chuckled Kinko. "Nothing so grand as this."

"And so, perhaps, in an even briefer time, your accomplishments will be lost?"

"No doubt."

"And all your striving and dreaming...?"

"...will disappear forever, without the notice of future
generations," replied Kinko.

"So?"

"So my life ultimately means nothing. I am of no
importance."

"Yes," said the old man. "And there is some freedom in that,
is there not?"

"Yes," replied Kinko, breathing more deeply than before.
"There is great freedom."

"Your life means nothing, and you are of no importance,"
the old man repeated. And then, striding quickly over to Kinko,
and taking his chin in his hand, he looked at him with eyes that
seemed red with fire. "And, at the very same time, you are

priceless and unique." Dropping Kinko's chin, he quickly turned away.

"You—and every sentient being—will live a life that no one else can live. You can give the world a gift no one else can offer. Like this unknown *daimyo,* your life could enrich the lives of thousands, or alter the flow of history. And then you will be gone, and your name will disappear. So, my son, you must bring every bit of passion and skill that you possess to your every endeavor. And then let it go, as a tree releases a leaf in the autumn. If you can hold these two truths together, you will truly live."

Kinko dropped his eyes to the ground, reflecting. He must have dozed momentarily, for his head snapped up from his reflection. The old man was gone. A gentle morning light warmed the winter sky.

Returning to Eko-*in* in time for breakfast, Kinko joined the monks for prayer and spent the day doing a variety of work tasks. After the evening meal and prayers, he sought out Akira Kendo and talked about the past two days in the graveyard. After finishing his story, Kinko sat silently, while Kendo sat with his characteristically closed eyes.

Finally, Kinko asked, "*Shishō*—the old man—was he a real person, or a spirit, or a vision, or just a dream?"

Kendo sat for a moment, and then without opening his eyes, said, "Did you learn something from your conversation with him?"

"Of course!"

"Then I wonder if your question matters? It was a gift."

THE SOUND OF
ENLIGHTENMENT

Most of the following week, at Kendo's direction, Kurosawa spent his days in intense *zazen* practice. He joined the rest of the community for meals and prayer services, but Kendo excused him from other work, directing him to spend the rest of his time meditating and playing *Mukaiji*. Every evening, the two men would meet in Kendo's room to discuss his meditation and to play *shakuhachi* together.

One night, after playing, Kendo looked at Kinko and said, "About two hundred years ago there lived a very famous tea master named Sen no Rikyū. He was the tea master for both Oda Nobunaga and Toyotomi Hideyoshi, who ruled Japan before the Tokugawa. He described the tea ceremony as *ichi-go, ichi-e*: 'one moment, one meeting.'" The night was cold and quiet, as Kurosawa waited.

"What he meant by that phrase is that even though the rituals of the tea ceremony are incredibly precise, scripted, and unwavering, a wise tea master will engage in every tea gathering as a completely unique encounter. They should treat it as if they are going through the motions for the very first—and very last—time. Every meeting is freighted with its own significance. It has never happened before and it will never happen again.

"Bring that mindset to your playing. Every night, we play *Mukaiji* and every night you play it perfectly. And always the same. But each night is different. Each night *you* are different. Each night *I* am different. Each night you must play the *Mukaiji* required for *that* night and no other.

"You have played this music long enough that it is part of you. Now you can be an artist. Now you can play *your Mukaiji*. You know all the notes and phrasing, you know the pauses and the dynamics. Now play it as yours—yours tonight, and just tonight. Tomorrow night you will play as yours tomorrow night. Maybe there's a longer pause—more *ma*—somewhere. Perhaps a phrase gets greater emphasis tonight because that's the phrase that needs it tonight. 'Ichi-go, ichi-e.' As the great poet Basho taught, 'Abide by the rules, then throw them out! —only then may you achieve true freedom.'"

After several days of intensive *zazen* sitting, Kurosawa said to Kendo at their nightly meeting—with a little frustration— "*Shishō*, I have been working hard at my meditation this week, but I'm not sure that I feel markedly different; certainly, I don't feel like I'm making progress towards 'enlightenment.'"

Unexpectedly, Kendo erupted in a belly-deep laugh. "Kurosawa, my dear friend, have you not realized yet that we do not sit *zazen* so that we can become enlightened? We sit *zazen*—everyone sits *zazen*—*because* we are enlightened. We are all born with Buddha-nature, and we sit as an expression of our enlightenment. *Zazen* is the work of a Buddha.

"You do not need to 'work hard at your meditation.' Just meditate. You cannot bring an agenda to meditation. We sit *zazen* because we possess a Buddha-nature; it is already a part of us. We practice because we are not always aware of who we are. But we do not seek to accomplish anything in our sitting. Once we have begun sitting *zazen*, we have accomplished it. As the great master Dōgen says, 'Wisdom is seeking wisdom.' It is that easy."

This idea caused Kurosawa some discomfort. He wondered if, perhaps, it was too difficult for him to give up the idea that hard work was at the heart of spiritual growth. In any case, in a somewhat belligerent tone he continued, "Then I am not sure that I understand Tanaka's obsession with *ro-buki*. Didn't he say that playing the same tone over and over again was a means of working towards 'enlightenment?'"

Kendo laughed again. "I'm not sure that I would want to interpret what Tanaka thought, but the process of practice prepares us to receive enlightenment. It does not *cause* enlightenment; it prepares the field for growth. I recall a very old—and probably apocryphal—story from Zen tradition. Centuries ago, in Zen's Japanese infancy, a nobleman from Kyoto asked a Zen monk to come to the emperor's capital to teach. The old monk traveled the long road to Kyoto, eventually arriving at the court of the noble. His first night there, the nobleman, surrounded by his courtiers, asked, 'Master, what is Zen?' The old man took out a *shakuhachi*, blew a single, long note, and said, 'That is Zen.' And then he turned and departed the court.

"For a thousand years—back at least as far as the *Surangama Sutra*—our Buddhist teachers have instructed us on the importance of sound as a tool to open up the spirit. This is why we have the tradition from India of chanting single Sanskrit syllables in meditation, and why we chant sutras instead of simply reading them. Teachers in the Fuke tradition have long believed that the quality of a single sound (*ichion*)— apart from any broader musical construction—can trigger enlightenment."

Kendo paused for a moment, taking a deep breath. The sound of snow falling off the roof broke the silence outside the window.

"When our Shingon founder, Kobo Daishi, returned to Japan from China, among his many learnings, he brought us the gift of Zen poetry. Zen poetry—like *shakuhachi* music— seeks to point beyond itself, to guide the listener or reader, to the silence behind the words, to spark the moment of enlightenment. Kobo Daishi taught that the perfectly chosen and placed word can contain all the power of the entire poem. That one word has the ability—by itself—to bring about a moment of enlightenment.

"In *honkyoku*, of course, we play more than a single note. But generally, the notes are fairly long and drawn out, so that we get the chance to focus on one note at a time. For me, by trying to make each note as perfect as I can—*ichion*—I make the entire piece more beautiful. Now, I'm not sure how much of that was in Fumon Tanaka's mind in his emphasis on *ro-buki*, but I suspect that many of those ideas were present."

The days moved on, and Kurosawa continued his intense regimen of sitting *zazen* and *shakuhachi* playing. Given the fact that all he did was sit, he was surprisingly exhausted at the end of the day. At times, it felt like early morning *suburi* with Tanaka when there was no way to lift the *jo* even one more time. But like *suburi*, when he could not sit for a single additional minute in meditation, he would relax the hold of his conscious mind and refocus on the breath coming from his *hara*.

One day, all his disparate learnings came together while he played *Mukaiji* again. He played with the kind of controlled abandon of Tanaka and tried to maintain an awareness of the uniqueness of that performance, listening for just what that moment might call forth from his playing. He felt his mind slow, as though it were stepping back to watch some other person playing.

He set down the *shakuhachi* and closed his eyes. Opening them slightly, he watched his breath, completely absorbed in the present moment. He felt the cool air penetrate the depth of his lungs. He was aware of the sunlight playfully dancing along the sill of the window. He heard the nearby call of a waxwing echo his music in the temple garden. The cool breeze made his exposed arms tingle.

With his next breath, he felt swept away by the sense of power and openness that possessed his body. It was no longer his body and no longer separate from the things around him. He was part of a magnificent unity of creation, all connected and pulsing with life and energy. Overwhelmed with a deep sense of joy at the beauty of his vision, he felt a deep love for all people and a deep compassion for all sentient beings.

His spirit seemed to rise, looking down at the wondrous beauty of Eko-*in* with its monks engaged in the simple holiness of their daily rituals. Rising further, he observed the elegant grace of the entire network of temples on Kōya-san and the delicate artistry of their placement in Kobo Daishi's design of the complex. And rising further yet, he delighted in the majestic power of Mt. Kōya itself with the organic interplay of town, temples, and hermits scattered throughout its eight peaks, all working together as a living body. Every piece was perfect.

With another deep breath, Kurosawa came back to himself

and offered a prayer of gratitude for the life of the world. He continued to sit with a sense of joy and peace until the heavy brass bell called the community to evening prayer. Walking to the main hall, his senses seemed heightened: each tree branch etched in crystalline precision, each wafted breath of incense burst like colors in his mind. He carried this sense of wonder into the *zendo*, seeing each of the monks as a marvelous work of beauty, each one precious and unique.

The intensity of this experience continued through the remainder of the evening, beginning to fade as night approached. After dinner, he sat with Kendo and shared his afternoon experience. "*Shishō*," he ventured, "is this what 'enlightenment' feels like?"

Kinko expected Kendo to laugh, but the older man did not. Instead, he sat quietly, with his eyes closed. "What an interesting question," he finally responded without opening his eyes. "Our tradition tells us that enlightenment—*satori*—happens in a moment with a complete understanding of ourselves and our place in the universe.

"When the Buddha achieved enlightenment sitting under his bodhi tree, in a single moment he understood his whole life —including all his previous incarnations—and the nature of all existence. And that moment of awakening continued for his entire life. It has happened in such a way for many Buddhas and bodhisattvas in the centuries since.

"Personally, however, I have never encountered such a person. I do not doubt that they exist, but I have never met one. I more often meet men and women who have moments of deep insight—moments of 'enlightenment'—but which fade. They are real and powerful and transformative, but they are rarely permanent. They remind us that we all have within us a Buddha-nature. Seeking enlightenment is not a goal towards which we strive, but is our very essence we seek to uncover."

Kendo paused, as though considering how to better get through to a recalcitrant child.

"Great warriors can diffuse a fight before it occurs because they have trained so relentlessly that they sense when someone plans to attack. Their awareness is continual, an ideal we call *zanshin*— 'remaining mind.' Only the greatest masters have that sort of awareness. But the goal is to work towards that level of ongoing mindfulness. My old *Shishō* used to say that everyone gets off balance sometimes, but the master regains his balance before anyone realizes he has lost it.

"Likewise, in the quest for enlightenment, we all have moments of deep insight and clarity. But then we lose them. Maturation towards Buddha-hood—for most of us—is a process of lengthening those moments of insight and clarity. So, celebrate moments like this afternoon. And then examine what made it possible and continue that practice.

"You will probably never recreate that feeling exactly, but you will develop habits that place you in a frame of mind where enlightenment will happen. Spiritual practice, after all, simply cultivates the ground for enlightenment. We do not find enlightenment; we create an environment where it can find us. A gardener does not grow plants; a gardener creates the space that facilitates growth. Whether something grows or not is ultimately beyond the gardener's control, but every master gardener has learned what produces the best results.

"And now, my friend, I want to echo Fumon Tanaka: you are welcome to make this temple the place where you pursue your enlightenment, or continue on your path to Edo and seek your *satori* that way. But you need to decide what the next chapter of your life looks like."

This statement was not a surprise to Kurosawa; he knew it was coming and that it was the right question. "Thank you, *Shishō*, for your wisdom and guidance. I, too, believe that this is the point at which I should draw my time here to an end. I would be grateful for a day or two to collect myself and prepare for the journey."

Akira Kendo bowed. "This temple is your home until you are ready to go."

In truth, Kurosawa had very little to do before leaving; but he was loath to be on his way. The months here on Mt. Kōya were unexpected and transforming. How little he anticipated what would happen when he reluctantly accepted the commission to travel south from Kyoto for Minzan Zenji. He knew now why the abbot had sent him; and as reluctantly as he was to come, he was now even more reluctant to leave.

In his heart, he feared that returning to the world he knew was to risk losing all that he had learned. He feared falling back into the comfortable routines that shaped his life before coming here. And he would not let that happen. He would re-enter the world as the person that he became in this place. He was resolved.

Kinko spent the next two days bidding farewell to the friends he made on the mountain, and visiting the graveyard and Kobo Daishi's mausoleum once more. On the day of his departure, he joined the monks for breakfast and morning prayer and then met Akira Kendo for a final *shakuhachi* lesson. After playing through *Mukaiji* one last time, Kendo set his *shakuhachi* down, closed his eyes, and smiled.

"Ah, quite a dramatic difference over a short time. You are a gifted musician, my friend. I will miss our time together."

"Thank you so much for your generosity of spirit, *Shishō*. I am a different person than the one that arrived at your temple three months ago."

Kendo laughed. "Not so very different. Any work we did here was a subtle refining of the gifted person that you brought to us. As you go, remember the words of the great sword master

Musashi in his wonderful Book of Five Rings: 'You must study these things.' Over and over again, as he writes about a specific sword technique, he ends the description by saying, 'You must study these things.'

"His point is that for a technique to be 'learned,' the martial artist must practice it over and over and over until it is so much a part of him that he doesn't have to think about it. He simply does it. It is never adequate for a martial artist to learn a technique and move on to something else. It is the same for a monk: every time we learn a thing, we must practice it over and over, just like doing *suburi*. When it is so ingrained that it is part of who we are, then we can say that we 'know' it.

"You have learned a great deal over the past months. Too much, frankly, to incorporate into who you are. So please continue to reflect on what you have learned, and continue to practice. Practice your *suburi*. Practice your *ro-buki*. Occasionally, even practice some *misogi*. Tanaka was right when he told you, 'Every day is an endeavor of spiritual significance.' Remember that. And trust yourself and your wisdom, as you re-enter the world of the *komusō*."

"I'm not sure what it means to be *komusō* for me anymore. The road before me is wreathed in fog, and I can barely put one foot before the other. Yet... I suppose... I am at peace with doing just that."

"Kurosawa, that is all any of us can ever do."

The two friends bowed deeply to one another. As he turned to leave his teacher, Kinko said. "I will continue to work on blowing a sound that will bring enlightenment, *Shishō*; but— if you will not tell Brother Tanaka—I think that I will also try to make that sound beautiful." Kendo closed his eyes, smiled, and nodded.

The morning was bright and cool, and the monks of Eko-*in* went about their duties like any other day. Hoisting his pack on his back, laden with three *shakuhachi*, and taking his mother's staff in his hand, Kinko Kurosawa bade farewell to the little temple. He followed the main road to the great Daimon Gate, and passing through, began to make his way down the mountain, noticing on the trees, the first buds of the coming spring.

AWAITING CHERRY BLOSSOMS

TEMPLE OF MUSIC

Climbing down Mt. Kōya, Kurosawa's heart was as free and light as he could remember. As the altitude decreased, the signs of spring became more plentiful. The thin snow underfoot when he left the temple disappeared entirely. Early buds on the trees blended into a gentle green haze across the mountain forest. Immersed in the beauty of the walk and praying the sacred Sanskrit syllables written on the stone pillars along the path, he gave little thought to the rest of his journey until he arrived at the village of Kudoyama.

Once there, he realized that his unacknowledged plan involved returning north to Kyoto, so that he could join the heavily traveled Tokaido Road to Edo. On the spur of the moment, however, he decided that since he was already so far south on the Kii Peninsula, it might be nice to travel due east and visit the Ise Jingu, the oldest and most revered Shinto shrine in Japan. From there, it would be easy enough to travel north and intercept the Tokaido near Nagoya.

Pleased with the idea of following in the footsteps of Kichiku on the famous pilgrimage where he received *Mukaiji* in a dream, he stopped for a brief mid-day meal in a small tavern and obtained directions east from the landlord. No roads traveled directly to Ise and the route would be mountainous; so the journey—which he estimated was over a hundred miles—would take him a week or more.

After his meal, he struck out on his route east. The road wound its way from valleys lush with nascent spring growth to cold, lofty mountain passes still covered in snow. Small scattered villages provided inns and shrines most nights, although he was forced to sleep out in the open twice. Traveling was slow, but Kinko was not in a particular hurry and the beautiful, solitary landscape gave him ample time for reflection.

The mountain forests were rich and verdant and alive with sound. Brooks swollen by melting snow cascaded down mountainsides, sweeping away winter's detritus. Choruses of birds welcomed spring's warming airs. Kinko recalled Tanaka's words, "There is music in everything," and tried to follow his advice, imitating the bird songs on his *shakuhachi*. Passing a small roadside shrine, Kinko remembered the poet Basho's travel log, "I crawled among boulders to make my bows at shrines. The silence was profound. I sat, feeling my heart begin to open:

> Lonely stillness—
> a single cicada's cry
> sinking into stone.

Thus, the miles and the days quickly passed. Ise, on the far eastern coast of the Kii Peninsula, was the most popular pilgrimage site in all of Japan. Most of the traffic to and from the city came from the north, down the peninsula's eastern coast; so Kinko's road from the west was largely empty until he approached the city itself.

The emperors of Japan traced their lineage back to the sun goddess Amaterasu-Omikami. According to legend, over seventeen hundred years earlier, a royal princess, named Yamato-hime-no-mikoto, wandered Japan for twenty years to find a fitting place for the worship of the goddess. When she arrived in Ise, the goddess Amaterasu instructed her to establish a shrine. Since that time, an unmarried woman of the imperial family always served as the shrine's head priestess.

Over the centuries, a far-flung complex of 125 shrines and sub-shrines developed, collectively known as the Ise Jingū. This multitude of buildings clustered around two main shrines: Naiku and Geku. Naiku, the "inner shrine," honored the sun goddess Amaterasu herself. Geku, the "outer shrine," located about four miles away, was dedicated to Toyouke-Omikami, the goddess of the rice harvest.

Over the previous century, the number of pilgrims to the Ise Jingū grew dramatically, making it the most popular pilgrimage site in Japan. While Kinko was generally aware of the popularity of the pilgrimage to Ise, he was unprepared for the number of people he found there upon his arrival. The town had the feeling of a perpetual festival with groups of pilgrims—all dressed in white or festive clothing—arriving and departing continually.

The constant flow of pilgrims meant that rooms at inns were scarce. Many hung signs outside proclaiming that they were full. Along a quiet side street, Kinko found an inn with no such sign. He slid open the rice paper door and stepped inside the main room. Cramped and uncomfortably warm, the room smelled unpleasantly from (he hoped) years of spilled sake. Glancing expectantly at the waitress, she waved him over to a small table by a side wall well out of the main flow of traffic.

Although he had already walked for some time that day, he was not particularly hungry. When the waitress found her way back to him, he ordered several pieces of *narezushi* and a rice ball, as well as a bottle of sake. She brought the sake first, and after pouring a cup, he settled into his spot, enjoying the hum of the surrounding conversation.

A group of six at the next table were obviously on pilgrimage, conversing animatedly about the happenings in their home village. The youngest, a pretty young woman in white pilgrim robes, imbibing more sake than prudent, was proclaiming—slightly too loudly—her excitement about the next day's journey to the Jingū. Her youthfulness and her natural eyebrows indicated that she was unmarried, a condition she was attempting to remedy by focusing much of her exuberance on a somewhat sheepish-looking young man sitting opposite her.

Kinko smiled as he sipped his sake, observing the awkward mating ritual. When the food came, it was unexceptional but adequate. The closeness of the atmosphere, however, was uncomfortable, so Kinko finished quickly and, having secured a room for the night, departed for a walk around the town.

It was a cool spring evening with the sun recently set. Crowds of enthusiastic pilgrims shopped for *omamori* amulets and other mementos of their trip. Kinko wandered for some time, stopping twice to play and collect alms—a very successful enterprise in this religious atmosphere. Finally, he settled himself at a table on the porch of a tea shop, ordered some more sake and watched the flow of people.

He was struck by the obvious joy on the faces of the passers-by. Festive joy was not a regular aspect of life in a Zen temple. Zen monks were not unhappy; but theirs was a quiet, understated joy. Kinko realized that he had often been dismissive of the kind of religious expression that he saw here at Ise. As he watched, he felt a sense of self-reproach at his own arrogance.

Certainly, religion was a serious matter, but did it always have to be solemn? Was not joyful celebration an appropriate response to the gifts of the gods or Buddha? Why did it always feel as though he was such a drudge? Was it about control? An unwillingness to let himself go, even a little?

A group of pilgrims noisily strolled down the middle of the street singing a song in praise of Amaterasu. The words were unfamiliar to Kinko, but the tune was from an old folk song. On the spur of the moment, he stepped down from his seat, sat on the edge of the porch, and dangled his feet above the dirt road. Pulling out his *shakuhachi*, he began to play along with them. It was an energetic little tune, and he played with abandon. All the pilgrims clapped in time and smiled and waved to him.

He kept playing until the procession wound its way down the street and out of view. Then, sitting back up in his seat, he continued to sip his sake until the next group came down the road, and he played for them. He spent the evening like this, appreciating the smiles and thanks from those around him, until, tired and gratified, he returned to his inn.

Kinko arose with the golden spring sun the next morning, departing the still-quiet inn. Hoping to visit the main Naiku Shrine before the heavy crowds, he hurried out of the town of Ise for the village of Uji-tachi some three miles to the south. Soon, however, he discovered that he was not the only pilgrim with this idea and found himself in a long, snaking line of white-clad worshippers.

The line slowed in front of a lengthy section of wooden wall, behind which Kinko could see the thatched reed roof of an extended building. He could just see the structure itself, built of beautiful, aged cypress wood, while both ends of the reed roof ridge concluded dramatically in forked finials of the same cypress. He knew this must be the Naiku Shrine, but could not figure out why people bowed and prayed outside the wall. As he got closer, he asked a small group.

The grandfather of the family laughed good-naturedly. "No one can go into the shrine itself; that is where the sacred mirror of Amaterasu resides: the gift from the goddess to the imperial family." As the man spoke, Kinko finally understood Basho's haiku:

Behind Ise Shrine,
unseen, hidden by the fence,
Buddha enters Nirvana

Kinko joined the other pilgrims in their prayers before taking a few hours to wander through the beautiful forest paths that led to many of the small sub-shrines. The day was glorious for walking, and Kinko basked in the sunshine while he prayed and played. As evening approached, he realized that he had not eaten all day and stopped at a tavern on the way back to Ise and his lodgings.

The great Tokaido Road lay a two days' march to the north, at the edge of the Kii Peninsula. Kinko planned to take the scenic road along the coastline of the Ise Bay and meet the Tokaido at the castle town of Kameyama. The air was cool and bright along the shore, and he reached the Tokaido on the third day, joining the stream of travelers moving between the great cities of Kyoto and Edo.

Traveling on the Tokaido was simpler and much faster than any part of his journey thus far. The road was broad and in good repair. Inns were numerous, generally clustered around the check-point stations. Even with some occasional rain, Kinko made good time. Day after day passed smoothly, as rain gave way to the joyous spring sun. Without incident, he journeyed through the cities of Kuwana, Nagoya, Okazaki, and Yoshida.

Late in the afternoon on a cloudless spring day, Kurosawa entered a small village. He was a day outside of the castle town of Hamamatsu, home to a Fuke Temple named Fudai-*ji*, a renowned temple in *komusō* circles for its rich history of music. While most temples were associated with a piece or two of *honkyoku* music, Fudai-*ji* was home to no fewer than eleven pieces of original music. Azaleas in a riot of colors wreathed the road into the village, and Kurosawa slowed to take in their beauty and breathe the soft spring air.

Entering the hamlet, he saw a group of villagers harangue three older men who stood on a low platform and tried in vain to quiet the crowd. As Kinko approached, one of the angry group noticed him. The man nudged his neighbor, who nudged another, and soon the entire mob fell silent and stood watching Kurosawa with hostile eyes. Some fingered the farm tools that they held in their hands.

Mindful of the animosity, but unaware of its origin, Kinko stopped and removed his *tengai* basket, smiling. He approached the group slowly. "The blessing of the Buddha on you, Friends. I apologize if I have interrupted you on this beautiful afternoon."

The attitude of the group remained hostile, though Kurosawa thought that he detected a hint of doubt in some of their eyes.

A large man, who appeared to be a leader of the group, stepped forward and replied aggressively, "As a matter of fact, it is you that we are arguing about just now."

His words confused Kurosawa. "I'm sorry, but I don't understand. What can you be arguing about that has to do with me?"

"Yesterday, two of your fellow *komusō* came through the

village, begging as usual." The man spat the words out. "With Fudai-*ji* so close, we see your like often enough. These two also said that they were from Fudai-*ji*. When their collections were insufficient, they bullied and harassed our villagers. They even beat a few of us, and its death for us if we raise a hand to a samurai even in self-defense." Ending in an eruption of outrage, the man barked, "You claim to be seeking charity when your begging is little better than extortion!"

The large man slumped back into the group after his outpoured venom. His neighbor then added, "So we are here because these members of our village council—charged with our safety—simply let the *komusō* monks leave with the money that they extorted! They could have either paid off the *komusō* with our tax money or they could have threatened them with complaints to the Fudai-*ji* temple. They could have even sought help from our lord. But they did nothing!"

Stunned and mortified by the actions of his fellow monks, Kinko was silent. He was not naïve and knew that many *komusō* could be thuggish and overbearing, but this was criminal. Without thinking, he dropped to his knees and bowed his head to the ground.

"Good people, you have my deepest apologies for the reprehensible actions of my compatriots. Men become *komusō* for many reasons, and not all are noble or holy. But please know that this behavior is a deep affront to our beliefs, and that I will do everything in my power to rectify this dishonor on our sect."

Raising his head, he saw the stunned looks on the faces of the men who had never seen a samurai bow to a peasant and did not know how to respond. "Honorable *Obo-san*, we are grateful for your apologies," said the large man. "But they do us no practical good."

Kinko stood up and took the bag of coins from his belt—all his money—and tossed it to the man. "I have traveled far and the Buddha has blessed me from many generous hands. Please accept the fruits of my playing as a small repayment for the violence done to you." Kinko was fairly certain that the two rogue monks could not have extorted so much from these poor farmers, so the act of generosity would hopefully go a long way to redeeming the reputation of the Fuke. "I trust that you will see the appropriate villagers are repaid."

The large man—still stunned—bowed to Kurosawa. "It shall be done, *Obo-san*. We are grateful for your help."

The awkward silence was broken by the smaller man who stepped forward. "Honorable *Obo-san*, I own the small tavern at the far side of the town. Evening is falling. Please be my guest tonight."

"I would be grateful for the shelter, brother, but—as you know—I have no funds to pay you."

At this, the group laughed, and immediately the tension that laid so heavily upon them lifted. As a group, the men joined Kinko and the tavern keeper in walking down the road. They all crowded about a table, and soon food and sake flowed freely.

The village, named Shimo-Ujiie, was a farming community selling its produce in the town of Hamamatsu. Since the temple of Fudai-*ji* maintained close ties with the Lord of Hamamatsu, the villagers were eager to not incur the wrath of the temple for fear of offending their lord.

After the sake began to loosen the farmers' tongues—and the three village elders had taken their leave—the group voiced their anger at the elders. Their village leaders should never have given the *komusō* free rein to abuse the farmers. The elders could certainly have threatened the monks with a formal complaint to Fudai-*ji* as well as the local lord. It became clear to Kurosawa that the anger he experienced on entering the village was as focused as much on the village elders as it was on the *komusō* themselves.

It was late before the last of the villagers wobbled out of the tavern, and Kurosawa was able to retire to his room. Despite the drinking and his weariness, his mind swirled with reflections on the day. He sat and meditated for a while before drifting into a deep sleep.

Kinko departed from Shimo-Ujiie as a clear, cool dawn was breaking, wanting to arrive at Fudai-*ji* before too late in the day. He was only on the road a few hours and passed through two small villages. When he arrived at a third village, he noticed a worried-looking tavern keeper who swept his front porch while glancing back inside the tavern. On a hunch, Kurosawa took off his *tengai*, climbed the steps, and entered the building.

As he suspected, he saw two hung-over *komusō* at the back of the room. One leaned back on the rear legs of his seat, while his burly companion pawed a young woman who must have been the proprietor's daughter. Kinko slipped off his pack, leaned it with his staff just inside the doorway, and walked directly back to the two men.

Without a word, his left foot swept the unbalanced chair from under the first drunken monk, who fell heavily backward, knocking his head hard against the floor. Simultaneously, Kinko struck the other monk with his back fist. The young woman fled to her father. The first monk was slow to get up, and Kinko grabbed the second monk by his top-knot and pulled his head back to expose his neck. Placing the point of his *tanto* in the soft flesh just under the man's chin, slightly harder than he intended in his excessive anger and haste, he caused a drop of deep red blood to roll casually down the monk's neck.

"You two have caused me enough trouble for one day," he

SONG OF THE SAMURAI

hissed into the second man's ear. "You have cost me significant
money paying back the villagers from Shimo-Ujiie, and you
cost me goodwill wherever I go. Come with me." Then he
turned to the first monk, who was picking himself up and
rubbing his head. "Collect your things and meet us outside."
Keeping hold of the man's topknot and his knife to the man's
throat, they walked outside, where Kurosawa grabbed the man's
bag of coins and pushed him down the steps.

Kinko retrieved his pack and staff and waited in the
doorway for the other man to join them. Down in the street
with the two monks, under the eyes of the innkeeper and his
neighbors, Kurosawa said, "Because of my expenses incurred
on your behalf," he held out the man's bag of coins,"I am
claiming this pittance. Now go, and I will follow up by
reporting your extortion to your abbot."

The two *komusō* eyed Kurosawa angrily, apparently
debating whether to attack him. *Wakizashi* short swords were
thrust in their belts, but Kinko held his heavily shod staff. Their
hangovers finally tipped the balance, and the two turned to
walk off down the road towards Hamamatsu. Kinko breathed a
sigh of relief and turned to the innkeeper. "I apologize for the
boorish behavior of my brethren," he bowed. "Can I offer you
any money as compensation?"

"You could compensate me with the honor of your
company for breakfast," the older man said. Kurosawa followed
him into the main room, where the man's daughter and wife
brought them both some miso soup, rice, and dried bonito.
"Thank you, *Obo-san*, for intervening just now. I doubt that
they would have hurt the girl, but your intervention was a relief
all the same."

"It infuriates me to see monks abuse their position," Kinko
returned with some intensity.

"Well," replied his new friend, "you probably know better

291

than most that the *komusō* are a mixed lot. Some are certainly religious men, but most—in my experience—are just samurai waiting for a new job. They're angry with their place in the world, and they take it out on whoever happens to be handy. Those two were no worse than most; better than some."

"I'm grateful for your patience and hospitality," said Kinko, rising, "but I must be on my way now."

"Be careful on the road, *Obo-san*. And when you get to Fudai-*ji*. You made at least two enemies today, and they will be looking for a chance to get even."

Kurosawa nodded, collected his things, and set off down the road, following the path of the other two monks. He kept a wary eye out for trouble.

He arrived several uneventful hours later in Hamamatsu and received directions from the checkpoint guards to the southern end of town where Fudai-*ji* lay. As Kurosawa neared the location, he was not surprised to notice several thuggish-looking men loitering outside the temple gate. Wishing to avoid more difficulties, he turned abruptly and skirted the perimeter wall of the temple complex. As he expected, there was a small gate in the rear of the temple, which—to his gratification—was unlocked. He entered and made his way through the rear gardens to what appeared to be the main administrative building of the complex.

The abbot was a squat man of modest height. His head was large enough that it seemed disproportionate to the rest of his body, and—combined with an unusually broad mouth—gave him a vaguely frog-like appearance, arrayed in his formal robes. He welcomed the traveler, and—after learning of Kurosawa's destination—seemed eager to ingratiate himself with Ichigetsu-*ji*'s new instructor. Upon hearing of Kurosawa's desire to learn the *honkyoku* pieces native to Fudai-*ji*, the abbot was quick to volunteer the services of his senior instructor.

As he prepared to take his leave, Kurosawa turned to the abbot. "By the way, Lord Abbot, I should mention that I had a little run-in with two of your monks earlier today." The abbot raised his eyebrows in question. Kurosawa described the conflict at Shimo-Ujiie, and the subsequent altercation that morning. As he spoke, the abbot shook his head sadly.

"I know the two brothers you mean," he said. "They are difficult problems. I will speak to them again this evening. It is hard running a religious institution with people who are here for non-religious reasons, as you will find out when you get to Ichigetsu-*ji*. Still, I believe that we are providing a service to both them and the community. They are better here—within our structures—than roaming the countryside, where they would likely become brigands or mercenaries, further destabilizing the region."

"They are little more than brigands now!" Kinko responded with more energy than he intended. "And they undermine our standing as a religious order."

"They may behave as brigands at times, and yet they are less dangerous to the community carrying a *shakuhachi* than they would be walking down the street with two swords on their hips and spoiling for a fight. With a little structure from us, they are more ready to transition back into a stable situation, serving some local lord.

"I suspect that you will find this to be the case when you join the staff of Ichigetsu-*ji*. In Edo, there are even more *rōnin* seeking entrance to our order. The structured life of the temple, and the music that we teach them, is a service to the shogun and the broader society. I guess that this will be an important part of your new role."

When Kurosawa had arrived at the abbot's office, he was

full of enthusiasm: having outwitted the thugs at the front gate, anticipating learning some new music, and with the end of his journey in sight. As he trudged from the meeting, a wave of discouragement rolled over him. For months, he envisioned teaching at Ichigetsu-*ji* as the solution to all his problems: re-establishing his reputation and occupying a position from which to refine the quality of *honkyoku* playing for the temple, and perhaps even the entire sect.

Hearing this abbot, however, it sounded more like a job of babysitting ruffians and making life easier for the *bakufu* than of cultivating the spiritual discipline of the *shakuhachi*. But perhaps he was being overly cynical. After all, he had taught for enough time to know that students arrived with different needs: some chaffed to deepen their musicianship, ready to blossom, while others were sullen and recalcitrant and in need of a kick in the rear.

Leaving the headquarters building, Kinko set off to find Fudai-*ji*'s senior instructor. He did not anticipate starting immediately, but wanted to introduce himself and set up a schedule. When he found the instructor, the latter was in the midst of a lesson. As convention demanded, Kurosawa simply knelt and listened to the teaching.

Fudai-*ji*'s instructor was a superlative musician, as well as a gifted teacher. When the lesson was over and the student departed, Kurosawa introduced himself to the instructor, who seemed delighted at the chance to share some of Fudai-*ji*'s *honkyoku* with the new instructor of Ichigetsu-*ji*. The two men agreed to begin the next day.

The teacher escorted Kurosawa to the evening *zazen* session and then to dinner. In the large refectory, Kinko saw the two monks from that morning glare at him. They were even more hostile-looking when the abbot's assistant came to escort them to the abbot for their reprimand.

The next morning, the two teachers settled in to work. Given the significant number of *honkyoku* from the temple, Kurosawa knew that he needed to write down the notation for the pieces in his music journal. As he listened to Fudai-*ji*'s instructor, the deep beauty of the temple's music impressed him. He was quite taken by a piece called *Tsuru no Sugomori* ("Nesting of the Cranes"), as well as a piece called *Takiochi* ("Waterfall"). Both pieces seemed to capture Fumon Tanaka's ideal of the music found in nature.

Kurosawa was also deeply affected by the temple's version of the three oldest *honkyoku*: *Kokû, Kyorei,* and—of course —*Mukaiji*. Every temple taught slightly different versions of these pieces, but Fudai-*ji*'s versions seemed to have great simplicity combined with great depth, along with an air of antiquity. He decided that from that moment, he would only play these new versions.

There was an enormous amount of music to learn, even in a cursory way, and the days flew by. At the end of a week, intellectually exhausted but content, he was ready to continue his expedition. And so, on a brisk, clear spring morning, he bade farewell to the temple and set out on the last leg of his journey.

UNEXPECTED COMPANY, REDUX

From Hamamatsu the Tokaido Road bent northwards on its journey to Edo following the coast. The traveling was easy, and over the following week Kinko passed quickly through Kakegawa, Fuchu, and Numazu. Just outside of the town of Mishima, the Tokaido rose steeply up Mt. Hakone and wound its way towards the Hakone Pass, which marked the entranceway into Kantō—the broad province surrounding Edo. As the crossing point into the Kanto region, this barrier checkpoint—the tenth station on the Tokaido—was much larger and more heavily guarded than the other stations. Soldiers carefully checked every traveler's baggage and travel permits. Kurosawa knew from fellow travelers to anticipate a long wait, along with thorough scrutiny.

The walk-up Mt. Hakone was beautiful, and at several points splendid views opened up overlooking Lake Ashi. As the morning wore on, however, it became overcast. The traffic was heavier here, and as he approached the checkpoint, it began to rain softly—a nurturing spring rain. He joined a line of travelers awaiting their turn at the gate with traveling papers in hand. His *tengai* basket provided him with some modest protection from the rain and allowed him to eavesdrop on the surrounding conversations.

Passing through the Hakone Checkpoint itself was unexpectedly easy. The guards were most interested in monitoring the movement of weapons or women. Upper-class women were closely monitored because a rebellious *daimyo* might try to smuggle his wife, concubines, and children out of Edo before any revolt. So guards were particularly careful checking the traveling papers of women leaving the Kantō region. An unaccompanied monk seeking entrance *into* Kantō barely received a second look.

Even so, as Kinko walked through the gate, he experienced a vague sense of unease. He carefully looked around him, but did not see anything alarming or out of the ordinary. Most of the inns and taverns around the checkpoint were on the Kyoto side he just left. But, as evening fell and the rain seemed heavier, he decided to look for a place to spend the night, settling on a large, clean-looking inn near the barrier.

As he entered, the main room was filling with the evening's clientele, also driven in by the rain. Still unsure about his plans, Kinko decided to sit and order a pot of tea. As usual, he took a table with his back to a side wall from which he could watch both the door and the street through the nearby window. Consequently, he saw the source of his unease long before she saw him. Entering the tavern door was Rokujo accompanied by Jun. Though dressed in an ordinary travel cloak, she caught the attention of many of the men near the door. Ignoring their stares, she scanned the room and noticed Kinko against the wall. With a brilliant smile, she walked over to him and bowed. Rising from the bow, she let her hand brush tantalizingly against his.

"Kinko, it's so good to see you!"

"It is lovely to see you as well, Rokujo." Was it? He was unsure. He looked into those arresting eyes, the color of a slate sky. She was as beautiful and intoxicating as ever, but there was some undercurrent that left Kinko wary. As though speaking in his ear, he heard Fumon Tanaka's voice, "When you can still yourself enough to pay attention, you will be aware when danger is near." What was the danger, he wondered?

"How in the world did you end up here?" he continued. "I assumed that you would have left for Edo ages ago."

"Well, I ended up remaining with my cousins for longer than I anticipated. When I was ready to go, I heard at Myoan-*ji* that you had left for that temple down south in Kii Provence. I waited for some time longer, hoping that we could travel together, but when you never returned, I just left. I always kept an eye out for you on the road though," she added, smiling sweetly. "How wonderful that we'll at least have a little more time together."

"Yes... what a surprising stroke of luck."

"Are you staying here?"

"I am. I was about to take a room when you arrived."

"Wonderful. Might I join you for dinner later?"

"That would be delightful."

Smiling again, she bowed and left the tavern. He watched her, smiling at the number of eyes that followed her out the door. Finishing his tea, he arranged for a room with the proprietor, deciding to pay a little extra for the indulgence of a room to himself. He first went to the room and unpacked a little more than usual to let his belongings dry. Then he sat *zazen* for a while to calm his spirit.

Sometime later, he heard the increasing murmur of conversation from the room downstairs. He descended and found a table for dinner. Rokujo joined him a short time later, and the two chatted over a well-prepared dinner of raw seafood *narezushi* and daikon. As they finished up their food and ordered tea, a *biwa* player and a *shinobue* player got up to perform. They were quite good, and much of the conversation in the room quieted to listen to them.

Suddenly, Rokujo grabbed his arm, eagerly suggesting, "Oh, Kinko, you must join them!" He tried to demur, but she was quite insistent, pleading, "It has been so very long since I heard you play." Almost forced from his seat, he made his way to the other side of the room, where he sat next to the performers. When they ended their song, they nodded at his request to join them. Agreeing on a song, the three commenced, to the enthusiastic response of the audience.

The trio played a couple of songs together, and as they started on the third, Kinko noticed that Rokujo no longer watched from their table. Quickly, he scanned the room and could not see her anywhere. Bowing to the musicians while they played, he slipped off the bench and made his way to the stairs leading to the tavern's upper floor. He took off his sandals and quietly ascended the broad wooden staircase. Turning right at the top, quickly and silently he walked down the hall to his room.

Sliding open the door, he saw Rokujo sifting through the contents of his pack. As the door opened, she started and with one fluid motion drew a long knife strapped to the inside of her leg. "I have two men who can be here in a moment, if I call out," she hissed. "I have no desire to see blood spilt tonight."

Oddly—given the gravity of the situation—her surprise and the venom in her voice struck Kinko as humorous. His mind was as untroubled as a mountain pond; he nearly laughed out loud. It was all now so obvious. How did he miss it through their days of travel together? Holding up both of his hands in a sign of his acquiescence, he slowly entered the room and moved away from the door, so that she had an unimpeded exit. He knelt on the floor and watched her. "So, I'm curious," he queried, "how did you orchestrate our first meeting so long ago in Akashi?"

She flinched, pausing, apparently unsure how much he realized. Keeping the knife pointed at him, she responded, "That was fairly easy. Anyone traveling from Kyushu to Kyoto would need to come through Akashi. It was a simple matter to watch the check-point for a *komusō*; there aren't that many along the San'yōdō. The city is large enough to remain in for some time without attracting attention, but small enough to keep an eye on the comings and goings. I lodged at the Gatehouse Inn, since it is the first inn of any significance once you enter the city. It seemed like a likely place for you to stop when you arrived.

"After you appeared, it was a simple matter to concoct an apparent confrontation with two local thugs in my employ. Your innate sense of chivalry—and your samurai ego—were sure to do the rest. The morons that I hired were supposed to have stopped us in some deserted place after we left the city and robbed you of your pack. Then I could part from you at the next convenient town, and you would be none-the-wiser. Instead, you had them arrested, and I needed to develop an alternate plan."

Kurosawa nodded; it all made sense. He followed up, "Why a *komusō*? What made you think that a monk would be carrying anything of importance?"

"Several months earlier, during the summer, the shogun's checkpoint guards stopped a messenger on the San'yōdō carrying a letter from Kyushu to Edo. The letter was unaddressed, but its contents were clearly intended for a *daimyo* residing in Edo and included plans to smuggle the *daimyo's* family out of the capital. The only reason for that would be as preparation for a conspiracy or revolt of some kind.

"The messenger killed himself before our people could question him so we never learned the name of the intended recipient. But we did know that the messenger appeared to have come from the area of Hakata. We sent several spies to Kyushu to supplement our intelligence resources there. One of them relayed the information that a *komusō* monk would be coming to Edo with another message from the traitors.

"We sent two officers to waylay any *komusō* coming down the San'yōdō, and they did attempt to stop one—you, I assume. The monk overpowered both of them and stole their travel documentation, resulting in a long delay in our ability to respond." At this news, another puzzle piece fell into place for Kurosawa. "Knowing that we had lost considerable time in this search, I decided to wait at Akashi and waylay any *komusō* who traveled that direction. You were much longer than I anticipated, and I was beginning to worry that I had missed you entirely."

"And the story you told me in Kyoto? About your fleeing your contract in the pleasure quarter of Fukuyama?"

She smiled. "Well, that was partly true. My family did sell me to a house of assignation, but it was in the pleasure quarter of Edo—the *yoshiwara*. And the lord who bought my contract did not want me for his third wife, but for the shogun's intelligence service—the *metsuke*. I have been in their employ ever since."

Kurosawa nodded; all the pieces fit. "Has it occurred to you that you did indeed miss the correct *komusō* in Akashi and that you have been following the wrong man?"

"It did, once you left Kyoto, and I was able to ascertain that you had not taken one of the roads to Edo. You were lost to my contacts for a very long time. And yet here you are, having gone to considerable trouble to approach Edo by a circuitous route, thus reinforcing my suspicions."

Kurosawa laughed. "If I were the messenger you seek, why would I have taken all the time to disappear into the Kii Peninsula, only to walk through the most heavily guarded post-station on the entire Tokaido Road? The truth is, you missed the messenger in Akashi, and you have been following the wrong man ever since." He laughed again, this time at the tiny hint of doubt in her eyes.

"That's not possible," she hissed.

"Well, it's an easy question to resolve: have you found any messages yet? Go ahead and look." He motioned to his pack. "You know well enough that is all I carry."

Keeping the knife pointed at him, she continued pawing through the pack until in frustration she turned it upside down and dumped its contents onto the floor of the room. She kicked his belongings to the side and rifled through the papers, carefully examining his "three seals": the *honsoku* booklet of the Fuke, his identity paper, and his travel permit. Suddenly, holding up a small booklet of paper, she crowed, "And what is this? Something written in a code of some sort!"

Kurosawa laughed. "It is indeed a code: that is my notebook of the various *honkyoku* music pieces that I have acquired along my way to Edo. Shall I show you?"

As she tossed him the booklet, he drew his *shakuhachi* slowly from his belt and opened the book to its first page. Pointing out the name of the piece of music and the temple from which it came, he explained to her his musical notation system.

"I remember from the night in Osaka when I searched this, there were other papers," she demanded.

"Yes, there was a packet of papers from the abbot of Itchōken-*ji* to his superior at Myoan-*ji* in Kyoto, which I left with the abbot there. If you return to Kyoto, I do not doubt that Minzan Zenji would be happy to verify that. He would probably even show you the papers," Kurosawa said, somewhat smugly, appreciating the growing doubt in Rokujo's eyes.

Fiercely, she sliced open the sides of his pack with her knife, looking for hidden cavities. She rechecked all the other items in the pack with a rising air of agitation. Finally, she threw the tattered backpack aside and turned to him. "You must have hidden it amongst your clothes. Strip!"

Kinko rose, and piece by piece, took off everything he wore, then tossed each over to Rokujo as he removed them. She pawed over each piece and finally pointed at his loincloth. "That too," she insisted, although not inspecting it too closely. Sitting dejectedly on the floor, she let the knife slip from her hand. "It must be here," she lamented under her breath. "I cannot have been wrong this whole time!"

At long last, she turned back to him. "Listen, if you have passed the message on to someone else, I can make sure that you are handsomely rewarded for any information. You will bear no punishment for this affair. In assisting me, you will be helping the shogun and the country."

Kurosawa tried to look as sincere as possible, although it was a little harder while sitting naked on the floor. "I am loyal to the shogunate," he replied, "and wish I could help you, Rokujo, but I am afraid that you simply latched onto the wrong *komusō*. I am sorry."

Shaking her head in disbelief, Rokujo arose and slipped the dagger into the sheath on her leg. "Well, there'll be hell to pay for this." She reached inside her sleeve and tossed him a silver coin. "Buy yourself a better pack for the rest of your trip. I doubt that we shall meet again, and I shan't say that I'll miss you. I won't. You're dull and rustic, and I doubt that you'll make much of a life for yourself in Edo. But good luck all the same." Turning away, she slid the door open and disappeared down the hall.

Kinko sat there for some time. The lit taper cast flickering shadows over his naked body and the detritus of his pack strewn about the room. After a long while, he sighed, smiled to himself and thought, "Well, she's not wrong: I am dull and rustic, and I will probably not make much of myself in Edo. And she's right that we won't miss seeing each other. Ah, well, she was lovely."

Slowly, he re-assembled his belongings. After tying on his loincloth and slipping on a light pair of linen pants, he neatly folded everything else up and put it in a pile. Then he stacked his papers together. Lastly, he made a pile of all the other odds and ends that he carried with him.

That done, he sat quietly in *seiza* for a long time. Was it *zazen*? He was not trying to quiet his mind or seek enlightenment, but was fully present to the beauty and irony of this moment. He tried to remember when the pieces of Rokujo's story stopped fitting together and marveled at how long he ignored his instincts about her. What had he also ignored in his relationship with Taka? With Matsu? "I am so often a mystery to myself," he reflected, "how can I ever know another?"

At length, he opened his eyes, went over to the far corner of his room and pulled back the edge of the tatami mat that covered the floor. He reclaimed the letter that he had hidden there earlier that afternoon, just after seeing Rokujo enter the tavern. The letter given to him by his father.

As he knew, the letter possessed no address. Carefully, Kinko slid his *tanto* through the unmarked wax seal. Deliberately, he unfolded the paper. Here, too, there was no salutation or date, but—given his father's directions to hand it to no one but his uncle—this seemed like a wise precaution. Kinko certainly recognized his father's calligraphy. The text read:

"Our support here gathers; the critical players are

sympathetic, but worried about their families. You must make arrangements for spiriting families from Edo at the crucial moment. We believe that your best chances lie upon the Koshu Kaido, it being less policed than the Tokaido. Also, we have allies in Kotu who may be helpful once you get that far. Send me notice as soon as you have planned the escape. Nothing can happen here until that part of the plan is in place. Be joyful: the day nears when our beloved island will be free from the tyrant's grasp."

Kurosawa knew that the letter was not from his father; neither was it intended for his uncle. Both his father and his uncle were only low-ranking retainers in the households of modestly influential lords. Were the letters between those lords? Or were they between the *daimyos* whom those lords served? Or were his father and uncle acting on behalf of other lords or *daimyos*, seeking to ingratiate themselves with other noble houses? There was no way to tell. The only certainty was that his father and uncle were being used to shield some ambitious lords.

Not that his father lacked culpability. Kinko was fully aware that his father would have eagerly accepted his role in this conspiracy. His incessant ambition to raise the Kurosawa family up the ladder of samurai status would have been motivation enough. Taking on a highly secret, dangerous, and delicate mission on behalf of a lord would place him in the inner circle of retainers, giving him opportunities for advancement and wealth. The risk to his wife and children would hardly cross his mind.

The risk to Kinko's own life. Kinko sat and let the full import of his father's action settle on him like wet snow. If Rokujo found this letter, he would have been killed. Actually,

he would have been tortured and then killed. Tortured merci-
lessly until he betrayed his own family. He sighed... the
madness of it all.

Yet now he was unsure exactly where his duty lay. His filial
duty demanded that he take the letter to his uncle and let their
plot unfold. He understood how the *daimyos* on Kyushu
bridled at the heavy hand of the remote shogun. He sympa-
thized with their yearning for freedom. And he, too, desired a
better life for his mother and sister.

His duty to the emperor demanded that he turn the letter
over to the authorities of the shogunate. As oppressive as the
rule of the shogun felt to the *daimyo*, Kinko now believed that it
provided valuable security and stability for the country. Roads
were safe to travel; the economy was prosperous; the arts flour-
ished. And the shogun's reign ended decades of internecine
clan violence across the breadth of Japan. Life was better for
many people, particularly those who were most vulnerable.

Back and forth, Kurosawa's mind ran, trying to untangle the
web of duties and responsibilities that were an inevitable
element of samurai life. Then he stopped. He picked up Ikkei's
shakuhachi and played *Mukaiji*. He played it again and then
stopped and sat. He listened carefully to what he felt and what
he heard inside himself.

And then—with a feeling of perfect balance—he folded the
letter back up, held it in the flame of the lamp and watched it
turn to ash.

THE CENTER OF THE WORLD

The next morning, his mind still quiet, Kinko gathered all his belongings into his cloak and carried the improvised bag over his shoulder. Hakone being a stop for travelers, it was easy to find a shop where he could spend Rokujo's money on a new pack. Beyond Hakone, the Tokaido Road plunged through heavy forests of oak, cedar, and maple, dropping from the highest point on the highway to the lowest: Odawara, by the sea. Occasionally, during the descent, the trees opened up which allowed a view of Mt. Fuji off to the west. The highway itself followed an eastward direction and cut across the northern edge of the Izu Peninsula.

Kinko was only about four days away from Edo, and the miles passed quickly. The Tokaido was notably more crowded now, nearing the great metropolis. Soon after he passed through the post station at Kawasaki—the second station on the Tokaido —villages clustered so closely together that it was difficult to discern where one ended and the next began.

Approaching the city proper, he could sense the movement of the wheels of power turning, lifting some and crushing others. It had a relentless, brooding atmosphere. The energy of the metropolis was different from anywhere Kinko knew; it was brilliant and passionate, and dark and ominous. As clearly as he felt it on Kōya-san, he knew that great spiritual forces were at work here.

A century and a half before Kurosawa's arrival, Edo had been a small fishing village. When Ieyasu Tokugawa came to power after defeating his rivals at the battle of Sekigahara, Kyoto remained as the formal capital of the emperor, but all the administration of the shogun's *bakufu* moved to Edo. In an astonishingly short time, the little fishing village on the banks of the Sumida River erupted into the largest city in Japan, perhaps the largest in the entire world.

Home to over a million people, the size of the city was dizzying to the newly arrived *komusō*. Because he was curious about his new city, once he passed the final checkpoint station —the Shinagawa-*juku*—Kinko continued to follow the Tokaido for the next few miles to its conclusion at the Nihonbashi Bridge in the heart of the city. The Nihonbashi was the beginning point of the two major highways between Tokyo and Kyoto, and the center of a thriving commercial district.

A large fish market occupied the space below the bridge, on the banks of the Nihonbashi River, although this late in the day, there was not much activity. Kinko followed the riot of sights and sounds to the door of a massive, three-story building facing the river. A tiled roof extended over the first-floor walkway above which a sign read *"Echigo-ya."* Entering, Kinko found himself in a dry-goods store larger than he could have imagined. The area devoted to kimonos alone was more space than Kinko had ever seen for a single shop. Hundreds upon hundreds of brilliantly colored fabrics hung in a dazzling display to meet any person's taste.

Having spent most of his adulthood in temples, the frenetic

combination of sound and color and movement overwhelmed Kinko: it felt much like he imagined the chaos of a battlefield might. He backed out of the doors and stood on the roofed walkway by the street. Needing to clear his mind, and in need of some money, he took out Ikkei's *shakuhachi* and began to play.

Mindful of his friend Harushige's observation so many months ago, as well as the wisdom of Fumon Tanaka, he made no effort to collect a crowd by playing popular songs. He simply started playing some *honkyoku* as his offering to those passing by. An unexpected number of people stopped to listen to the ancient music, and many contributed as he passed around his begging bowl. Feeling more secure financially, Kinko made his way down the street and soaked in the sights and smells of the metropolis.

The sun dipped low in the sky when Kinko realized that he should look for Ichigetsu-*ji*. He asked several people without any success: there were so many temples and shrines in Edo, that no one could know them all. Eventually, he passed a large, prosperous-looking Shinto temple and entered, hoping someone could point him in the right direction.

He was fortunate to find a line of priests and monks exiting their evening service. He singled out one with an air of authority and approached him. "Excuse me, *Obo-san*, this is my first day in Edo, and I am trying to find the Fuke headquarters temple called Ichigetsu-*ji*."

The old man smiled and pointed to the northwest. "Well, my brother, it's about 12 miles in that direction."

Kurosawa gaped in disbelief. "Oh my," was all he could think to say. "And is its sister temple, Reihō-*ji*, any closer?"

Still smiling, the priest pointed off to the west. "Reihō-*ji* is about 30 miles in that direction." This time, the priest could not help laughing at Kurosawa's crestfallen face.

"But they are both supposed to be in Edo!" Kurosawa blurted out.

Still chuckling, the old priest replied, "Edo is a very large city, and I'm not sure that I—who have lived here all my life—could tell you where exactly it ends. Ichigetsu-*ji* is close enough to be considered part of the city. Reihō-*ji* is technically in the city of Ome; but if you were to travel to it, I suspect that you would not find much countryside between here and there."

The old priest laid his hand on Kurosawa's shoulder, as though in parting; but stopped, adding, "You are new to the city, my friend. Why not spend the night here in Kanda Myōjin? We've just finished our evening prayer service and are going to eat. Join us for the meal and stay in one of our guest rooms. I'm sure that our abbot would be willing to extend hospitality to one of our Buddhist brothers."

With that, the old man guided him into the refectory, where Kinko gratefully joined the community for dinner. They were all interested in hearing about Kinko's travels, and he shared some *shakuhachi* playing with them before they let him retire to the guest quarters. Kurosawa attended the community prayer service the next morning, making a small contribution to honor their hospitality before continuing on his way.

Before heading north to Ichigetsu-*ji*, his new friend suggested that he travel south a mile or so and see the shogun's palace. Being the heart of the *bakufu*, Edo Castle would help orient Kurosawa to Edo as a whole. And so, on a pleasant but cloudy morning, Kinko Kurosawa left on a sightseeing tour of his new city.

It was easy to find the Edo Castle as it completely dominated the urban landscape and was visible from some distance away. The castle was so large that it was divided into different wards like its own small city, each ward clustered around one of the castle citadels. The central citadel was six stories tall and the wall around the whole complex was miles long, surrounded by a huge moat. A shopkeeper told Kinko that the extracted soil from the moat had helped to reclaim marshland from Edo Bay on the southern edge of the city. The moats on the east of the complex adjoined the Kanda River which allowed ships direct access to the castle.

The shogun's mandate that all *daimyo* maintain a residence in Edo resulted in a breathtaking number of massive estates surrounding the castle rampart, primarily in the neighborhoods to the south and east. Large and complex, they generally contained gardens and multiple buildings, none of which were visible to Kinko behind their high walls.

As he strolled past these miniature fortresses, Kurosawa's ear caught the sound of *shakuhachi* music nearby. He followed the sound for a block to the south and came upon an open square with a small crowd gathered around a skilled *shakuhachi* player. He played a piece called *Hifumi Hachigaishi*—"returning the begging bowl"—as the *komusō* collected offerings.

Kurosawa watched for a few minutes while this process ended. As the *komusō* prepared to leave, he noticed Kurosawa, with a slight start. The man bowed and began playing *yobitake-uketake* in recognition of their meeting. Kinko played the response back, and the two approached each other.

"Forgive me, brother," the other said stiffly, "but I believe that you are in the wrong area."

"I'm sorry," Kurosawa stammered in surprise. "I'm not sure what you mean."

"I mean," intoned the other, as though speaking to a child, "that *I* am assigned to the south castle district today. You must be in the wrong place."

Kurosawa removed the *tengai* from his head. "I apologize

for the misunderstanding. I have just arrived in Edo and am not familiar with the protocols of Ichigetsu-*ji*."

"Are you not expected to register at the main Fuke temple when you arrive in a new city?" the monk growled.

"Certainly," responded Kurosawa, trying to keep from becoming defensive, "but I arrived yesterday and didn't realize how far away Ichigetsu-*ji* was."

The other *komusō* relaxed a little. "Oh, the city is quite a bit larger than most people expect when they arrive. Tell me, where do you come from?"

"My name is Kinko Kurosawa, and I have arrived from Kuzaki-*ji* in Nagasaki."

On hearing this, the other monk opened his eyes wide and exclaimed, "You are to be our new teacher! We have been anticipating your arrival for some time."

At this, Kinko felt a little guilty. "I should have been here earlier, but I took a detour south to Kōya-san on my way."

"How wonderful to see the holy mountain," the other replied. And then, realizing his breach of etiquette, he bowed. "Forgive me, *Shishō*, my name is Nakai Shimura, and I am a *jizume* at Ichigetsu-*ji*."

"I am not familiar with the term '*jizume*.' What does it mean?"

"Most temples divide their members into *kyogai* monks and *jūshoku* priests with the latter being the permanent residents. Ichigetsu-*ji* is so large and has so many permanent residents that we have two ranks: the *jūshoku* are still the senior priests, and *jizume* are the junior members of the residential staff. We are assigned specific areas in which to play and beg so that we can cover the city more efficiently and avoid competing with one another. My area today is here south of the castle, and I was about to move to the east a few blocks. Would you like to join me?"

"Absolutely," Kinko enthused.

The two men walked east towards the Kanda River. Along the way, Nakai Shimura introduced Kurosawa to some Edo street food called *tempura*, which was fresh fish fried in a light batter. Kinko was immediately smitten. In a few blocks, Shimura stopped in another open square. He unwrapped his *shakuhachi* and looked shyly at Kinko. "Would you like to play with me, *Shishō?*"

"With pleasure," Kinko bowed.

He pulled out his teaching flute, and the two played together in unison for some time, while a large crowd gathered. They took up a collection, after which—since Kurosawa now possessed a better sense of Shimura's strengths as a player—he pulled out Ikkei's longer *shakuhachi*, and they played some duets. While familiar with solo *shakuhachi* players, most of the crowd had not seen a duet before and responded enthusiastically.

After taking the second collection, Shimura exclaimed, "This is enough money for me to stop for the day. But, if you're willing, we could go to one more location and get enough money for a nice dinner!" The young monk seemed less militant about Kurosawa formally registering his presence at Ichigetsu-*ji* now with the prospect of food.

Kinko agreed, and the two of them set off. After playing another round of music in a different spot, Shimura said, "Let's eat; I know just the place!"

He led Kinko through a maze of streets to the northwest. It was quite a long walk, a couple of miles at least when they stopped in front of a restaurant called San'ya.

San'ya—or "Three Valleys"—was one of the standard works in the *shakuhachi* repertoire, so the restaurant's name seemed fortuitous and made Kinko feel more comfortable in this strange city. "This place is more expensive than I can afford often," Shimura whispered conspiratorially. "But you helped me pull in quite a haul today, so you should at least get to sample the best food the city has to offer."

It was earlier than the traditional dinner hour, but the San'ya was still doing a brisk business. The two monks squeezed around a small side table, and Kinko let Shimura order for them both. As the food arrived, Kinko appreciated his new friend's choice of venue. Shimura, he learned, grew up in a small town to the north of Edo, where his father was the priest of the local Rinzai temple. He planned to return and serve there after spending some time at Ichigetsu-ji. Kinko, in turn, shared his history at Kuzaki-ji and recounted his long journey to Edo.

As night fell and the restaurant became more crowded, Kurosawa began to wonder about where they would spend the night. "I assume when it is your alms rotation in the city, you can't return all the way to the temple?" he inquired.

"Oh, no! It would take a full day walking down to the castle and back to the temple again. When we come to beg, we spend a night or two close to the castle before heading back to the temple. Sometimes we stay with friends that we have made in the city or often at one of the Rinzai temples closer to the city center. Tonight I thought we might stay at Rinsho-in, a lovely temple to the west of us."

The two men talked and sipped sake for some time, when Kinko said, "I was impressed by your playing today and by the quality of your *shakuhachi*. Did you make it yourself?"

Shimura laughed. "Sadly no. We learn the rudiments of flute-making at the temple. But most of us purchase our *shakuhachi* from Koji Yamada, who makes them over in the Sumida district. He used to be a monk at Ichigetsu-ji and now makes flutes that he sells to the temple monks. He's not too far out of the way on our route; perhaps I can take you by to meet him as we travel tomorrow."

"I would love that," Kurosawa answered.

The two monks chatted easily for some time more, before making their way to the nearby Rinsho-*in*, a charming, modest temple with exposed wood beams and a quiet garden, settled under the shadow of the massive Tendai temple of Kan'ei-*ji*. Although it was late by the time the two reached Rinsho, the gate-keeper was clearly used to *komusō* arriving at odd hours. They made their way to the guest quarters and quickly fell asleep.

In the morning, Shimura introduced Kurosawa to two other monks from Ichigetsu-*ji* spending the night at the temple. The four men joined the Rinzai monks for their morning meditation and breakfast, after which they departed for their playing assignments for the day. Kurosawa again accompanied Shimura in playing and begging in the area south of Edo Castle. Again, the two men performed duets together and collected enough alms for Shimura to meet his begging goal early. So, shortly after midday, they set off for Ichigetsu-*ji*.

Winding their way through the maze of streets, they found a bridge across the Sumida River. On the far side, the neighbor-hoods were less congested than west of the river, although still urban. After traveling east for some time, Shimura turned north, and in a few blocks stopped in front of a broad two-story building with a sign that read "Kotos: for sale or rent."

The two men stepped into the shop to find several kotos on display in the shop's front room. The 13-stringed instruments were six feet long and over a foot wide, so only six of them were set up for playing, but many others leaned vertically against the walls of the shop. In a backroom, Kurosawa could hear two kotos playing in what was clearly a music lesson. Through a doorway to the right, under the *noren* curtain, he could make out the workshop where the instruments were made.

Staffing the shop was a woman of about 30 with lively eyes and a ready smile. She wore a deep blue kimono covered in a dragonfly pattern and beamed in recognition at Shimura as he walked in. "Good afternoon, little sister," he said cheerily. "I hope that you and your parents are well."

"Very well, indeed, Shimura," she replied, bowing.

"This is my new colleague, Kinko Kurosawa, who is joining us at Ichigetsu-*ji*." The woman bowed to Kinko, who returned the greeting. "We are here to see Yamada; and if he is not too busy, I'd also love to have my friend meet your father."

"Of course, Shimura. Please wait a moment." With that, she disappeared through the *noren* curtain. Moments later, she raised the curtain and gestured for the monks to enter. As Shimura led the way, he bowed to an old man bent over a work table, gluing together two long sheets of paulownia wood.

"The blessings of Buddha on you, my friend Misawa," boomed the monk. The older man smiled and shuffled over. He was probably no older than sixty, although he was so severely stooped from years of working bent over a table that he looked much older. His eyes, however, were sharp and penetrating.

"It is good to see you, Shimura. I have three new kotos for you to bless, if you have the time."

"I would be happy to, Misawa. Let me first introduce my new friend, Kinko Kurosawa. He has arrived all the way from Nagasaki to instruct us in *shakuhachi*."

"Ah, wonderful!" said the old man. "We must play together! I love playing the koto with a good *shakuhachi* player. Much of the time, however, I must make do with Shimura," he added with an affectionate twinkle in his eye.

Turning to Kurosawa, Shimura said, "Shimada Misawa is a

distant relative of the great koto player and composer Kengyo Yatsuhashi. I tell you this to save him the trouble, as he would undoubtedly have found occasion for mentioning it to you soon."

The old man laughed and slapped Shimura on the shoulder.

Shimura continued, "I came today to introduce Kurosawa to Yamada; do you know if he's here?"

"He's working upstairs," said Misawa. "Go on up."

"When we're done, I'll come down and we'll get those kotos blessed."

Shimura led Kurosawa to a door at the rear of the workshop and up a narrow flight of stairs. As they ascended, Shimura said quietly, "Misawa is a wonderful koto-maker and a fine player; but his wife, Shino, is the real musician. Make sure that you get the chance to play with her at some point. Their daughter Setsu, whom you met in the shop, is also a fine player." At the top of the staircase, he stopped and knocked at the door. "Yamada, it's me Shimura. I've brought a friend." They stood there on the top step for a moment and listened to approaching footsteps.

The man who opened the door also seemed to be around 60, but he was both tall, and his posture made him appear even taller. Intense brown eyes sat under an unkempt mop of grey hair. The old monk bowed. "It's good to see you, Shimura; I've missed you the last time or two that you dropped by. Who is this that you've brought me?"

"This is Kinko Kurosawa who has traveled from Nagasaki to be an instructor with us. He was admiring my *shakuhachi* yesterday, and I brought him by to meet you while we were on the way to the temple."

"It is good to meet you, Kurosawa. Your reputation precedes you, and I look forward to working with you." Yamada

—perhaps out of tact, perhaps indifference—did not ask to hear Kurosawa play. "Welcome to my workshop," he said, inviting the two travelers in with a wave.

The room was small and cramped. Against the far wall were wide and deep shelves full of hundreds of bamboo culms. The culms on the bottom seemed the freshest and became drier higher on the shelving. Once they worked their way to the top, they were ready to become *shakuhachi*. Against the adjoining wall was a set of long, narrow shelving holding countless tools: heavy iron rods with files at the end, more delicate files, knives for an infinite variety of specific detailed work, *ji* paste for adjusting the interior bore, and lacquers for giving the bore a hard, waterproof finish. Through a small door in the remaining wall was Yamada's bedroom.

Examining several *shakuhachi* in the formation process, Kurosawa noted the high quality of Yamada's work. He tentatively asked if he could try one or two. Yamada waved a hand in permission and returned, "Might I also try your flutes?" looking at the three poking out of Kurosawa's pack.

The three monks then settled into their own quiet worlds: examining, playing, and exploring the various flutes in the workshop. Eventually, Yamada broke the silence. "These two *shakuhachi* are beautifully made and tuned," as he turned Kinko's teaching flute and Ikkei's flute appreciatively in his hands. Holding the latter, he noted, "I don't make too many long *shakuhachi*, but this has a wonderfully rich tone and a substantive feel in the hand. This one," as he picked up Tanaka's long *shakuhachi*, "is an absurd size. It also requires a great deal of finishing on the bore to make it playable," he added as an afterthought.

Kinko laughed, and said, "Absolutely not! Refining that monstrous flute would break the heart of an old monk on Kōya-san, and I wouldn't do that for the world. It serves its purpose just as it is." Yamada looked at Kurosawa curiously as he handed the *shakuhachi* back to him.

"There's clearly a story there," he said. "I'll look forward to hearing it at some point." Kinko spent the next hour questioning Yamada about his flute-making and appreciating the subtlety of his workmanship.

A soft knock on the door interrupted their conversation. Setsu entered, "Mama says that it's too late to walk on to Ichigetsu-*ji* this afternoon, so you should join us for dinner and spend the night here."

After they gratefully accepted her offer, and she retreated down the stairs, Shimura leaned over and whispered to Kinko, "I was hoping we might be here long enough to merit a dinner invitation. Mama-san is a wonderful cook."

The three men spent some more time talking in Yamada's workshop until Setsu summoned them to dinner. The Misawa family owned the entire building which was quite large. The ground floor was dedicated to the shop, the workshop, and a large practice room where the mother and daughter taught. Yamada rented a small, sectioned-off part of the upper floor for his *shakuhachi* workshop and bedroom, while the rest served as the family residence.

Dinner was upstairs in the family living quarters. As they made their way back through the koto shop and up the other set of stairs, Shimura whispered to Kurosawa, "Remember what I told you and make sure you play with Misawa's wife, Shino. She's an instructor in the Ikuta school. That was her that you heard teaching in the back room when we arrived."

As soon as he saw her, Kurosawa realized immediately that Shino Misawa was in no danger of being overshadowed by her talented husband. She was a tall, elegant woman, a few years younger than Shimada, but not many. She wore her beautiful long silver hair in the style of a much younger woman, but it did not seem incongruous. She clearly both adored and appreciated her husband and always deferred when engaging him. But she was also a force in her own right and was fully engaged in the conversation with her three guests.

In addition to being a musician, Shino Misawa was—as Shimura noted—a wonderful cook and laid out a magnificent dinner for her guests. The centerpiece was an udon soup with cabbage, daikon radish, edamame, and freshly made tofu. She supplemented that with gyoza, rice, vegetable tempura, and some smoked fish. Throughout the evening, she gently guided the conversation to include everyone around the table. Kurosawa found her presence quite compelling.

The sake flowed freely, and it was not too long before the conversation turned to music. There was much debate about the relative gifts of various composers, compositions, and players. Soon the conversation—and the sake bottles—moved downstairs to the shop, where the six kotos were already set up. With three koto players and three *shakuhachi* players, everyone played, and the music was extraordinary. Kinko rarely enjoyed himself so much.

His inhibitions loosened by the ample sake, Kurosawa shared stories of his teacher Ikkei and his longer *shakuhachi,* as well as of his time with Tanaka and his making the long flute. Shino loved hearing about Tanaka and about Kurosawa's experience on Kōya-san. She practiced *zazen* herself and appeared fascinated with the disciplines of the hermit.

The conversation and music lasted deep into the night, until at last, fatigue laid its iron hand on the whole company. Shino and Setsu set out futons for Kurosawa and Shimura in the large practice room on the first floor and bid them good night. With very little conversation, the two visitors quickly drifted off to sleep.

. . .

The monks were up early the next morning; but not as early as Shino and Setsu who had breakfast waiting for them. The meal was quiet and leisurely with the song of a nearby ringed plover drifting through the window on a cool morning breeze. After sharing tea, the two monks thanked their hosts and prepared to leave for the temple. Parting at the door, Kinko said to Shino, "Thank you so much for your hospitality. It was a deep pleasure to spend time with your family. You have made Edo feel like home."

Shino took Kinko's hand in both of hers and looked him long in the eye, responding, "This is your home whenever you feel the need of one."

The two men set off down the road with several more miles to go before reaching the temple. For some time they walked in silence, listening to the conversation of the birds, each lost in his own thoughts. "What a wonderful family," Kurosawa finally said. "Thank you for taking me to visit. It has been a while since I have eaten so well or enjoyed such spirited conversation and music."

"Yes, they are wonderful. Misawa's kotos are well-regarded throughout Edo, and Shino is widely appreciated as a teacher. As you heard last night, Setsu is also an accomplished player, and she, too, is beginning to develop a reputation as a teacher."

"She seems old to be home with her parents still," Kinko observed.

"Ah, that's a sad story," Shimura said. "She was married as a young woman to a merchant of the town, but the marriage did not last long. Her husband felt that she was not sufficiently submissive and made life unpleasant enough that she requested a letter of divorce. I don't doubt that she is her mother's daughter in that regard, but a man must be terribly insecure to be threatened by a woman of talent and opinion. In any case, she has never remarried and seems content living with her parents. She should be financially secure teaching music."

The two lapsed into a comfortable silence as they continued walking. This far out from the center of Edo, neighborhoods began to feel more like independent villages and the quality of the air became clearer, away from the fires and open garbage found nearer the heart of the city.

As mid-day approached, the monks emerged from a copse of trees, and there, on the crest of a hill, stood a magnificent temple. Its high whitewashed walls and massive iron-shod, oak gate reflected the brilliant sun. Both men stopped for a moment and in response to Kinko's wordless inquiry, Shimura answered, "Yes, that is Ichigetsu-*ji*. Welcome home."

A NEW HOME

C limbing the street, Kinko paid close attention to each of the buildings along the way. These were the stores, taverns, artisan shops, and food stalls that would populate his life for years to come. He explored each passing face, knowing them to be players in a drama of which they were presently unaware.

Passing through the gates of the temple felt like waking from a long, surreal dream. Here was a life he knew; a comfortably familiar life. Every person was a stranger, but he could look at each monk and recognize what role he played in this pulsing, moving, endlessly changing organism. He smiled at friends as yet unmade.

Shimura shepherded him through the people to the main administration building. "No doubt you will find the abbot eager to welcome you to your new position. It was a joy spending the last few days with you, Kurosawa. You are an extraordinary musician and I look forward to learning from you."

"Making the transition to this place has been immeasurably

easier having you as a guide," Kinko replied. "I am very grateful to you, Shimura." The two men bowed.

Kurosawa introduced himself to the scribe at the door and surrendered his identity papers. The man returned shortly and ushered Kurosawa down a long hall and then slid open the door to a surprisingly modest office. There sat a man of about 50 with a powerful build and a round, intelligent face, topped by a salt-and-pepper topknot. He looked up directly into Kurosawa's eyes with an expression of unquestioned authority, and introduced himself as the abbot, Ganryo Shuza.

He appraised Kurosawa for some moments with a look that revealed nothing. Then, inviting his guest to take a seat, he said, "We have been expecting you here for some time, Kurosawa. I'm glad that you have made the trip safely." The implied question was obvious, and Kurosawa—not wanting to appear obtuse —answered it directly.

"Without intending to do so, I have made this journey into a pilgrimage, spending a considerable time on Kōya-san, *Osho*. I apologize if this inconvenienced the temple."

Still inscrutable, the abbot replied, "Well, I hope that your time there will be to the benefit of our community. Tell me a little of yourself, Kurosawa, and a little about this pilgrimage."

Kinko shared his family history and an overview of his time at Kuzaki-*ji*. He also briefly spoke of his trip and of Minzan Zenji sending him to Kokoku-*ji* and his time on Kōya-san. The abbot listened in silence.

"An interesting tale," he finally said. "I appreciate the way that you used your time on Kōya-san and hope that will enrich the teaching you do. Now I want to ask you a delicate question: I assumed that your *komusō* papers would identify you as a *jūshoku* priest, yet they name you as a simple lay monk. This fact—combined with the cryptic letter from your abbot, implying that he is not unhappy to have you leave—tells me that there was a problem of some sort. Can you enlighten me on its nature?"

Kurosawa was both mortified and unsurprised at the turn in the conversation. Having no desire to obfuscate, he told the abbot simply and directly about his affair with Matsu Ekken and the abbot's response. Ganryo Shuza again sat listening. Eventually, he said, "Well, I appreciate your honesty, Kurosawa. People are prone to mistakes, and—hopefully—the wise among us learn from them. Overly righteous people are prone to ignore that. It is one of the reasons that I have never particularly liked your abbot in Nagasaki.

"Nonetheless, it makes my judgment here more complicated. I would like for us to get to know each other better before making any permanent decisions. For the present, I would like you to join our teaching staff as an additional teacher, rather than as head teacher. There are four instructors here and three at Reihō-ji. Get to know them, do some teaching, and give some thought as to how you would organize our work here. Let us meet again in a few weeks. My assistant will give you your credentials as a *jizume*, which is our term for the junior level of the full-time temple staff—though not a priest—and will show you the room where you will stay."

Ganryo Shuza rang a small bell, and moments later the door slid open and the abbot's assistant ushered Kurosawa out. As he walked down the hall, he could hear the abbot speaking in a low voice. The assistant scurried ahead of Kurosawa and slid open the door to his small office, which overflowed with papers. The assistant filled out the proper identification paper, handed it to Kurosawa, and edged past him back out into the hall, where he set off—Kurosawa in tow—to the staff living quarters.

A long, low structure which sat between the administrative bundling and the much larger monk's quarters housed the quarters for the *jizume*. A covered porch ran the length of the front with a doorway at either end. Climbing the steps, Kinko followed the assistant down a long passage to the rear of the building. The assistant slid open a door in the rear-most hall-way, and Kurosawa entered a pleasant room with a window on the back garden, furnished with a futon, a *zafu* cushion, and a low table with writing implements.

"Please feel free to wander anywhere in the temple complex, Kurosawa. This afternoon you will find lessons going on, as well as *budo* practice in the exercise yard. The bell will summon you to the evening *zazen* session, followed by dinner. Tomorrow morning, after *sui-zen* practice, the *shakuhachi* teaching staff will meet together in the top room of the music building. Please be prompt."

After the assistant slid the door closed again, Kinko set down his belongings and sat cross-legged on the *zafu*. The abbot's decision was disappointing, but not surprising. Ganryo Shuza seemed a reasonable, prudent leader, one whom he could comfortably follow. He took out Ikkei's *shakuhachi* and began to play. After playing long enough that he had hallowed the living space, he set aside his flute and went out to explore the temple.

By Fuke standards, Ichigetsu-*ji* was enormous with dozens of buildings scattered over a large, enclosed campus. Numerous small shrines dotted the grounds along with several small, immaculate gardens. Kinko was not in a particular mood to chat with people at the moment and so maintained a dignified silence, merely bowing to the monks he met. As evening fell, he joined the community in *zazen*. The enormous size of the community struck Kurosawa, seeing them all gathered together. At dinner, he joined a table with several other *jizume* monks and was introduced to the group by his friend Nakai Shimura.

The next morning, the bell which summoned the community to *zazen* awoke Kurosawa before dawn. Breakfast afterward was a boisterous affair, and Kurosawa again joined the table of his fellow *jizume*. Following breakfast, there was a brief session of community *shakuhachi* playing. This was technically a time of *sui-zen*—blowing meditation—though, in truth, there was nothing meditative about it.

In Kurosawa's experience, *shakuhachi* playing in large groups was rarely a good idea. The instrument was so temperamental that playing solo was hard enough; playing duets was effective only if two very good performers collaborated. But a mass of monks of varying skill levels—a charitable phrase for the collection at this temple—was always a cacophony. Kurosawa watched the army of monks trying to play together—or in some cases, not trying at all—and shook his head at the futility. The group was an odd assortment of humanity. Some were fine players; others at least attempted to follow along and create music; but a great number of the men appeared to care very little for the discipline at all, and barely pretended to play.

If the rank-and-file monks of Ichigetsu-*ji* were of dubious musical commitment, at least the teaching staff were experienced and competent. He met with the four other teachers in a room on the top floor of the music building shortly after the community *sui-zen*. The building was two stories tall, the first floor occupied by two large group training rooms. On the second floor were rooms of various sizes for individual or small group lessons. It was in one of these rooms that the teachers met every morning to plan out the day's teaching schedule.

As they entered, they joked good-naturedly about the playing at the *sui-zen* session just finished and poked fun at various monks that they all knew and taught. They welcomed Kurosawa as one of their own with barely an acknowledgment they had not met before. As they divvied up the classes for the day, they merely asked about his preferences. To their surprise

—as perhaps his own—his only request was to have some time free in the afternoon for *budo* practice on the exercise field.

His first class of the day was a large group of beginners, taught in one of the spacious music halls on the first floor. "How many monks should I expect? And how do you normally approach the classes?" Kinko inquired of the other teachers.

"Anywhere from twenty to fifty monks, depending on the day," one answered. "And we usually work on *Kyorei* with them, occasionally *Kokû*, just for variety. Both are important enough for the monks to need to know them and simple enough to focus on sound production and refinement." This seemed like good advice to Kinko and was similar to what he did with groups of new monks at Kuzaki-*ji*.

A little while later, Kurosawa settled himself on a platform at the front of the room and watched the monks file in. He noted the surprise on their faces at a new teacher. When the room was full and everyone settled down, he said, "My name is Kinko Kurosawa, and I am new here, coming from Kuzaki-*ji* in Nagasaki. I will be your instructor today. Let us begin by blowing *ro* as loudly as you can for ten minutes."

The students looked confused by this direction and cast furtive, questioning glances at one another. Kinko picked up his *shakuhachi* and began to blow, long and loud. Gradually, the students followed his example; at which point, he put his flute down and wandered among the rows, listening. He adjusted one man's posture here and someone else's instrument position there.

He walked past two burly samurai, who did not appear to be taking the exercise particularly seriously. He stopped before the first one. "If you are as pathetic a warrior as you are a musician, you may not know this..." As he spoke, the man tensed, looking furious, "...but a good strong breath is fundamental to *budo*. If you blow on the exercise field or—even worse—on the battlefield, like you are now, you are a dead man. Blow your *shakuhachi* like you are striking with a sword. Blow with energy. Blow with commitment."

He turned away, ignoring the man's red, angry face. Speaking to no one in particular, Kurosawa raised his voice, "You are not here this morning to learn a piece of music. You are not here to become musicians. You are here because this spiritual practice makes us better Buddhists, better warriors, better people. If you are only here to learn this flute," he raised his *shakuhachi* in his hand, "you are wasting your time and mine.

"You are here so that this flute can teach you to be a better monk. I am not your teacher; this," again, he held the *shakuhachi* aloft, "is your teacher. Bring to this practice everything that you bring to your weapons training as a samurai. Then you will be ready to learn." This captured their attention. And after continuing their *ro-buki* for the proscribed ten minutes, he began to teach *Kyorei*.

The rest of the lessons that day went smoothly and Kurosawa enjoyed both the work and the people. The level of activity in the temple surprised him, never seeing so many Fuke gathered in one place. It all felt so busy, not like the slower, more contemplative pace of the other temples he visited.

His fellow residents accepted his presence and position without question, and over the following days, he began to develop relationships with many of the monks. He enjoyed the daily routine and found the quality of the martial training exceptional. On his first day there, the *jo* instructor complimented him on his expertise with the staff and invited him to assist with teaching, a responsibility that Kinko gladly accepted.

Temple policy permitted the better musicians within the community to practice with a teacher of their choice. It did not take too many days for Kurosawa's reputation to spread. He had barely settled into the rhythm of the temple before his teaching schedule was full, and he needed to teach the more advanced students in small groups. If this caused any resentment with the other instructors, it was not noticeable. They were all as pleasant and collegial as possible in their morning meetings.

While many monks were fine players, the majority—*rōnin* waiting for a new post—possessed barely any ability to play at all. These "temporary" monks, as Kurosawa termed them to himself, were required to attend the large group lessons in the morning. The temple structure and discipline provided its members with an implicit recommendation unavailable to the average *rōnin* seeking employment. And the "temporary" monks knew that the harder they worked, the more quickly they would find employment with some lord, who looked to the staff to provide recommendations.

The frequency of lords seeking new retainers was one of the reasons for the overall busyness of the temple. Throughout each day, messengers from the estates in Edo arrived seeking recommendations for samurai. Occasionally a lord would arrive in person, accompanied by his retinue, for a first-hand look at samurai for hire.

In addition to these visits, Kurosawa noticed a significant number of visitors and messengers bearing the triple hollyhock crest of the shogun. Many of these messengers were welcomed at the gates with familiarity, making their way directly to the administration building—and often to the office of the abbot himself. This traffic surprised Kurosawa, though he did not give it too much thought.

. . .

A few weeks after Kurosawa joined the temple, the abbot's assistant attended the instructors' morning meeting. He patiently sat while the teachers discussed the playing of various monks. Only when they began to discuss the day's teaching schedule did he speak. "Brothers, the abbot has requested that Kurosawa-san travel to Reihō-*ji* for a few days and get to know their instructors as well. Please arrange the teaching schedule to accommodate for his absence."

Preparing for this trip, Kurosawa was again surprised at the distance he needed to travel. Having heard all his life as a *komusō* that Ichigetsu-*ji* and Reihō-*ji* were both located in Edo, he expected them to be very close to one another. In actuality, Reihō-*ji* was nearly fifty miles distant, taking the better part of three days to walk. As it happened, two other monks were traveling to their sister temple that day, so Kurosawa joined their party to make the trip.

It was a pleasant journey, and Kinko enjoyed getting to know his traveling companions, as well as learning the route from experienced brethren. On the afternoon of their second day, it began to rain, but it was the light rain of early spring and comfortable for walking.

Arriving at Reihō-*ji* on the third day, Kurosawa found a more modest-sized temple, much like his home temple in Nagasaki. Being farther out from the center of Edo, it was a quieter setting and far less busy than Ichigetsu-*ji*. Kinko laughed, remembering that Nagate Chikuzen's quest to Kokoku-*ji* was to uncover some history that would give Reihō-*ji* an enhanced status relative to its sister temple. That was a vain and hopeless quest, Kinko decided.

Immediately upon their arrival, all three of the monks made their way to greet the abbot. He was a diminutive man who seemed edgy and ready to take offense at the brothers from his sister/rival temple. Nonetheless, he graciously welcomed them and invited Kurosawa to join the teaching staff meeting the following morning. In answer to his inquiry, Kinko discovered that his friend Nagate Chikuzen now oversaw the work of the temple library. After following his colleagues to the guest quarters, where he deposited his pack, Kinko hurried off in search of his comrade.

To his surprise, the modest complex of Reihō-*ji* housed a very large and beautiful library. He found several monks there copying out sutra scrolls—a common spiritual discipline among Buddhists—as well as other documents. Chikuzen appeared before too long, and his face lit up like a lamp on a darkened night upon seeing his friend.

He immediately abandoned his duties and took Kinko's arm to guide him back to his office in the bowels of the library building. "It's so good to see you, Kurasawa," his friend exuded. "I thought about you often on the long trip from Kokoku-*ji*. Your advice about the manuscripts, by the way, was exactly right. I did not mention anything of my discoveries in my official report, but verbally mentioned them to a senior *jūshoku* priest on the abbot's council. For my discretion, I assume—and also because I did manage to uncover a few other items of interest—shortly afterward the abbot promoted me to this post, heading the library!"

"Congratulations, Chikuzen. That is good news indeed and well-deserved. This is the perfect place for you. Please show me around your domain."

And with that, Chikuzen led Kinko on a tour of the library, followed by a tour of the temple complex. It was a wonderful place with beautiful old buildings and a closer-knit community than Ichigetsu-*ji*. At dinner, after the evening *zazen* session, Chikuzen introduced Kurosawa to many of the other monks and priests.

In the morning, Kurosawa met with the three senior music

instructors and listened to their planning for the day's *shakuhachi* teaching. He taught some of the classes himself, to get to know the monks and to assess the temple's teaching structures. By the second day, the other teachers deferred to Kurosawa as the *de facto* leader, and two of the three asked him if they might have some private lessons; a request he was happy to honor.

After dinner at the close of his third day, Kurosawa sat on the porch of the guest quarters with Nagate Chikuzen who told him, "You have made quite an impression on the musicians here, Kurosawa. I am so glad that you took the time to visit with us."

"I'm glad to have been able to catch up with you, Chikuzen, and am delighted at the role you have carved out for yourself. And while I could easily stay, I suspect that I am needed at Ichigetsu-*ji*."

"I understand; but the more regularly you visit, the happier that we shall be here."

The trip back to Ichigetsu-*ji* was pleasant and uneventful. On the third day of the trip, he took a slight detour to visit Koji Yamada and the Misawa family. He spent some time helping Yamada in his workshop and was again struck by the skill of his craftsmanship. He correctly calculated how long he would need to stay working there to garner an invitation to dinner, and the five of them spent another wonderful evening playing music together.

Upon his return to Ichigetsu-*ji*, he was directed to report to the abbot. This was the first time meeting alone since their initial introduction. Ganryo Shuza was in good spirits as he welcomed Kurosawa into his office and invited him to take a seat. "Tell me about your trip to Reihō-*ji*," he commanded. Kurosawa reported on his teaching and his general impressions of the temple. Throughout his account, the abbot sagely nodded his head.

At the end of the narrative, the abbot sat thinking for a few minutes, before saying, "You have done well over the past month, Kurosawa; better than I had hoped. You have also impressed many of the members of my council, both with your musicianship and your impact on our community.

"After consultation with several temple leaders, I would like to invite you to play for the full council tomorrow afternoon as part of our discernment process in choosing a head instructor." The abbot said these last words very formally, as though they were part of an official proclamation. When he finished, he smiled broadly at Kurosawa. "We're looking forward to our time with you," he added, in a more friendly tone.

The time crawled until the next evening's meeting. That morning, all the teachers wished him well with genuine enthusiasm and members of the abbot's council sat in on some of his lessons. Finally, at the appointed time—his teaching *shakuhachi* in hand—he entered the administrative building and was ushered upstairs to a small room down the hall from the main council chamber. He did not have to wait too long before he was summoned to the chamber itself, where he was greeted by a line of the senior priests, sitting unsmiling before him.

"Please sit, Kurosawa," said the secretary of the council. "We are grateful for your presence with us and eager to hear you perform. Please play us something."

Even at this distance from Kōya-san, Kurosawa flinched slightly on behalf of his friend Fumon Tanaka at the term "perform." He had already decided that he would play *Mukaiji* for them. More than anything, he wanted—he needed—to play this piece like he used to play it back at Kuzaki-*ji*. He wanted it to be flawless, beautiful. He wanted them to hear it and know—know deep in their souls—that this was how the piece was meant to be played. He wanted their souls to sing, to rest, to rise to the Buddha. He wanted them to praise him.

But he also realized that he could not. That would be a betrayal of his entire journey. If he played that way, the last months would be in vain: all the wisdom gleaned painfully on his knees in the freshly fallen snow; all work to find himself, to understand, to gaze into the dark shadow places of his soul. All that, gone. Lost to a single moment of ego.

And so he played "Flute on a Misty Sea." Played it as only he could now. Played with the full awareness of who he was. Played so that every foible, every flaw, every shred that made him himself was on full display. Played as Brother Tanaka taught him to play. Played as Brother Kendo would want him to play. Played as only Kinko Kurosawa could play, because it captured all of who he was. It was excruciating. It was freeing. And as it was happening, he saw all his dreams plunge off of a cliff into an abyss whose bottom was dark and unknown. As he played, he closed his eyes, not wanting to see the looks on the faces of the men before him.

When he finished, an awkward silence filled the room. This was not what the abbot and council expected to hear—wanted to hear. This was raw, and passionate, and vulnerable, and true. Observing their faces, Kinko saw that some were shocked, some offended, some uncomfortable, some mesmerized. It was not the music or the teacher that they expected, and they didn't know how to respond.

Finally, the abbot, having looked around the room to see if anyone wanted to speak, said, "Thank you, Kurosawa, for sharing with us. If you will follow the attendant, we have much to discuss."

The attendant directed Kurosawa to the small room down

the hall from the abbot's council chamber, where he sat on a *zafu* cushion. The attendant left him there for some time and eventually brought him a pot of green tea. Kurosawa could hear the conversation down the hall ebb and flow like the rhythm of the sea, sometimes quite animated and at others a gentle murmur.

As the evening progressed, Kurosawa heard the bell for dinner and the distant babble of the monks moving towards the refectory. The attendant slid open the door and knelt, then said, "The abbot has instructed me to send you to dinner and evening meditation. He will summon you tomorrow."

This was not what Kurosawa expected. He knew in his core that if he had arrived at Ichigetsu-*ji* as the musician he was when he left Kyūshū, he would have been embraced with open arms by the temple's grateful leadership. He also knew that he was a far better musician—and a far better monk—now than when his journey started.

He anticipated that the way that he played would make some of the priests uncomfortable. He fully expected that some would raise objections to his appointment. But—if he was honest—he also hoped that the quality of his playing would shine through so clearly that it would sweep away any opposition. He did not want there to be any doubt that he deserved the position. Frustrated and embarrassed, he made his way to the dining hall. He noted that none of the abbot's council joined the community for dinner.

He slept poorly that night and arose long before dawn. With the rest of the temple still in slumber's tender embrace, he made his way to the training field. There, with his staff, he began the *suburi* practice that had been such an unwavering daily touchstone during his time on Kōya-san. Over and over, the staff rose and fell with a gentle hiss.

His body was sweaty and aching by the time he trudged to

the temple baths and relaxed for a few minutes in the scalding hot water. But his mind was clear and peaceful. He dressed in time to join the bleary-eyed monks for the morning *zazen* session followed by breakfast.

Shortly after breakfast, the abbot's attendant found Kurosawa and said, "The abbot would like to see you now." Kurosawa followed the young man back to the abbot's quarters and climbed the steps to the council chamber. Upon entering, he was surprised to find the abbot sitting alone, waiting for him.

"Kurosawa, please join me." He motioned to an empty cushion next to him. "I am sorry to keep you waiting for so long." He paused before continuing. "Truthfully, you were not quite what any of us were expecting last night. And a few of us were not sure what to make of you. Can you talk to me about your style of playing?"

After his experiences at Ichigetsu-*ji* over the past month, Kurosawa was comfortable sharing with the abbot and launched into the story of his journey from Kyoto to Kōya-san and some of the things that he learned from Fumon Tanaka and Akira Kendo. He talked about his own journey of self-understanding and the quest for Buddha-hood through one sound.

The abbot listened without interrupting. Kinko appreciated the silence of the older man, recognizing again the wisdom of one willing to listen. Finally, the abbot responded. "I am grateful for the honesty of your sharing and for the wisdom that you have absorbed along your journey. It may need some tempering to fit in here at Ichigetsu-*ji*. But I think that you bring the gifts that our temple needs right now."

The air seemed to hang heavy with significance. Then he continued. "I would like to reinstate you as a *jūshoku* priest and invite you to take a seat on our council as head music instructor."

RESTORATION

Kurosawa settled into his new role as easily as he settled into his new rooms. All the other instructors appeared to acknowledge his role without hesitation or resentment. He took charge of the morning meetings and immediately broadened the conversation beyond scheduling. He raised questions about the best way to teach the large numbers of beginners. They explored how to cultivate the better students to create a level of junior instructors. They deliberated about including the *honkyoku* from other temples into a new teaching curriculum.

Shortly after he moved into his new role, he was summoned to the abbot's office. Ganryo Shuza greeted Kurosawa with a broad smile and patted him companionably on the shoulder as he invited him to sit. "Well, Kurosawa, you seem to be well-ensconced in your position. Everything I hear seems very positive."

"Thank you, Lord Abbot."

"As you consider restructuring the music teaching here at

the temple, I thought that it might be useful for you to hear about the reasons that I invited you here originally."

Kurosawa waited expectantly.

"As the largest and most prominent Fuke temple in the land, we get many more monks than anywhere else, both entering and leaving the order. The shogun—who I have had the honor of meeting—sees our order as one of the best tools at his disposal for creating structure and oversight for the many *rōnin* that range across our land. The *bakufu* funnels as many of them as possible to Fuke temples—this one primarily—to keep them under better control. While that is useful for the *bakufu*, it makes it very difficult for us, in that we have a constant stream of samurai flowing through our gates, many of whom have little real interest in monastic life.

"I believe that the best way to instill both discipline and refinement is through music. I have, as you know, some very strong players, but we needed a real master musician to raise the overall standard of our music program and give it a comprehensive structure. I sent letters around the country, and you were recommended by several sources. I am pleased to see that they were right: you bring to our music program exactly what I needed."

As the abbot talked, Kurosawa found himself uneasy that the needs of the *bakufu* seemed to dominate the abbot's priorities, but he appreciated the desire to provide structure and discipline to a large, revolving assemblage of samurai. A different abbot might place more emphasis on the spiritual growth of the community, but spiritual matters were—in Kurosawa's experience—generally not the forte of the leaders of religious organizations.

The two men continued to talk into the early evening about Kurosawa's ideas for developing the music program and the abbot's various suggestions. The abbot was, by his own admission, not a strong musician and deferred to Kurosawa on the musical issues, while he kept Kurosawa focused on the goal of engaging and cultivating large numbers of samurai.

Over the weeks that followed Kurosawa continued this strategizing work with the help of his senior teachers. He also gave them individual lessons for their own musical and spiritual growth. At the same time, he assisted with the *jo* training on the exercise fields, which both allowed him to get to know the monks better and gain some additional credibility with the samurai who were newer and valued martial strength over musicianship.

Kurosawa grew in confidence in his role at Ichigetsu-*ji* as he established new friendships among the priests and senior resident monks. His quarters were comfortable. His position allowed him to set his own schedule. He was deferred to. He was flattered.

He enjoyed working with the abbot and his council. While the conversations were too often dominated by *bakufu* politics, he appreciated the opportunity to shape the life of the temple community. The other members of the council seemed more world-weary and cynical than he might have hoped, but that did not keep Kurosawa from contributing his share of cynical, world-weary comments in the discussions.

In his more genuine moments, he acknowledged that he was not practicing with Tanaka's great *shakuhachi*, and he knew that the reason for this was his fear that the people around him would not understand the discipline's significance. He slept as late as the other monks and did not practice *suburi* to keep his body honed. And while he advocated *ro-buki* practice for the other monks, he was not doing it himself.

But—he reasoned—these spiritual disciplines would return in time. Now, his priority was to establish himself. He needed to build credibility with the resident staff of the temple. There was much work to do. And, after all, hadn't he earned a little respite from the heavy discipline of Kōya-san? That kind of rigor would set him apart here in Edo in a way that would not be helpful to the work he was doing. The other monks would perceive him as pretentious and overweening.

On a glorious spring morning with the gardens flowering and birds singing in perfect concinnity, Kurosawa was summoned again to the office of the abbot. Kurosawa slid open the door to the office and knelt before Ganryo Shuza. "What can I do for you, my Lord Abbot?" he asked.

"I have a rare honor for you, Kurosawa. Your musical gifts have come to the attention of Lord Omura of the shogun's high council. And he has requested that you come and teach a *shakuhachi* lesson to a group of his retainers." This was a request so unusual that Kurosawa was not sure what to make of it.

"My Lord Abbot," he inquired, bowing, "why does Lord Omura desire his retainers to play *shakuhachi*?"

"He has a great love for the instrument; that is enough for you to know. I am surprised that you would hesitate to share our great gift with a broader audience."

"I do not hesitate, exactly. I am merely surprised and curious."

Ganryo Shuza reflected for a few moments. "Kurosawa, Lord Omura is high in the esteem of the shogun. His favor will yield great benefits to this temple and our order. It could also occasion great benefits for you personally. You have come to his attention. He could bring you to the shogun's attention. This could be a great boon to you and your family. Please, just do as I ask."

Kurosawa bowed and left the abbot's office.

He left the next morning with the group of monks assigned to play in Edo for the next few days. Not knowing how long he would be, he stowed a few things in his pack, and—on impulse —stuck in Tanaka's *shakuhachi*, which he had not picked up since he had arrived at the temple. A pleasant walk brought the group to the city by the early afternoon. Kurosawa made his way to the neighborhood of *daimyo* residences immediately east of Edo Castle. A few questions of passing samurai directed him to the estate of Lord Omura.

It was a massive compound surrounded by high, white-washed walls. The soldiers clearly expected Kurosawa and immediately ushered him through the front gate, from which a samurai guard led him to the main living quarters. The estate was as well fortified as a minor castle with a large number of guard barracks, stables, and training facilities.

He entered the main house and left his pack in the care of the attendant at the door. Another attendant led Kinko up to a second-floor room where Lord Omura was meeting with several senior advisors. Lord Omura was a man of modest height, but broad in the chest, and rather broad in the belly as well. He was bald with a purple birthmark on the left side of his head, just encroaching on his face.

Acknowledging Kurosawa's presence with a nod, he finished up his business with the advisors and dismissed them. Then, facing Kurosawa, he smiled with practiced ease. "I am honored to have a teacher of your standing to work with a few of my retainers," he said smoothly. "They have received some *shakuhachi* training, but need refining. Please let me know if there is anything that you need from me." He bowed and nodded to the assistant who led Kurosawa out of the room.

Kurosawa followed the man down the hall to another large audience chamber where the assistant invited Kurosawa to sit. "I will collect the retainers whom Lord Omura would like you to teach," he said and backed out of the room. Kurosawa sat appreciating the elegance of the room, and shortly the attendant arrived with six imposing-looking samurai.

As each of the men entered the room, Kurosawa took note of their powerful builds and graceful motion. Each of these men, he immediately recognized, was an accomplished warrior. They all knelt in *seiza* before him. As soon as they settled, the samurai on the end—their obvious leader—spoke.

"We are honored to have you here to teach us, *Shishō*. My colleagues and I are eager to learn. We have all received some teaching, so you may dispense with the rudiments."

Kurosawa bowed and replied, "It is my honor to be in this illustrious estate as your teacher. Let us begin by blowing *ro* for a few minutes." He began to blow and the others followed suit. They could all play the note, but their playing was indifferent. After listening to each one and making minor corrections in posture or embrasure, Kurosawa said, "Let us practice *Kyorei*," whereupon he began teaching the venerable old piece.

To his surprise, the samurai engaged with tepid enthusiasm; all the energy fled the room. They followed his instruction for some minutes, but without any apparent interest. He had just made it through a basic description of each of the phrases when the leader ventured, "This is very helpful, *Shishō*, but I hoped that you might teach my men *yobitake-uketake*."

Kurosawa stopped. Everything made sense now. *Yobitake-uketake* was a piece without any interesting historical or musical merit. It was important for one reason and one reason only: it allowed true *komusō* to recognize one another on the road. The men sitting before him were Tokugawa spies, preparing to travel under the guise of *komusō* monks. They needed to know *yobitake-uketake* in case they met any other *komusō* on their travels.

Kurosawa smiled blandly at the leader. "I'm sorry, but that

is a piece that we are only allowed to teach to *komusō* in the temple. And, honestly, it's not an interesting piece musically. If your men are not enjoying *Kyorei*, I'd be happy to teach them something else."

The leader's face tightened, and his mask of congeniality fell away. "I'm sure that our lord was quite explicit with your abbot about what he desired. *Yobitake-uketake* is what we need to learn. Please teach."

The situation was quickly progressing from uncomfortable to dangerous. He could not confront six armed warriors, much less in their own lord's estate. He needed to act quickly and decisively. Standing up, *shakuhachi* in hand, Kurosawa replied to the leader, "If this was the understanding, I will need to hear it directly from the mouth of Lord Omura. Please excuse me for a moment. I will be right back."

As he stood, the leader started to stand as well. Kurosawa put up a hand to indicate that he did not require accompaniment. Before the other man could speak or consult with the other samurai, Kurosawa quickly strode from the room, and down the hall in the direction of Lord Omura's audience chamber. He did not go into the chamber, of course, but—nodding to the guards—turned right and walked down the stairs.

He reclaimed his pack and exited the building. Striding purposefully, without looking to either side, he made his way through the estate complex and out the front gates into the crowded boulevard. Feeling momentarily safe, he took a few deep breaths and looked around to make sure no one followed. He walked to the end of the block and turned down a side street, all the while keeping an eye out for any pursuers. Unsure where to go or what to do, he made his way back towards Ichigetsu-*ji*.

He wandered in the general direction of the temple, avoiding the main roads, in case Omura's retainers pursued him. After he had walked an hour or so—without being aware of deciding to do so—he left the route to the temple and turned towards the house of the Misawa family. He was not sure why or who he wanted to speak with, but it felt like the place he needed to be.

A brilliant orange sun hung low on the horizon as he turned into their gate. Setsu gathered herbs from the garden plot out front and smiled broadly as she ushered him into the house. Shino was busy cooking and insisted that he join them for dinner. She called into the workshop, "Shimada, go invite Koji to dinner; tell him that our friend Kurosawa will be joining us."

Soon, the five of them had gathered around the low table for a merry dinner. After some pleasant banter, Shino turned to Kinko. "It is always a joy to have you with us, Kurosawa, but you seem preoccupied; is there something on your mind?" Kinko took a deep breath and then launched into his story. Afterwards, the table was quiet and thoughtful.

Koji Yamada finally broke the silence, "Well, this never happened to me, but it doesn't surprise me much. Our relationship with the *bakufu* has always been too comfortable and too much in the *bakufu's* interest for my taste. My personal feeling is that we should give up some of the perks of the connection and place a higher value on our independence."

Shimada Misawa chuckled, "It makes me glad that the *koto* is not a more portable instrument."

"But what should I do?" Kinko wondered aloud to the room in general. "I'm sure there'll be hell to pay when I get back to the temple, and what happens when the request comes again?" He put his head in his hands in despair. There was an awkward silence in the room.

"I wish I had some useful advice to offer you, my friend," consoled Yamada. "But the truth is that I was never particularly comfortable with life in the temple, and I was never as invested in it as you, so leaving was easy."

After a few more minutes, Shimada suggested, "Why don't we play some music together and see if something comes to us."

The rest of the evening drifted away in a current of music, not as energetic and boisterous as their previous evenings together, but—for Kinko, at least—beautiful and healing.

Kinko spent the night on a futon in Yamada's workshop. When the two men were alone, Yamada said to him, "Kurosawa, I was glad to see you today for my own personal reasons. I know that we do not know each other well, but I need to make a trip north to see my family in Mutsu Province—where we have a strong *shakuhachi* history. I don't know how long I'll be gone and would appreciate it if you could find someone connected to the temple who might want to rent my room for an interim period. I can't afford to pay Misawa for the space, but I don't want to lose it either. Can you make some inquiries?"

"I'd be happy to, Yamada. I'll let you know what I find out."

The next morning, he joined the family for breakfast and then sipped tea with Shino, while Setsu opened the shop and Shimada cloistered himself in the workshop.

"Perhaps it is none of my business, Kurosawa," she began, "but I am curious about what you were hoping for in life at Ichigetsu-*ji*? I recall your telling us on your first visit that several monks warned you about the challenges you might face here, and yet you came. Why would you do that rather than simply stay in a position in Nagasaki that you knew and loved?" Her eyes, locked on his, invited authenticity.

Kinko sighed. "Well, staying in Nagasaki was not an option for me." And with that, he plunged into the story of his expulsion from Kuzaki-*ji* and the journey to Edo—this time with less focus on the events and more focus on what he had learned about himself. Shino listened carefully without interruption.

At the end of the tale, she sat for a few moments, eventually commenting, "So it sounds as if you were more ambivalent about temple life than I understood before."

"What do you mean?"

"Well, from what you've just described, you didn't particularly like your abbot in Nagasaki and found his lieutenants smug and arrogant. At the same time, you felt superior to the other monks who seemed 'less religious' than you and to your peers who were not as intellectually or musically gifted as you. And to cap it all off, it sounds like your best friend was a Christian."

Kinko reflected quietly.

"I'm not trying to be difficult," Shino added. "I'm just wondering if your affair might have been—to some degree—an expression of self-sabotage? And, likewise, it seems as though your current dilemma stems from the tension between what you might have reasonably expected and what you were hoping for, despite warnings to the contrary."

Kinko nodded. "That and my own vanity: thinking that my talent—and the work that I did on Kōya-san—could transform the situation."

Shino's laugh was as clear as a spring brook dancing over a stone bed. "Well, that's a common foible among gifted people; and living in a household of gifted people, I know that one all too well. Can I offer you some advice?"

"Of course; I think that's why I'm here."

"I think so, too. Gifts from the Buddha are rarely offered randomly. You have received many gifts over the course of your journey here during the past year, and I think that those gifts were intended to prepare you for the questions that you now face. What have you learned about yourself and your art that can guide you at this point?"

"I have learned an enormous amount about my art, but I'm not sure that will help me in navigating temple politics."

"But you didn't just learn about your art: you learned that your playing teaches you about yourself. What is your playing teaching you now?"

Kinko walked slowly through the quiet morning streets on the way back to the temple. Anxious about what he might face when he returned, he forced himself to reflect on Shino Misawa's questions. What was his playing teaching him now? It did not feel like it was teaching him anything, and maybe that was an answer in itself. His thoughts fell on Tanaka's *shakuhachi,* unplayed since arriving at Ichigetsu-*ji.* "Why?" he wondered aloud.

He knew the answer: because he risked embarrassment. And he had justified this affront to his old teacher by believing that once he "established" himself, he could risk playing as he knew that he should. In his interview with the council, he had risked sharing a little of himself through his playing, but only a little. He was still performing. He was still unwilling to risk his "reputation" by sharing himself, who he was now after Koya-san, in front of this community of relative strangers. Perhaps, as Akira Kendo suggested, his newfound insights were not well enough integrated into who he was.

As he neared the precincts of the temple, he felt the hair on the back of his neck prickle. Foreboding lay thick and heavy in the air. He took off his *tengai*—feeling the need for peripheral vision —and stuck it in his pack, from which he drew Tanaka's long *shakuhachi.* He played it as he walked slowly down the street. In the middle of the block, he stopped. This was the place, the center. He looked carefully around. A moment passed. Another.

Then two figures detached themselves from a darkened doorway to his right, both carrying the two swords of samurai. Cloth masks covered the lower parts of their faces, but Kurosawa immediately recognized the cat-like movements of the men from Lord Omura's estate. The height of the first one matched that of the group's leader. In his monk's robes and carrying a pack, Kinko could never outrun the two unencumbered men. He stood still and centered his breath, sliding one foot slightly behind the other.

The two men approached, their hands resting lightly on the hilts of their swords. Kinko let his pack slide off his back to his feet. He held Tanaka's long flute in front of him with both hands like a *katana* and waited for the two to come within striking range. There was no way to win such a contest, but Tanaka's *shakuhachi* was as nearly as long and heavy as a *katana,* and a mid-day fight on a trafficked street would draw soldiers quickly. It was his only hope.

The two men appeared to make the same calculation. "Your instincts have saved you today, *komusō,*" said the familiar voice. "But you made an enemy yesterday, and you would do well to rectify your mistake. You may not have a second chance." Then, without another word, both men turned away and sauntered down the street, pulling away their masks after turning their heads.

When Kurosawa reached the temple shortly thereafter, he immediately sought out the abbot. He was ushered into the abbot's office, where he found Ganryo Shuza furious. "What the hell happened at Lord Omura's?" he barked as soon as Kurosawa seated himself. Kinko told him the whole story, adding, "I did not talk to Lord Omura directly, assuming that he would repeat what his head spy told me, and I was unwilling to teach *yobitake-uketake* without having a conversation with you." He bowed. "Is it possible that Lord Omura misunder-stood the nature of that music?"

The abbot rolled his eyes, as his face slightly softened. "No Kurosawa, Lord Omura understands perfectly well the purpose of *yobitake-uketake*; that is why he wants the shogun's agents to know it. He wants them to be able to travel disguised as *komusō*."

"But why would you allow him to violate the integrity of our order in that way?" asked Kinko, shocked to hear the abbot speak so directly.

"Because we benefit by keeping the *bakufu* happy, and this is part of the price we pay."

"I know that the shogun's agents sometimes masquerade as *komusō*—I have reprimanded one of them myself—and I know there is nothing we can do to prevent that; but why would we facilitate it?"

Becoming exasperated, Shuza snapped back, "Because when the shogun wants something, the shogun gets it. You can take a principled stand, but then you get replaced—or arrested, or killed—and someone less principled will do what the shogun wants anyway. That's the way power works."

"How do we know that this is what the shogun wants? That it's not a whim of Lord Omura? Is there a way of appealing our case?"

The abbot shook his head. "That's not the way Edo works, Kurosawa. If I possessed other high-placed benefactors who could argue against Omura on the shogun's inner council, that might be possible. But I don't, and it would involve expending an enormous amount of political capital to make it happen. And Lord Omura would just find some other way to get what he wants. The harsh reality is that the integrity of our insignifi-cant Buddhist sect does not count for much in Edo Castle."

"Well, as insignificant as it is, my integrity means something to me," Kurosawa reacted, his voice rising. "You can find some other teacher to do Lord Omura's dirty work."

"How very convenient for you," the abbot sarcastically replied. "Our order may be morally compromised, but at least you don't have to dirty your hands with it; that must feel very comfortable. But it is not that simple either. You are our senior instructor. Lord Omura knows that and asked specifically for your help. To send him a lower-ranking teacher would be a direct affront. And when this is over, will it really matter who teaches the shogun's agents? They will be taught. They will masquerade at *komusō* monks. And life will move on."

The abbot's face took on a benevolent expression. "Kurosawa, do you not realize what an opportunity is before you? Being of service to Lord Omura will open countless doors to you. It could even result in being able to play for the shogun himself. You could move in political circles beyond your wildest dreams with opportunities for preferment for both you and your family members. This could be a whole new chapter in the history of the Kurosawa family."

KINTSUGI

A deep mantle of despair settled on Kurosawa as he left the abbot's office. This whole journey—all the music he learned from the temples along the way, all his work on Kōya-san—was now to be prostituted for political gain. He thought of his father and laughed: this would be an answered prayer for the elder Kurosawa. Looking around at the monks bustling from one duty to the next—happy, fulfilled—he felt deeply alone.

Without a clear direction, Kinko found himself walking up the huge wooden staircase of the main hall, the *butsuden*. In a Zen temple, this shrine to the Buddha was less frequented than the zendo where the daily meditations took place, and Kinko found himself alone in the vast, open chamber before the statue of the Buddha.

Kneeling, he rested for some time and let his mind calm and his breath lengthen. Slowly, he brought the *shakuhachi* to his lips and played *Mukaiji*. He played with power and control and passion. He poured all of himself into the music and when

SONG OF THE SAMURAI

completed, he was empty and sat without thought or feeling. Simply present in the moment.

He rose with a sudden sense of clarity. Leaving the *butsuden*, he walked over to the senior staff quarters and collected some of his things in his pack. Walking down the hallway to one of his instructor's rooms, he knocked and slid the door open. "I am going to take a few days and check in on our colleagues at Reihō-*ji*," he said. "Could you coordinate classes while I'm gone?"

"Of course, *Shishō*. May Buddha go with you."

"May he, indeed," Kurosawa answered.

Passing the administration building on his way out of the temple, he asked the attendant on duty to inform the abbot that he was traveling to Reihō-*ji* for the next few days on a supervisory visit. Strictly speaking, he should have sought approval for such a trip first, but Kurosawa did not anticipate the abbot would object. And—in any case—he was in no mood for more conversation with Ganryo Shuza.

The journey to Reihō-*ji* would be a welcome chance to clear his head and to get the advice of his friend, Nagate Chikuzen. The afternoon was overcast and humid as Kinko departed the temple gate. It was late enough in the afternoon that it might have made better sense for him to stay the night and leave early the next morning. But Kinko was anxious to put some miles between himself and the abbot.

He set off down the road, passing through streets of bustling people as they talked and laughed in tea houses and called to friends and neighbors. The spring had been a cool one, and the cherry blossoms were late; but as he walked, he noticed that they were on the verge of blooming. He took his time walking, aware that the time to reflect might be more valuable than a quick journey.

As evening fell, he looked for some place to stay and found a modest-looking inn to his liking. He dined in the main room and spent the evening quietly sipping sake and watching the flirting, arguing, and laughing of his fellow travelers and the locals. It was calming, and he tried to keep from dwelling on the problems before him, trusting that on some unconscious level, his mind worked on the problem.

The next two days passed easily, and he arrived at Reihō-*ji* by mid-morning on the fourth day to the greetings of many friends. He spent the day helping with the teaching duties of the temple and joined the community for evening *zazen* and dinner. After dinner, Nagate Chikuzen brought out a pot of tea and sat with Kinko in the cool evening twilight. "Well, my friend, I am delighted to see you again, but it feels like this visit is more than just part of the regular teaching cycle."

"It is, Chikuzen. I'm frustrated and discouraged, and I'm not sure what to do about it. I need the advice of a wise friend." And so Kinko launched into the saga of the past few days. Chikuzen listened closely and expressed appropriate alarm at the encounters with Lord Omura's men and outrage at the abbot's response.

After Kinko finished, Chikuzen said, "What a discouraging story! Although, honestly, not a surprising one. Having spent a lot of time poring over the early documents of our order, there has always been an unhealthy comity between our order and the *bakufu*. It stems from our early leaders' deep need for legitimization within the Buddhist community and the shogun exploiting that need.

"In a broader context, throughout Japanese history, you find the leaders of Buddhist orders getting deeply involved in the political machinations of their times, almost always to the detriment of the religious life of their communities. Despite his own royal lineage, the Buddha always eschewed political power and instructed his disciples to surrender all signs of social status and rank."

Chikuzen paused for a moment, appearing to let the fragrant spring evening wash over him.

"Abbots—particularly abbots of major temples—are men of great rank and power, and most are willing to make significant moral compromises to maintain or enhance that status. Most—I hope—do this with good intentions, to further the work of the temple or the order, but their moral compromises degrade the integrity of our community."

"That has been my experience as well," Kinko admitted, "though Minzan Zenji in Kyoto might be an exception."

"So the question for you is: what role do you want to play in that system? There are people of great integrity who advise their abbots and try to ameliorate the impact of politics on temple life; I hope that I am one of those. There are others—like your friend Fumon Tanaka—who choose to never compromise themselves and eschew the politics of the temple entirely. Where are you in this picture? Where do you feel led? Where do you feel closest to the Buddha? Where do you find joy?"

Kinko looked at his friend with new eyes. For most of their friendship, he had felt like the senior partner. But Chikuzen was the teacher now, summing up with great clarity the struggle he faced.

"From a selfish standpoint," Chikuzen added, "I hope that you will stay in your role. I would love to keep you as a colleague, and I know that our instructors here are already growing under your mentorship. But please don't interpret that as pressure from me. You need to follow the path before you."

Kinko smiled and nodded. "I have enjoyed working with them and teaching them. They are fine musicians and fine people. I would like to not give that up." Having spoken what needed to be spoken, the two friends let the conversation drift along different avenues, each taking comfort in the other's presence.

Kurosawa stayed for two more days, while he taught and reflected in the quieter space of Reihō-ji. The morning he left, a gentle rain began to fall. Grey clouds blanketed the sky, and the riotous chatter of early morning birds filled the warm air.

Chikuzen walked him to the gate. "I will pray for your enlightenment on this issue, my brother. Come here when you need to." They bowed, and Kinko set out for Ichigetsu-ji.

The rain was soft but steady throughout the morning, and Kinko played Ikkei's *shakuhachi* while he walked. He stopped around mid-day on a more densely populated stretch of road to collect alms. On the second day out, he turned south to find his way back to the Misawa family home. Shino greeted him in the front shop, took his wet outer garments, and invited him in for tea. He could hear Setsu teaching a *koto* student in the back practice room and caught a glimpse of Shimada in his workshop.

As soon as her daughter finished teaching and returned to the shop, Shino ushered Kinko upstairs to the residential part of the house, where she made a pot of green tea for the two of them. When they had settled, she offered him the tea in a small ceramic cup with a deep, rustic brown glaze. The cup looked old, drawn from a pool of timeless memory. Down one side, circling the base and rising up the other side, was a thin line of gold binding pieces that had been broken.

Kinko sipped the tea and then examined the cup closely. "This repair technique is called *kintsugi*, isn't it?" he asked her.

"Yes. It's very beautiful, is it not?"

"It is. I have heard of the technique before, but never seen it done. Honestly, it always seemed like a counterintuitive craft: to repair a piece of ordinary pottery with gold adhesive: one spends more money on the repair than one would need to spend on a new cup. The cup is still broken, and the repair highlights the break itself."

"But that is the point!" exclaimed Shino. "Binding the pieces together in gold is a way of honoring the original work, as well as the history that has brought it to this point. This cup was my grandmother's. She gave it to my mother, who passed it on to me. Early in our marriage, Shimada broke the cup. I was furious with him, of course; but if I had thrown it away and bought a new one, all that history would be lost. By repairing it in gold, I have the chance to celebrate my mother and grandmother, as well as remember the highs and lows of my marriage. All this brings me great joy."

"But why," queried Kinko, "would you take joy in remembering that your husband broke a precious family heirloom?"

"Because that is part of the story that has brought us—and this cup—to this very moment. And all that is precious. I would not change one part of that journey. And this cup celebrates all of it."

Unconvinced by her explanation, to Kinko it felt like a rationalization for the loss of a valued family legacy. "Forgive me for my impertinence, but is not the breaking of this heirloom a matter of great sorrow?"

"When it happened, it was. But now it is part of the cup's history—and mine. All history is messy. If we only acknowledge those pieces of our history that are without flaw, we will have a very stunted view of ourselves. We are all flawed and broken by life in various ways. We can choose to try to cover those flaws over, or we can celebrate them for making us who we are." She looked at the cup, smiling at some unspoken memory, before continuing.

"*Kintsugi* is the art of celebrating the flaws, of highlighting them, of showing them with pride. The flaws outlined in gold declare, 'The very part of me that is broken is what makes me unique and beautiful.' Any cup can be perfect. Only this one—handed down by my grandmother, broken by my husband—is the one that I have shared tea in with you. It is our places of brokenness that make us who we are."

Kinko turned the cup in his hand around, appreciating for the first time its flawed beauty. "Thank you, Shino, for sharing your grandmother's cup with me. It makes drinking this tea richer. I am grateful for your wisdom."

"You have come here, however, because of the conflict that you told me about last week, did you not?"

"I did. But I think that you have already answered my question."

Shino smiled and affectionately patted his hand. "I am glad. Go see Koji, and the two of you can join us for dinner."

Kinko spent the rest of the afternoon working with Koji Yamada on some *shakuhachi* that he was finishing. As they worked, Kinko said, "Koji, you asked me last week about finding someone who might rent your rooms from you while you travel. I think that I have found someone."

"Excellent! Who it is?"

"Me," said Kinko simply.

Koji stared at him for some time without speaking. Then he smiled ruefully. "Well, I can't pretend surprise. At least this works out well for me; you can help continue my business! You are a very good flute-maker."

Kinko smiled. "I will do my humble best."

The two joined the Misawa family for dinner, who were delighted to hear about their new tenant. They spent another magical evening together of conversation and music, Kinko's heart strangely at ease.

As Kurosawa approached Ichigetsu-*ji*, he felt his anxiety rise. He was not worried about an attack by Lord Omura's men, although that was a slight possibility. He was, however, extremely uneasy about his conversation with Ganryo Shuza. He arrived at the temple without incident by mid-morning and immediately sought out one of the senior instructors to get a report on the past week. Afterward, he checked in at the administrative building to inform the abbot of his arrival.

He was ushered in immediately to meet with the abbot, who wore a peevish, vexed look. Without any preliminaries, he launched into the conversation. "Well, you have certainly taken your time! And you left me in a very awkward position with Lord Omura. I trust you have come to your senses?"

"I think I have," Kurosawa replied. "I am resigning from my position on the council and withdrawing my membership in the temple."

Ganryo Shuza sat in stunned silence for a moment. "I'm not sure that you understand what you are doing, Kurosawa. You have worked hard your entire life to come to this moment, to come to this place. You are relatively young and in one of the most important roles in our entire Fuke order. You can impact the musical life of the *komusō* for generations. You could move in the highest circles of the land." The words seemed to spill forth from the abbot, tripping over each other in their haste.

"Besides that, I need you to continue the work you have begun. You know my hopes and dreams for the work of Ichigetsu-*ji*. I have waited a year for you to arrive, and now you plan to throw that away, simply because you have one slightly distasteful task to do? Where would you even live? This makes no sense."

"I appreciate that this may not make sense to you, but it makes sense to me. You navigate a complex world of privilege and power, and I respect your ability to do that while trying to maintain your personal integrity and the integrity of our order. But that is not the world of which I wish to be part. I will live where our *shakuhachi*-maker Koji Yamada lives. Our great founder, Fuke, loved to be with the common people—to laugh with them, celebrate with them, to weep with them, to teach them. That life appeals to me. The great Rinzai master and *shakuhachi* player Ikkyu—after his enlightenment—also left his temple to avoid its political machinations, and lived as a homeless wanderer among the common people."

"But you forget that Ikkyu ultimately became the abbot of a temple himself and died in that position."

"He did—but reluctantly and later in life. That is not my journey now. Here is my proposal to you: let me relinquish my priestly orders and leave the temple. I will formally become a member of Reihō-ji as a *kyogai* lay monk. That will give you the ability to tell Lord Omura that I am no longer under your authority, nor at the temple. I will teach the monks of both Ichigetsu-ji and Reihō-ji for a salary to be agreed upon. In this capacity, I can continue to help you shape the musical and spiritual life of our order. I think that meets all your needs as well as mine."

The abbot exploded. "You are presumptuous, arrogant, and disloyal, Kinko Kurosawa! How dare you dictate terms to me! We do not hire music instructors; they are part of the leadership of our community. I am the abbot of the most important and powerful Fuke temple in all Japan. I meet with great lords and ministers, even the shogun himself. You are an insignificant nobody from a backward island. Get out of my sight, and I will summon you when I want to hear from you again."

Kinko—who refrained from smiling at the similarity between the abbot's diatribe and his last conversation with Rokujo—went back to his room, unloaded his pack and sat for a while. Becoming restless, he picked up Tanaka's long *shakuhachi* and walked over to the *butsuden*, where he knelt in front of the statue of Buddha, who sat serenely with his eyes shut and his hand raised in benediction. "Lord Buddha, your unworthy servant kneels before you, desirous of your wisdom. Share with me some tiny ray of enlightenment." He sat for some time, focused on his breath and tried to keep his feverish heart still.

Finally, he picked up Tanaka's *shakuhachi* and began to blow *ro-buki*. He blew gently at first, then harder and harder, louder and louder, until the single note filled the space. He felt as though he were trying to blow the walls down. Coming back to himself, he noticed two of his younger students watch him curiously from the front door of the *butsuden*. He nodded to them and continued meditating, his heart beginning to center.

There was an eerie quiet about the next few days. He fell back into his routine: meeting with the other teachers in the morning for planning sessions; teaching and organizing lessons; assisting with *jo* practice on the exercise fields; and joining the community at *zazen* sessions and meals. But a heavy weight in the air stifled creativity and joy.

Finally, the day came when the abbot summoned Kurosawa back to his office. "Have you thought about our conversation?" he growled.

"I think that when we ended our last conversation, I had proposed how we might resolve this situation. That still seems the best solution to me; have you considered it?"

"I have—and discussed it with the council. The universal

opinion is that there is no need to do things differently than we have done them before, and that you should curb your arrogance. Several members of the council suggested that Lord Omura might help reform your attitude."

The threat hung there in the air between them. Kurosawa assumed that there would be some test of wills, but he did not anticipate that it would be this crude.

"Very well," said Kurosawa. "I thank you for the opportunity you have offered, my Lord Abbot. May the blessings of Buddha be upon you." He arose and drew from the pocket in his sleeve his identification papers certifying his status as a *jūshoku* priest. He set them on the abbot's table, bowed, and left the office.

Slowly and deliberately, he walked to his room and loaded all his belongings into his pack. He found one of his senior instructors and told him that he was leaving the temple and asked him to lead the morning planning sessions. The shock on his colleague's face gave him some gratification, petty satisfaction though it was. Without speaking to anyone else, he walked out into the streets of Edo. As he looked a last time at the temple gates, he suddenly remembered his dream on Kōya-san. Smiling to himself, he turned and walked away, leaving his dreams like so much debris by the side of the road.

He made the journey to Reihō-ji as quickly as possible, feeling a deep desire to bring closure to this chapter of his life. He was well-known now to the abbot, who expressed his sadness that Kurosawa would not be teaching his instructors. But he was also delighted to have him transfer his membership to Reihō-ji, seeing it as some small coup over the abbot of Ichigetsu-ji. He willingly granted Kurosawa the status of *kyogai* lay monk that the latter requested.

With tears on both sides, Kinko took leave of his friend Nagate Chikuzen. "We will see each other soon, Kurosawa," he said earnestly. "Nothing about our meeting has been accidental." Kinko was less sure of this assertion, but bowed deeply to his friend.

"We will see each other soon," he agreed.

He left Reihō-*ji* early on a warm spring morning and hoped that it was an omen when he saw his first cherry blossom of the season. It was hard not to revel in the explosion of color that enveloped him on his way back to the Misawa household. He pulled out his *shakuhachi* and found himself playing with unusual freedom and joy as he walked. It felt like that wondrous time when he was first learning the instrument as a young man.

A golden sun hung low in the sky on the second day when he arrived at the Misawa home. Setsu was getting ready to close up the shop when he entered the door. Greeting him with a broad smile, she bowed and said, "It is good to have you home, Kurosawa. My mother is entertaining a guest upstairs who has come to speak with you."

Curious, Kinko climbed the narrow wooden stairs and was pleased to see Shino's smiling face. She sat beside the cooking fire, serving tea to the Ichigetsu-*ji* instructor with whom he had spoken before his departure. Upon entering the room, the instructor sprang to his feet and bowed. "It is good to see you, Shishō," he began. "I was a little worried; I have never seen the abbot so furious as after you left. He called an emergency meeting of the council, which then met with all the temple instructors."

Kinko waited.

"The abbot has sent me here to tell you that your proposal is acceptable to the council, and he would like to meet with you to sort out the details."

Kinko bowed. "I am grateful for whatever words you and the others shared to alter the abbot's perspective." His colleague also bowed and smiled.

"We all acknowledged a degree of self-interest in the matter, *Shishō*." Grinning, he added, "No one really wants your old job."

"Please tell the abbot that I will visit him in the next few days."

The young monk bowed. "With pleasure, *Shishō*. I will look forward to seeing you and continuing our lessons. And now, I must get started. I would like to spend the night back in the temple."

Kinko was not inclined to persuade him to remain, and so sent him on his way, with a little food for the journey provided by Shino. He sat with her sipping tea and recounting the events of the last few days while she prepared dinner for him and the family. They shared a pleasant, but subdued evening together, everyone sorting out how this new arrangement would unfold.

Climbing the stairs to Yamada's workshop after dinner, Kinko suddenly knew deep in his bones that he was in the right place. Walking through the workshop to the small, vacated bedroom, unseen before now, Kinko was delighted to find that the window overlooked the garden in the back of the house. Even without lamplight, the bright waxing moon cast a cool luminescence on the room.

Kurosawa knelt by the open window. Moonlight shone through the branches of the weeping cherry tree just outside his window, making glow the newly emerged pink blossoms. Even as he looked, he could feel his heartbeat slow and his spirit settle. He closed his eyes and breathed deeply. Opening them again, he gazed at the moon and thought of Basho's words:

"The moon and sun are eternal travelers. Even the years
wander on.
A lifetime adrift in a boat, or in old age leading a tired horse
into the years,
every day is a journey, and the journey itself is home."

AFTERWORD

Kinko Kurosawa (1710-1771) was born in the Kuroda region of Kyushu and was a member of the Kuzaki-*ji* Temple in Nagasaki. He traveled extensively, under the commission of Ichigetsu-*ji* Temple in Edo, collecting *honkyoku* music from Fuke temples all over Japan. Ultimately, the 36 pieces he collected became the core repertoire of the *Kinko-ryu shakuhachi* school, still active today.

Kurosawa's actual diaries were destroyed in an air raid on Tokyo in 1944. This novel is not historical, but is inspired by his remarkable life. All of the places in the novel are (or were) actual places, many of which we know that he visited. Other than Kurosawa himself, and his teacher Ikkei, all of the other characters are creations of the author's imagination. Any resemblance to actual people—living or dead—is purely coincidental.

All translations of Basho's works are from *Narrow Road to the Interior: And Other Writings*, translated by Sam Hamill (Shambhala Classics).

GLOSSARY

Anata: technically, "you," although also used as a term of intimacy, "Darling"

Bakufu: the government structures serving the shogun

Biwa: a short-necked, fretted lute

Bodhisattva: one who has achieved enlightenment, but forgoes Nirvana to help others

Bokken: a long wooden practice sword, meant to resemble a *katana*

Budo: the "way of the warrior," the practice of martial arts

Butsuden: the main sanctuary of a Buddhist temple, housing a statue of the Buddha

Daimyo: a feudal lord, who was a vassal of the shogun

Fuke: a subsect within the Rinzai Buddhist school, who used the *shakuhachi*

Gedan kamae: a sword position, with the weapon held low and pointed at the ground

Gūji: an honorific for a Shinto priest

Hara: the source of the body's energy, about two inches below the navel

369

Haori: a traditional hip-length jacket, often worn over a kimono

Hashi: or *yojo* is the generic name for a prostitute

Hoki: a spiritual tool

Honkyoku: "original music," the traditional Zen music for the *shakuhachi*

Honshu: the main island of Japan, and the location of Kyoto and Edo

Honsoku: a booklet of Fuke beliefs and practices carried by a *komusō*

Jizo: a small statue of a *bodhisattva,* protecting travelers and children

Jo: a wooden practice staff about five feet long

Jisume: "senior monk," a temple position between a *kyogai* and a *jūshoku*

Jūshoku: a priest in a temple, generally a permanent resident

Kaido: a major roadway

Kaiin: *komusō* identification papers

Kamae: technically "posture," used in *budo* practice to refer to a particular stance

Kami: The Shinto term for "god," many of whom are associated with nature

Kannon: Buddhist goddess of mercy

Katana: a long sword, often one of two swords carried by a samurai

Kintsugi: a technique for repairing broken pottery using a gold or silver adhesive

Koan: a paradoxical story or riddle upon which to focus during meditation

Kokû: "Empty Sky," one of the three oldest shakuhachi pieces

Komusō: a monk of the Fuke order, a sect of the Rinzai School

Koshi: a second-ranked courtesan

Koto: a six foot long, thirteen-stringed, plucked instrument

Kyorei: "Hollow Bell," one of the three oldest *shakuhachi* pieces

Kyogai: a lay monk, often in a temple on a temporary basis

Kyushu: the southernmost of the four main islands of Japan, off the tip of Honshu

Ma: silence, the empty space between notes

Minyo: folk music

Misogi: a Shinto practice of ritual purification, often practiced under a waterfall

Mukaiji: "Flute on a Misty Sea," one of the three oldest *shakuhachi* pieces

Narezushi: a pickled fish that was a precursor to *sushi*

Noren: a fabric divider hung in doorways, between rooms, or in windows

Obi: a wide belt, holding a kimono together

Obo: a generic title for a monk or priest

O-juzu: Japanese Buddhist prayer beads

Onigiri: rice cake, typically containing a savory or sweet filling

Onsen: a hot spring, and often the bathhouse associated with it

Rinzai: one of three major branches of Zen Buddhism in Japan

Rōnin: a masterless samurai, without a lord

Samsāra: the endlessly recurring cycle of birth, existence, death, and rebirth

Samue: monk's work clothing, trousers and shirt

Shakuhachi: a bamboo, end-blown flute, generally 21 inches long (54.5 cm)

Shamisen: a long-necked, three-stringed, fretless lute

Shinobue: a high-pitched, transverse-blown flute

Shishō: a term of respect for a teacher

Shogun: the military ruler of Japan, ostensibly under the authority of the emperor

Shōtō: a short wooden practice sword, meant to resemble the *wakizashi*

Sotōba: a narrow strip of wood affixed to a gravestone, usually in honor of an event

Suburi: a repetitive cutting exercise using a sword or staff

Suizen: the discipline of the *komusō*, blowing meditation

Tayu: a first-ranked courtesan

Tanto: a dagger, generally worn at the back of the waist

Tengai: a reed-woven basket worn over the head of a *komusō* monk as a sign of humility

Tengu: a mountain spirit or demon

Tsubone: a third-ranked courtesan

Tsūin: a travel permit carried by a *komusō*

Ukiyo: the "floating world," referring to the arts and culture of the pleasure quarter

Wakizashi: a short sword, often one of two swords carried by a samurai

Yoshiwara: the specific name for the pleasure quarter in Edo

Yukaku: the generic name for a "pleasure quarter"

Yukata: a light casual *kimono*

Zafu: a round cushion used for seated meditation

Zazen: sitting meditation

Zendo: the large temple room in which group meditation takes place

DISCUSSION QUESTIONS

THE KOMUSŌ:

1. Were you aware that there was a Zen tradition that used music as a meditation tool? Have you used music to meditate?
2. Were you surprised that same-sex relationships were common among samurai? As in ancient Sparta, these relationships often had a mentoring element to them, with one partner much older than the other. Such relationships were also a common element of temple life.
3. Talk about a time when something you had been dreading actually happened. Can you relate to Kinko's crisis?

THE SUMMONS:

1. Were you surprised that members of a Zen monastic order would engage in martial practice? How does this impact your understanding of the religion?
2. We often criticize religious organizations for how they address (or fail to address) sexual lapses among leaders. How do you feel about the temple Abbot's solution to Kinko's situation?
3. How did Ikkei's words to Kurosawa strike you? Are his comments too harsh? Do they resonate with what you know of Kinko thus far?

AN EVENING IN NAGASAKI:

1. How did you feel about Kinko's solution to communicating with Matsu?
2. Were you aware that Christian missionaries reached Japan as early as the sixteenth century? What are some of the connecting points between Christianity and Buddhism?
3. Ikkei advises Kinko to spend time among the less fortunate on his journey. Both Buddhist and Christian traditions teach that holiness and enlightenment are to be found among marginalized people. Why is that? Have you experienced this in your own life?

CALLING BAMBOO:

1. In the shogun's policy of *sankin kotai*, the families of the ruling *daimyo* were effectively held hostage to ensure the lord's obedience. How would it feel to have a family held hostage by the government? How might you respond?

2. Fuke monks supported themselves and their temples through begging. Like the Franciscans in Christian tradition, they saw a spiritual benefit to mendicancy. What do you think those benefits might be? What is your experience of needing to ask someone for something?

3. Reflect on Kurosawa's interaction with the old monk who tends the shrine where he and Shizu spend the night. Are there places where theological/philosophical rigor might be problematic from a spiritual standpoint?

HOMECOMING:

1. Was it surprising to learn that farmers were on the second rung of Japan's social hierarchy and that merchants–no matter how wealthy–were at the bottom? What might have been some of the reasons for that?

2. Kinko's relationship with his father is a challenging one. Have you experienced families where one child is markedly preferred to the other? What factors might explain the elder Kurosawa's treatment of his younger son?

3. Reflect on Kinko's relationship with his sister. What is her role in holding the family together?

PASSAGE TO HONSHU:

1. Leaving his family home, Kinko realizes that he is being pursued by retainers of the Ekken family. How does this impact his journey and his mindset?
2. Kinko defuses the tension in his inn by playing some folk tunes and involving his fellow travelers in some entertainment. Does this demonstrate any growth or change in Kinko as a character?
3. The first quarter of the book ends by noting that summer has turned to autumn. Much Japanese poetry and music emphasize the turning of the seasons. How does this add to the narrative of the story?

LIGHTS IN A GRAVEYARD:

1. The tale of "Hoichi the Earless" is a very old Japanese story made known to the West in the writings of Lafcadio Hearn. What does the story tell us about a Japanese understanding of music?
2. Kurosawa and the monks at the Akama Shrine believe that Kurosawa's offering of music has the power to aid souls in their cycle to rebirth. How might this be different or similar to other religious traditions which offer prayers for the dead?
3. What do you make of Kurosawa's experience of the dancing lights and the torch?

SWORDS IN THE MOONLIGHT:

1. Kurosawa is starting to figure out that he is in real danger at this point in the story. What are the most worrisome elements of this confrontation with the two samurai?
2. Our hero is generally an introvert and enjoys his own company. Did his decision to join Asano's group make sense in light of his danger?

RŌNIN:

1. The story of the 47 *Rōnin* is famous in the West as well as in Japan. Were you familiar with the story before now? Did anything surprise you in Asano's retelling of it?
2. Much film and literature depict *rōnin* as romantic, adventurous figures. What surprised you about the group of *rōnin* in this chapter?
3. Kurosawa is surprised and confused by Asano's appraisal of his playing. Why does he respond so defensively to his friend's observations?

DANCING BY LANTERN LIGHT:

1. Kinko is quickly welcomed into the bustling Asano family. How does he respond? What is he learning from them?
2. Had you encountered the term "pleasure quarter" before? If so, what did you know about it? What

did you learn? What surprised you about the structures of the pleasure quarter?

3. Kinko's relationship with Taka takes him by surprise. Why is it important? What has he learned from her and their time in the pleasure quarter?

LIGHTNING FROM A CLEAR SKY:

1. In Edo period Japan, the vast majority of the buildings were made of wood due to the risk of earthquakes, so fires could spread quickly. How do you respond to Kinko's impetuous rush to save his friend?

2. To save the young Asano, Kinko instinctively turns to the Samurai of his own class. What does he learn from this experience?

3. A significant virtual for a samurai was to be mentally prepared for death. How do you see this (or not see it) in how Kinko responds to the death of his friend?

UNEXPECTED COMPANY:

1. How do you respond to Kurosawa's treatment of the spy masquerading as a *komusō*?

2. Kinko intervenes when he sees two ruffians accosting two women travelers. How would you describe the relationship that develops between Rokujo and Kurosawa? Is it more than simply utilitarian for both?

3. The Fuke-*shu* is an unusual sect in Zen Buddhist tradition. What do you think of their founding

story? Are there anything in their traditions that surprise you?

TEMPLE OF LIGHT AND DARKNESS:

1. Kinko believed his time with Rokujo was behind him. When she shows up unexpectedly at Myoan-*ji*, was it a surprise? How did you react to the explanation of her behavior?
2. It has been a long time since anyone taught Kurosawa anything about playing the *shakuhachi*. What has he learned from Minzan Zenji? How might this be important his journey?
3. Why do you think that the abbot wants to send Kinko in the opposite direction from Edo?

A NIGHT AMONG FOXES:

1. Following the abbot's direction, Kinko goes to meditate all night at a mountain shrine, only to find his goals thwarted. Have you ever sought out a specific spiritual experience only to find your hopes frustrated? What did you learn?
2. Kurosawa has a surprising insight at the Fushimi-inari shrine that gives him a broader perspective. What does he realize and why is it important?
3. Kinko's journey now takes an unexpected turn (literally and figuratively). Why might this be important at this stage in the narrative?

DISCUSSION QUESTIONS

THE ROAD SOUTH:

1. Chikuzen has been sent to Kokoku-*ji* to explore whether something in the history of his home temple might increase its status. Does it surprise you that religious institutions would jockey for position with each other? What might that mean for Kurosawa when he arrives in Edo?
2. Chikuzen discovers some uncomfortable revelations about the origins of the Fuke sect in his research. History often makes us uncomfortable. Reflect on a time when you discovered a historical truth that changed how you understood something.

HOUSE OF A THOUSAND LAMPS:

1. Like Minzan Zenji in Kyoto, Kurosawa acknowledges Akira Kendo as a teacher. Minzan Zenji is clearly the superior musician. What traits do Kendo and Zenji have in common? How do they relate to Kinko differently?
2. Kurosawa is clearly frustrated at his initial interaction with Kendo. Why is he frustrated? What is he resisting?
3. The mausoleum of Kobo Daishi is the spiritual heart of Koya-San. What would it feel like to see a lamp that had been continually lit for over a thousand years? How do you respond to the idea that Kobo Daishi never died, but entered into a state of perfect meditation eternally?

MISOGI:

1. Virtually every religious tradition has its version of the odd, irascible hermit. How does Tanaka compare to similar characters you may be familiar with?

2. Tanaka ridicules Kinko's playing, just as Kinko is perplexed by Tanaka's. What accounts for these wildly different approaches to music?

3. How does Tanaka's martial practice relate to his musical discipline?

4. Many religious traditions have the concept of "spiritual warfare." What do you make of Tanaka's understanding of his role in protecting the monastic community of Koya-san?

THE TENGU:

1. In many traditional Japanese disciplines, the student learns by copying the master unquestioningly. This is a markedly different approach than education in the West. How does Tanaka's chiding of Kinko feel to you?

2. Tanaka gives Kinko a flute after meditating over it, knowing that "it will be a good partner." Do inanimate objects have spiritual dimensions to them? Where else have you seen this idea?

3. As he becomes more spiritually centered, Kinko begins to remember his dreams better. Do you remember your dreams? Do they provide insight into emotional struggles you might be having?

4. Tanaka perceives a spiritual attack on the mountain in the midst of a storm. What do you think about his belief? Do spiritual attacks occur? Do they have physical manifestations?

5. Kinko also has an unsettling experience that seems to blend both spiritual and physical. How do you understand what happened to him?

CITY OF THE DEAD:

1. Kendo's way of questioning always takes Kinko by surprise. Do you have people in your life who do that for you? What does it feel like?

2. Graveyards often gift us with a broader perspective, a sense of history. In the vast necropolis on Koya-san, Kinko is gifted in this way and also with a very specific vision: What does the old monk say to Kinko, and what does Kinko learn?

3. Have you ever sat in a graveyard at night? What did it feel like?

THE SOUND OF ENLIGHTENMENT:

1. Many Japanese arts have embraced the tea ceremony ideal of *ichi-go, ichi-e*: 'one moment, one meeting.' The goal is to bring to every interaction the feeling that it has never happened before and will never happen again. What would it look like to bring this mindset into well-worn, familiar interactions?

2. Kendo describes meditation as the process of recognizing the Buddha nature in ourselves, a

concept that echoes a Christian understanding of grace. What would it look like to claim our inherent divinity, rather than make spiritual disciplines an ordeal?

3. As he meditates, Kinko experiences a sense of transcendence and connection with everything around him. Have you ever had such an experience? What did you carry away from it?

TEMPLE OF MUSIC:

1. On his way to Edo, Kinko takes a brief detour to the most significant pilgrimage site in Japan: Ise. Have you ever been on a religious pilgrimage? What significance did it have for you?

2. The joyfulness of the pilgrims visiting Ise strikes Kurosawa, who notes how much of his own tradition is solemn. We often associate religious experience with being quiet and contemplative. Have you ever participated in a religious event that was festive and exuberant. How did it feel?

3. Kinko defuses a tense situation with the villagers of Shimo-Ujiie by embracing the Buddhist virtue of humility. Have there been occasions in your life in which a person's humility shifted the dynamics in a positive way? Why is that?

4. Kurosawa Kinko is primarily known today for founding the Kinko-*ryu* school of *shakuhachi* playing. He began this process by collecting *shakuhachi* music from different temples around the country. We see him beginning to engage this process with intentionality at Fudai-*ji* temple.

Have you had places in your life where you stumbled unexpectedly on something that became central to who you are?

UNEXPECTED COMPANY, REDUX:

1. When Rokujo reappears at Hakone, did any red flags get raised for you? Was the revelation at the end of the chapter a surprise?
2. After he meets Rokujo again, Kinko remembers Fumon Tanaka's advice to "still yourself enough to pay attention." Have you found yourself in a fraught position and been able to solve it by staying calm and centered? How can we get to this place in everyday life?
3. Kinko is caught in a classic feudal Japanese struggle of conflicting loyalties. How does he resolve this for himself? Is it a satisfying resolution?

THE CENTER OF THE WORLD:

1. Edo, in Kinko's day, was the largest city in the world, with over a million residents. Kinko is somewhat overwhelmed upon arriving. How do you think this impacts his understanding of his journey?
2. On the way from central Edo to Ichigetsu-*ji*, Kinko is embraced by the Misawa family, as well as the *shakuhachi* maker Koji Yamada. Reflect on his relationship with this family. What role might they play in Kinko's life?

3. Finally, after nearly a year of traveling, Kurosawa finally arrives at his destination. How do you think he feels? What are your hopes and anxieties for him?

A NEW HOME:

1. Kurosawa's initial hopes are disappointed when the abbot appoints him as a simple teacher, rather than as head instructor. How does he respond? How do you feel about the abbot's decision?
2. As Kurosawa begins his teaching duties at Ichigetsu-*ji*, we see him incorporate some of the things he learned from Fumon Tanaka on Koya-san. What of Tanaka's teaching is he passing on? How do the monks he is teaching respond?
3. At the end of this chapter, Kurosawa has the choice to "play it safe" and audition in the way everyone expects him to, or risk showing what he has learned on his pilgrimage. How do you react to his decision? Does this represent a change from the Kurosawa that we met at the beginning of the book?

RESTORATION:

1. Politics rarely has a positive impact on religion, and in this chapter Kurosawa begins to see some of that. This is obvious, and yet it seems to take Kinko by surprise. Why do you think that is?
2. As Kinko settles into his new role, he becomes rather lax in engaging in the disciplines that were

part of his life on Koya-san. What disciplines are important to your spiritual life? What helps you stay engaged with them?

3. Kurosawa ultimately finds himself in a position that is so morally distasteful that he feels no option but to refuse. How do you feel about his decision? How to respond emotionally to the abbots counter-arguments?

KINTSUGI:

1. By this last chapter of the book, Kurosawa and his friend Chikuzen have had a role reversal, with Chikuzen becoming the wise counselor. What does this tell you about the two friends? Are Chikuzen's words helpful to Kinko?

2. The Japanese art of Kintsugi repair becomes a metaphor for Kinko's journey. What does he come to understand in his conversation with Shino Misawa? How does it shape his decision?

3. How do you feel about Kinko's ultimate decision? Does it feel like the right outcome after his year-long journey? Is it satisfying?

NOTES

THE KOMUSŌ

1. For simplicity's sake, the author has used the western pattern for names throughout the novel, in which the given name precedes the family name; in Japan, the family name always comes first.

ABOUT RUNNING WILD PRESS

Running Wild Press publishes stories that cross genres with great stories and writing. RIZE publishes great genre stories written by people of color and by authors who identify with other marginalized groups. Our team consists of:

Lisa Diane Kastner, Founder and Executive Editor
Cody Cisco, Acquisitions Editor, RIZE
Rebecca Dimyan, Editor
Andrew DiPrinzio, Editor
Cecilia Kennedy, Editor
Barbara Lockwood, Editor
Chris Major, Editor
Cody Sisco, Editor
Chih Wang, Editor
Benjamin White, Editor
Peter A. Wright, Editor
Lisa Montagne, Director of Education
Lara Macaione, Director of Marketing
Joelle Mitchell, Head of Licensing

Pulp Art Studios, Cover Design
Standout Books, Interior Design
Polgarus Studios, Interior Design

Learn more about us and our stories at www.
runningwildpress.com

Loved this story and want more? Follow us at www.
runningwildpress.com
www.facebook.com/runningwildpress,
on Twitter @lisadkastner @RunWildBooks